T0146750

The Special Ones

sb white

authorHOUSE®

AuthorHouse™
1663 Liberty Drive
Bloomington, IN 47403
www.authorhouse.com
Phone: 1 (800) 839-8640

Published by AuthorHouse   10/15/2016

ISBN: 978-1-5246-1553-6 (sc)
ISBN: 978-1-5246-1552-9 (e)

Library of Congress Control Number: 2016917195

Print information available on the last page.

For Zandra

CONTENTS

PART I

PART II

PART III

PART I

The Training

CHAPTER I

"Way to go, Manx. It's your best time ever." Wren's voice was filled with excitement as she watched the muscled yellow cat leap from a high ramp to land on the floor of the barn and then swiftly change into a girl.

The inside of the large barn resembled an obstacle course and was filled with ramps that led to various levels of boards inside the building. Across the length of the floor were over-and-under hurdles; climbing ropes hung from the rafters; and mats were placed to one side to practice agility and defense tactics.

Breathing hard, the girl called Manx leaned over to catch her breath. Her long yellow hair had come loose from the braid at the back of her neck. With anxious green eyes, she looked toward a tall man standing nearby, waiting for him to acknowledge her effort.

The man stepped forward, leaned down to pat her shoulder, and said, "Congratulations, Manx. You have done well." The man looked around at the other children in the large barn and told them, "Gather around, my special ones. I have something important to tell you."

The children moved quickly to comply. Boxer, a twelve-year-old boy, was tall and slim with dark hair and eyes, and he resembled the tall man. Battle, age eleven, had wide shoulders and a stout build. His hair was steel-gray in color, and his eyes were a piercing blue. Wren, an eight-year-old girl with brown hair and eyes was the smallest of the group. And Manx was ten. The children fondly called the man Grand Pierre, and they had lived with him and Aunt May on the farm for the past five years.

Grand Pierre looked at the children and told them, "Each of you has mastered your unique skills and excelled at physical challenges. I cannot teach you any more."

Confusion began to cover the children's faces, but they stayed silent.

Grand Pierre continued. "Tonight we will celebrate with a special dinner, and tomorrow we are going on an outing."

The children looked at each other and grinned, excited about the celebration that would be a change from their usual sparse meal. The children never went hungry, but they also never left uneaten food on their plates.

"Will Aunt May make a dessert for us?" Wren could not wait to find out.

Aunt May had taught the children to call them Grand Pierre and Aunt May and not by their real names, knowing that the names of Piers and Maileen could give them away.

Grand Pierre chuckled and replied, "I'm sure she will have a special treat to celebrate your graduation. Now go and clean up for dinner."

As Grand Pierre opened the barn doors, the last light of day filled the barn, and the children hurried down the path that led to a large two-story house.

As promised, Aunt May had baked a special cake with frosting for dessert. After the empty dinner plates had been carried into the kitchen, Boxer said to Grand Pierre, "You said we are going on a trip tomorrow. Where are we going?"

Grand Pierre motioned for everyone to come into the living room. The children gathered around Grand Pierre's chair, anxious to hear his response, for outings were rare occasions. When they went on trips to learn about the forest and the animals that lived there, they were never allowed to reveal their special skills. All of their training sessions were held in the old barn, with the doors tightly closed.

Grand Pierre considered his answer and then said, "It's the final test you must pass. Now off to bed and get to sleep. Tomorrow could be a long day."

Knowing it was useless to try to pry more information out of Grand Pierre, the children said their good-nights and climbed the wooden stairs to their bedrooms. It would be hard for them to get to sleep. Wondering where they were going and what final test Grand Pierre would have for them kept them awake long into the night.

The children had finished their breakfast and were waiting outside for Grand Pierre. Manx and Wren were swinging on a wooden swing on the front porch. Boxer and Battle were in the yard practicing defense tactics.

"You're too slow." Boxer laughed as he jumped out of Battle's reach and spun around, catching Battle by surprise and tripping him, causing him to fall backward.

As Boxer reached down to help Battle up, Grand Pierre came around the side of the house. He was driving a vehicle with four tall wheels and a large cage affixed to the rear. There were no doors on the vehicle, and inside were two seats in front and a large bench across the back. Grand Pierre referred to the vehicle as "the transport."

"Climb in, children," Grand Pierre said when he had stopped the transport.

"Where are we going?" Battle asked as he climbed onto the bench beside the two girls. Being the oldest, Boxer always sat in front with Grand Pierre.

"Not far. The transport's energy source is becoming weak," Grand Pierre answered.

Once the children were seated, Grand Pierre pushed a knoblike button, and the transport silently rolled forward.

It was a treat for the children to be outside enjoying the warmth from the sun and seeing the variety of vegetation that populated the dense forest. Wren especially liked the bright-green trees with tendrils that spiraled from their tops to the ground. Battle pointed out massive, orange-striped leaves that grew from some of the plants. Manx loved the purple-flowered trees and always picked some flowers to bring back for Aunt May.

Boxer watched the dense forest, looking for animals, but he did not see any. Early mornings or late evenings were the best times to find animals eating the large leaves—or the ones who hunted the leaf-eaters. "I don't remember going this way before," he commented as the transport climbed the steep trail to reach the top of the mountain.

The mountain could be seen from the barn, but this was the first time Grand Pierre had gone this way. Once the transport had made it to the top, the mountain leveled off into a flat, rocky area.

"Hold on tight," Grand Pierre warned as the transport started down a steep trail on the side opposite the one they had come up. The trail ran downward into a narrow valley with a stream running through the middle.

Grand Pierre stopped the transport beside the stream. He looked around and said, "This should do nicely. Boxer, bring the food. We will lunch downstream. Come, children." He motioned for them to follow as he walked away. When they reached an open area, Grand Pierre stopped and told them, "We'll eat here."

For lunch Aunt May had packed buttered rolls and slices of yellow melon that grew near the farm. When they were finished eating, Grand Pierre stood and said, "My special ones, for five years we have lived on the farm, and during this time you have learned to master your special talents, become efficient in physical skills, and excel in all your studies. Each of you is different from the others, but you are also very much alike. You have trained hard and now must become a team, depend on each other, and always remember your Cs."

Grand Pierre looked at Boxer, who said, "Control."

Then at Battle, who said, "Cooperation."

Then at Manx, who said, "Caution."

Then at Wren, who said, "Curiosity."

Grand Pierre nodded. "Very good. You must remember to always *control* your powers, work as a team through *cooperation*, be *cautious* before you act, and be *curious* if you feel something needs explaining. You will make a great team. Boxer, you are the oldest and have advanced in leadership. Battle, you have a military heritage, both mental and physical. Manx has a technical understanding of how things work. And Wren, you have a special way of getting others to trust you. Soon you will have to depend on these skills to survive. I will leave now."

Grand Pierre started to walk away, and Manx jumped up and gasped, "Are you leaving us here?"

Grand Pierre faced the stunned group and explained. "Your final test is to work together as a team and find your way back to the farm. Tomorrow you will move to the Adoran settlement and will live at a place for children. Aunt May and I must leave too; the farm is no longer safe. I will explain more once you get back. Remember your *Cs*." Then Grand Pierre walked away from the shocked children.

"Maybe we can follow him," Wren uttered as she watched the tall man disappear. "The transport doesn't go fast."

"I don't think that's part of the test," Boxer replied and placed a hand on Wren's shoulder to stop her from running after Grand Pierre.

Once Grand Pierre was out of sight, Battle said, "We can go back the way we came. What do you remember?"

"I was looking at all the flowers and not watching the road," Manx admitted.

"I couldn't see anything but the tall trees," Wren added.

Boxer motioned for the others to gather around. He said, "If we return to where the transport parked by the stream, we can follow the tracks back up the mountain. Once we're on top, we can find the way through the forest that leads to the farm."

They all agreed that this was a good plan.

Boxer told Battle, "You take the lead, and I'll bring up the rear." Battle stood and started upstream, with the others trailing single-file behind.

A short time later, Battle held up his hand to signal a stop. He pointed to the ground and said, "Here is where the transport turned around and went that way toward the mountain."

Boxer looked toward the mountain. "Let's make our way to the top, and then we can decide what to do next."

Battle studied the area and pointed. "We can save time if we go this way and not follow the transport's tracks. It will be a steeper climb but faster."

"I agree." Boxer nodded and then looked at Wren and asked, "Can you make it?"

"Of course," Wren huffed. She then ordered Battle, "Lead on, commander," making everyone laugh.

The children finally reached the mountaintop and collapsed on the ground, breathing hard. The climb had been steeper than it looked, but it had saved them valuable time.

Wren sat up and said, "I could use a drink of water."

After a few minutes' rest, Boxer stood up. "I'm going to scout around and see if I recognize any trails leading down."

"Don't go far," Manx warned. "I don't think we're alone." Her inherited catlike senses told her that they were being watched. Her warning caused Battle to begin to pace back and forth while looking around.

"Let's all go and stay together," Wren cautioned, and she took hold of Manx's hand.

Boxer led the way across the top of the mountain. He stopped at the edge to look around and said, "There are several trails to go down. Do you recognize anything?"

"On the way up I remember seeing a large tree with huge purple flowers," Manx eagerly said.

"I can fly and look for the tree," Wren offered, looking up at Boxer. His hesitation caused her to add, "It will save us time and keep us from getting lost."

Battle stepped up beside Boxer, looked out across the forest below, and said, "It looks safe from here."

"Wren, make one circle and fly back," Boxer said firmly, giving in to her suggestion.

"Okay," Wren answered. She ran forward, held out her arms and jumped, instantly transforming into a brown bird with red feathers across the breast.

Flapping her wings to gain height, Wren made a small circle over the others and then flew away. The others watched anxiously as Wren became smaller in the blue sky. She flew halfway across the forest canopy and circled around. Suddenly she dove downward and then flew back up, chirping a detection signal.

"She did it!" exclaimed Manx, and the three children started down the mountain to where Wren circled a tall tree.

They were about halfway to their destination when a noise came from overhead. Startled by the swooshing sound, the three children looked up to see a large predator bird called a *vivan* flying directly toward Wren.

Manx screamed for Wren to dive, but Wren was too far away to hear. From a running leap, Boxer changed into a big black dog and howled a loud danger warning.

From their training sessions with Grand Pierre, Wren recognized Boxer's danger howl, and she glanced down to see Manx signaling her to dive. In one swift motion, Wren folded in her wings, as Grand Pierre had taught her, and aimed toward the flowering tree. The large vivan came closer, and Wren knew it was coming for her.

Wren tightened in her wings and dove even faster. The large tree with purple flowers was coming fast, and Wren knew she would crash at this speed, but she could not break the dive because the vivan was closing in on her. Tree or vivan snack? Wren chose the tree. The top branches knocked Wren to one side and then the other as she crashed toward the ground, but she had escaped the predator's sharp talons and instant death.

Wren continued to bounce from branch to branch until she fell from the bottom limb and changed back into a girl, landing hard on her back, winded from the impact. Scratches from the tree limbs covered her arms, and her shirt was torn in places. Wren sighed with relief.

Grand Pierre had tried to explain the changing process. Plain clothes merged into their animal forms, but they could not be holding other items when they changed. This discussion had occurred after Battle, trying to beat his record, had forgotten to drop a rope he was carrying—and changed. When he changed back, he still had the rope—but not his clothes. As Battle ran for cover, Grand Pierre said that the process was not quite perfected. Since then, they had all been careful to check before they changed forms.

Boxer raced up, leaped, and quickly changed from the sleek black dog. He knelt beside Wren and asked, "Are you hurt?" His dark eyes filled with worry.

Wren slowly pushed herself up and managed to whisper, "I don't think anything is broken." Still shaking from the close call, she looked at Boxer, hugged him, and said, "You saved me. Without your warning, I would not have escaped."

Manx and Battle ran up and asked, "Is Wren okay?"

"She just has the wind knocked out of her," Boxer told them.

Wren looked over at Manx and said in a shaky voice, "I found the tree." Everyone laughed, now that the scare with the vivan was over.

Manx pointed ahead. "We came down this way. We should go soon. Someone or something is following us."

"Wren can ride on my shoulders," Battle said.

Wren stood up, took a few steps, and said, "I'm okay—I think." And then she winced.

"Let me carry you until we are out of the forest," Battle said, and he lifted Wren up on his wide shoulders.

The children hurried through the forest until they came to a narrow path that Boxer recognized. He pointed. "If we follow this path, we will come out behind the barn."

"I can walk now. My ankle feels better," Wren said, and Battle lifted her down.

With Boxer in the lead, they started down the narrow path, single file.

"Something is following us," Manx warned.

When a low growl echoed around them, Boxer took hold of Wren's hand.

"You go ahead with the girls," Battle told Boxer. "I'll follow behind."

Battle turned to face the bushes where the growl had come from. He waited, and then jumped—instantly changing into a wide, doglike animal with thick armor-like hide across his muscled body and massive head. The steel-gray hairs on his neck stood up as he issued a warning growl, the meaning of which was clear: come any closer, and you will have to deal with me. Battle waited in animal form, and hearing no challenge to his warning, he turned and followed the path. When he caught up to the others, he changed back.

"I can see the house!" Wren shouted and ran ahead.

The other children looked at each other, grinned, and chased after her.

As they all jumped onto the porch, Grand Pierre opened the door and exclaimed, "Back before dark, my special ones! Very good, very good. Any problems?"

"It was a piece of cake," Boxer answered.

"Cake!" Wren looked up at Grand Pierre. "I hope there is some left. I could use a piece."

Grand Pierre noticed Wren's scratches and her disheveled appearance, but he didn't comment.

CHAPTER 2

After the children had washed up and eaten dinner, everyone went into the living room. Grand Pierre and Aunt May sat on a worn couch, and the children sat on the floor in a circle around them.

Grand Pierre said, "First, I want to say how very proud I am of you and how quickly you made it back to the farm. Now I must prepare you for tomorrow and the changes you will face. I'm not sure if you remember anything about the time before we came to live at the farm, but I must tell you your past to prepare you for the future."

Boxer lifted his hand and said, "I remember loud noises, and people running and yelling, and you and Aunt May getting us out of a burning building. Sometimes I think it was just a bad dream."

Grand Pierre answered, "No, Boxer, it was no dream. Aunt May and I were very lucky to escape with you children. Aunt May and I came to this planet with a scientific team whose goal was to alter clones developed on our own planet with specific animal traits from this planet. We chose Adoran after searching for a planet with an atmosphere like our own and a varied selection of animals. This was a critical requirement for the altered children to survive when we would return to Ulterion."

14

Grand Pierre paused and looked at the astonished faces of the children.

He continued. "I have always called you 'the special ones,' and now you know why. The scientific team set up a secret laboratory in the mountains. Aunt May worked in the nursery with the children, and I was one of the research scientists. On our home planet of Ulterion, others like us were being hunted and killed by our enemy. The rogues had developed robotic soldiers by combining mental abilities with highly developed androids. These androids were programmed to identify us by our genetics, and when they identified us, they tried to kill us.

"We had become desperate, and the idea of combining a clone with animal traits was intended to develop a new genetic code that the robots would not recognize. The goal was to use the altered clones to infiltrate and discover our enemy's plans. These robotic soldiers followed us to this planet and attacked and destroyed our laboratory, and they have been in control of the Adoran settlement since then. I have been warned that the robots have learned about this farm, which is why we must leave."

Manx was confused. "Are you saying that we are experiments? A cross between a clone and an animal?"

Aunt May spoke up. "Cloning is how the children of Ulterion are created, and they are very special. Each clone is given specific skills to fill his or her role on Ulterion. All defects have been eliminated, making them perfect. You are the very best of Ulterion."

"So we are half clone and half animal." Battle was beginning to understand.

"That's not entirely correct," Grand Pierre answered. "We combined only the animal traits needed for specific requirements, like stealth and cunning, or heightened senses, or physical abilities. By combining the required animal traits with Ulterion qualities of leadership, technology, science, military, or strategy, you inherited the best of both species. This is why Boxer and Battle are different, even though both were given specific dog traits. Boxer has Ulterion leadership qualities, and Battle has Ulterion military qualities, and their specific animal traits are designed to enhance them."

"Do we have names other than the ones you call us?" Boxer questioned.

Grand Pierre shook his head sadly. "Each clone had an assigned number based on the animal trait it was to be combined with. Boxer, you were I-32; and Battle, you were I-67. The 100 series was for doglike traits. The 200 series was for catlike traits, like Manx. The 300 series was rodents; and the 400 series was avian—like you, Wren. The 500 series was kept secret. Only a few scientists worked in that lab, and they did not discuss what they were doing."

"If I am number I-32, and Battle is number I-67, where are all the others clones with doglike traits?" Boxer wondered aloud.

Grand Pierre looked away and sighed heavily. Aunt May placed her hand on his arm. She looked at Boxer and said sadly, "We lost so many little ones. Many didn't survive the birth process, and others lived only a few hours or days."

"Are we the only ones left?" Battle asked.

Grand Pierre looked at Battle and replied, "We don't know. When the research facility was invaded by the robotic soldiers, they killed many of our team members and tore the facility apart, looking for our research material. When they started fires to destroy the labs, everyone was desperate to escape and told the children to run. I know of some scientists who escaped and are hiding in the settlement, but I know of no children."

"Why did those robot things come here?" Wren grumbled.

"The Rogue leaders on Ulterion must have learned of our research project," Grand Pierre answered. "When the robots arrived, they knew to look for the research files."

"How did you get to this planet?" Manx quizzed.

"We came in a large research vessel and set up our laboratory in the mountains so the Adorans would not know of our presence. They are not as advanced as we are, and we were afraid of their reaction because we do look somewhat different. We are tall and thin, and most of the Adorans are shorter and have darker coloring. This mountain region was where most of the animal population could be found, and I am not aware of settlements other than this one. Adoran is not a large planet. When the robotic soldiers arrived in their warship, they attacked the laboratory. A few of the scientists escaped in our research vessel, and we don't know what happened to them—if the vessel was destroyed, or if they made it back to Ulterion."

Grand Pierre and Aunt May looked solemnly at each other, and the children could see the sadness in their faces at the loss of their friends and the children in the fiery attack by the robotic soldiers.

"You must miss your home," Wren said. "Is Ulterion a pretty planet like Adoran?"

Aunt May answered, "At one time it was a beautiful planet—until the rogues started the wars. Everyone had to move underground for protection from the robots, and much of the planet has been destroyed by all the fighting. Creating clones that could survive outside because of their animal instincts—and still have the knowledge to infiltrate the rogues' headquarters—was an important project. The rogues looked no different from the rest of us, but they had changed their genetics years ago to allow them to live longer. I think they were worried about the planet becoming overpopulated, which was why they developed the robots to wipe us out." Aunt May shook her head sadly.

Grand Pierre looked at the children and sternly told them, "Never think of yourselves as anything but the best qualities of Ulterion combined with the uniqueness of your animal skills. You are the *special ones*, and now you must help free the Adoran settlement from the robots' cruel rule. I wish we had more time, but tomorrow Aunt May and I will take you to a children's home on the outskirts of the settlement. Father Brion is from the settlement and runs the children's home. He is aware of your special skills and is one of the leaders of the opposition formed to defeat the robots. He will continue your training because you have much to learn about the robots and the settlement. Never reveal your skills to anyone, and if you are discovered by the robots, run and hide—and get a message to Father Brion. Don't trust anyone, as the Adorans live in fear and will turn you in for food or favors. Now, off to your rooms, pack your things, and get some sleep. We must leave as soon as it's light enough to drive the transport."

The children slowly climbed the stairs to their rooms, lost in thought over everything they had learned.

In the boys' room, Boxer packed the books that Grand Pierre had given him, and Battle packed the throwing sweepers he'd made. To advance Battle's military training, Grand Pierre had assigned him a task to develop a defensive weapon.

"We don't have much to pack after living here for five years," Battle said to Boxer, looking at their meager belongings stacked on their beds. Boxer glanced around at the sparsely filled room and agreed. They had little to leave behind.

In the girls' room, Manx packed the sketches she'd drawn of the different forest flowers. She told Wren how sad she was at this moment, saying that she would miss the trips into the forest. Then she checked the drawers to make sure all of their clothes were in their sacks. Aunt May had sewn their plain shirts and pants.

Wren carefully wrapped a shirt around the mirror Aunt May had given her. She looked at Manx with tear-filled eyes. "I can't believe we have to leave the farm. I shall miss Aunt May and Grand Pierre."

Manx wrapped her arms around Wren, sharing her sadness. This was the only home they knew, and tomorrow they would leave everything familiar behind.

Just before the first light of day, Aunt May woke the children and hurried them downstairs. Each carried a sack filled with their possessions. When the children stepped outside, the transport was waiting, and the rear cage was filled with various items from the house.

"You will have to hold your own bags," Grand Pierre told the children as they climbed onto the bench seat, crowding together so all four could sit.

Aunt May sat in the front seat, and it was the first time the children had seen her in the transport. She had never accompanied them on their training trips.

"I think we have everything, or as much as the transport can carry," Grand Pierre said as he climbed into the driver's seat. He took one last look at the big, old house and admitted, "I shall miss our home. I am sorry our exit has been so rushed." Then he pushed the button to start the transport, and it rolled down the narrow path.

"If some of the other scientists who escaped are living among the Adorans, why didn't we leave before now?" Manx asked.

"After being attacked by the robots, the Adorans didn't trust anyone. Once they learned they had nothing to fear from the scientists—and the scientists had knowledge of the robots and how to avoid them—they began to work together. That is how the opposition began. Not all of the Adorans are part of the opposition, because they fear the robots. Only the opposition leaders know the real purpose of the research facility and about you children. Brion is one of the leaders and is anxious for your help."

"Why did you call him 'Father Brion' before?" Boxer asked.

"That is part of his cover," Grand Pierre replied as he guided the transport down the narrow trail. "Being manager of the children's home gives him access to the settlement to meet with others aligned with the cause. He has learned where the robots' headquarters are located, obtained maps to the settlement, and created routes to avoid the night patrols. The robots will destroy any place if they think someone living there is against them. So far, the orphanage has been left alone. The Adorans are a peaceful people and had never encountered anything as fierce and cruel as the robots before."

"Are there other children living at the place where we are going?" Wren asked.

"Yes," Grand Pierre said. "When the robots attacked the settlement, some of the Adorans tried to fight back and were killed. The children with Father Brion had been left with no one to care for them."

"I'm sad for them," Wren said. A worried look covered her face. "Do you think they will like us?"

Grand Pierre turned and smiled. "How could anyone not like you, little Wren?"

It was early morning when the transport rolled out of the forest. The ride had taken about one hour. Grand Pierre stopped the transport when a large valley came into view. The children could see various structures that filled the valley below. Many were box-shaped with large doors, others looked roundish with pointed roofs, and some resembled the farmhouse. Roads crisscrossed the valley, creating a large grid-like pattern.

"This place is huge!" Battle exclaimed as he sat forward for a better view.

"Many of the buildings look burned," Boxer noted.

"That is from the robots' searches," Grand Pierre said. "The larger buildings were businesses, the round ones were used for storage, and most of the homes have been ruined. The settlement has almost been destroyed by the robots, and there have been no repairs since the invasion. We must hurry before we are seen. Hold on. The orphanage is at this end of the settlement and downhill from here." Grand Pierre turned the transport down a narrow, bumpy trail.

"You know your way around," Manx said. "Is it because of all the trips you took every few days?"

Grand Pierre looked over at Aunt May, who said, "I told you that you weren't as sneaky as you thought. Nothing got past these four."

"That's because you trained us so well!" Wren chirped, making Grand Pierre chuckle.

The trail ended at a large compound. There was a long main building with four smaller buildings in front of it. The buildings were made of logs, stained with grime from years of neglect. The roofs were patched with various items. Grand Pierre drove the transport behind the main building. It was early morning, and the orphanage looked deserted. A small door in the back of the building opened, and a man stepped out and motioned them forward.

"Bring your things, children," Grand Pierre said and stepped from the transport.

Aunt May stood beside the transport, her eyes filled with tears, and tightly hugged each of the children as they climbed out.

"Hurry," Grand Pierre ordered in a hushed voice.

When they reached the door, Grand Pierre quickly made introductions. "This is Father Brion. He will teach you about the robots and train you for your missions. Work as a team and always remember your Cs. Aunt May and I can't stay in the settlement and must get to safety before the robots discover us. Good-bye, my special ones."

Then Grand Pierre hurried to the transport and drove away.

The Orphanage

CHAPTER 3

"Come in, come in." Father Brion motioned as he held the door open.

He shut and bolted the door when all four children were safely inside. Father Brion was a head shorter than Grand Pierre, with bushy hair that stuck out in all directions and thick eyebrows. He wore a long brown coat with wide sleeves.

He whispered, "You have much to learn in a short time. Follow me, and bring your things."

Father Brion seemed to scurry instead of walk as he led the children down a narrow hall at the back of building. When he came to a door at the end of the hall, he stopped and turned to the children. "You must be very careful at all times—what you say and what you do," he cautioned. "You must avoid any hint of suspicion that could bring the robots. You will be staying in a small pod directly across from this door. It's not as big as the pods the other children stay in, but you will be able to stay together. The secret entrance to the basement is directly under this door. That is where I have stored the maps and material critical for your missions, and we can work on your missions unseen."

Father Brion opened the door and looked outside. Satisfied that no one was around, he stepped outside and hurried across a narrow path running alongside the main building. He stopped at the back of a small wooden structure and unlocked a short, narrow door. Father Brion bent over as he went through the door. Boxer, Battle, and Manx ducked inside as well, and Wren was able to walk through without bending over.

It was dark inside the room, and Father Brion stepped over to a window and pushed aside the tattered drapes blocking the light. He turned and looked closely at each of the children.

He held out his stubby hand to Boxer and said, "Boxer, I am very grateful to have your assistance in planning the missions."

Then he took Battle's hand and told him, "Piers—or, as you call him, Grand Pierre—has told me of your outstanding military skills. Your input on how to disable the robots is a critical need."

His grin was lopsided as he looked at Manx and admitted, "With all the strange technology from the scientists that I must learn how to use, I am happy to have you on the team."

Then Father Brion placed his hand on Wren's shoulder. "Little Wren, I hear you are one very brave girl."

Then he straightened up and said, "Welcome, each of you. We have two meals a day at the orphanage: one in the morning and the other at evening. Snacks can be found in the kitchen if you can convince Marta, our cook, that you need one. You will meet Marta and Sola today. Sola is my assistant and runs the orphanage for me. Both are very trustworthy if you ever need help. Try to blend in with the other children. You are not as different-looking as the scientists are, which is why Piers felt it critical that you stay here and help with the missions. Piers has done an excellent job with your schooling.

You are far advanced over the other children living here. We used to have classes for the orphans, but I cannot get anyone from the settlement to come and help any longer. The children work on assignments that Sola gives them, but it is not an ideal learning solution. Pod one is where the boys stay, and the girls are in pod two."

Father Brion glanced around. "I'm sorry the pod isn't nicer, but this building was used for storage. Sola managed to move the beds in for you. At least you will be together. Unpack and settle in and always use the front door to enter or leave your pod. Come to the main building when you hear Marta ring the bell for first meal. I will get with you soon to begin work on your missions."

Father Brion nodded and quietly slipped out the small rear door, leaving the children alone inside.

Manx dropped her bag to the floor and looked around. "Wood floor, wood walls, wood beds. I think we are in the wood pod."

"It's not too bad, and we can fix it up," Wren said, trying to make the best of the situation. "It's small and sort of cozy."

"At least we have a window," Battle added as he looked out into a large open yard. Across the yard he could see the other buildings where the children stayed.

"You girls take the two beds in the back," Boxer said. "Battle and I will sleep in front. We can block the small door with that table so no one will notice it—in case we have visitors." Boxer was thinking of what Father Brion had said, and he wanted to keep the hidden entrance to the basement a secret.

There were two small wooden shelves above each bed and the children began unpacking. "We can put your flower drawings on the walls," Wren told Manx as they unpacked and placed their clothes on the shelves.

Boxer finished arranging his few books on one of the shelves above his bed. Grand Pierre had found the old books in the farmhouse, and one of them contained drawings of the forest and animals. The book Boxer like best and read the most was a book about the solar system, which named the sun and stars and the planet Adoran. Grand Pierre had always smiled when Boxer had read to him from this book, and now Boxer understood why. The Adoran writer who had created the book was far from correct in his assumptions about how the solar system worked. Boxer loved the old books, for they were an important part of his childhood.

It didn't take Battle long to refold his clothes in small, neat squares and place them on a shelf. On the other shelf he arranged his sweepers, lined up in a straight row. Battle liked everything neat and in its place. At the farm, one of the tricks the girls played to get even with Battle or to annoy him was to mess up his neat piles and even lines. This usually happened when Battle gave the girls static about trying harder or completing their challenges quicker. Battle was a great taskmaster, but he was always the hardest on himself—a part of his military heritage.

A loud clanging noise startled Boxer and hurt his ears. He looked at the others and cautioned, "Don't forget: we're orphans, and we were dropped off last night because our grandfather cannot care for us any longer. Remember our *C*s. Now, let's go eat—and meet the other children."

As the oldest of the four, Boxer was the leader of his group. Now he knew the reason for his ease at leading and organizing. It came from his Ulterion heritage.

"I'm so excited, I don't think I can eat a thing!" Wren exclaimed as the four children stepped outside. Boxer closed the door to the pod and led the way to the main building.

Battle sniffed the air. "Something smells good." It had been hours since Aunt May had woken them, and he was hungry.

"Let's stay together," Manx said and took hold of Wren's hand. She felt uneasy but was unsure why, especially at a home for orphaned children.

Boxer paused before opening the main door and looked at the others. "Ready?"

The three nodded their heads, and with Boxer in the lead, the special ones entered the large dining room. The room went silent as all the children stopped eating and turned to stare at the newcomers.

A short, plump woman stepped from the kitchen, wiping her hands on the apron tied around her ample waist, and exclaimed, "You must be the children Father Brion said came to the orphanage last night!" A smile crinkled her face in welcome. Then she said to the children sitting at the table eating their breakfast, "Everyone say hello to our newest members."

There were eight children seated at a long, battered table: five girls and three boys, all of various ages. All stared at the newcomers without saying a word.

"I'm Marta, the cook, and everyone who eats helps with cleanup. That's my rule. Sit down, and I'll bring your food." Marta pointed to the vacant end of the table.

After the four newcomers were seated, Wren leaned out and shyly smiled at the other children around the table. The smallest of the girls smiled back from across the table, but the older girls glared at Wren. The three boys when back to eating their breakfast.

"The food looks good." Battle broke the silence in the room as Marta placed a heaping plate of food in front of him. He was hungry and picked up his fork and began to eat.

Boxer and Manx both said thank you and stared at the large amount of food on their plates.

"Eat it all. The next meal isn't until evening," Marta told them when she noticed them looking at their plates. Then she hurried back into the kitchen.

"Hi, everyone. My name is Wren." Wren eagerly looked around the table at the other children, not bothering to eat.

The only response to Wren's greeting was from the youngest girl, who was sitting on the other side of Boxer. The girl looked back at Wren and said, "I'm Karry." She was smaller than Wren, with dark circles under her eyes, and had been pushing the food around her plate.

The oldest of the girls mumbled to the two girls sitting on either side of her, but it was still loud enough for everyone to hear. "Who cares?" The three girls all laughed at the snide remark and then went back to their meals.

The girl sitting on the other side of Karry didn't look up but kept slowly eating. "She can't talk." Karry pointed to the silent girl next to her. "No one knows her name. They call her the dummy." Karry pointed to the three older girls, who now glared at her.

"That's not very nice," Wren said, causing the three older girls to turn their menacing eyes on her.

"This is going really well," Manx whispered to Boxer.

A boy who looked older than Boxer demanded, "Where did you come from? You didn't come from the settlement, or I would have seen you before."

It was clear from the forceful tone of his voice that he was the established leader at the orphanage. The boy's limp brown hair hung in strings around his face, and his fingernails were dirty. His clothes looked like he had worn them for days. Battle looked over the wiry boy, assessing his strength, and knew that he would not be a problem for him or Boxer, even though the boy was trying to assert his authority.

Boxer answered, "From a farm beyond the forest. Our grandfather could not care for us any longer and brought us here last night."

"Where beyond the forest?" the boy challenged Boxer.

Boxer shrugged his shoulders. "We have never left the farm before, so I couldn't say. We're just glad to have a place to live and to be able to stay together."

"That's right," Manx said.

"So, are you brothers and sisters? You sure don't look alike." The older boy continued to stare at them with a puzzled expression.

"We're more like cousins," Manx clarified. "What's your name?" she sweetly asked the rude boy, causing Battle to smile at her deviousness.

The boy paused as if deciding whether to answer Manx or not. Finally he said, "I'm Lester, and he is Barten, and then Ray." He pointed to the boy sitting next to him first, and then to a boy with curly, reddish hair seated across the table from him. "What are your names?" Lester asked Manx.

Manx responded, "I'm Manx. Boxer is the oldest, and then Battle. And Wren already introduced herself." She pointed out each of them.

"Those are stupid names," said the oldest girl loudly, causing everyone to look at her.

Battle clenched his fists under the table but stayed quiet.

Manx looked directly at the rude girl and replied in a firm voice, "Our grandfather named us, and they are not stupid names."

The girl gave Manx a scowl that clearly said she still thought they were stupid names, and then she went back to eating. Manx bristled and sensed that this girl was not to be trusted.

Battle looked over at the rude girl and said, "You know our names. So, what are yours?"

The girl stared at Battle with hard eyes and finally said, "I'm Vera, and she's Jonne, and she's Dortha." Vera pointed to a girl on each side of her, and both Jonne and Dortha looked at Battle with a devious smirk. From the girls' hostility, it was clear that the newcomers were not welcome here, though they weren't sure why.

Marta walked back into the dining room and announced, "Time to clean up," breaking the tense feeling around the table.

CHAPTER 4

When the cleanup chores were finished, the orphanage children left without offering to show the newcomers around.

Boxer suggested, "Let's walk around and get to know the place."

When they were alone outside, Battle stated, "We must be careful. I don't trust any of them. I felt real hostility from those boys."

"The girls were just as bad," Manx added.

"Not all of them," Wren said. "Karry seems nice, and I feel sorry for the quiet girl. I'm going to call her Bunny because calling anyone 'dummy' is not nice." Wren paused and then asked, "Why didn't they like us?"

Manx thought for a moment. "Maybe they miss their homes and families and didn't want to have to live here."

"Even so, that's no reason to treat others like they treated us," Battle said. "I don't think Lester cares about anyone but himself."

As the special ones walked around the orphanage grounds, they were curious about the three smaller buildings in front of the main building.

"Those must be pods one, two, and three. Our little one is three and a half," Manx joked.

As they crossed in front of the first pod, they could hear Lester talking. "The boys must stay in there," Boxer noted.

The next pod they came to had the door open, and even though the pod was larger, the inside looked much like theirs. Vera jumped from the bed where she was sitting and slammed the door, saying, "Go away. You are not allowed in here."

"Anyone want to guess whose pod that is?" Manx grimaced.

"Why don't they want us to come in?" Wren asked.

Boxer warned, "Wren, those girls are very unfriendly. Don't go around them unless one of us is with you."

Wren sighed. "The orphanage doesn't seem like a very nice place to live."

"Boxer," Father Brion called and waved from the door of the main building. "May I see you?"

Boxer turned to the others and told them, "I will meet you later in our pod." Then he hurried off to meet Father Brion.

"Look, there are swings," Wren said. "Bunny is in one. Can I go over?" She pointed at the edge of the yard near their pod and looked at Manx and Battle, waiting for an answer.

"Okay," Manx agreed. Then she added, "I'll get my tablet and sit under the tree and draw while you swing."

"I'll practice throwing my sweepers by our pod," Battle said as they walked to their pod at the back of the compound. He let Manx know that he would be on watch.

Wren skipped toward the swings and smiled as she sat in the swing next to the silent girl. Both girls moved their feet back and forth in unison to keep their swings moving. After a few swings back and forth, Wren looked at the girl and said, "This is fun. I've never been on a swing before."

The girl kept her head down and concentrated on her feet.

"I've decided to call you Bunny," Wren told her. "It's a much nicer name, and I love cuddly little bunnies, even though I've never seen one. Have you ever seen a bunny?" Wren chattered away as the two girls continued to swing.

The silent girl smiled and looked over at Wren and nodded her head.

"Wow, are you lucky! Did you see it here?" Wren asked excitedly.

The girl shook her head no and pointed toward the forest.

"Did you come from the forest too?" Wren was curious about the silent girl with blonde hair and pale-blue eyes. The girl nodded, and Wren jumped from the swing and said, "I want to tell Manx. She is over by that big tree, drawing. Want to come?"

Wren held out her hand. The girl hesitated and then jumped down and took hold of Wren's hand. The girl was taller than Wren and very slim for her height.

"Bunny likes her new name, and she has actually seen a real bunny," Wren told Manx as the two girls sat down beside her.

Manx looked at the silent girl and told her, "Bunny is a great name, and it suits you perfectly. Is it okay if we call you Bunny?"

The girl smiled at Manx and nodded her head. Manx took a sheet of paper, and in a few quick strokes she drew a bunny with long ears, a wrinkled nose, whiskers, and two big, round eyes. When Manx finished the drawing, she handed it to Bunny and said, "A bunny for Bunny."

Bunny took the drawing and held it against her chest.

"She likes it!" Wren exclaimed.

Manx stood up and told Wren, "Let's go finish unpacking. Boxer should be back soon."

"See you later, Bunny," Wren said as she hopped away with Manx.

Battle was sitting at the small table when the two girls walked into the pod. He looked up and asked, "Any sign of Boxer?"

Manx shook her head no as she joined him at the table. Wren went over to the window and stood on her toes to look outside. She announced, "Here he comes."

When Boxer entered the pod, he shut the door and told Wren, "Keep watch at the window in case someone comes around." He sat down at the table with Battle and Manx and told them, "Father Brion showed me the secret entrance to the basement, and the maps of the settlement. Tomorrow he is going on rounds to pick up food and supplies, and I'm to go with him. He wants me to learn my way around the settlement and the patrol routes of the robots as quickly as possible."

"What if you see one?" Battle asked in a worried tone. "Do you think it will recognize you as a threat?"

"I won't know until I meet one," Boxer responded.

"You must be careful and have an escape plan. You won't be able to come back here, and we will have to leave too. We should decide on a place to meet up in case something happens." Battle's military instincts were kicking in.

"I can see a lot of trees down the road," Wren said, standing higher on her toes to get a better view. "We could hide there." The other children joined her at the window.

"The trees are far enough away that we won't be seen from the orphanage, but they're close enough for us to get to in a hurry," Battle said, considering. "The tall trees can act as our meeting place if we're ever forced to escape."

The next day after first meal was over, the special ones were waiting out front when they heard a rumbling noise and watched Father Brion drive a battered vehicle out of pod three and around to the main building. The big, noisy vehicle looked strange to the special ones, and they stared at it. They had only seen Grand Pierre's transport, and this thing was twice as big.

Father Brion stopped the gray machine and motioned to Boxer. "Get in the truck. We must leave now to complete the rounds before second meal."

Boxer turned to Battle. "Stay alert, and watch out for Wren and Manx."

Battle understood Boxer's concern and told him, "We'll stay around our pod until you get back."

As Father Brion drove the truck away, he explained that he had to be careful and stay on the main roads to avoid suspicion by the robots. He asked Boxer if he had memorized the grids and main roads. Boxer said that he had, including certain locations Brion had marked with an X. In these locations, Brion would make contact with other members of the opposition while picking up any items left out for the orphanage. He would leave notes with questions to be answered, or answer questions left for him. At times, one of the men would help Brion load the truck and secretly discuss things that needed to be accomplished.

Boxer saw very few people outside, but he did notice faces staring from windows. Up close, the settlement was in shambles. Many of the homes were not livable and were without doors and windows, and some had collapsed. From all the destruction, Boxer wondered how the settlement had managed to survive for the past five years.

As they watched Boxer and Father Brion drive away, Wren noticed Karry and Bunny on the swings and hurried to join them, her happy chatter filling the air. The other children kept to themselves, totally ignoring the newcomers.

"I'm glad Wren has made friends," Manx said to Battle and then added, "I'll get my drawing tablet and sit and watch Wren."

Inside the pod, Battle took the sweepers from the shelf and showed them to Manx. "Depending on where you hold it when you throw it, it will strike the target in a different way," he explained. "It can fly over something like a wall and then drop down on the target. Or change your hold, and it will fly low under something and then rise up and hit the target. There are hidden blades for cutting if needed."

"This is great," Manx said. "I'm impressed with your ingenuity. If you threw one of your sweepers at someone, the strength of your throw would knock him out." Manx was reaching for her drawing table and chalk when Wren came into the pod, looking despondent.

"I thought you were swinging with Bunny and Karry," Manx stated.

Wren flopped down on her bed. "Vera came over and said they had work to do in their pod, and she made them leave."

It was easy to see Wren's disappointment, so Battle suggested, "Why don't we go for a walk to the trees and explore. I would like to check it out and make sure it will work for our escape place."

Wren's mood immediately brightened, and she jumped from her bed. "Okay."

Placing his sweepers on the shelf in a straight line, Battle closed the door to the pod and joined Manx and Wren out front.

As they walked past pod one, Lester stepped out and demanded, "Where are you going?" Manx bristled at Lester's tone of voice.

Battle stopped in front of Lester. "Just taking a walk. Do you want to come with us?" Lester was the taller of the two boys, but Battle's width and muscles made Lester look smaller.

Lester sneered. "No, and don't get lost, 'cause no one will come to find you."

"We won't," Battle answered, keeping his tone flat and not rising to Lester's challenge. Then he rejoined Wren and Manx to continue down the dusty road.

When they were far enough away from Lester, Manx asked, "Why did you invite him?"

Battle smiled and answered, "It was a test. I wanted to see what he would do. And you need to keep your enemies close."

Wren looked up at Battle. "Is Lester our enemy?"

Battle responded, "He isn't our friend."

The stand of tall trees was bigger than it had looked from the orphanage, and the trees formed a circle. The area inside the circle was shaded, and the trees continued into the forest beyond.

Battle paced around inside the circle and said, "This is a great place to hide, and we can escape to the forest from here."

"Maybe we will see a real bunny." Wren was busy looking under the thick brush.

"Can we get back to the orphanage through the forest?" Manx asked. "I'd like to avoid Lester, if possible.

"Probably, but we should return by the road. I know Lester is watching us, and I don't want him to get suspicious and follow us here."

Manx agreed. "We don't want anyone else to know about this place."

"Wren!" Battle called, not seeing that she was searching for a real bunny nearby. "We should start back and wash up for second meal!"

When the three reached the orphanage, Battle and Manx started talking loudly. Wren frowned at their strange behavior, not understanding that this was to let Lester know they were back.

"Look!" Wren said. "That big truck is in pod three. Boxer is back." She pointed and hurried to their pod.

CHAPTER 5

$\mathcal{W}$hen the three entered their pod, Manx stopped and held out her hand and said, "Wait."

The pod looked exactly as they had left it, but Manx walked to each bed and sniffed. "Lester was in here and searched the place," she said. "Battle, check under the beds. Wren, make sure all your things are here."

Wren hurried to her shelves and looked closely and told Manx, "Everything is here."

"Mine too," Manx said after checking her shelves.

Battle looked at Manx. "Boxer's and my stuff is all here, but my sweepers aren't the way I placed them when we left."

Just then, Marta rang the bell for second meal. As Battle, Manx, and Wren entered the large dining room, they looked around for Boxer. They saw him seated at the table with a boy who had dark hair, a pointy face, and two very large front teeth. The young boy's looks were peculiar, but they suited him.

"How was your trip with Father Brion?" Battle asked as he sat down at the table across from Boxer.

"It was interesting," Boxer answered, but his look said that he had more to say later.

"Who's the newcomer?" Manx asked as she sat down by Battle. Wren climbed onto the bench beside her.

"He was waiting at one of Father Brion's stops with a note asking Father Brion to care for him. He hasn't said a word, so I'm not sure of his name." Boxer smiled at the boy and added, "Father Brion is going to put him in pod one with the other boys. He said there is plenty of room for him."

"Lucky him," Battle mumbled to Manx.

"We need to talk after we eat," Manx told Boxer as the other children from the orphanage came into the dining room and found places at the long table. If Lester noticed Manx's glare aimed at him, he didn't let on.

"Hi, Karry. Hi, Bunny." Wren leaned out to great her new friends.

Neither girl answered Wren's greeting, and they silently sat down at the table, keeping their heads bowed. Vera sat down at the other end of the table with a smug look on her face. She had heard Wren's greeting and watched the two small girls ignore it.

Manx immediately knew Vera had something to do with Karry and Bunny's changed behavior. Jonne and Dortha looked over at Wren and Manx with expressions that mirrored Vera's nasty smirk.

There was little talk at the table as the children ate their meal. After the dishes were cleared, Father Brion walked into the room followed by a thin woman with short brown hair. "She must be Sola," Manx whispered to Boxer.

"Children." Father Brion clapped his hands to get everyone's attention. "We have a new member joining our family." Father Brion pointed to the young boy, who looked ready to bolt. Father Brion paused and then said, "I'm afraid I don't know his name."

"Great. Another dummy," Vera exclaimed loudly.

"Vera, you know that is not acceptable," Sola sternly told her.

Vera rudely answered back, "Let Wren name him. She's so good at it."

"We could call him Bucky," Lester said and then turned to make sure his followers laughed at his mean joke.

Father Brion said, "Enough of this. Perhaps a time-out in the pods would be appropriate."

"What's the difference?" Lester said, his tone defiant. "All we ever do is stay in our pod. This place is boring."

"I'm sorry you feel that way, Lester." Sola stepped forward and faced him. "I am open to any suggestions for activities."

Lester shrugged and turned to Barten and Ray and scoffed, "Let's go to our pod."

"Show our newest member to the boys' pod and help him settle in," Sola told Lester.

Lester huffed and looked around. "Where are his things?"

"He didn't bring any with him," Sola answered. "I'll get him some bedding and clothes from the locker."

It was starting to get dark as the children left the main building and walked to their pod. "I feel sorry for the new boy having to live in pod one with those creeps," Manx exclaimed after she shut the door. The others agreed with her.

Boxer closed the tattered drapes that hung over the window and pulled the small wooden table into the middle of the room. There were only three chairs, and Boxer said, "I'll stand so I can listen at the door in case we have visitors."

One of Boxer's animal traits was his highly developed hearing. Because he could hear sounds from far distances, Grand Pierre had made special bracelets for Manx and Wren to wear. When the girls rubbed their bracelets, they emitted a sound so high-pitched that only Boxer could hear it. The two girls had worn their bracelets since arriving at the farm, and neither had ever taken them off, in case they became separated or lost. All four special ones could see in the dark as well as in the light. This was another one of their unique animal skills.

When Boxer was sure no one was sneaking around the pod, he looked at the others with a concerned expression. "Things are not good in the settlement. Because of all the robots' restrictions, the people have not been allowed to grow crops or hunt for game, and food has become scarce. The rogue leaders shut down the power at night, leaving the settlement in the dark, and everyone is under a curfew. Donations for the orphanage have almost stopped, and Father Brion isn't sure how long he can keep the orphanage open. If he has to close it, he will lose the ability to make rounds and meet with others in the settlement who are working to overthrow the robots. For this reason we must speed up our training and help Father Brion retrieve data from the robots' headquarters. After dark we can sneak out the small door and get to the basement's hidden entrance under the main building without being seen. Only two or three of us will go at one time, as someone must always stand guard."

"I agree that we need to stand watch," Manx said. "Our pod was searched today by Lester." She grimaced.

"Are you sure it was Lester?" Boxer asked.

"Yes. Lester has a stink all to himself!" Manx huffed.

"I don't think Wren should be left alone to guard," Battle said. "If we have trouble, it will come from Lester or Vera or their goons. They would not hesitate to hurt anyone smaller than they are."

Manx stated, "I know that Karry and Bunny are afraid of Vera. She must have really scared them; both girls were frightened at second meal and barely ate."

Boxer continued, "Tomorrow Battle and I will meet with Father Brion. He wants Battle to figure out how to disable the robots, since they are programmed for military use. Today Father Brion drove around as much of the settlement as possible without causing suspicion. It helped me learn the patrol routes the guards use. So far, there has been no sign that the rogue leaders are aware of any opposition activities. Manx, you need to learn how to operate the device the researchers rescued from their facility. It will be your job to get inside the robots' headquarters and use this device. Let's all get some sleep. Starting tomorrow, we will be busy planning the missions."

The following days fell into a schedule for the special ones. Between first and second meals, they spent their time reviewing what they learned in the basement the night before. Boxer drew maps for the others to gain knowledge of the settlement and to recognize certain roads and buildings, including the fastest routes to the hideout.

From information provided by the opposition team, Battle figured out how to avoid the robots when he determined that they always swept the area they were searching from right to left and never in the back.

Manx and Father Brion spent hours figuring out the various settings on a round, metal device given to them by the researchers called a com-nit. If they aligned the strange symbols on the com-nit in certain positions, it changed the use of the device. Manx figured out how to align the symbols to capture images. It would be her task to find documents or drawings and record them. From the images, the researchers could translate the documents for the opposition.

Father Brion warned Manx, "Never leave any sign that you were in their headquarters, or the rogue leaders will change buildings and routes, and we don't have time to get new information."

The other children in the orphanage had not missed the special ones between meals. After first meal, where they ignored the special ones, they went back to their pods to work on the day's assignment from Sola. Or Lester and Vera and their goons, as Battle called their followers, would stand around and whisper and then laugh out loud.

Boxer told his companions to say that they were working on lessons, if they were ever asked about their absence, but Lester and Vera had not shown any interest in them. After second meal, eaten in silence, all of the children would return to their pods before the power was turned off, leaving the orphanage in darkness.

After the third night of meetings with Father Brion, Manx returned to the pod and told Boxer, "I started to feel like I was being watched. Battle and I searched the basement and around outside, but we didn't see anyone."

Boxer replied, "We will have to be extra careful, but I know the other children have not left their pods after dark. I've been listening."

Manx shivered. "I know when I'm being watched."

The following day on the way to first meal, Wren grumbled to Manx, "I wish I could play with Karry and Bunny." For the past three days, the two girls had refused to look at Wren or answer her greetings.

"Why don't you sit with them at breakfast?" Manx told Wren.

"You think it's okay?" Wren asked.

"Of course. We can sit where we want for meals."

The dining room was empty when Manx and Wren entered the room, and Wren hopped, birdlike, from one foot to the other as she watched the door for her friends.

"Here they come," Wren announced excitedly.

When Karry and Bunny entered the room, Wren hurried over and took hold of their hands and told them, "Manx said I could sit with you during meal." Karry looked ready to cry and tried to pull her hand away.

Manx walked over and looked at the frightened girls and told them, "Go ahead and sit down. It will be okay."

With bowed heads, Karry and Bunny hesitantly followed Wren to the table. Wren climbed onto the bench and motioned Karry to one side of her and Bunny to the other. Manx could sense that the two girls were scared. Wren chattered away, telling the two girls how much she'd missed them and suggesting that maybe they could swing after meal. Wren's excitement didn't carry over to Karry, who sat there shaking.

The door banged open, and Vera entered the dining room followed by Jonne and Dortha. Vera stopped and her mouth dropped open when she saw Wren seated between Karry and Bunny.

"What is going on?" she demanded loudly, stomping toward the quivering girls.

Before Vera could reach the table, Manx jumped up and in one swift leap landed in front of Vera, blocking her way. "Do you have a problem?" Manx's voice was a low hiss.

One look at Manx's face caused Vera to step back.

Manx warned Vera, "There is *no* assigned seating for meals. Everyone can sit where they want."

"We'll see," Vera answered. She turned and walked around the table and sat down across from Wren.

Neither Karry nor Bunny looked up when Vera sat down. Jonne and Dortha followed behind Vera and dutifully sat on each side of her.

"As soon as the meal is over, go back to the pod," Vera ordered, looking directly at the two smaller girls.

Swiftly Manx jumped onto the bench beside Karry, leaned over the table, and glared at Vera. Manx crouched, ready to spring. "After the meal the girls are going to swing." She began to roll her fingers across the wooden table, her sharp nails making a clicking sound.

Vera sneered, "Do you think you're a cat?" She forced a laugh, but her face lost all color when Manx hissed, catlike, in her face.

Manx moved back to sit beside Karry, constantly watching Vera the way a cat watches a mouse. She sensed Vera's fear. "Just so you know," she said, "I'll be with the girls by the swings."

All of the boys entered the dining room together and hurried to the table as Marta carried in plates of food, unaware of the scene being played out between Vera and Manx.

After the meal was over and the dishes had been carried into the kitchen, Manx told Boxer in a voice loud enough for everyone to hear, "I'm taking Wren, Karry, and Bunny to the swings. I'll be there if you need me."

With ringing ears and a confused expression, Boxer replied, "Thanks."

Manx hid a smile as she watched Vera storm out of the dining room trailed by Jonne and Dortha.

Boxer noticed the pointy-faced boy coming from the kitchen and waved to him. "How are you doing? Did you get settled into pod one?"

The boy smiled and nodded his head and walked outside without saying a word. As far as Boxer knew, the boy still had not said a word. Boxer considered going after the boy to make sure he wasn't being hassled by Lester, but he had to get back to his own pod to finish the plans for tomorrow night's mission. It would be the special ones' first mission, and tonight he would go over the final details with Father Brion.

Manx sat under the tree and watched the three young girls swing, marveling at Wren's nonstop chatter. A few minutes later, Wren hopped off her swing and skipped over to Manx.

"Looks like you're having fun," Manx told Wren.

Wren sighed. "Well, something is wrong with Karry. She won't talk to me."

"Why don't you ask the girls to come and sit, and maybe we can find out why?" Manx replied, although she already knew who was responsible for their fearful behavior.

Wren hurried to the swings and returned with Karry and Bunny.

"Hi, girls," Manx said. "Come here and sit down. I bet you could use a rest after swinging." She smiled at the two girls. When they sat down, Manx took hold of each of their hands and squeezed them to get the girls to look at her. "Wren and I have been worried about you." When Karry didn't say a word, Manx continued. "I know Vera has done something to frighten you and make you to stay away from Wren. Karry, won't you please tell me about it?"

Karry looked at Manx. Tears filled her eyes, and her small chin began to quiver. Manx reached out and held Karry as she began to sob. Karry cried so hard that her tears soaked Manx's shirt. Wren held Bunny's hand as they watched Karry weep in Manx's arms.

When Karry finally stopped crying, Manx dried the little girl's face and said, "Karry, what has Vera done to you and Bunny? She shouldn't be allowed to scare others."

Karry sighed loudly, looked around, and then whispered, "She said she would have the metal men come and take us away."

Manx was confused. "Metal men?" she repeated.

Wren chirped, "Those robot guys Grand Pierre told us about."

"Oh!" Manx now understood Vera's threat. She had heard the stories from Grand Pierre and Father Brion, but so far she had not seen a robot.

Manx asked Karry, "Have the metal men come around the orphanage?"

Both Karry and Bunny nodded their heads.

"When?" Manx asked. She was sure Father Brion didn't know about this because he'd said the orphanage had been left alone.

"After dark Lester goes and talks to them," Karry answered.

"Do you know how many times Lester has met with them?" Manx questioned.

Karry shrugged her thin shoulders. "Some nights. I can see them from the window."

Manx knew that Boxer and Father Brion must be told. They would need to start watching Lester and find out what he was up to, which was definitely not good.

When Manx was worried, she had a habit of turning the thin metal bracelet on her wrist—the one that Grand Pierre had made for her and Wren. As she turned the bracelet, she immediately knew what to do. She felt for the hidden lock and pushed. The bracelet snapped open.

"Hold out your arm," Manx ordered Karry. Manx pushed up the sleeve of Karry's shirt and placed and locked the bracelet above her elbow. "This is a special bracelet. Do not let anyone else see it." Manx looked hard at Karry to make sure she understood that it was important. Karry nodded her head that she understood. "If you and Bunny are ever taken or lost, rub the bracelet like this, and keep rubbing it. We will find you. Keep rubbing the bracelet. Do you understand?" Manx was putting all her energy into rubbing the thin silver band—and wishing it was Vera's neck she had between her hands.

Boxer crashed out of the pod and frantically looked around, and Battle was behind him with an anxious expression on his face. Then Boxer and Battle raced to the large tree where the girls sat.

"What's wrong?" Boxer exclaimed with a confused expression, seeing Manx sitting under the tree still rubbing the bracelet that was now on Karry's arm.

Manx realized that she was responsible for Boxer and Battle's sudden appearance. She stopped rubbing the bracelet and pulled down Karry's sleeve. "See how it works?" she said. "You girls are not alone. We will find you."

A relieved Karry smiled up at Manx and then reached out and hugged her around the neck. Boxer and Battle stepped back, watching the girls, knowing that Manx would explain later what was going on.

Manx stood up, brushed at her clothes, and then reached out and took hold of each girl's hand. "One more thing," she said. "You must eat all of your meals from now on to grow big and strong, and then Vera can't scare you anymore. Promise me?"

With grateful expressions, Karry and Bunny nodded to Manx.

"We need to go to our pod and do some work, but we will see you both at second meal." Manx promised.

The small girls smiled and waved good-bye to Wren. Holding hands, they skipped back to the swings.

Once inside their pod with the door closed, Boxer asked Manx, "What was that about? And do you think it was a good idea to take off your bracelet?"

Manx gravely answered, "It was necessary."

Then she told Boxer and Battle about Vera threatening the girls and Lester's secret night meetings with the robots.

Mission 1

CHAPTER 6

*P*lans for the first mission were completed, and last night Father Brion and Boxer had gone over the details again. Today after first meal, Boxer would go with Father Brion on rounds to get one final look at the two-story building that was the rogues' headquarters. The opposition leaders were counting on Manx to discover information about the robots' mission on Adoran.

It had been five years since the scientific facility had been raided and the robots had taken control of the settlement. Father Brion had told Boxer that the scientists were concerned that the robots had not returned to Ulterion after completing their mission. It had been suggested that the rogues might be planning to make a permanent colony on Adoran, and as the months passed, this worry increased.

This morning, before Boxer left with Father Brion, he told the others he would return as soon as possible, but it would take extra time to scout the rogue headquarters during the day. Father Brion did not want to alarm the robots; if he did, he would be stopped and searched.

Battle anxiously paced around their pod. He was worried about Boxer meeting a robot that could detect Boxer's Ulterion heritage. If that happened, Boxer would have to escape, and the mission would be over before it had begun. The special ones would have to leave the orphanage to avoid being found by the robots.

Manx sat under the large tree, waiting for Boxer to return. She was watching Wren play with Karry and Bunny. The two young girls seemed more relaxed and not fearful as before. Manx bristled at the thought of Vera threatening the two girls and scaring them with the robotic soldiers.

Manx worried about tonight's mission, knowing she would have to break into the rogues' headquarters and find information that would help defeat the robots. She also worried about the rogues making a permanent colony on this peaceful planet. It would mean the destruction of the Adoran way of life. She would do her best to help the opposition team defeat the cruel robots. Manx decided to return to the pod and review the headquarters layout again. She and Wren would enter the building tonight while Battle and Boxer stood guard outside. Her time inside would be limited, and she wanted to be as prepared as possible. Manx was anxious to finally put her special skills to use.

Manx had trained with Grand Pierre for the past five years, and she now understood his dedication. Like the others, Manx was far advanced in knowledge, reasoning, and physical skills. The special ones were healthier, stronger, and more intelligent than the children living at the orphanage. Grand Pierre and Aunt May had given their all to prepare the special ones.

Aunt May had once mentioned that Boxer was almost fully grown, and that by age twelve children were considered adults. Manx had not given Aunt May's comment much thought until now, and she decided that Aunt May had been referring to Ulterion ages. Boxer was as tall as Grand Pierre, much taller than Father Brion, and as mature as any adult.

Manx had learned that Lester was fourteen and the oldest at the orphanage. When he reached fifteen years, he would have to leave. Lester lacked maturity and tried to intimidate anyone smaller than himself. He wouldn't have a chance if he ever challenged Boxer, and a part of her wished he would.

Manx stood up and brushed the leaves from her clothes. She froze and looked around, feeling as if she was being watched, but she did not see anyone. She shook her head, thinking her catlike senses were overreacting. Her confrontation with Vera, along with the tension over tonight's mission, had them in high gear. Manx called to Wren, saying they needed to go and study their lessons. Wren hopped from her swing, told her friends that she would see them later, and hurried to catch up with Manx. When they entered their pod, Manx shut the door and pulled the drapes over the window before unrolling the paper that detailed the building's layout.

As soon as second meal was over, the special ones hurried to their pod to go over the mission one last time. Tonight they would sneak out of their pod after the settlement went dark. Boxer reviewed the details: Three dogs were penned in cages behind the two-story building. At night the dogs would be turned loose to roam the picket-fenced yard. Battle would draw the dogs to him so Manx could get in. Boxer would stand lookout for the patrol guards. Wren would find a way in so that Manx could search for information before the patrol returned.

Manx looked at the com-nit that could capture images. The scientists could retrieve and interpret the images because they understood the rogues' language; it was almost identical to their own. Each of the special ones had a part in the mission, but Manx knew that if she didn't find something useful, the mission would be considered a failure. She closed the com-nit and placed it in the special holder with a strap so she could carry it around her neck. Father Brion had designed the holder to leave her hands free. Manx was a strong and formidable opponent, both as a girl and as a cat, and the use of her hands was critical.

Boxer stood at the door and signaled for quiet. From now on, they would use the hand signs Grand Pierre had taught them. The orphanage had gone dark, and Battle looked out the window and motioned that it was all clear. Boxer nodded and quietly opened the door, stepped out, and listened. This was the shortest way to the forest. When he signaled the others to go, Battle stepped out and ran to the nearby trees to stand watch. Boxer closed the door after Manx and Wren had slipped out and silently made their way to where Battle watched.

Manx's heightened senses caused her to glance around. Boxer joined the others and motioned them into single file. Wren stepped behind Boxer, Manx came next, and Battle came last as they crept through the trees. Boxer stayed hidden in the trees until they were past the orphanage and then ran along the side of a road that led into the settlement. The special ones made no noise, their steps sure in the dark night. They had no fear of running or tripping on unseen objects.

Boxer held his hand up, signaling them to stop. The special ones had kept a steady pace to reach a vacant area across from the rogue headquarters. No one was breathing hard from the long run, for they were all in excellent physical shape.

Boxer knelt down, and the others formed a circle around him. He whispered, "The dogs are loose. Manx, the fastest way in is over the back fence. From there you can jump on top of the dogs' cages and reach the top floor roof where it extends over the back porch. Wren, according to the opposition's surveillance, a window on the top floor is open, signal Manx when you find it. Battle will go to the front and draw the dogs there. The patrol is due anytime, and once they are past, we will have about thirty minutes before they return. Stay hidden until the patrol passes."

Battle looked down the road and whispered, "Here they come."

The special ones were anxious to see the machines with manlike features. Silently, side by side, two large metal creatures rolled down the road. They resembled men from the waist up and were attached to a large platform with wide treads on each side that moved them forward. When they passed by, they turned right and then left, shining bright beams of light from the tops of their heads across the road.

Each guard wore a uniform with various weapons attached across the front. The top of each head was covered by a metal cap, and a narrow piece of the metal extended down the back of each one's neck. In a strange way, their movements and eyes made them seem alive. Grand Pierre had said that the robots were programmed to interact with people and would respond to orders from the rogue leaders—without feeling—no matter what they did or who they hurt.

When the robots rolled out of sight, Boxer signaled his companions to go, and he leaped forward and changed into a large black dog.

Battle jumped and changed into a wide, armor-plated mastiff and loped across the road to the fence and began pacing.

Wren extended her arms, changing into a bird, and flew toward the roof of the two-story building.

Manx crouched and sprang forward, swiftly changing into the muscled yellow cat. She made no sound as she ran to the back of the building and leaped the fence.

Battle made a yelp like he was injured, and all three dogs raced toward the sound. Manx jumped on top of the dog cages and then to the roof of the back porch, her padded paws not making a sound. Manx heard a series of chirps and knew that Wren had spotted the open window. Manx ran to the window, jumped inside, and changed.

Manx stood in the middle of the dark room and looked around. Tables and chairs were scattered about, and on the back wall she saw two tall cabinets. Manx took the com-nit from the holder and aligned the symbols. She quickly went to each of the tables to see if any items had been left out on them, but all the tables had been cleared off. Manx hurried to the back of the room to search the cabinets. So intense was her concentration that she didn't hear the commotion at the front fence.

Each tall cabinet had four drawers that pulled out, and remembering the Cs, Manx cautiously looked around for any alarms or trip wires. She found none. She slowly opened the top drawer of the first cabinet. It was filled with what looked like parts, but she couldn't tell what they were for. She captured an image of the parts and carefully closed the drawer.

Manx discovered that the other three drawers all contained parts, but each drawer held different-looking ones. She captured images of the drawers and then moved to the second cabinet. She paused before opening the top drawer of the second cabinet, for she had heard Wren's warning: two fast chirps repeated twice. It was a signal to hurry and get out.

Manx knew she had only been in the room seven minutes. Each of the special ones had been taught how to track time in their minds like a stopwatch. It was an important part of controlling a situation. If they hadn't finished the task Grand Pierre had given them within the allotted time, they had failed the test.

Manx opened the second cabinet's top drawer and found it full of stacks of papers. She stared at the stacks, not sure if they were useful or not. There were three stacks that came to the top of the drawer. It would take her hours to capture an image of each paper—and besides, the stacks looked dusty. Manx captured an image of the drawer and moved to the second drawer—when Wren chirped another warning.

The second drawer held two folders, and Manx lifted them out and sat them on the floor. She opened the first folder; it held a paper filled with columns and rows of symbols that resembled the ones on the com-nit. Manx quickly captured the paper's image and put it back the same way she'd found it. She opened the second folder and found a folded paper. She unfolded it and saw that it looked like a map. She quickly captured its image, refolded the paper, and put both folders back in the cabinet.

As she started to open the third drawer, Wren flew through the window and changed and shouted, "Manx, we have to go! Battle and Boxer are having trouble with the dogs. Haven't you heard?"

Startled, Manx shook her head. "I have two drawers left." She pulled open the third drawer, and like the top drawer, it was filled with papers that looked like they had been shoved in without any order. Manx captured the drawer's image.

Wren ran back to the window just as Boxer issued a retreat howl. "We have to go now!" Wren yelled. She changed into the brown bird and flew out the window.

Manx knew time had run out, but she needed to inspect the final drawer, and she opened it. Her mouth dropped when she saw a device wedged inside that looked like the com-nit, only much larger. She could tell it belonged to the scientists. It was too large for her to carry, so she captured an image of it, closed the drawer, and ran to the window.

Manx couldn't see the front of the building, but from all the barking and growling, it sounded like there were a dozen dogs, not just the three penned in the yard. Manx could tell that Battle and Boxer were not part of the deafening riot.

Manx secured the com-nit in the pouch around her neck and jumped out the window, changing into the yellow cat. She ran to the back and jumped onto the porch and then on top of the cages. She crouched and leaped, clearing the fence and landing on the hard ground.

Manx could see two beams of light coming down the road. The patrol guards had returned with their sirens blaring. Between the dogs' barking and the sirens' wailing, Manx was sure the noise could be heard all the way to the orphanage.

Manx raced to the side of the building and could see Battle and Boxer waiting across the road in the vacant area. Wren was perched in a tree. The three guard dogs were in a vicious panic, snarling and growling and trying to dig out of the fenced yard. If the robots searched the ground by the fence, they would notice Battle's tracks and follow them across the road.

Manx decided to control the situation. Dogs usually hated cats and would go to great lengths to harm them.

Just as the two patrol guards rolled to a stop in front of the panicked dogs, Manx leaped into a nearby tree and cried a very loud *meow*.

The crazed dogs began another barking binge. Manx jumped to the ground, puffed out her fur so the robots could easily see her, and again meowed as loud as she could. She turned and ran along the side of the fence, causing the obnoxious trio of hounds to chase after her. Giving one final meow for the guards' benefit, Manx jumped high into a tree and watched the dogs slide to a stop at the end of the fence, knocking into each other and howling with frustration.

Manx was stunned when she heard one of the guards say in a metallic-sounding voice, "It's just a cat that has the dogs going crazy. Maybe we should shoot it."

The other guard answered, "I think we should shoot the stupid dogs."

Then the warning sirens stopped, a "situation clear" was announced, and the patrol guards turned and headed back down the road.

Manx waited until the two patrol guards were out of sight and then circled around the building to avoid upsetting the dogs again. Then she crossed the road to join the others in the vacant area.

"Good thinking, Manx. You fooled the patrol guards." Boxer had changed back.

Manx and Battle did the same. Wren hopped from the tree and changed when she landed on the ground.

"I didn't know those monsters could talk," Manx uttered and shook her head in amazement.

Battle added, "They were communicating with the rogue leaders. The warning sirens and 'all clear' signals were sent and received somewhere else, not here. There must be another building that is being used by the rogue leaders, and we must tell Father Brion."

"We need to leave," Boxer said, and he started running toward the orphanage.

CHAPTER 7

$\mathcal{T}$he special ones reached the tree circle hideout and paused to catch their breath. Since leaving the vacant area across from the robot headquarters, they had run all the way without stopping. Because of the trouble with the dogs, the mission had taken longer than planned. Boxer held his hand up, signaling quiet, and crept toward the orphanage.

He returned and whispered, "Lester is meeting with the patrol guards outside of pod one. He is whispering so low I can't make out what he is saying. Let's change to avoid detection and make our way back to our pod through the forest."

All of them changed into their animal forms and slowly crept away, staying hidden in the trees. Wren perched on Battle's shoulder, not wanting to fly at night and attract attention. Manx looked around intently; the feeling of being watched had returned.

Making no sound, the special ones made their way through the dense forest and stopped across from their pod. When they changed back, they could still see the guards' search beams by pod one.

"Can we get to our pod without the guards seeing us?" Wren asked anxiously.

"Not until they leave," Boxer replied softly. He did not want the guards' sensors to pick up any movement.

"I would like to know what Lester is telling those guards," Battle said in a low growl.

Finally the patrol guards turned, pointed their lights down the road, and silently rolled away. Lester went back inside. The special ones were surprised when the door to their pod opened and someone whispered, "It's safe. Hurry."

Thinking it was Father Brion waiting for them to return, the special ones ran toward the open door. All four were speechless when the pointy-faced boy closed the door once they were safely inside.

The boy looked at them and exclaimed, "Wow, you are full of surprises. I knew you had secrets, but I never would have imagined what I just saw."

Stunned, the special ones froze in place and stared at the boy. Boxer broke the silence. "You can talk."

"How did you see us in the dark?" Battle wanted to know.

Glaring at the boy, Manx declared, "You're the one who has been watching us."

Wren collapsed on her bed and sighed, "I'm exhausted, and my feet hurt."

Battle stepped in front of the boy and in a menacing voice told him, "You'd better start explaining what you are doing in our pod."

The boy didn't look intimated by Battle's glare. He just shrugged his narrow shoulders. "Waiting for you to get back," he said. "When those guards showed up and Lester went to meet them, I started to get worried."

Confused, Boxer asked, "You saw us leave?" He knew there had been no one around when they'd left. Neither he nor Battle had seen or heard anyone.

"I can be sneaky too," the boy replied with a sly grin, exposing his two large front teeth.

Manx said, "I need to get the com-nit to Father Brion," and she removed the pouch from her neck. She looked at Boxer, not sure how much to say in front of their intruder.

The boy looked at Manx and said, "Father Brion is in the basement, pacing. You should let him know that you are back and everyone is safe."

Manx glared at the boy and hissed. "You sure seem to know everything that's going on around here."

The boy put a finger to the side of his head and said, "I see and observe." Then he grinned at Manx. "Have your kitty senses been tingling?"

Boxer moved the table away from the small door and opened it. "Manx, tell Father Brion everything you saw in the headquarters. Battle and I need to have a chat with this funny guy."

After Manx left, Boxer placed his hand on the boy's shoulder and looked at Battle. "What should we do with him?"

Battle shrugged. "It depends on how he answers our questions."

"Now, hold on. I'm on your side." The boy tried to wiggle free of Boxer's hold as Battle pulled a chair from the table. With a push from Boxer, the boy sat down hard in the wooden chair. When the chair stopped rocking, the boy placed his arms on the table, folded his hands, and said, "Ready when you are."

Boxer and Battle joined the boy at the table while Wren watched from her bed. "Why did you let everyone think you couldn't talk?" Boxer asked first.

The boy gave another grin and lifted his hands up. "So I wouldn't have to answer a bunch of questions."

"How did you sneak out of pod one without Lester or the other boys hearing you?" Battle asked next.

"Those duds snore so loud they wouldn't hear a tree crash to the ground. Besides, I sleep in the back of the pod and make the blankets look like I'm under there. I snuck out when everything went dark." The boy seemed to be enjoying himself.

"If Lester finds out you can talk and have been sneaking out of the pod at night, he will give you trouble and might even hurt you," Battle warned.

The boy shrugged, unconcerned. "I'm not afraid of Lester, and Ray isn't so bad. He talks to me. He really misses his family and only goes along with Lester to be left alone. He warned me not to make Lester mad because he has a really bad temper."

The small door opened, and Manx crept back into the pod. She looked at Boxer and said, "Father Brion is anxious to get the images to the scientists and is leaving now. He said to tell everyone, 'Good job.'"

Boxer pointed to the boy and asked Manx, "Did you tell him about our little surprise?"

"No. He was anxious to leave, and I didn't want to distract him," Manx answered. She glared at the pointy-faced boy, "What is your name?"

The boy wrinkled his nose, scratched his head and admitted, "I don't have one."

"Where were you living before you came here?" Manx demanded.

"With this tall guy who hardly talked. We hid out in old buildings, and people came and brought us food. One day he took me to a place and told me to wait there. He said someone would pick me up. Then Father Brion and Boxer came in the truck." The boy looked around and admitted, "I like it here at the orphanage. It's fun, and the food is good."

"For someone who sees and observes, you don't seem to know much, and if the tall person didn't talk much, who taught you?" Manx was not buying the boy's story, remembering Father Brion's warning about not trusting anyone from the settlement.

The boy leaned toward her, raised his eyebrows, and replied, "I listen a lot."

The boy's story still wasn't making sense to Manx, and she hissed with frustration. "How can you watch us but we don't know you're around? You're not invisible."

The strange boy looked down at his hands and mumbled words that Manx didn't understand.

"What did you say?" she demanded and leaned over the table to stare in the boy's face.

The boy looked up at Manx, nose to nose, and admitted, "Because I'm sort of like you." His answer shocked everyone, and they stared at him with open mouths.

"Show us," Boxer demanded, and for the first time the boy looked frightened.

"Now," Battle ordered.

The boy's narrow shoulders shook, and then he collapsed in the chair and changed into a dark-gray rat with a pointed noise, two large front teeth, and a long tail. Scared, the rat jumped from the chair and raced across the floor to disappear through a small hole in the wall. Stunned, the special ones looked at each other, trying to adjust to what they had just witnessed.

Finally Boxer uttered, "A 300 survived. I wish Grand Pierre was here."

Outside at the window a voice whispered, "Can I come back in? And what is a 300?"

Battle opened the door for the boy. "I guess you really are one of us."

"We need to give him a name," Wren chirped from her bed. "Since he's a mouse, we can call him Mickey."

"Yuck. Mickey Mouse. What kind of a name is that?" The boy nixed Wren's suggestion.

"Actually, he is a rat or rodent, to be specific," Boxer explained.

"Rat. That's a good name for you." Manx grimaced at the boy, still upset about his spying on them and getting away with it.

"No, thanks," the boy replied. Then his face lit up, and he exclaimed, "I know. Since I'm a rodent, call me Dent." He looked around the room expectantly, and one by one the special ones agreed that Dent seemed like a good name for the pointy-faced boy with two large front teeth.

"We need to get some sleep," Boxer said. "It's almost morning. What should we do about Dent?"

"Nothing," Dent said. "Let me keep acting like I can't talk because everyone ignores me and leaves me alone."

Battle agreed. "Good idea. Maybe you can find out what Lester is telling the robots. Everyone, we will keep Dent our secret."

"Can we call him Dent at meals?" Wren asked.

Battle sighed. "Sure. We'll tell everyone that you named him too." And everyone laughed.

Boxer turned to Dent, and his tone became serious. "At night, meet us here in the pod. We can teach you what Grand Pierre taught us, and you can let us know about Lester's meetings with the robots. As far as the other children know, we are not friends, and we don't hang out. It will work better that way."

CHAPTER 8

The following morning, the special ones slept through first meal, not hearing Marta ring the bell. Their first mission had almost failed because the dogs had not been contained, and with the added Dent dilemma, recent events had left them beyond tired.

They awoke at the cheery announcement, "You'd better wake up. You'll soon have a visitor." Dent was standing in the middle of the pod, which caused Manx to sit up in her bed and groggily rub her eyes.

"What did you say?" Manx mumbled.

"Marta is on her way, bringing food," Dent replied with a grin on his face and his two front teeth prominent.

Hearing of the arrival of Marta, Boxer and Battle jumped out of bed, running fingers through their messy hair. Wren stirred under her quilt but made no move to get up. There was a quiet rap at the door, and Boxer looked at Dent and whispered, "Thanks." Dent changed into the gray rat and exited the way he'd entered.

Boxer opened the door to see Marta with a tray of rolls. "Sorry we missed first meal," Boxer told her as he took the tray.

Marta smiled and winked. "I told the other children that you were not feeling well when they asked where you were.

Bring the tray back later. Sorry it's not more, but supplies are running short."

"Thanks. We really appreciate you doing this for us," Boxer told Marta as she left for the main building.

Boxer placed the tray on the table and said, "While we eat, we can review the mission and what went wrong. The main problem was the dogs. I didn't account for their rabid reaction to Battle and alerting the guards. It was poor planning on my part, and we were lucky the guards bought Manx's ruse that a cat was the cause of the dogs' behavior. We won't get away with it again."

"Don't be so hard on yourself," Battle said as he bit into a roll. "Neither Father Brion nor I figured the dogs would be a problem."

"I almost didn't have enough time to complete the search," Manx said, "and the last drawer may be the most important. When I told Father Brion what I'd seen, he couldn't wait to tell the scientists. I think the large device may be what they're looking for and could be used to defeat the robots."

Wren crawled out from under her quilt and slowly sat up. Her tangled hair hid most of her face. Manx handed her a roll filled with some kind of spread, and Wren pulled it open and frowned. "Don't ask; just eat," Manx told her.

Wren pushed the roll back together and took a bite. "Not bad."

While they ate, they agreed that overall their first mission was a success and had gone mostly as planned. But they had been lucky, and the next mission must be planned better because they could not count on fooling the robots again.

That evening when the special ones entered the large dining room for second meal, Lester loudly said, "You must have made a speedy recovery; none of you look sick to me."

As they sat down at the table, Manx looked over at Lester and groaned. "It was a stomach thing."

Vera and her two sidekicks glared at Manx but didn't say a word.

"Sure." Lester sneered as Marta placed plates of food on the table, and then he sneered at his plate and grumbled, "The meals keep getting worse."

Boxer noticed that there was not as much food on their plates as there had been when they'd first arrived at the orphanage, and there was not as much variety as before, but he was thankful they had food to eat. He smiled as he watched Karry and Bunny eat every morsel on their plates. The two young girls were beginning to look healthier, thanks to Manx. Vera had not given the girls any problems, as far as he knew, and if Wren ever found out that she had, he was sure she would tell them.

After second meal cleanup, the special ones went back to their pod, looking forward to a full night of sleep. Father Brion had not returned, so they would not be meeting with him tonight.

A short time after the orphanage went dark, Dent appeared in the pod and changed. He warned, "You'd better watch out for Lester. He ranted until lights went out about you four not being sick and trying to figure out what you are up to. He may be stupid enough to tell the guards something to get you in trouble."

"Think he smells a rat?" Manx joked, causing Dent to wrinkle his nose at her. They seemed to enjoy teasing each other. Manx and Dent were the same height, but Manx was muscled and Dent was slimmer.

Battle answered, "Keep a watch on Lester, and let us know if he tries anything. We may have to set a trap for him to make him look suspicious." He was already thinking of a way to make Lester look guilty.

Boxer told Dent to sit at the table and began telling him about the scientific expedition from Ulterion, the cloning project to combine specific animal traits, and the arrival of the robots. Dent listened intently and didn't interrupt Boxer, which was a surprise to Manx.

When Boxer told about their training on the farm by Grand Pierre and Aunt May, Dent finally spoke. "You were lucky. I apparently escaped with the tall man, and all I can remember is hiding and scrounging for food. Finally, others started coming around and would bring supplies and talk with the tall man. I didn't hear a lot of what they talked about, but it seemed like they were making plans. They would bring him papers to read, and he would write on them and give them back. I don't think the tall man told them anything about me except that I was an orphan and needed someplace to live."

"Did the tall man know of your special talent?" Boxer quizzed.

Dent nodded his head. "He said never to use it unless to escape."

"He probably saved your life," Boxer said with a thoughtful look. "Only a couple of the opposition leaders know what was really going on at the scientific facility. Grand Pierre told us never to reveal our special talents to anyone, and to use them to get away if we were threatened. Fear and not understanding our differences may cause the Adorans not to trust us. The tall man must have been part of the scientific team and joined the others hiding in the settlement."

The four children took turns teaching Dent about the Cs Grand Pierre had taught them. Boxer explained control;

Battle explained cooperation; Manx explained caution; and Wren explained curiosity.

Dent was impressed. "Excellent," he said. "If we remember our *C*s, that should keep us out of trouble." He hesitated. "But I need my own *C* to feel like I belong."

Manx groaned. "I knew he was going to be trouble."

Wren chirped, "How about *cute?*" Dent made a face at her.

"He's always making jokes," Battle said. "What about *comic?*"

Manx stared at Dent and suggested, "*Cocky.*"

"Thanks a lot," Dent grumbled at their suggestions.

Boxer looked at Dent and said, "*Concealment.*"

"Concealment." Dent smiled. "I like it, and it works for all of us. We must always *conceal* our special talents. Now I feel like part of the team."

From teaching Dent, Boxer knew that he had a highly developed intelligence that came from his Ulterion heritage, but he could not figure out Dent's specific skill. Dent seemed to understand everything they taught him, and he retained it, never once asking for anything to be repeated.

Three days had passed since the first mission, and Boxer went to the main building to find out if Father Brion had returned. The large dining room was empty, but he could hear Marta and Sola talking in the kitchen. Boxer stopped and listened. He didn't need to be in the same room to hear that they were concerned because there was only enough food to last another day. He stepped into the kitchen, and the two women turned toward him.

Sola asked, "Boxer, do you need something?"

"I came to find out if Father Brion had returned, and I heard you talking about the food shortage. In the forest where we lived with Grand Pierre, there are plenty of fruits, berries, and vegetables growing wild. I used to help Aunt May pick them for meals. I know the way there, and it will solve the food problem until Father Brion returns."

Sola looked at Marta, who said, "This sounds like a solution to our problem."

Sola turned to Boxer. "Father Brion didn't take the truck. I can drive it if you're sure you can find the way."

Boxer nodded. "I'm positive."

"It would be a good outing for the children," Sola decided. "And the back of the truck has rails for them to ride safely. Marta, ring the signal bell for the children, and I'll let them know we will be going on an outing today."

When all the children were settled in the back of the truck, Boxer and Battle secured the rails. Sola had stressed the importance of staying seated until the truck stopped or there would be no further outings.

Manx sat across from Wren, who was seated between Karry and Bunny, and their faces gleamed with anticipation. Vera sat in the front with Jonne and Dortha, all grumbling about getting their clothes dirty, and pretending to pick unclean items from their shirts.

Manx knew that Vera and her two followers never did anything that could get them dirty. The only reason they helped with meal cleanup was Marta's rule: if you ate, you helped clean up. Karry had told Wren that all those girls did was lie on their beds and complain about everything.

Lester and the other boys sat in a line across the back. Boxer was inside the truck, seated between Sola and Marta. The big truck rumbled from the orphanage and down the narrow road that ran into the forest. The old truck went much faster than Grand Pierre's transport, and it wasn't long before Boxer pointed and told Sola to turn into a large field.

Once the truck had stopped and the rails had been removed, the children climbed out, each holding a sack to fill. Boxer pointed to where the wild berries grew, and it was decided that the girls would pick the berries. The taller boys would pull the round, yellow melons off the creon trees. Battle carried a shovel to dig the yalma roots that grew beneath the ground, and Ray and Dent would gather them. Sola would find the wild onions and greens to make salads.

It wasn't long before the children began returning to the truck with their sacks full of vegetables and fruits. As Marta oversaw the loading of the truck, she turned to Boxer. "Thanks for bringing us here. You have saved the orphanage. As long as we have food, we can keep it open."

Boxer understood her hidden message and the importance of the orphanage for Father Brion and the opposition.

As the children climbed into the truck to return to the orphanage, Manx looked around and didn't see Wren. Wren had been picking berries with Bunny and Karry, but she was not with them now. Manx asked Karry, "Do you know where Wren is?"

Karry answered, "She said she would be right back, and she went into the trees."

Manx glanced around, and still not seeing any sign of Wren, she hurried toward the area where the three girls had been picking berries. When she reached the wild berry bushes, she felt uneasy and called out, "Wren, it's time to leave."

Manx was about to alert Boxer and Battle that Wren was missing, when Wren answered, "I'll be right there."

Relief that Wren was all right caused Manx to exhale. She was unaware that she had been holding her breath. Wren walked from the trees and took Manx's hand, and the two girls ran to the waiting truck. Manx frowned with concern on the trip back, as Wren had given no explanation for her absence, causing Manx to wonder what she had been doing.

Second meal that day was a cheerful occasion for everyone. Sola thanked the children for gathering the fruits and vegetables, and Marta had baked pies from the wild berries. Lester and Vera were almost nice as they gobbled down their heaping plates of food.

After cleanup Manx noticed Wren leaving the large dining room, and she watched out the window as the younger girl hurried toward their pod. She noticed that Wren's shirt bulged in the front. Again Manx frowned, wondering what she was up to.

Later, when Manx entered their pod with Boxer and Battle, Wren was sitting on her bed, looking innocent, and her shirt had shrunk back to normal. Manx meant to question Wren, worried that she was doing something that would get her into trouble.

Manx forgot about that when Dent suddenly appeared in the room and changed. "Rat patrol checking in." Everyone laughed. Dent reported that so far Lester had not met with the robots and was now snoring loudly with his stomach bulging from the big meal.

The special ones spent the next hour teaching Dent more about their unique skills and answering his questions. Each night he had another list of questions—some of which the special ones could not answer because they were too technical or were about Ulterion.

The next morning Father Brion joined the children at the table, saying how fortunate they were to have an abundance of food once again. Boxer thought he looked tired as he watched him eat. While the children were cleaning the tables, Father Brion whispered to Boxer to meet him in the basement as soon as he and the others could slip away. On the way back to the pod, Boxer told Battle, Manx, and Wren about Father Brion's request.

"I was going to swing with Karry and Bunny," Wren said. "Do I have to go?"

When they were back in the pod, Boxer told her, "I'm concerned about you playing with the girls without one of us watching you."

Dent made his appearance and told Boxer, "I can keep watch from the trees, and no one will notice me. If Vera comes around, I'll signal you."

"It could work," Battle agreed. "And Vera will think one of us will be watching Wren."

Boxer told Wren, "Stay by the swings where Dent can see you, and don't go anywhere else."

"Okay," Wren promised as she hurried to play with her friends.

"Rodent on guard." Enjoying his new role, Dent clicked his heels together, saluted, and changed into the large gray rat to guard Wren.

Boxer, Battle, and Manx quietly snuck out the back and climbed down the steps into the basement. Father Brion turned when he saw them and exclaimed, "I have great news. The images Manx captured held important information, and we have been asked to plan two more missions.

"First, we need to go back to the robots' headquarters and retrieve the large device in the bottom drawer. It was the master control of the systems in the laboratory, and Piers thinks it can be programmed to interrupt the robots' communications.

"Second, Boxer and I need to find the building the rogue leaders are using as their communication center. Once we identify the building, we need to find out what they are doing inside. One problem is that it will be manned day and night, and we will need a diversion to get inside.

"Third, a team of scientists is going to the secret laboratory to find out if the robots are still guarding it, and if any of the buildings survived the fires. No one has been back there since the raid. Manx, the two documents you captured are the robots' patrol schedules and communication frequencies. The folded document is a schematic detailing the robots' wiring. It is how they repair the robots from the cabinet of spare parts. The bottom floor of their headquarters must be where the robots are repaired. It will require a lot of work from us to plan and execute two more missions in a short time. Congratulations to you all. On your first mission you retrieved needed information to help the opposition." Father Brion's face beamed with pride.

Mission 2

CHAPTER 9

$\mathcal{T}$he special ones were in their pod, reviewing the plans for their second mission, when Boxer shocked them by saying that it had been thirty days since they'd come to the orphanage. Boxer had tracked the days by putting a mark each day in one of his books.

The special ones settled into a routine. Between meals they would come back to the pod and work on the mission details. At night they would meet with Father Brion in the basement to refine the details. Father Brion had extended the donation route, searching for the rogues' communication center. Boxer and Battle had slipped out twice after dark to scout out possibilities but had found both buildings empty.

Sola had taken the boys on another trip to gather fruits and vegetables. They had also found wild hens' eggs, and the orphanage pantry was stocked for another few weeks. Manx continued to watch Wren disappear each day after meals into the trees across from their pod with her pockets full. She would return a short time later looking happy—with her pockets empty. Manx debated whether to ask Wren what she was doing or wait for her to tell her on her own. It wasn't like Wren to keep secrets. She usually couldn't keep a secret for even a short time.

Vera had not bothered Karry and Bunny, and playtime for the three girls was a daily event. While the girls would swing, Wren's nonstop chatter filled the air. The special ones relaxed in their new routine, and Dent was on guard to warn them if Lester was up to something. Dent still didn't talk around the other children, but he made up for it when he was alone with the special ones. His teasing and joking kept them entertained, if not annoyed at times.

So far, Lester had not met with the patrol guards again and had left Dent alone, never noticing when he went missing after dark. Lester and Vera and their groupies finally stopped ragging Dent about his name. They had come up with many negative slurs and rhymes, which he ignored. He was proud of his name, and thanks to the nightly lessons, knew he was much smarter than those who ridiculed him. Ray was the only one who secretly told him he liked the name, which they all thought Wren had given him.

Manx was outside in front of the main building, making sure that Vera saw her when Father Brion and Boxer returned early from their scouting trip. Father Brion looked flustered. After parking the large truck in pod three, Manx watched the two hurry inside and knew they were heading for the basement. She glanced around to make sure Lester or Vera wasn't watching her, and then she slowly walked to the swings and told Wren it was time for studies. Wren told Karry and Bunny she would see them later at second meal.

Dent joined the others in the pod, anxious to find out what had upset Father Brion.

"I bet the patrol stopped them and made them return to the orphanage." Battle was worried as he paced back and forth in the small pod.

Boxer entered the pod, closed the door, and told Battle to keep watch out the window. He was excited. "We were near the edge of the settlement when a platform appeared out of nowhere and ordered Father Brion to return to the orphanage. When Father Brion asked the guard why, he responded that Father Brion had no business there and for now would not be allowed to drive the truck into the settlement. Luckily, we had picked up some supplies and food, and the guard saw it stacked in the back of the truck. I stayed inside the truck, so the guard didn't notice me."

Boxer paused took a deep breath and then continued. "On the map in the basement there is a large building set back from the main road, and the narrow road leading to the building is well used, with deep ruts from the platforms. Father Brion stopped the truck to get a better look at the building, pretending the truck was having engine trouble, and that was when the guard rolled up with sirens blaring and ordered him to leave the area immediately."

Boxer looked at the others and grinned. "I think we've found their communication center, but it will be hard to get close enough to verify. We must finalize plans for our second mission back to the rogues' headquarters to rescue the scientific device—and at the same time figure out how to make sure this building is their communication center."

"I could do a flyover and look inside, like Grand Pierre taught me," Wren said. "Are there trees around the building?"

"There are a few trees around the building," Boxer answered. "I'll talk to Father Brion tonight about having Wren do a flyover. It's a good idea, since there are no other buildings nearby."

Manx was concerned. "How will you get there without being seen?" she asked Wren. "And are there other birds in the trees? Remember the large vivan that swooped down on you before."

"I'll be careful and fly low," Wren promised.

"If Dent will keep watch tonight, Wren can join us in the basement, and we'll ask Father Brion," Boxer suggested.

Dent jumped to attention, saluted, and said, "Always ready to do my part."

Plans for the second mission were completed. When the patrol guards passed the robots' headquarters, Boxer, Battle, and Manx would go in. Wren would keep watch from the trees in the vacant area across the road.

Marta had figured out a way to put the dogs to sleep. She'd made treats filled with a sleeping powder she'd taken from the medicine chest at the orphanage. The treats would be dropped into the dogs' cages. Battle was sure the dogs would eat them because all of them looked half starved.

Manx would once again jump to the roof, enter through a window, retrieve the large device, and drop it to Boxer waiting on the ground. Father Brion had been given instructions from the scientists on how to align the com-nit—if there was enough time. Manx would open each of the drawers containing the spare parts and would slowly move the programmed device over the parts. A magnetic signal from the com-nit would make the spare parts useless for repairing the robots.

Battle would watch the dogs, and if they woke up, he would put them back to sleep. No one doubted Battle's ability against the three mongrels. Tomorrow night the special ones would engage in their second mission, and all were hopeful that this time everything would go as planned.

The special ones were sitting in their pod, waiting for the orphanage to go dark. Then they would sneak out and return to the robots' headquarters. They would travel the same route as before. Dent would stand watch at the orphanage, so they would not be surprised by a robot patrol as they had been before. Dent was diligent in keeping watch on Lester, and he continued to guard the three girls, making sure that Vera didn't threaten them.

As they waited to leave, Manx glanced over at Wren perched on her bed and humming to herself. It had become a routine that after meals Wren would disappear into the trees across from their pod with pockets bulging, and then return shortly afterward with pockets not bulging. Manx figured out that Wren was taking food to some animal. Wren's empathy with others was amazing. Manx had decided that after their second mission to the robots' headquarters was over, she would confront the young girl. It was apparent that Wren wasn't going to tell Manx what she was doing.

Battle looked out the window and announced, "It's time."

Boxer stood and said, "We'll cross to the trees, and then go single file to the vacant lot." He opened the door.

The special ones' pace was fast, and in no time they had reached the vacant area across from the robots' headquarters. Boxer held up his hand, signaling them to stop. The settlement was dark and eerily quiet. They had not seen anyone or heard anything moving.

Boxer signaled that it was time for the patrol guards to pass, and they all hid in the trees to avoid the guards' searching beams moving from right to left. Suddenly the road was brightly lit as the two patrol guards silently rolled past. Without their search lights, the special ones would have no warning that the patrol was near. Once the guards were past, Boxer motioned for Battle to go.

Stealthy Battle stepped from the trees, crossed the road, and circled around back to reach the dogs' cages. He counted the treats Marta had made; there were four for each dog. He tossed three treats in each cage and made a scratching sound just loud enough to draw the dog's attention. The dogs were loose, but once they caught the scent of the meaty treats, each ran to its own cage and quickly gulped them down, sniffing around for more.

In the cage farthest away, the dog started to come out, but then its legs wobbled and it bumped against the cage and fell down, knocked out by the sleeping powder. The middle dog's head slumped forward, and then it collapsed. Battle waited for the dog in the cage closest to him to succumb to the sleeping powder. It was the largest of the three dogs and might need another treat. Battle was about to toss in another treat when the dog suddenly sat down on his back end, and with a dazed look in its eyes, its front legs collapsed.

Battle whispered, "Go."

Boxer motioned for Manx to change, and both of them raced across the road and leaped high, clearing the fence and landing in front of the building. Boxer changed back, while Manx ran to the back and jumped on top of the dogs' cages and then to the roof of the back porch. She swiftly made her way to the side of the building and found the window she had used before. She paused to listen and then jumped through the window into the large upstairs room.

Manx didn't need light to see, and she knew where to go. She changed and hurried to the back wall where the cabinets stood. There would be no searching on this mission, for Manx knew her target. She knelt down in front of the cabinet and pulled open the bottom drawer. She lifted the large metal device and was surprised to find indentations on the side to carry it. It was four times the size of the one in the pouch around her neck and at least that much heavier. She was glad that Boxer would carry the heavy device back to the orphanage.

Carefully she made her way to the window and whispered, "I've got it."

Manx bent over and crawled outside. She didn't want to open the window further, afraid of leaving any sign that the rogue headquarters had been invaded.

Boxer was waiting on the ground below, and Manx dropped the heavy device to him. Manx pointed to the device around her neck and motioned that she was going back inside to disable the robots' spare parts. Boxer nodded, and Manx crawled back through the window and removed the device from the pouch. She aligned it as instructed, and now ready, she hurried to the back of the room.

Boxer carried the heavy device to the back of the yard. He heard a signal whistle from Battle and turned toward the sound.

"Over here," Battle whispered, crouched at the back corner of the fence. After the dogs were knocked out, he had made an opening in the fence large enough for Boxer to crawl through.

Once through the fence, Boxer asked, "How are the dogs?"

"Still sleeping but beginning to stir," Battle reported.

"Manx is disabling the spare parts. Watch for her. I'm going to see what is in the ground floor. All the windows have been blacked out, and that makes me curious. Guard this." Boxer placed the round device on the ground and crept back into the yard, stepped up on the back porch, and carefully opened a wide door that led into the ground-floor room.

Battle watched Manx jump out of the upstairs window and silently run to the back of the building, her paws not making a sound. She jumped to the dogs' cages and then to the ground. Battle stepped out and whispered, "Over here."

The largest dog tried to lift its head and whined; it had caught the scent of a cat. Manx hurried out the hole in the fence, removed the pouch from her neck, and changed. She picked up the pouch and ran across the road.

Boxer heard the large dog whine as it made an effort to stand on its wobbly legs. He backed out of the ground-floor door, pausing to make sure it was shut, a strained look on his face. Safely through the fence, he asked Battle, "Do you need help closing the hole?"

Battle replied, "I'm not going to close it. I'm going to push the fence back just enough that the dogs can't get through without some effort. I'll leave the rest of the treats outside the fence, and those mutts will go crazy wanting to get them and will push their way out. I'll meet you after I erase our tracks so the robots will see only the dogs."

Boxer ran across the road, carrying the heavy device, and joined Wren and Manx. They watched Battle sweep a tree branch back and forth, leaving no sign that they had been there. When Battle joined the others, he tossed the broken branch into the bushes. Boxer immediately gave the signal to run single file; he was anxious to get the large device back to the orphanage.

When they reached the hidden tree circle, Dent was waiting. "All clear," he whispered and followed behind Battle as they circled through the dark trees to their pod. As silently as they had left, the special ones entered their pod.

Once safely inside, Manx sighed. "I'm glad that's over."

Boxer said, "I'll take this device to Father Brion. He will want to get it to the scientists tonight, and I need to let him know what I saw in the ground-floor room. It was really disturbing." He left through the small back door.

Manx clasped the pouch around her neck. She had intended to give it to Boxer to take to the basement, but his strange comment about what he had seen on the ground floor had caused her to forget. Manx looked at Battle, and he shook his head. Clearly he had no idea what Boxer had seen.

Everyone was in bed when Boxer returned. The fast pace to the robots' headquarters and back had exhausted them, including Boxer. What he had seen on the ground floor had left him shaken, and he had needed to let Father Brion know. Boxer climbed into bed and was instantly asleep.

CHAPTER 10

*I*t was Marta's clanging of the bell to signal first meal that woke everyone. Slowly the four children crawled out of bed in their wrinkled clothes and stumbled outside, squinting their eyes in the bright sun. All were tired and moved at a snail's speed. They didn't talk, including Wren. But they didn't want to miss another meal and have Lester wondering why.

When they sat down at the long table, Battle muttered, "Maybe food will help."

Manx mumbled back, "Another four hours of sleep for me."

They all concentrated on eating when Marta set their plates on the table. After the dishes were cleared, the special ones walked back to their pod with a little more energy in their steps. Once inside the pod, Wren collapsed on her bed, and the other three sat at the small table.

Manx looked at Boxer and told him, "Father Brion was missing at meal, so he must have taken the device to the scientists last night. Now will you tell us what you saw that upset you?"

"Wait for me," Dent said after he'd changed from the gray rat and joined them in the pod.

Boxer looked around at the others. "The mission was a success and went as planned. Retrieving the device and

90

disabling the spare parts is a huge win for the opposition. The rogues will not be able to repair any of the broken guards. Now the scientists must find a way to disrupt communication between the guards and rogue leaders. This is a critical factor to retake the settlement and defeat the rogues."

Boxer paused and shook his head to clear his thoughts. "It was so weird that it still creeps me out. It was totally dark in the room, and there were three platforms with the guards disassembled, and parts were scattered all around. In the back was a different kind of robot standing next to a table. It wore clothes, like pants and shirts, but the head was missing. There were wires sticking up where the head should be. On the table I saw the head sitting there with the eyes open and watching me. The head looked alive but couldn't move because it had been removed from the body. I froze at the sight of it. It knew I was in the room, where I was standing, and was watching to see what I was going to do. I started to worry if it could still communicate and signal for help. Then the dogs started to wake up, and I backed out of there. That thing knew that I was in the room—but how?"

Boxer actually looked frightened. Finally he continued. "Father Brion left before dawn to deliver the device and ask about the robot I saw in the room. The body was tall and resembled Grand Pierre. It would be hard to defeat, since it's made of metal."

After hearing Boxer's story, no one said anything, not even Dent. Silence fill the pod.

During second meal, as Marta placed the plates of food on the table, she leaned over and whispered to Boxer to meet Father Brion in the basement after dark. Boxer was surprised that Father Brion had returned so quickly, and he nodded to Marta to let her know he understood.

After the orphanage went dark, Manx stayed with Wren in the pod, and Boxer and Battle left through the back door to meet Father Brion. After second meal, Dent had left the dining room, and no one had seen him since. Battle said that Dent was on Lester watch. It wasn't long before Boxer and Battle crept back into the pod and pushed the small table in front of the door.

Boxer looked at Wren and told her, "Tomorrow night we will make a reconnaissance of the communication building. The opposition leaders need this information to firm up the plans for our final mission. The man-like robot I saw at the repair depot is one of the rogue leaders, and there should be more inside the communication center. These rogues are more intelligent and give orders to the guards about when to change patrol routes or invade a house or even kill someone. The opposition is going to post watchers at the headquarters. They are anxious to find out if the repairs stop, if Manx was successful in disabling the parts."

The others quickly fell asleep, and Boxer listened to their breathing. He was still awake, going over the reconnaissance once again. Father Brion was restricted from driving the truck, and Boxer had determined that it took one hour of driving to reach the building at the far end of the settlement. As the large black dog, Boxer was fast, but to keep the pace of the truck for one hour was not possible, even for him. Boxer figured it would take him two hours to reach the area. He would carry Wren perched on his back, and when they reached the cover of the trees, he would rest while she did her flyover. They would leave the orphanage two hours before daybreak, as Boxer wasn't concerned about running at night and felt more comfortable concealed by the darkness. If he saw anyone on their way back, he would escape into the forest and return that way.

The next morning, Manx was waiting outside the pod for Wren to return from her secret trip into the forest. She had left as soon as first meal cleanup was completed, with her pockets bulging. Manx sat under one of the tall trees, drawing to pass the time.

When Wren stepped out of the trees, Manx called to her, startling the young girl. From the surprised look on her face, Wren knew she had been found out. Manx patted the ground next to her, making it clear that Wren should sit down.

Manx waited a long minute before she finally said, "I've been watching you sneak away after meals with food hidden in your clothes and then come back later without the food. I know you're feeding something, and I've been waiting for you to tell me. Apparently, you aren't going to, and I need to know what you're doing to make sure you're not going to get into trouble or hurt."

Wren looked back toward the forest, trying to decide, and from the stern tone of Manx's voice, she knew she had a dilemma. Wren wrinkled her face, took a large breath, and finally admitted, "I promised him I wouldn't tell."

"Whom did you promise?" Manx demanded, now becoming worried.

Wren sighed. "I call him Bear."

Manx was shocked, and her face showed it. "Who is Bear?" she demanded.

"Okay, I'll tell you," Wren reluctantly agreed. "I hope Bear doesn't get mad."

Boxer walked out of the pod and over to where the two girls sat and said, "Wren, you can't keep secrets from us."

Manx looked up and asked, "You heard us?"

Boxer grinned. "Of course." And he sat down with the girls.

The look he gave Wren caused her to continue. "When we were picking berries, I saw him standing in the trees and went to talk to him. He had been watching us on the farm but was afraid to show himself. It was Bear that Manx sensed tracking us. He wanted to know if Bunny was doing okay. He brought her to the orphanage after the robots raided the laboratory. He tried to take care of her, but it was too hard to find enough food to eat. He had watched Father Brion care for the children living here and had felt that Bunny would be safe."

"What?" Boxer exclaimed. "Are you saying that this boy and Bunny escaped from the laboratory?"

Wren shrugged her shoulders. "I guess so. But Bear isn't a boy. He's bigger than you and looks all grown up. He likes the food Marta cooks and is always hungry."

"He must have been part of the 500 series experiments that Grand Pierre told us about—and Bunny too." Boxer was stunned.

"Bear didn't call her Bunny, but he likes the name, and he said that I could call him Bear. I named him Bear because he looks like a bear—all big and wild with long brown hair. His clothes are mostly rags. I was wondering if Sola would have any extra big clothes in the storage room to give him. He sure could use some." Wren's admission caused Boxer and Manx to look at each other with astonished expressions on their faces.

"Ask Bear if he will meet with us tomorrow," Boxer told Wren. "Tell him he has nothing to fear, and like Dent, he and Bunny are one of us." Wren nodded in agreement.

It was two hours before dawn, and Boxer shook Wren's shoulder and whispered, "We need to leave to reach the communication center by first light."

Wren sat up and yawned and climbed from her bed. Battle and Manx watched at the door as Wren and Boxer crept out. "Be careful," Manx whispered.

When they reached the safety of the forest, Boxer told Wren, "Change and hop on my back and hold tight."

Both changed, and then Boxer—as the large black dog—ran from the safety of the forest and down the dark road. Boxer kept a steady pace, and his long strides brought them to the narrow road that led to the communication center just before dawn. He stopped in a cluster of trees along the road and listened. Not hearing any sounds, Boxer changed, and Wren did the same.

He whispered, "As soon as it's light, fly to those trees near the building and watch for movement. If there are rogues inside, count how many."

As soon as daylight brightened the sky, the birds perched in the trees began flying and chirping loudly, welcoming the new day. Boxer motioned, and Wren changed and flew from the cover of the trees to join the other birds. The other birds were small like Wren, and none of them gave her any notice.

Boxer watched Wren fly a circle around the trees nearest the building and then land on the top branch of the tallest tree. She wasn't very close, but she should be able to see inside now that it was light. Wren hopped from the high branch to a lower one, sat there for a minute, and then flew directly toward the building. Boxer nervously watched the small bird hover near a window and then begin to fly around the big wooden structure.

When Wren disappeared around the other side of the building, Boxer worried. What was she up to? Then he remembered the Cs Grand Pierre had taught them. Curiosity was her special C, and it certainly described her. Boxer let out a large breath of air when he saw a small brown bird with a red breast fly from the back of the building and head toward the trees where he hid. He continued to watch the large building, in case Wren had caught the attention of one of the rogues, but he did not see any sign of activity.

Wren hopped from an inside tree branch and changed and said, "I was having trouble seeing inside. When I flew around the building, I counted six tall robots, but I couldn't see into all the rooms. The ones I saw were sitting at tables with metal boxes in front of them, and it looked like they were doing something on the boxes."

"That's good, Wren, but flying around the building wasn't planned," Boxer said sternly. "I was worried about you."

Wren huffed back, "If I am going to contribute my share to the missions, you have to let me do what I need to do to complete my task."

Her spunk caused Boxer to smile. "Okay, as long as you don't get hurt. Are you ready to head back?" Wren nodded, and both changed. With Wren perched on his back, Boxer left the trees and started back toward the orphanage.

CHAPTER 11

$\mathcal{B}$oxer made a turn onto the long road that ran around the edge of the settlement and by the orphanage. It was still early morning, and he had not seen anyone. Suddenly a large pack of dogs came from behind one of the burned-out homes and started running straight for him, growling and snarling. Boxer heard Wren's warning chirp. She had seen the dogs.

Boxer was tired from hours of running, and he knew he couldn't outrun the energized dogs for long. The dogs were rested and extremely hungry. Boxer leaped from the road and headed for the dense forest to escape the starving pack. The dogs ran from the road, trailing him, howling louder as they sensed that their prey was fatigued.

The forest trail was narrow, and gnarly bushes covered the ground. In his haste to escape, Boxer tripped and stumbled. His legs were unsteady as he stood up. He checked to make sure Wren was okay and then ran farther into the forest. The hungry pack was gaining, its leader a large mongrel scarred from many fights. The narrow trail turned uphill, and Boxer was panting hard. How long before the dogs overtook him? Wren could fly to the safety of the trees, but he would not be able to defend himself against the pack of dogs for very long.

As the ravenous mongrel turned right behind Boxer, the bushes that hugged the trail shook violently, startling Boxer. After he ran by, a huge brown bear leaped out, completely blocking the narrow trail. The bear stood on its back legs and roared, stopping the lead dog in its tracks. The rest of the pack hurtled around the narrow turn and crashed into their leader. With one swipe of a gigantic paw, the huge bear sent the startled leader tumbling backward.

The bear roared again and bared its large teeth. None of the pack were willing to challenge a foe as fierce as the huge brown bear. The leader tried to back away from the bear, but the dog pile had the trail blocked. It only took one forward lunge from the enraged bear to cause the terrified dogs, in one motion, to leap up, spin around, and race down the trail as fast as they'd come up it, with the huge bear loping behind them.

Boxer heard Wren's loud chirp thanking Bear, her newest friend. Boxer gave a bark of thanks and continued toward the orphanage.

Boxer and Wren quietly sneaked into the pod and found it empty. There were two plates of food on the table, and each collapsed into a chair and began to eat. Both were tired and covered in dust from the long run, but their grumbling stomachs won out over cleaning up.

Boxer sighed and told Wren, "That was a close call with those dogs. If Bear hadn't stopped them, I could not have escaped. I can't wait to meet him and thank him myself."

Wren grinned. "I bet he chased those dogs all the way back to the settlement. He was really scary."

"I wouldn't want him mad at me," Boxer agreed as he continued to eat.

Battle entered the pod and exclaimed, "You made it in good time. Did you have any trouble?"

Boxer and Wren stared at Battle, unsure where to start.

Manx enter the pod and said, "I'm glad you're back. It wasn't fun staying behind and not knowing what was happening."

Just then, Dent appeared through the hole in the wall and changed. He held up his arms and gestured. "Ta-da! Guess who Lester met with last night."

Boxer quickly told about the trip to the communication center, the rogue leaders Wren had counted, and being chased on the way back by the pack of dogs—and Bear saving them.

Battle was shocked and asked, "How long has everyone but me known about Bear?"

"Manx and I just learned about him yesterday and didn't have time to tell you or Dent about him and Bunny," Boxer explained.

"I've always thought Bunny was smart and understood more than she let on," Manx told the others. "I never sensed her being that scared of Vera—not like Karry. I think Bunny is older than we thought, especially if she was with Bear in the secret lab. I just wish she could talk."

"What if Wren asks Bear if Bunny can talk?" Dent suggested.

"When I bring him food, I'll ask him about Bunny and if he will meet with us." Wren yawned widely and added, "Right now I just want to go to sleep."

"Good idea," Boxer agreed. Then he added, "I need to meet with Father Brion so he can inform the opposition leaders of what we learned today. For now we'll keep Bear and

Bunny a secret, like Dent. I wish I could talk to Grand Pierre and get his advice about what to do."

After the orphanage went dark, Boxer quietly left the pod to meet with Father Brion. After thinking it over, he asked for a meeting with Grand Pierre—or Piers, as Father Brion called him. After finding out that Dent was one of them—and now Bear and Bunny—Boxer was becoming concerned about keeping their special skills a secret.

Back in the pod, Boxer asked Wren to tell Bear that it was important that he meet with them. Dent was smart and listened intently whenever the others shared their training and knowledge. He was reliable and had become a valuable member of the team. Bunny wasn't a problem; she had been at the orphanage for at least three years and apparently had not inherited any animal traits. Bear could be a problem and had been watching them for some time.

Boxer understood Bear's hesitation to reveal himself. He had been able to survive since the secret laboratory was invaded by the robots. But would Bear be able to keep his secret when challenged? Boxer had witnessed firsthand what Bear was capable of. Bear felt responsible for Bunny, and if the small girl was ever threatened, Boxer was sure Bear would act before thinking.

The next morning after first meal, Wren returned from her trip into the forest to meet Bear. The others were waiting for her. She hopped up and said, "Tonight when it's dark, Bear said he will meet you over there in the trees." Wren pointed across from the pod.

She looked up at Boxer and told him, "Bear said to tell you you're welcome. He understood your bark of thanks when he chased off the dogs. He chased them out of the forest and watched to make sure they didn't return. And he said that Bunny can talk with her hands. Now can I go swing with Karry and Bunny?"

"Wren, thanks for taking the risk to meet Bear—and for being his friend," Boxer said. "I'll ask Sola if there are any clothes that would be large on me. Go and play. You've earned it." Boxer smiled at the brave girl and then watched as she skipped to the swings.

"I wonder what Bear meant when he said that Bunny can talk with her hands," Manx said as they walked into their pod. Both Battle and Boxer shook their heads. They had no idea.

Battle and Boxer were discussing ways to disarm the robots when Father Brion entered through the small door. His clothes were dirty, as were his face and hands, and since his hair had a tendency to stick out all over the place, it looked the same.

He pulled a chair up to the table, sat down, and breathed out, and said, "Boy, did I have a close call last night coming back from meeting with the opposition leaders. The patrols have doubled, and the spotters watching the headquarters said something is going on. Even some of the rogue leaders have been on site. They may have discovered that their spare parts are useless and are trying to figure out why. I had to hide along the roads and make my way back between patrols." Father Brion paused and looked ready to collapse. He looked at Boxer and said, "We need to go back to the communication center and retrieve one of the metal boxes. It is the final link to disabling their communications. Piers is coming to the orphanage later tonight. It will take some time for him to avoid the increased patrols."

Manx excitedly asked, "Can we all be there? I can't wait to see him."

"Since it will be after the orphanage has gone dark, it should be okay," Father Brion replied. Then he stood, saying he needed to clean up before second meal.

Once Father Brion had closed the small door, Boxer looked at the others. "We need to tell Grand Pierre about Dent and Bear and Bunny. There are too many of us to keep our secrets hidden for long, and if something should happen, we have to be able to reach him. The opposition has hidden the scientists for years. He and Aunt May must be staying with them."

Battle agreed. "We need an escape plan in case the robots discover us and the orphanage becomes unsafe."

Manx sighed. "And I was just getting to like Lester." The others smiled at her sarcastic remark.

Just then, Marta rang the bell for second meal. Manx jumped up and gasped. "Where's Wren?" She had been so intent on listening to Father Brion and so excited about seeing Grand Pierre that she had forgotten about her.

"I'm here," Wren chirped as she opened the door and waited for the others.

Father Brion missed second meal, and Battle whispered to Boxer that he must still be cleaning up. After clearing their dishes, the children returned to their pod, and Manx quizzed Wren. "Where were Karry and Bunny?"

Wren replied, "I don't know. I waited on the swings all afternoon, but they never came." This worried Manx, and she intended to mention it to Boxer and Battle.

Suddenly Dent appeared in the pod. "I can't stay long," he said. "I think Lester is meeting with the patrol again. Something is going on. He and Barten keep whispering. Then Vera and her goony girls came to the pod, and they all went outside, snickering like they were hiding something. When I find out more, I'll report back." Dent changed and scurried out the hole in the wall.

"Bear is waiting for us," Boxer said. "Let's go meet him." He picked up the pile of extra-large clothing Sola had given him, not asking why he needed it. With Boxer listening at the door, the special ones ran, one by one, to the safety of the trees.

Wren led the way and stopped in a small clearing. "Bear, it's okay to come out."

The nearby bushes rustled, and a grown boy taller than Boxer and as wide as Battle stepped out. His shaggy brown hair reached his shoulders, and a scowl covered his face. He didn't say a word but glanced around looking ready to bolt.

Wren hopped up and took Bear's hand. Her face was beaming as she made introductions. "Bear, this is Boxer and Battle and Manx." It was a strange sight to see the wild-looking boy being led by the small girl.

Boxer stepped forward and held out his hand. "I am very happy to meet you—and thank you for saving us." Bear slowly held out his hand, like he wasn't sure what to do.

"I know you feel strange being around others, and I hope you learn to trust us," said Boxer. "Wren said you took care of Bunny and have been watching out for her." Boxer's words eased the situation, and Bear relaxed a little.

Battle and Manx walked over. Both smiled and said hi and shook Bear's hand. Boxer handed Bear the clothing, and Bear took the clothes and growled, "Thank you."

Boxer continued. "The tall man we lived with on the farm, Grand Pierre, is meeting us tonight at the orphanage. He is one of the scientists that worked at the laboratory and escaped with us when it was invaded by the robots. We are going to tell him about you and Bunny—and one other boy named Dent, who now lives at the orphanage. I want to make sure you understand that you are not alone and that your secret is safe with us."

Boxer waited for Bear to respond, and when Bear stayed silent, Boxer said, "There are other scientists from the laboratory who escaped the attack and are hiding in the settlement. We are working with them to overthrow the robots. If the orphanage isn't safe for us any longer, and we have to leave, I'll make sure that Bunny gets to safety. If at any time you need to contact us, growl, and I'll hear you. As soon as possible, we would like you to come and live with us."

In a growly voice, Bear asked, "Do you know the names of the scientists hiding out?"

"No, but Grand Pierre will," Boxer replied. "Is there someone I can ask about?"

"Bunny had a special nurse who took care of her and could communicate with her by hand signs," Bear explained. "Her name is Francine. If she made it out, get Bunny to her."

Boxer nodded. "I'll ask about Francine. We need to get back. Grand Pierre will be here soon. Will you meet with one of us every day so we can keep you updated? We may need your help again."

Bear grinned when Boxer mentioned needing his help, and he agreed to meet them after first meal. The special ones hurried to their pod, and after making sure no one was watching, they left through the small door and crept to the basement.

CHAPTER 12

When the special ones entered the basement, Father Brion had a large map spread across a table and was studying it.

He looked up and said, "Piers should be here soon. We need some kind of diversion to get the rogue leaders out of the communication center to allow Manx to go in and retrieve one of the metal boxes."

He pointed to an area on the map not far from the big building set back from the road. "One option is to set a fire in this old field. All the dried grass should burn fast and create enough smoke to draw the rogues outside."

Battle studied the map. "It will work if the blaze is close enough for the rogues to feel threatened."

Before Battle could say more, the door to the basement opened, and a tall man came down the steps. In unison the children cried out, "Grand Pierre!"

Wren was first to reached the tall man, and he lifted her up and hugged her tight. "My little Wren, how I have missed hearing your voice." The tall man turned to the others and exclaimed, "Boxer, Battle, and Manx, all my special ones are here." Grand Pierre swallowed hard and his eyes glistened. "You look well. I wish Maileen could see you."

After Grand Pierre hugged each of them, he began to discuss ways to enter the communication center. It would difficult because of the rogue leaders inside. After several options were reviewed, setting the big field on fire seemed the best strategy to draw the rogues outside and allow Manx to get in.

Grand Pierre and Father Brion would meet with the opposition leaders and finalize the details. Grand Pierre stood and said that he must leave to avoid being seen by the patrols in the daylight.

Boxer stopped Grand Pierre. "We need to discuss a few things with you. First, we need an escape plan and directions to your hideout. There is a boy living here named Lester, and he has been meeting with the patrol guards. We are sure he is going to cause trouble for the orphanage and for us."

Grand Pierre listened and nodded his head. "I will make sure you can find our hideout."

"Second, is there a scientist living at the hideout who worked in the secret lab—someone named Francine?" Boxer asked.

Grand Pierre looked shocked. "Francine is there, but how does anyone know about her?"

Wren chirped, "This time we are going to shock you like you did to us."

Grand Pierre pulled out a chair, sat down, looked around at the special ones, and asked, "What have you four been up to?"

Manx answered, "It's just not us four. There are seven of us."

Grand Pierre's eyes widened, and he stuttered, "Seven special ones."

Then Boxer told him about Dent—about how quickly he learned everything and how he constantly asked questions—and how much they now relied on him.

Grand Pierre exclaimed, "A 300 survived. Remarkable."

Boxer continued. "A girl was brought to the orphanage about three years ago. Francine was her nurse, and we were told she can talk with her hands."

Grand Pierre explained. "She can sign. Francine was very fond of her and looked for the girl after the raid but did not find her. She will be very happy to learn that the girl survived and has been here at the orphanage."

"We need to get Bunny—that's the name Wren gave her—to safety as soon as possible," Boxer explained.

Grand Pierre thoughtfully rubbed at his chin. "Maybe Francine can come and get her, but if the robots find her, they are programmed to shoot on detection."

"There is one more who escaped from the secret lab," Boxer said, "and he is the one who got Bunny out. When it became too difficult for him to care for her, he brought her to the orphanage. Wren named him Bear." Boxer stared at Grand Pierre, watching his reaction.

Grand Pierre's mouth dropped open again, and he looked unable to speak. Finally he uttered, "He has to have been part of the 500 project in the secret laboratory."

Boxer wasn't sure how to describe the wild, shaggy boy to Grand Pierre. He finally gave up and said, "Wait until you meet him and see him in action."

Wren hopped onto Grand Pierre's knee and excitedly chirped, "Bear saved me and Boxer from a pack of mean dogs. They were trying to kill us, and he chased them out of the forest. Bear is sort of scary but nice too."

Wren looked up at Grand Pierre, waiting for him to say something, but Grand Pierre was speechless—which never happened. He stood up and asked, "Is that all?"

The special ones nodded their heads, knowing they had shocked him enough for one night.

Grand Pierre stopped at the top of the stairs, turned, and proclaimed, "My special ones, you have exceeded all my expectations."

The Rescue

CHAPTER 13

*I*t was another night short on sleep when Marta rang the bell signaling first meal. Groggily the special ones made their way to the dining room. Marta was carrying plates of food out of the kitchen when they entered.

After placing the plates on the table, Marta looked around and asked, "Where are Karry and Bunny?"

Manx gasped, realizing that the two girls had not been seen since yesterday at first meal. She had intended to mention it to Boxer, but with all the excitement of seeing Grand Pierre, she had forgotten.

Vera and her two goons, as Dent called them, ignored Marta's question and kept eating. Manx stood up and looked directly at Vera and demanded, "The girls haven't been seen since first meal yesterday, and Wren said they never showed up to swing either. Where were they at second meal and last night?"

Vera sneered back at Manx, her voice brittle. "It's not my job to watch them. Maybe they ran off."

Marta stepped beside Manx, pointed her finger at Vera, and told her, "It is the job of the older children to keep watch on the smaller ones. If they weren't in their beds last night, why didn't you tell us?"

Vera glanced at her two followers and said, "I can't remember if they were in their beds or not, can you?"

Both Jonne and Dortha tried to look as innocent as possible. They shook their heads and shrugged their shoulders like they had no clue. Manx could see that Lester was enjoying watching Marta get upset with Vera. She knew that he was somehow involved with the missing girls.

"I need to let Sola know immediately. We must find the girls." Marta hurried to the kitchen and returned with Sola.

Sola questioned the three scheming girls, again asking why they did not let her know the little girls were missing. She received the same denial from them as did Marta.

After cleanup duties were completed, Boxer noticed Dent lingering by the door. He motioned that he wanted to meet, and Boxer gave a slight nod to let him know he would meet him in their pod, hoping that Dent had information about the missing girls. The special ones were worried about Karry and Bunny, and they hurried to their pod. Dent was waiting inside when they opened the door.

Manx anxiously asked, "Do you know what happened to Karry and Bunny?"

Dent replied, "I think Vera and Lester have done something to them. Those two have been sneaking around, but I haven't been able to get close enough to hear what they are whispering about. Barten's involved, but I don't think Ray had anything to do with it because he has been keeping to himself. Ray may have heard them discussing it and didn't want to be part of it."

Manx sighed. "Vera's sneaky and may be trying to get back at me. But why harm the two girls?"

Dent said, "I think it's more than to get even. Lester is behind this."

"Do you think Ray will talk to us if we get him away from Lester?" Battle asked.

Dent thought for a moment and then answered, "He is afraid of Lester and remembers him from school before the robots arrived. Lester has always been a troublemaker and will pick on anyone he can. If Lester doesn't find out, Ray might tell you what he knows."

Manx looked at Boxer and asked, "Have you heard the signal from my bracelet?"

Boxer replied, "No. Either Karry forgot, or she isn't able to signal."

No one said a word, each of them worrying about the two small girls, and they didn't notice when Wren left through the small door in the back of the pod.

Marta began ringing the bell and continued until all the children came out of their pods and stood in front of the main building—except Wren. Sola announced that everyone would help search the orphanage grounds and buildings for Karry and Bunny. If the girls weren't found, then the search would be expanded. Sola said that Father Brion was away, and she would direct the search. The special ones knew that Father Brion was meeting with the opposition leaders.

Boxer stepped away from the others and stood and listened for the signal from the bracelet. He noticed Manx watching him and shook his head. He could hear no signal.

All of the buildings had been searched and everyone was making a final circle around the orphanage grounds. Sola walked over to Boxer and asked, "Do you have any suggestions as to where to search next?"

"I can't imagine that the girls left the orphanage on their own, or where they would go if they did. Someone caused them to disappear, and both Lester and Vera know something." Boxer's tone of voice left no doubt as to what he thought of Lester and Vera.

Battle walked over to Boxer, waited for Sola to leave, and then told him, "I just met with Ray behind our pod. Dent kept watch so no one saw us. He said that Lester and Vera had something to do with the disappearance of the two girls. Yesterday after first meal, Vera came to the pod and mentioned the girls, and then Lester and Barten left and didn't return for a while. He didn't know where they went, but when they came back, they met with Vera and her goons, and all were carrying on and laughing."

Boxer suggested, "We could try to track the girls' scent, but I think it's been too long, and any trace of which way they went would be gone."

Wren hurried over. "Did you find them?" From the strained looked on her face, it was obvious that she was very worried about her two friends.

Boxer said, "No, but we are not going to give up."

Wren wrinkled her face. "Bear asked if you would meet him. You know the place."

Now Boxer was worried, not knowing what Bear might do, and he was sure that Wren had told Bear about the missing girls. He looked around and motioned for the others to make their way back to the pod. If Bear became upset, then it would be a critical situation. Dent followed the special ones to their pod, pretending to be searching for the girls.

Once inside, Boxer said, "Bear asked to meet with us, and I'm sure Wren told him Bunny is missing." Boxer paused and looked over at Wren perched on her bed. She nodded her head. Boxer admitted, "I'm concerned about what Bear might do if he gets upset and can't control his powers."

Manx spoke up. "We need to let him know what is going on and see if he has any ideas of where to look for the girls. He may have heard Lester and Barten yesterday."

Battle added, "He can search the forest around the orphanage. If Lester and Barten weren't gone long, then the girls can't be far."

Manx sighed. "I keep hoping that Karry will signal with the bracelet. Both she and Bunny know what to do."

Boxer walked to the door. "No one will miss us for a while. Let's all go to meet with Bear, and together maybe we can find the girls."

When they entered the small clearing, Bear was pacing back and forth. The dark scowl on his face expressed his concern. He was tightly clenching his fists and growled, "Where is Bunny?"

"Wow! You sure are big," Dent exclaimed. "I'm glad you're on our team." Bear glared down at the pointy-faced boy, who said, "Just calm down. Between all of us, I'm sure we can find the girls."

Bear growled his response.

Boxer said, "Bunny and Karry haven't been seen since first meal yesterday, and we're sure the two older boys had something to do with their disappearance. The three girls that share the pod with them are in on it too. I'm not sure of the reason, unless it's to cause trouble for the orphanage."

"That could be the reason for Lester meeting with the patrol guards two nights in a row," Dent suggested. "If word gets out that children have gone missing, I'm sure the rogues will have reason to close the orphanage."

"Where will Lester and Barten go if the orphanage is closed?" Manx asked.

"I don't think they're worried about it and have been waiting to leave," Dent replied. "I heard Lester mention to Barten that it won't be long."

"Bear, you know the forest," Battle said. "Is there any place close by where the girls could be?"

Bear shook his head, and his wild hair flew around. "I will search today and let you know tonight. If the boys weren't gone that long, maybe they took the girls to one of the abandoned buildings in the settlement."

"That makes sense," said Manx. "If only Karry would signal."

Bear glared at Manx, and she quickly explained about the bracelet that Grand Pierre had made for her and Wren.

"You need to stay calm," Dent told Bear. "Hey, *calm* could be Bear's special *C*. He really needs to learn to stay calm."

"What are you talking about?" Bear glared down at Dent.

"We'll teach you." Dent grinned. "Each of us has a special word. Mine is *concealment*."

Battle sighed. "Lessons will come after we find the girls. Bear, you search the forest for any place where the girls may be hidden, and we'll talk to Sola to see if we can start searching the buildings closest to the orphanage. We'll meet you back here tonight. If you find something, give a roar. Boxer will hear it, and we'll meet you here."

When they returned to the orphanage, Boxer left to ask Sola about searching the buildings closest to the orphanage. The others waited by the swings. Wren sadly looked up at Manx and uttered, "I just hope they are all right."

Wren's sad face caused Manx to hug and reassure her. "With all of us looking, we will find them. This is just a mean plot by Lester to cause trouble for the orphanage."

Boxer returned and told them, "When I was talking with Sola, Lester came up. When Sola mentioned that we were going to start searching the nearby buildings, he got a funny look on his face. Dent, I need you to watch Lester and get close enough to hear if he talks to Barten or Vera. If he leaves the grounds, see which way he goes, and then come and get me. Be careful, and don't get caught."

"Dent on duty. I'll let you know as soon as I find out anything. I think time is running out for Lester." Dent turned and walked toward pod one, silently following behind Lester.

"If Wren flew over some of the closer buildings, do you think she could see anything?" Battle suggested.

"I doubt it," Boxer responded. "If the girls are inside a building, they would be hidden."

"What if I changed and searched the buildings?" Manx hated waiting around and not doing anything.

"It would take too long, and one of us should be with you in case you run into that dog pack." Boxer meant to say more, but he stopped and listened—and then grinned at the others.

Manx grabbed his arm. "It's the signal from the bracelet."

Boxer nodded and said, "Loud and clear and not far from here. The signal is just past the circle of trees."

Wren started hopping up and down. "I knew we would find them."

Battle cautioned, "We must be careful how we rescue them and not alert Lester. It's critical that we don't reveal our skills or the real reason we are at the orphanage."

"Battle is correct," Boxer said thoughtfully. "Battle and Wren, go and get Bear and meet us in the hidden tree circle. Manx and I will find the girls and take them there. I don't think it's safe to bring them back to the orphanage until we find out what Lester is up to. Maybe we can keep the girls hidden until Father Brion returns. Let's walk back to our pod and say we are going to rest before we start searching the settlement. I'll meet you there after I tell Sola what's happening so she isn't surprised."

CHAPTER 14

When Boxer entered the pod, he told Battle, "Push one of the beds in front of the door so no one can get in, and make sure the cover for the window is closed. We'll leave by the small door. Wren, if you call for Bear, he will hear you, but wait until you and Battle are far enough away from the orphanage so no one else can hear."

Manx opened the small door in the back of the pod, looked out, and motioned an "all clear." Then she climbed out, followed by Wren, Battle, and Boxer, who closed the door. The four made their way to the forest, and Boxer told Manx, "Karry hasn't stopped rubbing the bracelet. I wonder why she waited so long."

Then Boxer ran through the forest followed by Manx. Once past the circle of trees, the road turned, and they could not be seen from the orphanage. Boxer stopped and looked around, and not seeing any patrols, he said, "The signal is coming from that old building."

Boxer pointed ahead and ran across a wide, unkempt area filled with weeds, broken fences, and various forms of garbage. It was like one of Grand Pierre's agility tests for Manx, and she jumped and stepped sideways to avoid tripping on all the trash.

Boxer stopped when he reached the back of the building and listened. He whispered, "This way." He crept around the side of the building, saw a broken window, and crawled though. He helped Manx as she climbed inside to avoid getting cut on the shards of broken glass.

It was dark in the old building, and it stank of mildew and rotting things. Manx didn't want to know what the smelly things had once been, and she tried hard not to inhale the horrible stench, taking small breaths of air. Boxer came to an opening with stairs going down. He stopped and listened for any sound that would indicate that there was someone other than the two girls.

He motioned for Manx to move forward with care. Without making a sound, he started down the steep stairs, which were in much need of repair. The basement was pitch-black, but Boxer could see the two girls huddled in a corner. Their hands were tied, or had been; ropes dangled from their arms. Boxer whispered, "Be careful, and don't scare them."

Manx stepped in front of Boxer and softly whispered, "Karry, Bunny—it's Manx and Boxer. We came to get you out of here."

Karry cried out as Manx reached the small girl and took hold of her hands. "You and Bunny are safe now. Boxer and I are here, like I promised."

Manx untied the rope from Karry's arms, and Boxer did the same for Bunny. Manx started to throw the ropes to one side, but Boxer stopped her. He said, "Let's take them with us. I don't want to leave any sign that the girls were down here."

Manx never questioned Boxer's intelligence or his reasoning, and she handed him Karry's ropes to stuff in a pocket.

"I'm glad you finally rubbed the bracelet," Boxer told Karry. "Everyone has been very worried."

"Not everyone," Karry said. "Vera and Lester said if I called out or made any noise, the metal men outside would hear me and come get us." She still feared the metal men.

"There are no metal men outside," Manx reassured the frightened girl. "Lester and Vera lied to you." Then she asked her, "Why did you finally rub the bracelet?"

"Bunny said I should, and she untied our hands," Karry explained. "She said not to be afraid—that you would find us."

"Bunny can't talk." Manx was confused.

"Not out loud, but she held my hands and told me what to do," Karry answered.

"We need to go," Boxer said as he helped Bunny stand up. "Manx, help Karry up the steps, and I'll help Bunny. When we get outside, I'll carry Bunny on my back, and you take Karry. We can make faster time."

Carefully, Boxer and Manx helped the two girls from the littered basement. Boxer noticed a door that led outside and pushed it open. He paused at the door and listened, and then he lifted Bunny on his back and signaled for them to go. Manx followed, carrying Karry on her back.

When they reached the safety of the hidden tree circle, Battle, Wren, and Bear were waiting. Battle lifted Karry from Manx's back, and Bear hurried to Boxer and lifted Bunny and cradled her in his arms.

The others watched as Bunny tightly hugged the shaggy giant around the neck; her face glowing with happiness. She reached a hand out and touched Manx's face. Manx took hold of her hand and said, "You're welcome, Bunny."

"I told you she could talk," Karry told them.

Both girls had dirt-smeared faces, and their clothes were filthy, but happiness radiated from them after the ordeal they had been through.

Boxer quickly told Battle that Lester and Vera were responsible for the girls going missing, and it wasn't safe to take them back to the orphanage. He added, "I wish we could get in touch with Grand Pierre and take the girls to him. They would be safe, and Francine could take care of them."

Battle suggested, "What if we sneak them into the basement until Father Brion returns?"

Boxer agreed. "We can't stay here, and we need to get the girls to safety. If Lester goes back to find the girls, he isn't going to find any sign of them. I've got the ropes he tied them with. I wish I knew what he has planned."

Bear had been listening. "Bunny's nurse made it out?"

"Yes. Grand Pierre said that she looked for Bunny for a long time but never found her," Boxer explained.

"We must get Bunny to Francine as soon as possible," Bear insisted. "I can watch the basement from the forest, and if anyone comes around and tries to harm the girls again, it will be their last time."

Bunny and Karry were in the basement, sleeping after eating all of the food Sola had brought them. Manx had washed their faces and hands and had given them some of Wren's clothes to wear. Sola and Marta had been told about Lester and Vera's abduction of the two girls and had agreed to keep the girls hidden until Father Brion returned. Sola said Father Brion was planning to be back before dark.

The special ones were in front of the main building, pretending to be looking for the girls. Bear was on watch, hidden directly across from the basement door. Dent sauntered over and reported that Lester was in the pod, acting anxious, like he was waiting for something.

After Dent heard about the girls' rescue, and about Bear being on guard and saying that if Lester or Vera came around they would not be walking away, he said, "A Bear's gotta do what a Bear's gotta do. It will serve them right. Bunny and Karry could have come to harm in that old building, left there without food or water."

Marta rang the bell for second meal. The special ones turned to go inside and were startled when two patrol guards came rolling up with sirens blaring. Standing on the back of one guard's platform was a tall rogue leader.

Boxer gave the alert signal in case they were identified by the robots' sensors. The special ones edged to one side of building to give them quick access to escape to the forest if they were discovered.

The rogue leader stepped from the platform and stiffly walked toward the front of the building. Sola stepped from the porch and asked, "Do you want something?"

The rogue leader's walk was mechanical, and he jerked to a stop like he needed oil. When the leader spoke, it sounded like a recording. "I was told there are children missing."

The special ones weren't surprised by the leader's statement and had been expecting something like this to happen.

Before Sola could respond, Lester stepped up and pointed to Boxer. "I saw him sneaking around and followed him. He took the girls and hid them in an old building, and Vera saw it too." Vera stepped forward, nodding her head in agreement.

"Should we arrest him?" one of the guards asked.

"Wait just a minute. You are not arresting anyone on Lester's word." Sola's face had turned red with anger as she faced the rogue leader.

The leader stiffly turned to Lester and ordered, "Show us the building."

Lester nodded and turned to start down the road, walking fast.

The rogue leader stepped on the back of one guard's platform and ordered the other guard, "Make sure no one leaves."

The guard turned and rolled after Lester with the leader standing on the platform. The other guard watched Sola and the children from constantly moving eyes.

Manx glared at Vera, who slyly smiled. Barten, Jonne, and Dortha stood behind Vera with smirks on their faces. Boxer noticed that Ray had edged over to stand behind Battle.

The waiting seemed longer than the time it actually took for Lester to take the rogue leader to the building and return. Lester was sweating, and his face was red as he walked directly in front of the guard.

When they reached the orphanage, the rogue leader stiffly stepped from the platform and walked to where Sola stood. "I found no signs of the children. I searched the inside and the outside of the building."

Sola glared at the leader and said in a hard voice, "I told you not to believe anything Lester says. Honesty isn't one of his qualities. This isn't the first time Lester has caused problems."

Lester's jaw tightened as he listened to Sola's words. He was angry and couldn't do a thing about it.

The rogue leader turned to Vera and pointed. "Tell me again what you saw."

Vera turned white with fright and looked ready to faint. She pointed to Lester and stuttered, "I just said what he told me to."

Lester glared at Vera and looked ready to strangle her.

Just then Father Brion came walking down the road. He was dusty, and his arms were full of items for the orphanage. He stopped beside the rogue leader and placed the things he carried on the ground. "What is going on?" he asked.

Sola angrily replied, "Karry and Bunny are missing, and Lester just accused Boxer of taking them."

"No, no," said Father Brion. "Yesterday Karry's aunt learned that she was at the orphanage and came to take her to live with her. Karry asked if Bunny could come too, and the aunt agreed to take both girls. I had to leave for rounds and forgot to tell Sola. I am sorry for any trouble I caused, but without the use of the truck, it takes me longer to make rounds." Father Brion looked at the rogue leader. "If I could use the truck, it would allow me to return faster and avoid problems like this."

Dent moved closer to Manx and whispered, "We should give Father Brion an award for acting."

The rogue leader responded to Father Brion, "We will take it under consideration." Then he pushed a button on his chest and said, "Situation clear." He faced Lester and warned, "Do not give false information again." Then the leader stepped on the back of the platform, and both guards turned and rolled away.

Father Brion turned to Lester and sternly said, "After meal I will see you in my office and Vera you too!" Vera turned even whiter, and Lester stomped toward pod one with Barten right behind.

Father Brion looked at Boxer, wiped the sweat off his brow, and said, "It's been a *bear* of a day."

Boxer grinned, understanding how Father Brion had known what was happening and was able to trick the rogue leader. Bear had met Father Brion and warned him. Maybe Bear would be a good addition to the team after all.

Marta held two extra plates of food and looked around. Battle told her, "If those plates are extra, I know someone who really likes your cooking." Marta grinned and set the plates on the table by Battle.

The children hurried to finish their dinner. The situation with Lester and the robots had made the meal late and the food cold. Lester and Barten had not come to dinner, and Vera had kept her head down while eating, not making her usual snide remarks aimed at Manx.

After cleanup Battle told the others, "Wren and I will deliver these plates to Bear. I'm sure he's hungry." Wren beamed at the opportunity to see her big friend.

Boxer said, "I'm going to see Father Brion and will meet you back in the pod."

When Manx entered the pod, Dent was standing in the middle of the room. He looked at Manx and said, "Guess who left their pod?" His grin was big.

"Good riddance," Manx replied as she sat down on her bed. "I wonder where they went."

"I don't have a clue, but I think Lester was just waiting to cause trouble before he left. It sure backfired on him. He looked ready to kill Vera too." Dent laughed as he sat down at the table and crossed his legs.

"It's too bad he didn't have the chance," Manx replied. "She's as bad as he is. I wonder what Father Brion is going to do about those girls."

The small door in the back of the room opened, and Wren climbed in, looking happy. "I saw Bear, and then Boxer let me go into the basement to see Bunny and Karry. They are going to go live with Grand Pierre." Wren jumped onto her bed. "After dark, Bear is going to help Father Brion take the girls to meet Grand Pierre."

Manx was surprised. "When did Father Brion talk to Grand Pierre?"

Wren wrinkled her face in thought and said, "Maybe with the com-nit thing and that big one you took from the robots' headquarters. They can talk or signal or something."

"Interesting," Manx uttered. She wondered if Wren was right and they could communicate with Grand Pierre like the robots were able to do.

CHAPTER 15

The next morning after first meal and cleanup were over, Vera, Jonne, and Dortha disappeared to their pod after being sternly warned by Father Brion that if they caused any further trouble they would have to leave the orphanage.

Wren carried away two plates of food for Bear, and Manx walked beside her. With Lester gone, Manx didn't want Wren going off alone in case he sneaked back and tried to get even with them. It was a mystery why Lester was so aggressive toward them, but according to Ray, it was how Lester treated everyone he couldn't intimidate. Manx felt more at ease now, and the open hostility from Vera had stopped, but she still sensed that they had to be cautious.

Bear was waiting for the two girls in the open area, and he looked hungry. It didn't take him long to make two plates of food disappear. He thanked them as he handed the empty plates to Manx.

Wren couldn't wait to know. "Are Karry and Bunny safe?"

Bear looked down at Wren, nodded his shaggy head, and said, "Yes, and Francine was there too. Bunny was excited to see her. Karry told Francine that Bunny had told her—just by holding her hands—to signal with the bracelet. Francine said that Bunny was able to communicate by thoughts, and that was the reason she didn't talk. Only a few extremely brilliant scientists on Ulterion have this ability. Francine taught Bunny to talk through her hands so she could communicate with her. Francine told Father Brion that all of Bunny's tests exceeded all measurements, and with the right training, Bunny would excel in science."

Manx was stunned to hear about the brilliance of the blonde-haired girl with faint-blue eyes, and Wren said, "Wow."

At second meal Marta told Boxer that Father Brion wanted to meet with them that night, and Boxer knew the plans were finalized to retrieve one of the metal boxes. Father Brion had been surprised earlier in the day when one of the patrol guards had rolled up in front of the orphanage and announced that Father Brion would be allowed to drive the truck to pick up supplies, but he could not stray from the main roads or he would be shot. Then, after delivering the message—and the threat—the guard rolled away.

Boxer bristled, and Battle clenched his fists as they stood and watched the robot disappear. The knowledge that Father Brion would undoubtedly be killed—without thought or feeling—strengthened their determination to help the opposition defeat these mindless machines.

Boxer had learned from Marta that Father Brion had a family, but they had been killed during the invasion and his home destroyed. The pictures Father Brion carried of them in his mind were all he had left. Boxer understood the reason Father Brion devoted his time and daily risked his life for the opposition.

That night Dent agreed to stay with Wren in the pod while the others left to meet Father Brion. Dent mentioned to Boxer that they would have to get Ray to safety because if something went wrong trying to retrieve the metal box, there would be no way to get him out. The robots would not hesitate to kill him if they thought Ray was part of the opposition. Boxer would ask Father Brion if Ray could be dropped off at a safe house.

Boxer knew Marta and Sola had escape plans and would use them when the fight for freedom started. What would happen to Vera, Jonne, and Dortha, Boxer didn't know—or care, after what they had done to Karry and Bunny.

At night after the lights were powered down, Vera and the two other girls would not leave their pod. They were in fear for their lives, and their behavior had changed from rude and surly to nervous and jumpy. After the incident with Bunny and Karry, the three girls had told Sola that something was coming around at night, growling and scratching the outside walls, and rattling the door, trying to get in.

Sola had looked around the pod but had not seen any animal tracks. She told the girls that Lester might have come back to get even. The three girls were sure Lester could not make the low, menacing growls that kept them awake every night.

The special ones didn't offer an explanation, even though they knew the source of the girls' nightly fright. Bear was giving the three callous girls a taste of their own medicine for their horrid treatment of Karry and Bunny.

All of the special ones would go on the retrieval, whether they had an assigned task or not; Grand Pierre did not want to separate them. Grand Pierre would assist because of his knowledge of the rogue leaders. If the scientists could disrupt the communication signals, the robots would not function properly and could then be disabled. The latest count of rogue leaders and guards was ten, or maybe eleven. There might be one more guard, but no one knew how to tell them apart for a final count.

Father Brion looked anxious when Boxer, Battle, and Manx entered the basement. Papers were spread across the table. He stood back and said, "We are almost ready. Just a few more details, and then it will be time to execute."

The special ones could tell that Father Brion feared what would happen if the plan failed: execution.

Father Brion gathered his thoughts and continued. "Piers wanted me to let you know that the search team returned from the laboratory and reported that the buildings are intact. Only the actual labs were destroyed. After the robots are defeated, the Ulterions will move back to their facility, and there is plenty of room for everyone. The search team found the warship the robots arrived in, but nothing useful was left inside. Piers said it was like an empty container. The rogues had moved everything out."

Father Brion moved the papers aside, put the large map on the table, and pointed to a red X. "Here is where we will stage the fire. It is close enough to get the rogues' attention, and far enough away to hide what we bring to burn. Starting tonight, we will sneak in and stockpile wood treated with fuel that the rogues won't be able to put out before Manx retrieves one of the metal boxes. Piers will wait in an old building across the road. Battle, you will guard Manx in case she runs into trouble. Wren will wait with Piers and get a message to the others if plans change. It will take another two nights for the team to build up the scrap pile."

Father Brion looked at Boxer. "Tomorrow we'll take the truck and do rounds like normal."

"I need to talk to you about Ray," Boxer said. "If something goes wrong with the retrieval, he could be in danger from the robots."

Father Brion asked, "What about the silent boy Dent? Do we need to get him out?"

Boxer wondered how much he should say. "Dent is a big help to us and will go on the mission—and Bear too."

Father Brion looked confused. "As long as Piers agrees."

"Then we don't have a problem," Battle answered as the three special ones climbed from the basement.

The following morning at first meal, Father Brion told Boxer that he had made arrangements for Ray to be taken to safety, so Ray would go on rounds with them in the truck today. After cleanup Boxer told Ray to go and get his things and meet him by the truck.

Ray looked hesitant until Battle told him, "It's for your safety." Satisfied by Battle's explanation, Ray went to pack his few belongings.

Boxer looked at Dent. "Do you want to move into our pod? Now that Ray is gone, you will be alone."

Dent scratched his nose and said, "Nah. I'll be okay. Besides, I'm hardly there."

"Most of the time he's in our pod anyway," Battle joked.

Father Brion drove up in the old truck, and Ray and Boxer climbed in.

Manx looked around at the empty orphanage grounds. Vera and her two followers had disappeared inside their pod with the door shut, probably catching up on their sleep. Manx grinned at the thought of Bear continuing his nightly "prowl and growl," keeping the three girls awake, shaking, and scared.

"Do you want to swing?" she asked Wren.

Marta rang the bell for second meal just as Father Brion and Boxer returned from rounds—without Ray. Boxer joined the others as they walked into the dining room and sat down. Vera, Jonne, and Dortha sat at one end of the long table, and the special ones sat at the other end. Dent came in and sat down by Battle.

As Marta carried out the plates of food, she announced, "Sola wants to talk to everyone in the main room when cleanup duties are finished."

Vera looked over at Dent and demanded, "Where is Ray?"

Dent looked up at Vera, shrugged, and kept eating.

"Why is everyone leaving?" she exclaimed.

Battle stopped eating and looked at Vera. "We're still here."

Vera's old self returned when she spat out, "I wish I wasn't," causing Manx to hide a grin as she continued eating.

When Sola stepped into the room, the special ones waited on one side, Vera and her mates on the other. "I have sad news." Sola paused. "I'm afraid we have to close the orphanage. It is impossible to keep it open from the scant donations. Ray went to live in the settlement with another family. There are three openings at the work center, and Father Brion talked with the director today. Vera, Jonne, and Dortha, you will leave tomorrow after first meal and go to live at the center. Beds and meals are provided, and there is a variety of opportunities for work. The director will meet with each of you and decide where to place you."

Vera scowled at Sola, and Jonne and Dortha seemed frozen in place. Manx smiled. Work was not on Vera's agenda, or the other girls' either. Sola told the dazed girls, "Have your things packed and ready at first meal."

Sola turned to leave the room, and in a loud voice, Vera demanded, "What about them?" She pointed to the special ones.

Sola turned, looked directly at Vera, and sternly said, "Their grandfather contacted Father Brion, and in a few days he will be able to care for them again. He also agreed to have Dent live with them."

Sola abruptly turned and walked from the room. The look on her face clearly expressed her relief that she would not have to put up with Vera's bad-mannered behavior any longer. Try as she had to help the three girls, they had not been willing to help out. Rather, they had expected to be waited on.

Wren squeezed Manx's hand and exclaimed, "I just can't wait to see Grandfather."

Later that night Dent joined the special ones in their pod and said, "After tomorrow it will be just us five. Do you think Bear could stay in pod one with me? It's been a long time since he's had a real bed to sleep in, if you call these hard cots beds."

Boxer said, "As long as no one else sees him. After the robots are overthrown, we will all go to live with Grand Pierre at the facility. Grand Pierre is excited for all of us to be reunited."

Dent grinned. "It's too bad tonight is the last time Bear will be able to keep those horrid girls from sleeping."

Everyone agreed with him.

CHAPTER 16

$\mathcal{T}$he special ones once again packed their meager belongings. Manx watched Boxer make a final mark in his book before he placed it in his sack. The number of marks would equal sixty days since they'd come to live at the orphanage. They would carry their sacks to the basement, and if the robots destroyed the orphanage, maybe the basement would be spared. They placed their filled sacks by the small door just as Marta rang the bell signaling first meal.

The special ones and Dent were seated at the table when Vera, Jonne, and Dortha sluggishly walked through the door. They had never looked this bad. All three girls looked haggard, and from the dark circles under their eyes, they could have passed for raccoons. Each girl carried a bundle of clothes, which they pushed under the bench as they sat down. They were packed and ready to leave.

Manx grinned at Dent. She couldn't wait to ask him about last night and what mischief Bear had been up to.

Marta carried plates of hot food from the kitchen and set them on the table. She told Boxer, "Father Brion will meet with you when he gets back from taking the girls to the work center." She seemed to be having trouble holding back a large grin when she mentioned the girls and work in the same sentence.

It was late afternoon when Father Brion returned from the work center and drove the large truck behind the main building. He hurried down the back hallway and opened the door directly across from the special ones' pod. He stepped across and knocked on the small door. Battle opened the door.

Father Brion peered inside and saw the four sacks. "You are packed. Now carry your sacks to the basement. Then I need Boxer and Battle to load the truck. We are taking everything we can, in case the orphanage is destroyed. Once we are free from the robots, we can set up a new orphanage. If I leave soon, I will be able to get Sola and Marta to safety and miss the patrol."

After the large truck was loaded, Marta gave Boxer a box of food for their last meal at the orphanage. She looked at Boxer and Battle and assured them, "I'll see you soon." Then she hugged both boys.

When the large truck disappeared around the side of the building, Boxer shut the back door. The empty building echoed with his footsteps as he carried the box out the front. When he entered the pod, the others were waiting.

If they were worried, it didn't show. Dent joked as he helped pass out the food, pretending to give Bear another helping after each of them, so Bear would end up with seven servings to the others' one. Bear was enjoying Dent's humor, and he had a satisfied grin when Manx said that the three girls looked like a raccoon trio at morning meal.

After they'd finished eating, Boxer asked, "Does everyone know what to do, or do you want me to go over the plan again?"

Bear looked at Boxer and growled, "Kill the robots."

Dent lowered his voice and tried to match Bear's growl. "Kill them all."

Wren hopped up with fists raised and tried to speak in a low voice, but it sounded more like a squeak. "Death to the metal men," she said, making everyone bend over with laughter.

Boxer raised his hand and said, "Father Brion is back." He walked to the door and opened it and then looked out as Father Brion turned off the motor.

It had been a slow return to the orphanage. To avoid being seen by the patrols, Father Brion had been driving after dark on ruined roads without lights. He stepped from the truck and hurried inside the pod.

He looked around and said, "Sola and Marta are safe, and Ray said to tell everyone to be careful and that he can't wait to see you. His uncle Drew recognized him when he was taken to the hideout. Drew is one of the opposition leaders and was stunned to see Ray. He had been told that his brother's entire family had been killed during the raid. Ray has been helping organize the weapons to fight the robots."

Dent spoke up, shocking Father Brion. "That's great news. I knew Ray wasn't involved in Lester's deceitfulness."

Father Brion scowled at Dent, who grinned and shrugged his shoulders.

Father Brion looked at Boxer and asked, "Does everyone know what to do tomorrow? Once the fire draws the rogues outside, Manx will have a short time to get inside and retrieve one of the communication boxes."

Boxer affirmed, "We are ready."

"That's good. Now we must leave to avoid the guards. Drew has marked the back roads where the robots don't patrol. We should reach the building before light, and Piers and Drew will meet us there. Boxer knows the roads and will ride up front with me and read the map. The rest will ride in back. If we are stopped by the patrol, run and get to safety." Father Brion looked worried.

Boxer assured him, "We have a place to meet if something should happen. All of us have studied the map and know how to get there."

Father Brion took a large breath and then exhaled it. "Let's get going."

Bear wasn't happy at having to ride in the back of the truck. It was something he had never done, and he didn't like to be confined in a small space. As he climbed up, Dent explained, "If the guards stop the truck, jump out and run to safety."

Bear looked at Dent and growled, "I would never run away and leave any of you. We all escape together."

Dent grinned, and his two front teeth glistened in the dark. "Like I said, I'm glad you're on our side."

Bear climbed into the back of the truck, and Father Brion drove from the orphanage into the dark night.

The ride was slow, dusty, and bumpy, and the back roads were narrow, rutted, and full of holes. Father Brion grumbled to Boxer, "The roads were never like this before the robots invaded. The settlement was a wonderful place. The buildings were in good shape, the roads always repaired, and the fields full of crops. Our children ran and played without fear of being killed."

Father Brion didn't say any more, clearly remembering the family he had lost in the invasion. Being one of the opposition leaders was personal for Father Brion.

Father Brion sharply turned the steering wheel to avoid a large hole in the road, when Boxer ordered, "Stop." Boxer leaned out the window and then said, "Quick, pull over behind that building."

Father Brion spun the wheels, and the large truck bumped across a vacant lot to stop behind the building. Boxer motioned for him to turn off the motor, and they waited in the dark silence. Down the road came a patrol guard traveling alone. They usually travelled in pairs.

"That guard must be coming from the communication center," Father Brion whispered. "Why is it on this road?"

"Probably returning to headquarters," Boxer replied. Once the guard was far enough away not to hear the truck's rumbling motor, Boxer told Father Brion it was safe to continue.

"That was close," Father Brion uttered as the truck bounced back to the road. "It's not much farther, and I'll be glad when we get there."

Father Brion turned off the road, drove the truck over a garbage-littered field, and came to a stop behind a dark building. Everyone climbed quietly from the truck and entered through a door hidden by planks of wood to stop anyone from seeing inside. Once inside, Father Brion stumbled on the rickety floor. The special ones could easily see the broken boards.

Grand Pierre and Drew were in a long room with a window covered by old papers. On top of a table, a small light illuminated them. Drew looked like an older version of Ray, except for the gray sprinkled his reddish hair. He was slimmer than Father Brion but not much taller. Wrinkles formed around his brown eyes, and the clothes he wore were threadbare. He smiled when he noticed the special ones, which softened his features.

"Thank you for watching out for Ray," he told them. Then he turned back to the plans.

Boxer signaled an alert just before two men crept into the building and entered the room. Grand Pierre noticed Battle move into a defensive position and said, "These men are part of the opposition."

The men hurried to Drew, and one whispered, "Everything is ready. When we signal, Cray will light the fire."

Drew replied, "After the metal box is retrieved, I'll signal to start the fires in the settlement to mislead the patrols and allow us to get away."

When the sun became visible over the horizon, Drew asked the special ones, "Are you ready?"

Battle stood up and replied, "As we can be."

Grand Pierre cautioned, "Remember your Cs, and work as a team."

Drew turned to the two men. "Signal Cray to light the fire."

The special ones looked out the window toward a field full of stubble from crops long dead. They saw a small flame flicker, and as it grew larger, smoke began to curl into the air as the fire consumed the fuel-soaked wood.

"Impressive," Dent exclaimed as he watched the flames leap high.

Drew stood behind Dent and said, "Let's hope it impresses the rogues so they go to find out what's going on."

"Here they come." Dent was excited as he watched the tall rogue leaders walk stiltedly from the communication center toward the fire.

Battle counted. "That's four. How long do we wait for the others to come out?"

Boxer said, "Let's go and get as close as we can without being seen." He walked out of the room followed by Manx,

Battle, and Dent. When they were outside, Boxer noticed Dent. "What are you doing?" he whispered.

"I'm coming with you," Dent replied.

Boxer could hear the determination in Dent's voice. He motioned for single file and ran across the road to a small stand of trees. The other three ran behind him.

When they reached the trees, Battle pointed and whispered, "Look. Numbers five and six have left the building."

"Manx," Boxer said, "the second window is open. Get in and grab the closest metal box. Battle will be outside. Get it to him, and get out."

Manx nodded, swiftly changed into the yellow cat, leaped from the safety of the trees, and ran toward the open window. Battle checked to make sure that the rogues were still walking toward the billowing fire and then sprinted after Manx. Boxer kept count of the rogues. If one turned back, he would call out a danger signal for Manx and Battle.

Manx was fast, and she reached the open window and leaped through. She checked the room, and finding it empty, she changed. She hurried to the closest table with one of the metal-encased boxes.

Battle was not a fast runner, and he reached the window just as Manx leaned out holding the heavy box. Her arms trembled with the weight of it, and when she let go of it, she almost fell out the window after it. Battle caught the heavy box, turned, and started back to the road.

Manx grabbed the windowsill to steady herself and then dropped to the ground. She knew she didn't dare change where others could see her, so she ran after Battle. She smiled to herself. It was an easy in-and-out with the rogues out investigating the fire.

Manx reached the road and heard Boxer shout a warning signal. She froze in place, confused because the rogue leaders had not returned. Behind her a loud siren blared, and she heard a voice shouting, "Stop, or you will be killed."

Manx twisted around to see one of the platform guards pointing a gun at her. Manx knew it didn't matter to the robot that she was a young girl. If she moved, it would shoot her without hesitation. The guard stared at Manx with stone-hard eyes, waiting for further orders.

The rogue leaders were outside, unaware of what was happening. Manx trembled in fear and didn't know what to do. She couldn't escape the deadly gun aimed at her. She didn't dare change; it would give away their secret. Her heart pounded in her chest, and with terror-filled eyes, she stared at the man-like menace.

Suddenly the guard started twitching and acting weird. Its arms began jerking back and forth, its head tilted sideways, and then it spun around and faced backward.

"Run!" Boxer yelled from across the road, but Manx froze in place, staring at the bizarre, jerking guard.

Grand Pierre and Drew rushed down the road. They had seen the guard. Battle met Drew in the road, handed him the metal box, and turned to help Manx. Before Battle could reach her, a loud crackling noise came from the strangely jerking guard, followed by a small explosion that caused sparks to shoot from its eyes.

The guard's arms dropped useless to the side, and its head fell forward as a plume of black smoke curled from under the metal plate that extended down its back. From under the metal plate, a gray rat tumbled onto the platform, and as it fell to the road, it changed back into Dent.

Battle and Grand Pierre reached the slumped boy at the same time.

"He saved Manx," Battle declared.

"Help me lift him," Grand Pierre ordered. Then he cradled the boy in his arms as he loped back down the road. Dent raised up, coughed out black smoke, and collapsed back into Grand Pierre's arms.

Battle grabbed Manx by the arm and pulled her after Grand Pierre.

Father Brion motioned everyone to the truck. As Manx climbed into the back of the truck, she asked Grand Pierre, "Will Dent be okay?"

"I'm sure he will." Grand Pierre sounded hopeful.

Dent raised his head and looked at Manx, his two front teeth now black, and rasped, "It's hard to kill a rat."

Drew drove the old truck like a battle wagon. He raced across fields and down narrow roads to escape being seen by the rogue leaders.

The special ones held tight to the rails and couldn't talk over the loud grinding noise from the maxed-out motor. Boxer listened for any sound of pursuit from the robots, but unless they had their sirens blaring, he wouldn't have been able to hear them.

Manx kept one arm around Wren to make sure she didn't get bounced out. Bear pointed to a large fire that blazed high, and Battle could smell smoke coming from other fires throughout the settlement, all of them lit to confuse the robots and hide their own escape.

The large truck made a sharp turn and started going uphill. From the increased bouncing, Boxer knew they had left the road and were driving away from the settlement. He had kept track of the direction Drew was going, and they were at the far end of the settlement where the map showed a large forest. He knew that the scientists and opposition leaders had been hiding for years, and their hideout had never been discovered.

The old truck slowed as it made a series of sharp turns and continued upward. Suddenly it jerked to a stop, and Father Brion jumped out and ran to the front of the truck. He pushed open a wide, vine-covered gate to allow the truck to pass, and once through the gate, he pulled it shut. As he jumped back inside, he shouted, "We'll be at the caves soon."

Caves. No one had mentioned caves before, and they all wondered where there were caves large enough to hide the big truck.

The Caves

CHAPTER 17

The truck continued through the forest, following a rutted trail fenced by tall trees leaving barely enough room for the truck to pass. Gnarly branches grabbed its sides as it rolled by. After one last narrow turn, the truck rolled down a steep embankment and onto level ground.

Drew guided the truck under a large bluff that extended from the mountain above. He released his tight grip on the steering wheel and exhaled a large breath. "We did it!"

The special ones stood up in the back of the truck and were amazed by the bluff, which could only be seen from the ground. Anyone looking down from above would miss it. But it was all of the activity taking place under the bluff that left them speechless.

A field abundant with grass and wildflowers extended from the bluff, and children were playing there. A stream ran from the mountain, creating a small pond before it continued trickling through the field. Tables were nestled under the bluff, with men and women sitting there. A man was using an ax to cut logs into pieces. Shirts and pants were drying on rocks by the pond.

"This place is like a beehive," Manx exclaimed as she looked around.

Drew and Father Brion stepped from the truck. Both looked exhausted. Grand Pierre still cradled Dent in his arms, and Father Brion helped him climb from the truck. Dent appeared to be sleeping as Grand Pierre carried him into the caves.

One by one, the children climbed from the dusty truck. This was not what they had expected when Father Brion mentioned caves.

"Look! There's Marta," Wren shouted, pointing to a cooking area where blackened pots hung over a campfire and skillets sat on a rusty grill. From the aroma in the air, Marta was cooking breakfast.

Marta turned at hearing her name, and seeing the children, she hurried to them, wiping her hands on her apron. The jubilant group met her halfway, all happy to see her and anxious to enjoy her cooking.

"You made it!" Marta exclaimed as she hugged each one. "Any problems?"

"There was a patrol guard behind the building, which we didn't know about," Battle told her. "It almost killed Manx, but Dent took out the guard."

Marta looked around. "Where is Dent?"

Manx answered, "Grand Pierre carried him inside. He said Dent would be okay." Manx sighed and hoped that Grand Pierre was right.

Marta looked up at Bear and smiled. "So, you're the one Wren was taking food to. Bear is your name?"

Bear grinned and in a low voice told her, "You are a really good cook."

"Well, from now on you join everyone for meals and don't eat by yourself. I'd better get back, or breakfast will be charcoal." Marta turned and hurried back to the campfire.

Father Brion walked up and told them, "Go ahead and look around, but when Marta rings the bell, come quickly, or you will miss breakfast. After we finish eating, we will meet with Piers and go over the plan."

When Father Brion walked away, Manx turned to Boxer and grumbled, "What plan? I thought we completed our missions." She was still shaken over almost being killed—and the fact that Dent had risked his life to save hers. She worried about the pointy-faced boy who had become an important member of their team.

Boxer shrugged. "Apparently Grand Pierre thinks we can be of further use."

Battle said, "I'm interested in the caves. I want to look around."

The others agreed to explore the caves and find Grand Pierre.

"He went this way," Battle said when the opening in the mountain led to three different paths. He could smell the smoke from Dent's burned clothes and knew which path to take.

"This looks like one of Grand Pierre's mazes that he made us find our way out of," Wren commented as she followed behind Battle. "But then we were blindfolded."

"These caves extend a long way and must have been created by water that eventually became that small stream," Boxer explained as they walked farther into the caves. "I think it's the same stream where Grand Pierre left us to find our way back to the farm."

The caves didn't smell damp or musty. "These are nice," Bear muttered.

"Thinking of hibernating?" Manx teased, causing Bear to loudly "harrumph" in her ear, which made her jump.

Battle made another turn and then stopped by an opening. "In here," he said.

The children peered inside and were shocked to see that the cave resembled their old home. They saw Grand Pierre sitting in his chair next to a bed where Dent lay sleeping. The furnishings in the cave looked familiar because Grand Pierre had carried them in the transport from the farmhouse.

Grand Pierre looked up and said, "I wondered when you would find me." His grin was a welcome sight as they all crowded into the cave. Grand Pierre looked at the large shaggy boy and said, "Bear, I'm glad you're here. We have a problem, and I hope you can assist us."

"If it gets rid of those monsters, I'll do everything I can," Bear answered.

Grand Pierre said, "Your knowledge of the forest around the settlement will be most helpful to identify places for the repeaters. We needs trees that are tall enough to bounce the signals back and forth. We plan on blasting scrambled signals that will disrupt the guards. Once the guards are incapacitated, the opposition teams can disable them for good."

"How many of the guards and leaders are still active?" Battle asked.

"From the latest count—and it's hard to tell because they all look alike—there may be five patrol guards and six rogue leaders," Grand Pierre said. "Never think that the rogue leaders aren't dangerous, because they are—even more so than the guards. In a hand-to-hand fight, no one can defeat them."

A small, shaky voice whispered, "We have to find the rogues' weakness, like the exposed wiring under the patrol guard's metal plate."

Everyone turned toward the bed where Dent looked back at them.

"Dent!" Manx exclaimed. She was the first to reach him and took hold of his hand. "I've been so worried about you. You saved my life, and if something happened to you, I would never forgive myself."

Dent smiled at her with his front teeth now black and said, "It wasn't your fault. No one knew about that guard. It just happened."

Grand Pierre leaned down, placed his hand on Dent's brow, and looked hard into the boy's eyes, making sure there were no lingering effects from the explosion. He asked, "How did you know about the exposed wires?"

"I studied the wiring diagram with Battle. The rogues could be vulnerable too." Dent tried to sit up, but Grand Pierre placed his hand on Dent's chest and ordered him to rest.

Marta rang the bell to signal that it was time to eat, and Manx told Dent, "I'll bring your meal back here, and Wren and I will eat with you."

Dent's smile was lopsided as he watched everyone hurry away with Bear in the lead, not wanting to miss out on breakfast.

Manx and Wren carried their plates of food and a plate for Dent to the cave. Bear saw Bunny and Francine and went to sit with them. Battle sat by Ray; he wanted to know about the weapons that could be used against the robots. Grand Pierre introduced Boxer to Argies, the tall man who had originally rescued and cared for Dent. He was one of the Ulterion scientists and worked with Grand Pierre in the cloning lab.

Grand Pierre told Boxer that a total of six scientists had escaped and were living in the caves, along with about thirty Adorans who were hiding because they were part of the opposition. Boxer learned that the caves were connected by a vast underground system of tunnels that extended under one end of the settlement directly opposite from the orphanage. There was a hidden access under one of the buildings, which the opposition used to enter the settlement unseen. So far, no one other than the opposition members knew of the secret entrance or about the caves.

Manx, Wren, and Dent had just finished eating when Grand Pierre returned to the cave. He walked over to Dent. "How are you feeling?"

Dent grinned, exposing his two black teeth, and said, "Much better. The food really helped."

Grand Pierre smiled down at him. "That's good. I just met with Argies, the scientist who rescued you, and told him how you saved Wren. He wasn't surprised and said that you were quite intelligent. Now, if Manx and Wren will stay with you, I have a meeting with the opposition team to plan the final offense to defeat the robots."

Wren chirped, "You don't need us?"

Grand Pierre fondly smiled at the three children and told them, "Not this time. You three have done your part—and very well, I might add!" Then he turned and walked out of the cave.

Manx sighed. "I'm not sure if I feel good about not being involved. Not knowing what is happening is sometimes worse."

"It's probably too dangerous for us," Wren told Manx, who loudly replied, "But what about Boxer and Battle and Bear?"

Dent spoke up. "You should be more worried about the robots than those three."

CHAPTER 18

$\mathcal{B}$oxer, Battle, and Bear walked behind Grand Pierre into the cave that was being used as the opposition's headquarters. They sat down beside him on a hewn wooden bench. This was the largest of the caves and could easily fit thirty people inside.

Drew and Father Brion stood beside a table that was leaned on its side. Crudely drawn maps were pinned to the table. Ray was sitting in the front beside the two men responsible for the fires. Boxer counted twenty men in the room, including Grand Pierre, Battle, Bear, and himself. The men resembled Drew, with their mended clothes and worn shoes. The group was ragged looking, but their clothes were clean.

Grand Pierre and the other scientists were taller and slimmer than the men, but it was their pale skin and eyes that made them stand out from the tanned skin and darker features of the Adorans. Boxer noticed that there were no women in the room and decided that they must be taking care of the children.

Drew looked around the cave and, satisfied that everyone was there, began: "Status update for a communication box. One was successfully retrieved, and Piers and Argies now

have the items needed to disrupt the rogues' communication."
Thankful sighs were heard around the room.

Drew continued. "Status update for the disruption devices. Piers said it will take another day for Francine to complete the repeaters. Once they are ready, we need to install them to bounce the scrambled signals back and forth. As long as the repeaters stay operational, they will continue to send. Two-man teams will be assigned to disable each patrol guard and rogue leader. We won't know how the robots are affected until the scrambled signals are received, so you must be prepared for them to fight back.

One of the men sitting in the back raised his hand and asked, "How will we know where to find the robots and if the disruption works?"

Drew answered, "We have spotters at the communication center and headquarters tracking their locations. The guards have doubled patrols, so those are easy to track. One platform guard has been going between the two locations, and we're not sure why. One of the guards was disabled during the last mission, and now we know how to disable them if we can get close enough.

"The scientists have made blasting sticks to place under the guards' platforms. When exploded, one stick is powerful enough to overturn the guard. Place another stick under the metal plate on its neck, ignite it, and it will take out all its wiring. That will disable them all, and then we can take them apart.

"The rogue leaders have a higher intelligence and will need a different tactic. Defense weapons built into their bodies connect to their neural wiring, and they can engage these weapons without the use of hands. They also have the ability to use external weapons, like guns or knives. In the communication center they have a stock of weapons, and we cannot allow them to get to those weapons."

Cray, one of the men who had started the fires, asked, "What if we just burn the communication center down?"

Father Brion stepped forward and explained that the main problem was in getting close enough to place enough wood to catch the building on fire. And once they'd revealed their plan, the rogues would kill anyone near the building.

Another man challenged, "All our plans are based on the disruption signals working. What if it doesn't?" Other men in the room agreed with him.

Grand Pierre stood up and faced the group. "We are certain the disruption signals will work, but how long it will take for the rogues to change to another channel is something we don't know. Once we are given the go, every team must be in place and ready to disarm the robots. If we can stop the rogue leaders from accessing their communication devices, they won't be able to change to a different channel to command the guards, and they will not leave the communication center unattended again." Grand Pierre sat back down.

After all the men's concerns were addressed, plans were finalized. Tomorrow night the repeaters would be placed at the four corners of the settlement. Grand Pierre would program the communication box to blast out false signals. The two-man teams would be in place when Drew signaled *go*.

Anticipation covered the faces of the men in the room. Adoran had been a peaceful land before the robots had arrived, and it had never needed weapons. The scientists had shown the Adorans how to build blasting sticks. The teams assigned to the platform guards would have a total of four blasting sticks and axes to disassemble the robots. The teams assigned to the rogue leaders would carry heavy chains to bind the leaders' arms, and axes to disable them. Battle knew that the meager weapons of the opposition would not be adequate to defeat the robots, and success would depend on disrupting their communications.

Boxer and Bear met Grand Pierre and Drew in front by the table. Grand Pierre had drawn a red X across the settlement on the largest map. He looked at Bear and said, "You know the forest surrounding the settlement, and I need you to identify trees that are high enough to secure the repeaters at these locations."

He pointed to the four ends of the large X and then continued. "You and Boxer need to make sure the repeaters cannot be knocked out of the trees if they are discovered. The robots will have to shoot them to disable them, so hide them well."

Boxer studied the map and said, "We can go out the back of the building with the hidden entrance and reach the forest. Then we can stay hidden in the tree line and avoid the roads. When Bear picks out a tree, we will secure the repeater and continue around the settlement."

Boxer looked at Bear and asked, "Do you see any problems?"

"Here." Bear pointed at one end of the X. "Large trees in this area are scarce. When the robots arrived, they burned down a lot of the trees. There may not be any trees that will get the repeater high enough to bounce the signals."

"What about these buildings?" Drew asked and pointed at the map. "They are empty as far as I know."

"If we can get to the buildings unseen, we can place a repeater on the roof of one, but it may be visible to the guards' scans," Boxer commented as he studied the map.

Grand Pierre spoke up. "If there are no trees high and sturdy enough to hold the repeater, only use one of the buildings. We must keep the repeaters hidden and keep the signals bouncing as long as possible."

"Understood," Bear answered.

Boxer and Bear followed Grand Pierre from the meeting room. The plans were finalized, and they understood the importance of their part. Grand Pierre had assured Drew that if anyone could get the repeaters secured around the settlement in one night, it was Boxer and Bear.

Grand Pierre hurried along the narrow tunnel to his cave. He wanted to check on Dent. He was still worried about the boy and was amazed at his bravery and intelligence. Boxer and Bear were also anxious to see Dent. When the three entered Grand Pierre's cave, they found Dent sitting up in bed.

Boxer hurried over. "You look a lot better."

"Except for a couple of black teeth, I feel fine," Dent replied.

Boxer grinned at Dent and told him, "Those black teeth make you look mean."

"Grrrr," Dent growled, but it lacked the menace of Bear's growl.

Grand Pierre chuckled and said, "If you feel up to walking, I'll show everyone where they will sleep tonight."

Dent climbed out of the bed, stretched, took a couple of small steps, and said, "Everything seems to be working."

Grand Pierre motioned. "This way."

The three boys followed Grand Pierre down a narrow tunnel. He stopped by a small cave, and inside were four mats placed in a row. Wren and Manx would be sharing the cave next to Grand Pierre's with Aunt May. When Wren heard this, she hopped up and down, excited to see Aunt May again.

"Maileen is busy helping program the repeaters and will join us at evening meal," Grand Pierre said, trying to calm Wren.

The following day passed quietly. Everyone was anxious, waiting for the sun to disappear, and then the battle for Adoran would begin. The special ones were sitting under the bluff and were startled when Grand Pierre drove the transport from one of the caves. They gathered around the familiar vehicle, all asking questions at the same time.

Grand Pierre held his hand up. "Wait. One at a time. Yes, the transport is working, and we were able to replenish the fuel source from equipment rescued from our lab. Yes, I am using it tonight to carry the communication box to the orphanage. I decided that would be the safest place because the rogues think it is empty. Yes, I intend to leave after last meal, enter the settlement after dark, and make my way to the orphanage."

"You're going by yourself?" Battle asked. "What if you're caught by one of the guards?"

"Everyone else has a job to do," Grand Pierre explained.

"I'm coming with you," Battle said decidedly. "You will need help to avoid the patrols."

Grand Pierre agreed. "That is an excellent idea. I was concerned about avoiding the patrols."

Wren took hold of Grand Pierre's hand and reminded him, "Be careful, and remember your *Cs*."

The tall man smiled down at her. "Thank you, little Wren. I plan on being very cautious."

CHAPTER 19

$\mathcal{E}$vening meal was over, and Boxer and Bear were ready to leave, each carrying a pack strapped on his back that held two repeaters. The repeaters were larger than Boxer had imagined, and now he understood the need for trees tall enough to hide them.

Drew would lead the way through the network of tunnels. When they reached the hidden entrance in a building at the edge of the settlement, Drew would climb the narrow steps and enter first to make sure no one else was around. The repeaters were critical in defeating the robots.

Grand Pierre asked again, "You know where to place them?"

Boxer told him not to worry, that both he and Bear knew the exact locations. They would get the repeaters set up before daylight.

"Ready?" Drew asked, and Boxer and Bear, with determination in their voices, answered, "Ready," and followed Drew down a narrow tunnel.

Battle carried the heavy communication box to the transport and placed it in the cage in the back. He waited for Grand Pierre to finish talking with Argies and knew they were discussing escape options if the plan failed.

When they finished their conversation, Argies placed both hands on Grand Pierre's shoulders and said with assurance, "It will work."

Grand Pierre answered, "It must work." And then he climbed into the waiting transport.

The transport was smaller than the old truck and easily climbed the narrow trail. When they came to the vine-covered gate that hid the entrance, Battle jumped out and opened it. After the transport was through, he secured the gate and climbed into the front seat. The transport followed the steep, narrow trail up the mountain and quickly reached the top. When they reached the road, Grand Pierre stopped the transport.

The power had been shut off, and it was dark. Grand Pierre looked at Battle, who listened and looked around and then motioned *go*. Grand Pierre drove the transport onto the road that edged the settlement and ran past the orphanage. In the dark night, Battle was on high alert, for the patrol guards ran silent. Only their searching beams gave them away.

Back in the caves, Ray began distributing weapons. The teams would leave the caves one hour before dawn, go to the hidden entrance, silently make their way to their assigned hiding places, and wait for Drew's signal. The teams assigned to the rogue leaders would have a longer hike, but they could make it to the communication center before the sun announced the day of reckoning for the robots.

Drew and Father Brion would drive the old truck to the edge of the settlement and wait to give the *go* signal. Drew carried the com-nit, which would blink green when Grand Pierre was ready to broadcast the disruption signals. In the quiet morning, three long honks from the old truck would echo around the settlement and let the two-man teams know the battle for Adoran had begun.

"This way," Bear whispered to Boxer as they crept around the old building and stopped.

Boxer looked up at the roof. "This is the only building high enough for the repeater to work."

So far, they had evaded the night patrols, and the first two repeaters had been hidden in trees high above the rooftops. Boxer turned the repeaters on and set the dials exactly as Grand Pierre had shown him. The final repeater would be placed in one of the trees in the circle close to the orphanage.

"Give me a lift so I can climb onto the roof, and then hand me a repeater," Boxer said as he placed the pack on the ground.

Bear knelt down so Boxer could stand on his shoulders, and then he stood up, his strength so massive that even Boxer's weight didn't daunt him. Boxer reached out, grabbed the roof, and climbed on top, being careful not to make any noise. He leaned over and grasped the heavy repeater that Bear held above his head.

Boxer crept to the roof's highest point, careful to avoid all the broken boards. He stopped by a tall chimney, set the repeater down, and uncoiled a piece of cord. He wound the cord around the chimney and secured the repeater to it, making sure it was pointing in the correct direction. He switched the repeater on and set the dials. Satisfied, he turned to climb back down but kicked a loose board, which noisily tumbled off the steep roof and banged loudly when it hit the ground.

"Who's out there?" a voice yelled from inside the building. Boxer froze, not daring to take another step.

"It's probably those darn dogs again," said a second voice.

Boxer recognized the voices. They were Lester and Barten.

A door slammed open, and two figures stepped out, each holding a piece of wood as they looked around. Boxer was trapped on the roof and ducked down, knowing that if they saw him it would mean trouble for him.

A low, menacing growl broke the silence, and a huge brown bear lunged at the two figures. "It's the bear Vera told us about!" screamed Barten. He started to run back inside, but the bear blocked the door. "It's the one that kept whispering *Bunny!*" He shrieked and started shaking so hard that the stick dropped from his hand. He stumbled backward to escape the bear. From the roof, Boxer moaned, "Bunnnny," and Barten took off running down the road, screaming for his life.

Lester turned white with fear when the large bear started toward him. "I'm sorry!" he yelled in a quivering voice, and then he turned and raced down the road after the shrieking Barten.

Boxer jumped off the roof and ran behind the large bear to the safety of the trees. From all the noise Lester and Barten were making, any patrols in the area would chase after them. Bear changed and was trying hard not to laugh out loud at the sight of the two boys running and screaming down the road. Bear motioned for Boxer to follow as he led the way to the hidden tree circle.

Battle motioned *stop*. He listened, searched the road ahead, and then motioned *go*. Progress had been slow, and once they had barely avoided the patrol as it turned on the road directly in front of them. The guards had the ability to turn a full circle on their platforms, but they never searched the road behind them. Battle could see the tree circle and knew they were close.

Before Grand Pierre turned onto the road that led to the orphanage, Battle signaled *stop* and jumped from the transport. He stayed hidden in the trees as he crept toward the dark buildings. Battle had to make sure the buildings were empty before Grand Pierre drove the transport around back.

He ran to pod one and looked in the window—then pod two, and pod three, which was used for storage. Battle could see clearly that the rooms were empty. He ran beside the small pod he had shared with the others, listened at the rear door, pushed it open, and found it empty. Next, he checked the main building. He entered through the side door and crept down the back hall. He listened and heard no sound other than his own breathing. He looked into each room and then went outside to search the back of the building. Satisfied that they were alone, he ran back to the transport.

Battle lifted the heavy communication box, carried it inside, and set it on a table in the front room. Grand Pierre knelt down and started turning knobs. Blinking lights appeared on the front. Grand Pierre mumbled to himself, tweaking the various dials. He looked at Battle. "I have made contact with three of the repeaters, and when the last one comes online, I'll signal Drew."

Battle glanced out the window. The darkness had started to fade, and it would be light soon.

"Ah, here it is." Grand Pierre was elated. Boxer and Bear had secured all the repeaters. Grand Pierre lifted the com-nit he carried and spoke into it: "Ready."

Drew answered back, "It's a go."

Battle jumped. He'd heard a noise, like the opening of a door. He started to investigate, when Boxer hurried into the room followed by Bear.

Grand Pierre glanced up. "Good work. I have contact with all four repeaters. As soon as Drew gives the signal, I will start sending the false signals."

Boxer and Bear collapsed on an old couch, glad to rest after their long night's activities. Battle asked, "Did you have any problems."

"Nothing Bear couldn't handle," Boxer replied, causing Bear to grin. Then he told Battle about finding Lester and Barten in one of the buildings.

When the sun was fully visible above the horizon, three loud honks from the old truck's horn broke the morning silence. Grand Pierre bent over the metal box and press a red button, and green lights started blinking crazily. The three boys watched the box, expecting to hear sounds of some kind.

Boxer asked, "How do you know it's working?"

Grand Pierre glanced up. "The green lights are the robots' frequency, and the signal strength is strong. I hope it's enough to disable them."

Battle stood and paced the room. "I wish I knew what was happening." Boxer and Bear agreed. Waiting wasn't easy for them either.

"We should get you to safety in case the robots discover where the signals are coming from," Boxer told Grand Pierre.

Grand Pierre replied, "I can monitor from the com-nit. There is nothing more to do here."

"Let's take him to the tree circle," Battle suggested. "It's the safest place I can think of."

When they reached the circle, the com-nit beeped, and Grand Pierre answered, "I'm here."

Drew's voice sounded odd. "The disruption is working, and four of the patrol guards have been disabled. One man was hurt and taken to safety. The teams assigned to the rogues are having a harder time. The leaders aren't as affected by the disruption."

Grand Pierre replied, "I can increase the strength. Maybe it will help."

"Try it," Drew said and disconnected.

Battle looked at Boxer. "If you stay with Grand Pierre, Bear and I will go and fight the rogue leaders."

Grand Pierre started to say something, when a loud siren came from down the road. From the tree circle, everyone looked out to see a rogue leader standing on the platform of the last functioning guard. The platform turned erratically, heading toward the orphanage. The guard's hands were crazily swinging in circles, and its head leaned to one side. The rogue leader was driving the platform with one hand, its fingers inserted in the guard's eye sockets. With the other hand, it held itself upright on the platform.

Grand Pierre exclaimed, "They've figured out where the disruption is coming from. If that leader disables the communication box, Drew's men won't be able to defeat them."

When Grand Pierre finished talking, he was standing in the hidden tree circle alone.

CHAPTER 20

*B*attle and Bear rushed from the tree circle and changed, knowing they would need force and strength against the robots. Boxer chased after them but did not change. Not expecting a wide, armor-plated mastiff to rush up from behind, slam into the platform, and knock it over, the rogue leader was caught off guard. Bear lunged and grabbed the rogue leader around the waist and tore him from the platform.

The platform lay on its side, its skids continuing to roll, causing the erratically jerking guard to spin in a circle. The loose dirt created a whirlwind. Battle changed, and when the guard circled around, he grabbed the guard's head in his strong arms. The skids continued turning the platform, but Battle stiffened his legs and held tight to the guard's head.

The pressure from the turning skids and Battle's refusal to budge caused the guard's head to jerk loose from its body. Battle took a quick step backward to keep from falling and lifted the head in his hands, loose wires dangling from beneath. In disgust, Battle threw the mangled head to the ground. The final guard had been disabled.

Battle looked over to where Bear was circling the rogue leader, which was disrupted enough that it could not engage the weapons built into its body. The rogue kept stumbling as it faced the enraged bear.

Battle remembered the sweepers he always carried with him, and he took one out of his pocket. He turned it, and the razor-sharp blades popped out. He yelled, "Bear, back away!"

Bear growled, not wanting to let the rogue escape, but he stepped away when Battle pulled his arm back, aimed, and launched the sweeper. The sweeper made a whistling noise as it flew through the air to hit the rogue in the back of the neck. The sharp, spinning blades cut deep. The rogue stumbled and went down on its knees. It turned toward Battle with a look of unbelief that a boy could defeat a rogue. Then the rogue leader fell forward, unmoving on the ground.

Boxer had continued running into the main building and picked up the communication box. Careful to not change any of the settings, he carried the box through the building and out the back. He placed the box in the transport cage, jumped into the driver's seat, and drove from behind the building to the hidden tree circle. He stopped and called to Grand Pierre, "I've got the box. Let's take it to the communication center and see if the signal is stronger there."

Grand Pierre loped from the trees and climbed into the transport. "Good work," he told Boxer as they drove away.

Battle walked over and pulled the sweeper from the back of the rogue's neck. He inspected the wide gash, making sure that all the wires were completely severed and the rogue could not be repaired.

Bear changed and stood beside Battle, looking down at the motionless leader. "I'm impressed," he said. "That's a pretty amazing weapon."

Battle put the sweeper into his pocket. "It did the job."

Watching the transport disappear down the road, Bear asked, "If we turn the platform over, do you think you can drive it?"

They watched the skids spinning the platform in the dirt with the headless guard.

"It's worth a try," Battle answered.

Once the platform was righted, it started rolling away, and Battle jumped on the back. He looked at the various wires sticking up out of the guard's neck to see how they connected, selected two bright-orange ones, and touched them together. The skids stopped turning. He knew how to stop the platform. Now to make it go forward.

After a couple of wrong choices, he connected the blue wires, and the platform's skids rolled forward. "Jump on!" Battle shouted as he held the blue wires together. "This beats running after the transport," he told Bear as the two rolled down the road.

↓↳ ↓↳

Boxer stopped the transport beside the building across from the communication center. Grand Pierre hurried to the back of the transport and inspected the metal box. "The signals are still strong. Can you see the men or any of the rogues?" Grand Pierre asked.

Boxer stepped from the transport, looked around, and pointed. "There are men hiding in those trees and behind that ridge."

"Do you think you can get to them and find out the status of the rogues? They must be inside, trying to get the communications fixed." Boxer started to cross the road, when he saw the old truck bouncing across a field. Drew pulled up beside the transport and jumped out of the truck, followed by Father Brion.

Drew hurried over. "The spotters say that the rogues are in the building. They're having trouble moving and haven't used any of their built-in weapons. We lost track of the last guard and one of the rogue leaders. They escaped before we could contain them."

Boxer heard the sound of something approaching and warned, "Hide."

Everyone scrambled out of sight behind the building. They were speechless when they saw Battle and Bear riding on the back of a platform with a headless guard. Turning wasn't an easy task using just the wires, but Battle finally stopped the platform beside the old truck. He and Bear jumped down. "Thanks for waiting for us," he told Boxer with a big grin.

"Apparently you didn't need a ride." Boxer grinned back.

Grand Pierre told Drew, "I have a feeling that you no longer need to worry about the last guard or the rogue that escaped."

Seeing Drew arrive in the truck, one of the men hiding in the trees ran up and asked, "What's the plan? Do we go in after them?"

Drew thought for a moment. "Are you sure all the rogues are inside and unable to engage their weapons?"

"Positive," the man replied.

"Fire should drive them out," Drew responded. "Then, with the stronger signal, we can disable them. Have the men start throwing wood against the building and light it."

The man raced back toward the trees, shouting orders, and men on both sides of the building began tossing pieces of wood. Crashing noises filled the air as dried tree branches, wood planks, split logs, and broken furniture began piling against the sides of the building. Then the men tossed burning pieces of wood into the piles. Fire quickly engulfed the wooden building.

"What's taking them so long to come out?" Father Brion asked.

Just then, one of the leaders appeared at a window and fell outside. The rogue's movements were erratic, and when it tried to stand up, it fell again. Two men rushed forward, one carrying an axe, and the other a length of chain to bind the rogue's arms. When the rogue's arms were secure, the man ran forward, swinging the axe and burying it deep in the rogue's neck, cutting all the wires. The rogue didn't move as the two men dragged it away.

"One down," Drew said as more rogues stumbled from the burning building, barely able to stand. Once they were away from the fire, the men quickly disabled them.

When the last rogue leader was chained and its wires cut, Drew shouted, "It's over."

Everyone gathered around and watched the building burn to ashes. Then they started chanting: "Freedom! Freedom!"

The brave men gathered around, and Drew congratulated them for their courage in fighting the robots. When they heard that the robots had been defeated, others living in the settlement joined the celebration.

Drew announced to the rejoicing crowd they still had a lot of work ahead to rebuild the settlement. Tomorrow there would be a meeting at the work center. When Drew declared that tonight the power in the settlement would not be turned off, cheers rose from the crowd.

Drew thanked Grand Pierre and the scientists for their help, adding that without their knowledge they would never have been able to defeat the robots.

That evening the scientists and the special ones were seated in the front room of the orphanage. Drew, Ray, and Father Brion were there, and Drew thanked everyone again for their hard work and for risking their lives to defeat the robots.

It had been decided that the scientists and children would stay at the orphanage until they could move back to their facility in the mountains. Drew said a decision had been made to make sure everyone had a place to live, and there were no plans to reopen the orphanage. Father Brion told Wren that Karry was going to live with Marta and that Wren could visit her anytime, which caused Wren to hop excitedly around the room.

After Drew, Ray, and Father Brion left, Grand Pierre and the scientists started discussing Ulterion, wondering about the status of the war on their planet. This caused Boxer to remember the rogue leader at the headquarters building. He walked over to Grand Pierre and told him about the rogue's head still being alert, even without being attached to its body.

Grand Pierre replied, "Tomorrow we must go and make sure it is disabled." Reassured, Boxer joined the other special ones in the kitchen.

The special one sat at the large table, and Dent looked around and grinned. "Now we are six: Boxer, Battle, Manx, Wren, Bear, and Dent. We should give our team a name."

"The Special Six," Wren chirped, and Bear growled at her suggestion.

Grand Pierre had walked into the room and heard the topic being discussed. "What about the Secret Six?" he suggested.

"I'll vote for that," Battle answered.

"Me too," Boxer agreed, and it was decided. They would be the Secret Six.

Grand Pierre laughed and told them, "You will be a force to contend with."

The following day, Grand Pierre and Boxer drove the transport to the robots' headquarters, pushed open the wide doors, and walked in.

Grand Pierre said, "I'll contact Drew and make sure they completely destroy these guards."

They had left the doors open and could see the rogue's head sitting on the table with its eyes shut. Its body had not moved and was standing in the same place Boxer had seen it before.

Boxer said, "It knew I was here. It opened its eyes and stared at me."

Grand Pierre studied the head, picked it up, and turned it over. He told Boxer to hand him a tool, pointing to a clamping device. When Grand Pierre inserted the device into the rogue's neck, the eyes opened. He clamped the device and pulled hard to expose a group of wires. He took a knife from the table and cut the wires, and the rogue's eyes closed.

When the last rogue was disabled and could not communicate, a red light beneath the control panel of the robots' warship began flashing.

PART II

The Secret Six

CHAPTER 21

"*L*et's keep the drawings of the flowers together and put the animal drawings on the other wall," Wren suggested. She stood in the middle of the room, looking around, and then turned a full circle with eyes squinted, searching for just the right place.

"Good idea, Wren. We can decorate each wall different." Manx turned to the blonde-haired girl who was sitting on the edge of a bed, swinging her legs back and forth, and asked, "Bunny, do you like that idea?" Manx's technical skills were highly developed and her drawings very detailed. The flowers and animals she drew were complete to the petal or whisker.

Bunny smiled and nodded and motioned with her hands that the flower drawings should go on the wall opposite from her bed. She motioned that she would be able to see flowers when she woke each day. When the scientists and children had temporarily moved back to the orphanage, Francine had taught them how to interpret hand signs so Bunny could communicate with them.

The three girls now shared a large dorm room in the mountain facility. They had comfortable beds, very different from the hard cots they had slept on in the orphanage. The refurbished room was their new home, and they were anxious to decorate it with special touches that would make it their own.

A year had passed before the special ones and the scientists had been able to move permanently from the orphanage to the facility in the mountain. It had taken months of hard labor by the scientists and children to clean out the ransacked building and make it livable. The overall structure had not been destroyed, and the kitchen, dining room, and living quarters were intact. The girls shared one large room, and the boys had a similar one. Each of the scientists had been assigned a smaller private room.

The scientists were disappointed that the laboratories and all the equipment had been destroyed. The rogues had invaded the facility in an attempt to discover the purpose for the secret laboratory hidden on Adoran. All documents regarding the experiments had been destroyed by fire, and the scientists who had managed to escape in the research vessel had not been able to save any of the stored research results, which had stopped further testing.

The special ones were secretly pleased that no more children would be sacrificed, even though the scientists believed that the loss was worth the possibility of saving of their planet. After the research vessel had left Adoran space, the survivors had received no messages from those who had escaped, leaving the scientists on Adoran to wonder about the fate of their coworkers and friends.

The girls had just finished pinning the last animal drawing to the wall when they heard a knock at their door. A familiar voice asked if it was safe to enter their abode. All three girls grinned at Dent's nonstop teasing, and Manx hurried to open the door. Standing on the other side of the door were Dent,

Boxer, Battle, and Bear, and they trooped into the room and looked around.

"You've been busy," Dent said. "Your dorm looks great. Ours isn't exactly livable. We can't convince Bear to sleep in his bed."

Bear glared at him and replied in a low growl, "What if I put your bed outside?"

Wren exclaimed, "It's too cold. He would freeze."

Boxer noticed Manx's drawings and walked over to the wall with the animal sketches. He counted seven and said, "Good resemblance, Manx. You've captured each of us in a special way—even Dent's black teeth."

Boxer's remarks caused Dent to hurry over and stand before a drawing of a gray rat hiding in the trees—with two black front teeth. Dent studied the picture, turned to Manx, and grinned, exposing his blackened teeth. Bear sat down on the bed beside Bunny, causing the bed to sag in the middle.

Battle said, "We came to see if you need our help with anything. But your room looks great—not like the mess ours is still in."

Wren hopped over and said, "Aunt May found us the colorful quilts and rugs, and Grand Pierre brought the furniture." Each girl had a bed, a desk, and a small chest for their clothes, and with the drawings on the walls, the room was bright and cheerful.

Battle stared at the animal drawings and commented, "I'm not sure if the bunny drawing is accurate. I don't think Bunny inherited any animal skills, and I can't think of any purpose to combine a rabbit with a clone."

Manx walked over and explained, "I wanted to include Bunny with the rest of us so she wouldn't feel left out."

Wren chirped, "It was my idea."

Battle looked down at the smallest of the special ones and told her, "Now I understand. You would not want anyone to feel left out. Bunny is one of us, even if she doesn't have the animal inheritance."

Wren asked, "What good would a bunny be on a mission?"

Bear reached over and picked up Bunny, held her high in the air, and growled, "We could eat her." Then the wild-haired boy pretended to eat the slim, blue-eyed girl, causing her to twist away, silently laughing.

"Hey, Bear is very *caring* of Bunny," Dent exclaimed.

Pillows from the beds hit him as everyone yelled, "No more *C*s!"

The door to the girls' dorm room opened, and a tall man looked in and exclaimed, "What is going on in here? All the noise you're making woke everyone." The pillow throwing at Dent ceased as everyone hurried to greet Grand Pierre.

Wren took hold of his hand, pulled him into the room, and proudly said, "Look how nice we've made our room look."

"Manx, your drawings continue to improve, and the flowers are very precise." Grand Pierre stopped in front of the animals and studied each picture. "You have captured the essence of each trait—even Bunny's quiet demeanor."

Manx pulled out a chair from one of the desks for Grand Pierre to sit in and said, "Please tell us about Ulterion. You said you would, once we moved back here." The others also pleaded with him, anxious to know more about the planet, the war with the rogues, and the reason for their specific animal traits.

Grand Pierre took the seat Manx offered, rubbed his chin in thought, and began. "Many years ago, the people on Ulterion became upset with each other. There was one group of scientists who wanted to develop a super-race that would live forever through regeneration of their cells. Other scientists wanted to improve the Ulterion way of life through space exploration and automation. Finally, two separate factions emerged—the rogues and the Ulterions—and they could not settle their differences in a reasonable way. The rogues wanted to devote resources to the development of a super-race, and the Ulterions wanted to create a better way of life. The rogues began raiding the storage centers and stealing the resources they required—materials, equipment, whatever they needed. That was how the separation began and the war started.

"The rogues controlled one section of the planet and stayed there for many years, developing a superior being. The Ulterion scientists continued on their path of exploration and automation. With all the automation came the need to limit population growth, and that created the cloning facilities where only replacements were allowed to be born. By this time the Ulterions had moved underground. They had created an idyllic city with a controlled environment—air, temperature, and lighting—with laboratories and facilities for enjoyment and living. For years they had everything they needed, and they lived without thought of depleting the planet's resources. Then the resources began to run out.

"During this time the rogues continued to develop a super-race, and their failures became what you know as the robots. To keep the experiments alive, the rogue scientists turned them into machines that could be programmed to perform tasks. When the rogues had created the soldiers, platforms, and leaders, they began to attack. The cities above ground were support facilities and were the main targets, and when the Ulterions came to repair the damage, they were killed. This caused a major problem for the Ulterions because all the energy-generating plants were recharged by the sun. In response, the Ulterions increased their military presence. This story of people turning against each another and destroying their planet is not a pleasant one."

Grand Pierre paused and shook his head. "Since the robots have destroyed our labs and communication equipment, what has happened for the past twenty years would be a guess. Now, on to more pleasant items. Argies and Jacques have repaired the second transport, and we can drive both transports to the settlement tomorrow. I'm sure Drew will have plenty of work lined up for us. Marta asked if Wren could come and spend the day with Karry." Grand Pierre stood and told the group that they would leave for the settlement in the morning after the meal.

After telling the children about Ulterion history, Grand Pierre returned to his room. Many thoughts raced through his mind as he recalled the past twenty years on Adoran. With the exception of Dent, who was in his eleventh year, the other boys were considered grown and ready to assume the types of roles they had been cloned for: technical, leadership, military, scientific, and mechanical. The animal traits they'd inherited caused them to look very different from each other. Manx and Bunny were in their eleventh year, and Wren was in her ninth. Soon all the special ones would be grown. They were happy and had adjusted to their new life at the facility.

They got along—except for the times when Dent made Bear growl—and were very protective of each other. Dent had proved that when he'd risked his life for Manx. It was very rare when a clone inherited all of the desired skills, and Grand Pierre knew that Dent had. Dent excelled in learning, and once he read or was told something, he retained it.

In the past year, Bunny had gone through a growth spurt and was now as tall as Manx. Francine had explained that Bunny was the same age as Manx but was not sturdily built like Manx. Bunny had inherited the tall, slim build of the scientists. Bunny must have been cloned for the higher level of scientists, which was why she didn't talk, for highly developed scientists communicated by thought or telepathy.

Grand Pierre did worry about little Wren. Her instinct to care for everything and everyone could, and did, get her into trouble. She did not have the aggressive animal nature or the natural physical strength of the others. Grand Pierre had taught Wren ways to defend herself. To fly away and hide was her best protection. The concept of family had disappeared from Ulterion many years ago. Each of the children was special, and he cared for them all like the father they did not have, but he worried more about Wren.

CHAPTER 22

The following morning the four scientists were seated in one of the transports. Grand Pierre drove, and Argies sat up front. Berne and Jacques sat behind on the bench seat, and neither talked much unless it was about their work at the laboratory or what had happened on Ulterion since they had left. They seldom interacted with the special ones but would watch them during the times they were all together.

Manx had mentioned to Dent that it felt creepy having them watch her. Dent had replied that they were just curious to see how the special ones had matured. In their own way, the scientists were proud of the results of their work. Dent's remarks caused Manx to scowl at him. Proud or not, she did not like them watching her.

The special ones climbed into the second transport. Boxer drove, and Bear sat in front next to him. Battle, Dent, Manx, and Wren sat on the bench seat. Bunny stayed at the facilities with Francine and Aunt May. The children still affectionately referred to Grand Pierre and Aunt May as such, not using their Ulterion names.

A narrow road had been carved to wind down the mountainside into the settlement. It was wide enough for the transports to travel single file. This was the special ones' first trip to the settlement since moving to the facility. During the past year, their time had been spent repairing the damaged building. Grand Pierre had stayed in contact with Drew, and after the road had been completed, he had made several trips to the work center.

Grand Pierre had told everyone that the first thing the Adorans had done was to give the settlement a new name: Freedom. Everyone had agreed on this name to remember all the brave men and women who had died in the invasion, and as a reminder that they must be prepared. If the Ulterions and rogues had found their planet, others could too. It had been a huge shock for the Adorans to learn that other societies inhabited their universe and had to ability to travel through space. The Adorans had not learned to fly, or even realized the need of it.

The orphanage was now being used for storage, each of the pods holding items to rebuild businesses and homes. Everyone who was able to work was assigned to a team. Grand Pierre said Drew and Brion were doing an outstanding job of scheduling work. Ray was assigned to a cleanup team and drove the old truck around the settlement, removing piles of trash. The opposition fighters living in the caves had moved back into their abandoned homes, rebuilding while they lived there.

The work center located in the middle of the settlement was being used as the center of operations, providing food and daily assignments for the teams. Sola now ran the center, and Marta was the main cook. Until the meager herds of cows and goats repopulated and crops were planted and harvested, food was still scarce. A few chickens had been caught and were caged in pens for a daily supply of eggs.

Perkin, who had previously run the work center and had helped Brion establish his cover as orphanage director, was in charge of the power grid. Getting it repaired and stable was his assignment. Once the power grid was reliable, businesses that had been idle for years would be operational.

All the changes shocked the special ones when they stopped the transport. Many of the homes had been repaired, and the yards were clear of rubbish. People were walking around, laughing and talking. Potholes in the roads had been filled.

"What a change!" Boxer exclaimed as he jumped to the ground. "I never knew there were so many people living here. Everyone stayed hidden when the robots were in control."

Grand Pierre stepped from the transport, and Drew hurried from the work center to greet him. As the two men shook hands, Drew exclaimed, "You arrived at the right time. Perkin ran into some problems at the power plant, which I'm sure you can help with."

"Ah, what difficulties has Perkin encountered?" Grand Pierre asked.

"Something is arcing—or not arcing. I'm not exactly sure, but I know you will understand what he is saying and help him resolve it." Drew shook hands with the other scientists, greeted the children, and then led everyone to a door on one side of work center.

The room they entered had maps pinned to the walls with various colored lines. Boxer walked around and studied the maps. One was of the roads, and the red Xs were where the repair teams would be working. Another map showed the power grid that crisscrossed the settlement. The main plant was at the far end of the settlement near the building with the secret entrance to the caves. A third map had the various businesses color coded to make sure the critical ones would be powered up first.

Boxer turned to Drew and said, "Very impressive how you have everything lined out."

Drew replied, "Good. I have requested your help. Brion said you were outstanding in planning and implementing the missions."

Dent grinned at Manx, both of them having the same thought: Boxer was good because of his Ulterion cloning.

Manx felt a tug on her arm and looked down. "Will you help me find Marta?" Wren asked, anxious to see Karry.

Manx told Grand Pierre she would return after taking Wren to Marta. It was an easy task. Manx just followed the smell of food cooking to the large kitchen where Marta was giving orders to the other cooks regarding the evening meal.

Manx had to hide a smile when she saw Jonne and Dortha standing over a sink with their arms in a pile of suds, washing dishes. She wondered where Vera was but did not want to ask the two girls. As far as she was concerned, she never wanted to talk to them again.

Marta turned, noticed Manx and Wren in the doorway, and hurried over, wiping her hands on the apron around her waist. Marta gave both girls a hug and exclaimed, "I'm so happy to see you. You've both grown! Karry is waiting in the next room."

Marta led the girls to a room next to the kitchen where Karry was busy coloring with various pieces of chalk. Karry jumped up and ran to Wren, both girls squealing with joy.

Manx laughed at their delight and asked Marta, "Will they be okay by themselves?"

Marta understood Manx's concern, especially with Jonne and Dortha so close by. Marta's voice was firm. "Don't worry. I keep a close eye on Karry, especially after what happened before."

Manx knew that Marta would not let anything happen to the girls on her watch, and she left them to their play.

Manx walked into the scheduling room and heard Drew tell Grand Pierre, "The boxes are stacked on the ground floor along with some of the robotic parts. You should collect them today because things have started to disappear. It's not enough to cause concern, but we wonder who is doing it, and why."

When Grand Pierre asked what was missing, Drew answered that it was mostly food items and stored things, like blankets and other personal stuff.

Grand Pierre turned to Battle and said, "Take the transport and load the boxes and anything else that may be useful. Dent and Manx can help you. Bear and I are going with Perkin to determine the problem at the power plant."

Battle motioned for Dent and Manx to follow him, and when they climbed into the transport, Manx asked, "Where are we going?"

Battle replied as he drove away, "The old rogue headquarters. Drew stacked boxes of parts there. He wasn't sure if they were useful, and he didn't want to destroy them until Grand Pierre went through them. Drew said it looked like the building had been searched, and he wasn't sure if some of the parts had been taken or just moved."

Manx shivered. The rogues' headquarters brought back memories of the robots she would rather forget.

Battle stopped the transport in front of the building the rogues had used as their headquarters. The fence had been torn down, and the doors to the dog cages hung open. The building looked deserted.

"I wonder if they will tear it down," Manx said, hesitant to get out of the transport.

"Probably not," Dent said. "It's one of the better buildings in the settlement and hasn't been ruined like so many of the others."

"I wouldn't want to live here." Manx shuddered.

"The robots are gone," Battle assured her as he stepped from the transport. "Let's load the boxes and then go back to the work center. Maybe we can help one of the teams." He walked toward the empty building.

The transport's cage was quickly loaded with boxes of papers and two wooden crates of parts from the cabinets. Manx recognized the parts from the images she had captured. Dent was curious and looked around the large ground-floor room used as a repair depot. He asked Manx if she wanted to go upstairs, and she firmly replied that she would wait outside in the transport. Dent climbed the stairs to the second floor, curious to see the room where Manx had retrieved critical information for the opposition.

When Battle, Manx, and Dent returned, Boxer was studying the road repair map. He turned to them. "Barten and Lester were assigned to the road repair team, but no one has seen them for days, and I need to reassign their work. The crew leader said that one day they didn't show up, and no one knows what happened to them. They haven't been back for meals either. I asked why they'd been allowed in the settlement after abducting Karry, and the crew leader said they had convinced everyone that they were sorry. They had been allowed to stay if they didn't cause trouble."

"Maybe they fell into one of the large holes and were covered up," Manx suggested.

Boxer grinned and replied, "Highly unlikely, but a good solution."

Battle asked, "Is there anything I can do?"

Boxer suggested, "I know Ray was asking for extra help loading and unloading the scrap. He has to take it away from the settlement to burn it."

Battle eagerly agreed. "Assign me to Ray's team. I can load or unload whatever he needs."

"I'll leave a note for him to meet you here in the morning." Boxer could tell that Battle was anxious to meet Ray. The two had established a friendship at the orphanage.

"What about me?" Dent asked.

"You can help me," Boxer responded. "I need to get the crews better organized, and Drew wants me to track each day's completions."

CHAPTER 23

"Where is Bear?" Manx asked, looking around the room. "It's not like him to miss breakfast, and this isn't the first time either."

"Maybe he misses being alone," Wren suggested. "He was alone for a long time."

"Well, I'm going back to our room and do nothing," Manx exclaimed. "I have washed more dishes and swept more floors at the work center than I thought was possible." She walked from the dining room.

When Jonne and Dortha had left the work center one night and hadn't returned, Marta had asked Manx if she would help in the kitchen. Marta had told Manx that Vera had done the same thing weeks before. Marta said that this was strange because no one had seen the girls since they'd disappeared. And then she'd added, "Good riddance." Manx was sure the three girls were with Lester and Barten.

At the repaired facility, Aunt May did all the cooking, and Francine and Bunny handled the cleanup. They would not let anyone else help, saying it was their contribution to allow the scientists and children to enjoy their one day off each week.

"I'll wait for Bunny and then go outside," Wren told Manx, and she waited by the door.

Wren and Bunny enjoyed exploring the forest around the facility, with Wren constantly looking for a real bunny. She accompanied the others to the settlement one day a week to spend time with Karry. On the other days she stayed at the facility with Aunt May, Francine, and Bunny, helping out with chores that needed to be done.

Manx went back to the girls' dorm, straightened the beds, and placed the pillows on them. She sat down at her desk and took her drawing pad out, but she couldn't get started. She stared at the blank paper and finally decided to go and find Wren and Bunny. Maybe she would see something interesting outside to draw.

As she was leaving, Dent hurried to catch up with her. "Hey, wait for me!" he called as Manx opened the door. "Where are you going?"

Manx told him she was going to find something to draw. Together they walked in silence, which was a rarity for Dent, down one of the paths that ran into the mountain.

Suddenly Manx held her hand up and closed her fist, signaling *stop* and *quiet*. Manx listened and then crept behind a large tree, motioning for Dent to follow. She heard a low growling sound again as she crept forward. She halted when she saw Bunny standing beside a burly brown bear with her hand resting on its shoulder. The bear nodded his head and growled.

Dent took hold of Manx's arm and pulled her back down the path they had just come up. When they were far enough away, Manx exclaimed, "Why did you do that?"

Dent explained, "Don't you understand? Bunny and Bear are communicating. Apparently, when he is in animal form she can talk to him with her mind. His animal senses must allow him to understand what she is saying."

Manx was too stunned to reply.

"Let's go back inside and leave them alone," Dent said.

Once inside, Manx worriedly exclaimed, "Where's Wren? She said she was going to wait for Bunny and then go outside."

Manx and Dent hurried down the long hallway and saw Wren leave the kitchen. They rushed to meet her. "I thought you were going outside with Bunny," Manx gasped.

"We did, and then Bear came with a sack full of vegetables and berries. Aunt May said she wished she had some to cook, like when we lived at the farm, and Bear must have heard her. He gave them to me to take to her." Wren always explained things in her own special way, making everything sound so simple—though Manx's heart was still racing with worry for her.

"Aunt May is going to make a dessert for dinner. I'm going to let Bear know. He is outside with Bunny." Wren skipped away.

Manx told Dent she was going back to her room. She was frustrated because it seemed like a waste of time worrying about Wren, but they all did.

Wren returned to the girls room and exclaimed, "That's your best drawing ever!" causing Manx to jump from her chair.

Manx had been so engrossed in getting every detail correct that she hadn't heard Wren come into the room. She sat back down and studied the drawing of a slim, blonde-haired girl standing next to a big brown bear, her hand resting on the bear's shoulder, with the forest surrounding them.

Manx looked at the drawing. It really was the best one she had done.

Manx was curious, and she asked Wren, "Have you seen Bunny with Bear like this before?"

"Sure. That's how she talks to him." Wren shrugged her shoulders, not surprised the way Manx had been.

"Let's hang the drawing over Bunny's bed and surprise her," Wren suggested.

The evening meal reminded the special ones of the meals they'd shared with Grand Pierre and Aunt May on the farm, and between the scientists and children, there were no leftovers.

A few weeks later on the drive back to the facility, Boxer told the others that Drew had said that phase one of the rebuild was complete. The power grid was stable, thanks to Grand Pierre and Perkin, and Perkin was learning how to read the gauges to avoid any future problems. The men responsible for designing and building the plant powered by the underground stream had been killed by the robots when they'd refused to turn the power off at night. The rogue leaders had known enough to power it off at night and back on in the day, but that was all they'd ever done to maintain the plant.

All the large holes had been filled, and the roads were again drivable. The scrap and trash had been cleared, making the settlement look maintained. Fields had been planted, and the first crops should be in before the weather turned cold. Phase two would be the rebuilding of the businesses, now that the roads were fixed and the power grid was stable.

Battle mentioned, "Ray said Drew is becoming concerned because tools and weapons have disappeared, and boxes of food have gone missing from the work center." He waited, but no one responded. He continued, "Ray thinks Lester is behind it and is hiding somewhere with his followers. Ray and I stopped and searched a few of the empty buildings, but we found no sign of him or the girls. And there are others who have left. Ray said the ones leaving don't have families or care about rebuilding Freedom. Since no one has seen them during the day, I think they are using the cover of night for their raids. I was thinking about setting a trap for Lester. Anyone interested?" Battle grinned as he looked around.

They all eagerly nodded, accepting Battle's offer. "Tonight after meal, let's meet in the boys' dorm and create a plan," he said.

After the evening meal, Manx waited a short while in the girls' dorm. Then she stood up and told Wren and Bunny that she was going to the boys' dorm and would be back. When Wren asked why, Manx was evasive, and that was enough to engage Wren's curious nature.

"You're planning something," Wren said. She hopped off her bed and followed Manx out the door after telling Bunny that she would be back.

Manx quietly knocked on the door to the boys' room and then opened it. When she walked in, followed by Wren, Boxer frowned. Manx shrugged. "I told you it would be hard for me to get away."

Wren marched over to Boxer and with her hands on her hips told him, "You are planning something and trying to leave me out. No way!"

Battle spoke up. "It could be dangerous. We don't know what may happen."

Wren turned to Battle and huffed. "You should let me decide. I can take care of myself." This caused the others in the room to groan, which made Wren more determined than ever that she would not be left out.

Battle said, "Here's the situation. Lester—or whoever is behind the stealing—must be watching or have spies in the settlement. Ray said that things go missing each time something new is stored. The thieves think they're tricky because they only take a few items. They probably think no one has noticed since Drew hasn't said anything about it, hoping to catch them.

"There are empty crates in storage. I was thinking that we should mark them with signs that say 'Food for Work Center' and then make it look like the truck has broken down. Then Ray and I will walk back to the work center, make a big deal out of it, and say we can't get the truck running until the next day. If Lester has spies in the work center, or if someone is watching, it would be hard to miss the truck itself—or Ray and me carrying on about the old truck constantly breaking down." Battle paused and looked at the others in the room.

Boxer suggested, "If we do this tomorrow, which is the day before our rest day, we could go back after dark and keep watch on the truck. We won't be able to drive the transport, and we'll have to travel at night in animal form for speed. Dent won't be able to keep up, and Wren shouldn't fly at night."

Dent quickly said, "I can ride on Bear's shoulder. And you may need me if we find them and someone needs to get close."

Boxer nodded his agreement.

Wren looked at Boxer. "I'll ride with you," she said. "Besides, I can fly at night, and if someone needed to get back here fast, that would be me. We should tell Grand Pierre what we are planning, in case something goes wrong and we need his help."

Boxer sighed. "Wren is correct. We can't plan something like this and not tell him."

"We have a plan," Battle said. "Tomorrow Ray and I will go to the orphanage, mark the empty crates, load them in the truck, and then fake a breakdown. We can walk back to the command center and let everyone know that the truck broke down again. After dark we'll come back and hide in the tree circle and wait. Does everyone agree?"

Everyone agreed to the plan, and Dent announced, "The Secret Six have been activated."

The Trap

CHAPTER 24

The following morning as the special ones walked to the transports, Boxer told Grand Pierre that he needed to talk to him when they reached the work center. From Boxer's solemn manner, Grand Pierre knew that something was about to happen.

Dusk was turning into dark when the Secret Six quietly sneaked out the facility door that led outside. They ran, single file, around the building and into the forest with Boxer in the lead and Bear last.

When they were safely hidden in the forest, Boxer signaled them to stop. "Bear knows the forest and will lead the way. Let's change and follow Bear."

With Dent riding on Bear's shoulder, and Wren perched on Boxer's, the six made good time to the tree circle.

When they changed back, Bear growled at Dent, "You need to file your nails. I think you drew blood."

Dent replied, "Your hide is so tough it would break my teeth if I tried to bite you."

"Keep the noise down," Battle warned. He asked Boxer, "Can you hear anything?"

Boxer listened and shook his head no.

"Everyone, get some rest while we wait," Battle ordered, anxious to see if his plan would draw Lester out of hiding.

Battle stood watch, not taking his eyes off the old truck. The night was half over, and everyone was becoming restless trying to stay quiet. Manx looked at Dent and could tell that he was having a hard time going so long without talking. It seemed that Battle was the only one who had inherited the skill of silence.

Boxer stood up and motioned that he'd heard something. He crept beside Battle and looked toward the truck. Three shadows sneaked from behind pod one, hurried to the truck, and climbed in the back. Lester was easy to recognize, and the other two must be Barten and one of the guys who had left the work crews.

The others crowed behind Battle and Boxer, watching the scene at the truck. One of the crates was shoved against the side of the truck, and they heard one of the intruders grumble, "All three crates are empty. Someone else must have taken the food." Then they lifted the crates and threw them over the side to smash apart as they hit the ground.

Three shadows climbed from the back of the truck, not worrying about making noise. "We need that food. Find out from Karl who took it." They recognized Lester's voice. "You and Barten see if you can break into the work center and get us something to eat," he ordered. "I'm going to check around. Maybe they moved the food into one of the pods. Meet back at the trail before daylight."

Then Barten and the other shadow ran down the road toward the work center, and Lester ambled toward pod one. He pulled on the door and found it locked, and then he went to the window and tried to push it open.

"Why don't we grab him and take him to Drew," Manx whispered.

Battle answered, "Because we need to prove that he has the stolen the food and find where they are hiding it. I know Karl, and he is as sneaky as Lester. The leader of the road team said he sneaked off and slept more than he worked."

"What are we going to do now?" Wren questioned, tired from waiting around.

Battle responded, "There's nothing more we can do here besides watch Lester sneak around the orphanage. Ray and I made sure everything was locked tight."

"One of us should follow Lester to his hideout," Dent suggested.

Boxer said, "Bear you know the forest and how to get around without being seen. You follow Lester, but stay as far back as possible."

"I'll go with Bear, in case we need to get in close," Dent said.

Manx started to protest, but the look on Dent's face told everyone that he was concerned about Bear following Lester alone. And Manx was clearly hesitant about leaving Dent and Bear to their own devices.

"Be careful," Manx warned, and Dent grinned, adding that they would remember their Cs.

Boxer, Battle, Manx, and Wren changed into their animal forms and ran into the dark forest. Dent and Bear watched Lester.

When Lester walked away from the main building, kicking the ground, Dent knew he had not been able to break into any of the orphanage buildings. Battle and Ray had done a good job securing them.

Dent and Bear changed, and Dent scurried up on Bear's shoulder. Bear silently stalked Lester from the tree line, and Dent could feel the tenseness in him. He knew his large friend would like nothing better than to tear Lester to pieces because of what he had done to Bunny.

Bear growled so low that Dent almost missed it. Bear had stalked Lester around the settlement to the narrow trail that led to the caves. Lester had found the caves and was using the building at the edge of the settlement to sneak in and out of Freedom. Bear and Dent would tell Boxer that Drew needed to secure the hidden entrance to the caves. Lester had used the mountain trail tonight, thinking that they would be carrying back boxes of food.

Bear climbed down the steep mountainside and stopped at the edge of the tree line. He didn't dare go into the open area in front of the caves. Dent scurried to the ground and watched as Lester, Barten, and the third guy were met at the entrance to the caves by a small group. Dent recognized the girls: Vera, Jonne, and Dortha. The other three guys he didn't know, but with their grimy appearance and stringy hair, they could be Lester's twins.

Dent needed to talk to Bear, so he changed, and Bear did the same. "I need to sneak inside and find the stolen items," Dent said. "Then we will have proof. No one is going to pay any attention to a rat, and I'm sure there are other rats in the caves beside those two-legged ones."

"I'll wait here for you, but don't take long," Bear whispered. "It's getting light, and we need to leave or we'll be seen."

Dent changed and scurried from the trees, zigzagging his way to the caves, staying hidden in the tall grass. Lester and the others had gone inside, and Dent stayed against the cave wall as he scurried forward. Dent found six guys and three girls in the largest cave, sitting on the log benches. All were complaining about not having anything to eat.

Dent turned to scurry out of the large cave and find the items the group had stolen, but when he turned around, he was looking at the face of a very large cat glaring at him with hunger-filled eyes. The cat's lips drew back, exposing a mouth full of sharp, pointed teeth. The cat loudly meowed and hissed at Dent.

"Here, Kitty." Vera stood up to call the cat, and then screamed and pointed when she saw the gray rat.

Dent knew the cat would expect him to run away, so instead he ran directly at the cat. When he was nose to nose with the cat, he leaped as high as he could, clearing the cat and landing on its bushy tail. Dent couldn't resist: he sunk his sharp nails deep into the cat's tail before he raced out of the cave.

The cat shrieked in pain, and Vera rushed over and grabbed up the injured cat. "Kitty's bleeding!" Vera wailed as loud as Kitty.

"Kill that rat," Lester yelled. "It's probably been eating our food, as big as it is."

Six guys jumped up and chased after Dent, grabbing anything they could find to "kill that rat."

Before Dent could make it outside, two of the guys jumped in front of him, swinging pieces of wood and trying to smash him. Dent swerved from side to side to keep from being flattened like a pancake. Lester and the other three scraggly dudes ran up, trying to stomp on him with their dirt-covered shoes.

"Grab its tail!" someone yelled as Dent ran one way and then the other to avoid capture. Dent saw his chance to escape and raced between a pair of legs toward the open area in front of the caves. A piece of wood thrown from behind landed directly in front of him, causing Dent to skid to a stop. Then he was surrounded by Lester and his gang.

Holding tight to hurt Kitty, Vera edged to one side, not wanting to miss Lester and his goons kill the rat. She glanced up and saw Bear run from the trees. In two strides he changed into a huge brown bear, snarling as he charged directly at Lester.

Vera screamed, dropped Kitty, and pointed toward the stampeding brown monster.

Barten looked up and squealed, "That bear followed us here. Run for your lives."

Barten raced inside the caves, and everyone chased after him to escape the snarling beast.

Bear skidded to a stop and gave a final roar that echoed throughout the caves, and Dent scurried up his shoulder. Then Bear turned and loped to the safety of the forest and made his way back to the facility.

CHAPTER 25

It was early morning when Bear and Dent crept into the boys' dorm and crawled into bed. Both were exhausted from the night's activities. Bear had loped, without stopping, all the way back to the facility, and it had taken all of Dent's strength to hang on.

Between almost being Kitty's next meal and being the center of the "kill that rat" game, Dent's energy was spent. He had been lucky to escape the caves alive and with his tail in one piece. On the loping ride back to the facility, Dent tried to recall the exact order of the wild and scary events that had happened in the caves: Feed the kitty, kill the rat, avoid being pancaked by big stomping feet—and Bear to the rescue. Something was nagging at him, something he was forgetting, but he couldn't recall what it was.

The day was half over when Dent was nudged awake, and Manx whispered, "Wake up and tell us what you found out."

Groggily, Dent sat up in his bed and looked around. Everyone was standing around his bed, and Bear was snoring away undisturbed in his own bed.

Dent gave Manx a puzzled look, and she told him, "No one wants to wake Bear up."

Dent grinned and said, "I didn't know we'd inherited 'chicken' traits too." He climbed out of bed, walked over to Bear, and whispered, "Fooooood," which caused Bear to stir and give a low growl.

"I don't smell any food," Bear said as he opened his eyes.

Dent sat on his bed, inhaled a large breath, and then told the others about following Lester to the trail that led to the caves. He looked at Boxer and said, "Be sure to let Drew know to secure the entrance to the caves. It isn't a secret any longer."

Dent continued telling about following Lester to the caves, sneaking inside, and counting six goons, plus Vera and the other two horrids. Dent omitted the part about almost being Kitty's dinner and the "kill that rat" game.

Manx hissed. "I knew those girls had hooked up with Lester."

Dent looked down at his nails, saying that was all. It had been getting light, so he hadn't had time to search for the missing items.

Bear didn't correct or add anything to Dent's story, because neither of them wanted to admit that Dent had almost been killed in the caves.

"Aunt May saved your breakfast in the kitchen," Wren chirped, and Bear and Dent were happy to have the subject changed from their big cave adventure.

"Thanks, Wren. I'm starving, and Bear must be double starving." Dent turned to Bear, who had not said a word, and told him, "Let's go eat."

"I'm going to let Grand Pierre know about Lester and the caves," Battle said as he followed Dent and Bear from the room.

Battle walked from the sleeping area to the room where he had carried the boxes from the rogue headquarters. Grand

Pierre had papers arranged in stacks on a table, and he sat on a stool, studying a paper that looked to be a diagram of something. When Grand Pierre noticed Battle walk into the room, he placed the paper on the table and waited to hear the outcome from the trap.

Battle stood at attention as he reported about Lester and his two helpers raiding the truck, and then Bear and Dent following them to the caves where the others who had left the settlement were hiding out.

Grand Pierre asked if that was all, and Battle answered, "Yes."

Grand Pierre said it was a good mission, which made Battle smile. The children were always pleased when their teacher gave them praise.

The following day, the children drove alone in the transport to Freedom. Grand Pierre and the other scientists had completed all the tasks Drew had assigned them, and they were now working in the facility's communication center, trying to repair the damaged equipment.

Berne knew more than the other scientists regarding the specific hardware, and he and Francine had spent hours trying to repair the equipment. Francine, like Manx, had inherited technical skills, and she understood the communication protocols and how to send and receive signals.

Phase two of rebuilding Freedom had started. Dent continued to help Boxer schedule and track the crews' progress. Manx assisted Marta in the kitchen, and Battle and Bear rode with Ray in the big truck, delivering items for the various teams.

One day when they were unloading items for the road crew, Battle pointed out Karl to Bear and said that he was the snitch for Lester. When Battle had told Ray about Karl, Ray had informed his uncle, and Drew had assigned a man to watch Karl and find out what information he was passing to Lester.

Ray wanted Drew to run Karl out of Freedom. The work crew wouldn't miss him. Karl worked just enough to not be kicked off the team. Drew said it was better to know what Karl was doing and who he was meeting with. Drew was worried that Lester might have other snitches in Freedom.

When Boxer told Drew that Lester was using the caves as his hideout and was using the hidden entrance for his night raids, Drew had the cave entrance secured. It would have taken Bear and Battle working together to break through. Double layers of heavy wood planks had been nailed to the floor, and a guard had been assigned—both day and night—to make sure no one tried to remove the boards.

Drew also assigned men to guard the trail that led to the caves so that no one could go down or come up. If Lester was going to continue his night raids, he would have to find another way into Freedom. Since sealing off the entrance and trail, the theft problems had been resolved. Bear had gone back to the caves a few nights later and had found them empty.

It was their day off from working in Freedom, and everyone was enjoying a leisurely breakfast—except Bear. Dent commented that Bear was on "prowl patrol" whenever he missed breakfast.

Aunt May always kept Bear's food warm in the kitchen because he would eventually show up with berries to make a dessert. The vegetables, fruit, and eggs Bear found helped to stretch the food.

Wren watched Aunt May making breakfast and asked her why she liked to cook. Aunt May told her it was something she enjoyed doing. Creating recipes from the different foods was fun. She had never had the chance to learn to cook on Ulterion because all the daily meals were prepackaged with their required nutrients. Wren wrinkled her face, trying to understand what she meant.

The children were carrying their empty dishes into the kitchen when Bear walked in with a dark scowl on his face and no berries. It was easy to tell when Bear was upset; his face darkened, and he clenched his fists tight. He motioned for the others to follow him to the boys' dorm.

When everyone was in the room with the door closed, Bear told them, "I've found where Lester and his gang have moved. I went to pick berries for Aunt May and almost ran over Vera and those two girls. I was lucky they were busy picking berries and talking, so they didn't see me. I hid until they left because they would have seen me if I'd tried to get away."

Bear paused in thought for a moment and then continued. "They've moved into the old house where you lived with Grand Pierre, and they were gathering vegetables and fruit like we did at the orphanage."

Battle replied, "I was wondering where they were getting food."

"They must have tried to trap an animal, but I don't think they did. One of the girls said if they did kill something, she wasn't going to skin it. Vera said she wished Lester would kill 'that bear,' and she didn't care which one."

Bear's words puzzled everyone but Dent because Dent suddenly remembered what had been nagging at the back of his mind. It was a glimpse of Vera pointing toward the trees and screaming as loudly as she could, "He changed into a bear!" And then Barten had yelled for them to run for their lives, and everyone had stampeded back into the caves.

Dent groaned and held his head as he sat down on his bed, causing everyone to look at him and wonder what was wrong. He looked up and admitted, "We may have a problem."

Then he told them everything he had omitted before: about almost being Kitty's dinner, about the "kill that rat" rampage, about Bear coming to his rescue, and about what he had just remembered—Vera pointing and screaming, "He changed into a bear!"

Dent added that Lester and the others had been so intent on trying to kill him that they had only heard the word *bear* before turning and racing for their lives into the caves. It wouldn't have been long before Lester figured it out.

Boxer said, "I have been waiting for this to happen."

Battle said, "I wonder what Lester is planning now."

Manx said, "Do you think anyone will believe Vera?"

Wren said, "We need to let Grand Pierre know." And she hurried from the room.

Wren returned with Grand Pierre, and after hearing the complete story from Dent, Grand Pierre nodded his head. "Bear should stay at the facility from now on."

Bear growled, "No. If Lester tries something, I need to be with the others."

"Not knowing what he may be planning is a problem," Grand Pierre admitted.

"Who else knows about us?" Manx asked.

Grand Pierre replied, "Drew and Brion became aware of the real reason for the facility from overhearing the scientists in the caves worrying aloud about the children. I'm not sure if any others in Freedom have learned about the real purpose of the facility. I have been very secretive about your abilities, and those two are not aware of the exact animal traits each of you inherited."

"What should we do?" Battle wanted to be prepared.

"For now, let's proceed as normal," Grand Pierre said. "You will still help Drew with the work in Freedom, and I'll let the other scientists know to be on alert. If you suspect that anything is not right or seems off, let me know. And be careful."

Dent replied seriously, "And remember our *C*s." Grand Pierre left the room.

The Secret Six sat in a circle on the floor in the boys' dorm.

"If anything should happen while we are in Freedom, get to the hidden tree circle," Boxer said. "That will be our meeting place. Wren and Manx can signal with their bracelets if they are in trouble. If anyone calls for help, I'll find someplace to change and bark the danger alert. Does anyone have any other suggestions?"

No one had anything further to add, except saying to stay alert and watch out for traps Lester might be planning. They knew he would use this new knowledge to try to even the score with them.

Karry still had Manx's bracelet, and the small girl had not taken it off since Manx had placed it on her arm. Manx would ask Karry for the bracelet the next time Wren went to the work center to play with her.

Two days later, as the children walked to the transport, Battle signaled for them to stop. He walked around the transport and into the nearby trees and said, "Someone was snooping around the transport. They probably scoped the facility from the tree line but wanted a closer look at the transport. Wren, go and get Grand Pierre. I'm not sure it's safe to leave the facility unprotected."

While they waited, Battle turned to Boxer, Bear, and Dent and suggested, "I think we should post a guard outside at night. We can each take two-hour shifts, so no one will have to miss a lot of sleep."

Though Manx protested, Battle told her, "You need to stay with Wren and Bunny in case something does happen." It was decided that the four boys would stand watch, starting that night.

CHAPTER 26

After telling Wren she would have to cancel her day with Karry, and asking Bear to stay behind and guard the facility, Grand Pierre rode to Freedom with the children in the transport. Grand Pierre was concerned. He needed to talk to Drew and determine if Lester could cause problems for the children.

Drew and Grand Pierre stood beside the transport, discussing the situation concerning Lester. They did not see Ray walk up. After telling Drew that one of Lester's followers had witnessed Bear change and that the children's abilities might become an issue, Drew replied that he would keep watch for any sign of trouble. Ray did not want to interrupt, so he stood quietly and listened. And then he backed away.

Ray walked to the old truck where Battle and Boxer were waiting. They stopped talking when Ray came near. Battle told Boxer he would see him later and opened the door to the truck and climbed in.

That afternoon, on the ride back to the work center after completing the last trip to unload material for the road team, Battle told Ray, "You haven't said two words all day. Is something bothering you?"

Ray looked over at Battle and then drove the old truck off the road and stepped out. He walked around to the back. Battle climbed out of the truck and walked to where Ray stood.

Ray faced Battle and asked, "Is it true about you and the others?"

Battle paused, not sure how to answer. Ray was his friend, the only one he had—not counting the other special ones. Ray apparently had learned of their abilities, so Battle answered yes and watched for his reaction.

Ray shook his head to clear his thoughts and said, "I always thought you were different, not like the other children in the settlement. You stuck together like you had a secret." Ray laughed. "I guess you do."

Battle asked, "You're not worried that we're different?"

"No way. I think it's great—weird, but great." Ray stared at Battle and told him, "I have been wondering all day what each of you would look like—if you weren't you."

Battle grinned and replied, "That we keep secret—most of the time."

"Bear is a bear; that isn't hard to believe. I just wish I could have seen him go after Lester, and I wish he would have caught him." Ray looked at Battle and admitted, "It's great to have a friend like you that I could call if I needed help. I can call you?"

Battle replied, "That's what friends are for."

"Does it hurt? When you change, I mean," Ray quizzed Battle.

Battle laughed. "No. You have to understand that we've never known anything else. We didn't understand that we were any different until we came to the orphanage. Grand Pierre and Aunt May treated us like normal children, except for the training by Grand Pierre on how to control and when to use our abilities. Bear never had that opportunity, and when he gets upset, it's hard for him to stay in control. Dent quickly learned all the things Grand Pierre taught us."

"Amazing," Ray said.

On the drive back to the work center, Ray kept grinning at Battle and finally said, "I just wish I could see you in action."

Battle laughed. He had been honest with Ray, and he felt that their friendship was stronger because of it.

Phase two of Freedom's rebuild was on schedule. Boxer and Dent ran the work crews, leaving Drew time for organizing a leadership team in Freedom. As the days passed, the special ones relaxed. There had been no sign of Lester or his gang, and as far as anyone could tell, nothing further had gone missing. Grand Pierre agreed to allow Wren to go to the work center and spend one day each week with Karry.

After dinner the children walked back to their dorms, and Battle mentioned that there had been no sign that anyone had come back to scout the facility.

Suddenly there was a sound overhead like a strong gust of wind. It shook the doors, startling the children.

"Manx, take Wren and Bunny to the secure lab," Boxer ordered as he ran toward the main entrance with Battle, Dent, and Bear behind him. After learning that the facility had been searched, Grand Pierre had told Boxer the code to the lab.

Manx rushed into the girls' room and found Bunny sitting on her bed with a frightened look on her face. Manx took her hand and said, "Come with me. I need to get you and Wren to safety until we know what is happening."

Manx hurried Bunny and Wren down a hall that ended in a heavy metal door. Manx entered a code into a pad and, when she heard the lock click, pushed the door open. Battle and Bear had worked hard to clear the lab of broken equipment to make it safe, and when it was locked, the lab was a secure place to escape to if they were ever threatened. Once inside, Manx entered the code again, and the lock closed, securing them inside.

Grand Pierre arrived at the entrance the same time as Boxer. Boxer asked him, "What is going on?"

Grand Pierre's pale face looked even paler as he admitted, "A space vessel just landed."

Boxer understood Grand Pierre's fright and thought the robots had returned.

Francine ran up and exclaimed, "They've returned for us! I was able to make contact with the ship. It's from Ulterion."

Francine pushed her way past Grand Pierre. "Hurry, Piers. Let's greet our rescuers."

The other scientists were crowded together, all trying to get out the door at the same time. Boxer hung back, as did Battle, Bear, and Dent. The four walked to the area where the spaceship had landed and stared at the sleek, oval-shaped vessel.

The ship glimmered in the sun. It was not very large. A door opened, and a ramp extended to the ground. A tall man who could have been Grand Pierre's twin stepped out and looked around, shielding his eyes from the bright light.

He saw Grand Pierre and exclaimed, "Piers, my colleague! I have come for you." Then the tall man hurried down the ramp.

Grand Pierre met the man halfway, and they greeted each other with a hug, which was unusual because no signs of affection were ever made by the scientists. The man turned to the ship and waved to the ship's pilot that all was okay.

Grand Pierre started back to the facility as the other scientists crowded around, all asking questions at the same time.

Grand Pierre loudly said, "Let Aeron come inside before the light blinds him. Then we can have our questions answered."

The scientists followed Grand Pierre and Aeron to the dining room and sat down, excited to hear news from their home planet.

Boxer went to the lab and brought Manx, Wren, and Bunny back with him, and the children watched from the door.

Aunt May carried a glass of water and set it in front of Aeron. After he drank it all, he exclaimed, "I had forgotten how good water tastes."

Aeron looked around and said, "I am afraid we do not have much time. We must leave soon. The fuel source is weak, and we must make it back to Ulterion. This is the only ship left that is capable of space travel. All the others have been destroyed by the rogues, and their last ship blew up on the way here."

Francine said, "I don't understand. The rogues were coming back here?"

"There was a beacon here that started sending signals over a year ago," Aeron explained. "Apparently the rogues intended to relocate to Adoran because the situation on Ulterion has become quite bleak. The rogues chased us here from Ulterion. Our space team found a way to disrupt the warship's energy core and caused it to explode when the deep-space engine engaged. When we intercepted their communications, we learned that a few of our scientists were still alive. We have risked much to bring you back to Ulterion, and we can only stay on this planet an hour. The pilot is very firm about this and will have no problem leaving without us. He must get the ship back to Ulterion. If we can recreate our power supply, then we can refuel the ship for future use." After Aeron finished speaking, there were sighs of relief from some of the scientists—and stunned silence from others.

Aeron looked around and counted. "We can take all of you. Six is the maximum number of additional passengers the ship can hold. Only bring necessary items for the trip. Now hurry, and meet at the ship in one hour."

Grand Pierre stood up and asked, "What about the children? We can't leave them here."

Aeron looked puzzled. "Children survived the attacked?" He looked at the door where Grand Pierre pointed. "There is no room for them, so they must remain here."

Grand Pierre looked at the other scientists and told them, "Go pack your things. I need to speak with Aeron."

The scientists left the room, with the exception of Aunt May and Francine. Aunt May spoke first. "How can we leave the children with no one to watch out for them?"

Aeron replied, "All but two look grown. They can take responsibility for the others. On Ulterion, they would be joining their groups." His words lacked any feeling.

Francine exclaimed, "There is no way Bunny will survive. I've taught her hand signs, but she will never belong here."

Aeron looked shocked. "One is an ulta-mind? There have been no ultas that survived cloning in many years. It is unfortunate that we cannot take her."

Grand Pierre wanted confirmation. "Six is the number of passengers the ship can hold?" Aeron nodded, and Grand Pierre continued. "What is the status on Ulterion? Is everyone still living underground?"

Aeron looked puzzled and replied, "Of course. Where else would we live?"

"Then it is settled." Grand Pierre's voice was firm. He looked at Francine and said, "Get Bunny ready to leave. I will stay here with the children."

"No!" Both Francine and Aunt May gasped.

Aunt May knew how much Piers cared for the children, and that he would never abandon them on Adoran.

Francine knew that the only chance Bunny would have to continue to develop as an ulta was on Ulterion.

Grand Pierre waited with Aeron while the other scientists packed. He was concerned about their return, and he asked Aeron for the status of the planet and the war with the rogues.

Aeron hesitated before admitting that most of the planet was uninhabitable because of diminishing resources. Fumes from all the bombing had destroyed the air purifiers and had left a haze that the sunlight could not filter through to power the equipment. Equipment failure and breakdowns occurred daily, and maintenance had stopped because the robots would kill anyone who came outside. The robots survived on top because they didn't need to breathe."

Grand Pierre sighed. "It sounds bleak." And Aeron agreed.

Manx and Wren hugged Bunny good-bye, their eyes filled with tears as they watched her walk to the spaceship. Before she walked up the ramp, Bunny signed that she would keep Wren and Manx in her thoughts.

Wren ran back to the girls' room, trying to hold back tears. When she entered the room, she walked to Bunny's empty bed and started crying. Then she noticed that the drawing of Bunny and Bear was missing. Bunny had taken it with her.

When Manx walked toward the kitchen and heard voices, she wondered who was still in the facility. She had thought that all the scientists were on the ship. She stopped at the rear door of the communication room and saw Grand Pierre and Francine looking at the repaired equipment. Francine pointed as she spoke, and Grand Pierre nodded his head.

Manx felt Dent walk up beside her, and both silently watched Francine take Grand Pierre's face in her hands and say something. Manx was shocked when Grand Pierre placed his arms around Francine and held her tight. When Francine pulled away, she handed Grand Pierre the device that Manx had taken from the rogues' headquarters. Francine pointed to the device and said something. Then she kissed Grand Pierre and hurried out the front of the comm room and ran to the spaceship.

Manx waited until Grand Pierre had left. Then she said, "I never realized that Grand Pierre had feelings for Francine and she for him. I feel bad that they can't be with each other because he choose to stay here with us."

"I don't think feelings are encouraged on Ulterion," Dent commented.

"He gave up his life there to stay here," Manx murmured.

"The Secret Six would give up our lives for each other," Dent told her.

Manx turned and looked at Dent. "Like you did for me."

Dent grinned, exposing his two black front teeth, and told Manx, "I would risk my life every day for you."

As they turned to leave, Dent took hold of Manx's hand, and they walked hand in hand down the hall.

Dent told Manx, "Grand Pierre said he could make my teeth white again. He found something that would take the black out."

"Don't you dare!" Manx exclaimed. "I like your teeth just the way they are." She squeezed Dent's hand until he cried out, just to make sure he understood.

The Attack

CHAPTER 27

The following morning, Grand Pierre met the children in the dining room and told them, "We will all go to the work center today. I need to speak to Drew and let him know that my colleagues have returned to Ulterion." Grand Pierre was solemn and not his usual energetic self.

The children had talked in the boys' dorm late into the night until Wren fell asleep, and Boxer carried her to bed. They discussed their concerns about Lester trying to get back at them for making him look like a fool in front of the robots. Now that he had found this facility, they did not have any place else to go. Lester was living the old farmhouse, and the caves were not an option. They needed a safe place in case Lester and his gang of goons—Dent's description—tried something.

Boxer stated that it wasn't *if* it would happen but *when* it would happen. For this reason he told Grand Pierre, "We should not leave the facility unguarded, day or night. If Lester finds outs no one is here, he will try something."

Battle added, "We need to change up our schedules. We can't be predictable and have a set routine, like when we drive into Freedom. We should take one transport and keep one locked away."

"No one knows about the scientists leaving," Grand Pierre said, "and I need to let Drew know that my support for him will be limited. I do not have the skills the others did. My main area was genetic research. Drew will need to depend on the people in Freedom, going forward." He paused with a concerned look and said, "I fear we may have helped them too much and given them knowledge they were not ready for."

Battle responded, "You only showed them how to make use of their own resources, like the blasting sticks. They would have eventually figured it out, or something like it."

Boxer said, "Bear should stay and guard the facility. If Lester told Karl or his snitches, Bear is the only one he knows about. None of us should go out alone, just to be safe."

Battle argued, "I need to help Ray, since Bear won't be going. Besides, I'm safe with Ray. Manx should stay with Wren and come to the work center on the days she visits Karry. We need to let Marta know that she must find a replacement for Manx. Boxer and Dent will still manage the work crews until something changes."

"I agree with Battle," Boxer affirmed. "If something happens at the facility, Manx and Wren will be safe in the lab."

"Agreed," said Grand Pierre. "All of us will go except Bear. After today, Bear, Manx, Wren, and I will stay at the facility. We are running late and should get going." Grand Pierre hurried the others out of the room.

Boxer drove the spare transport into the storeroom and secured the door. He climbed into the front beside Grand Pierre, and Manx, Wren, Dent, and Battle sat on the bench.

When the transport rolled up to the work center, Drew and Ray were waiting by the old truck. Drew hurried over and said, "We were becoming concerned."

Grand Pierre stepped out and told Drew, "There is something I must tell you."

Ray asked Battle, "Are you ready?"

Battle looked at Boxer, and Boxer told him, "Go with Ray, and we'll see you later."

Battle nodded and climbed into the old truck.

Later that day when they returned to the facility, Grand Pierre asked the children to meet him in the dining area. After everyone was seated, he told them, "We must organize the duties, like cooking and cleaning and monitoring."

"Monitoring what?" Manx asked.

Grand Pierre explained. "Francine said that once she arrives on Ulterion, she will contact us. She showed me the equipment and the settings to monitor. We must have someone in the comm room each day, and I was thinking that would be Manx, since she will be staying with Wren. When Manx goes to Freedom, I will monitor for Francine's signal."

Manx looked excited. "I can't wait for you to show me. Besides, I don't want to spend time in a kitchen again."

Wren chirped, "Aunt May was teaching me how to cook, and I'm getting pretty good. I just have trouble understanding her directions, like how much stuff to put in."

Dent told Wren, "I can help you. I know the directions she used were in the Ulterion language. We can go over what you want to cook the night before and make sure you understand what to do."

"Bear can bring vegetables and fruit like he did for Aunt May." Wren excitedly hopped from one foot to the other.

"We'll all help with cleanup, like we did at the orphanage," Dent responded.

"How will we maintain our patrol schedule if we have duties when we get back?" Battle wanted to know.

Bear answered, "If I'm to stay here, I can patrol at night while everyone sleeps. Grand Pierre and Manx are around during the day, so I will sleep then. This will allow me to make trips at night for food and to check on Lester."

Grand Pierre rubbed his chin in thought. "That about covers everything. If we find something we have forgotten, we can discuss it at that time. Now, off to our beds."

The following morning as Boxer, Battle, and Dent walked to the transport, Bear stepped from the trees. "The road is clear, with no sign of Lester or his gang. I'll recheck the road before it's time for you to drive back and make sure it's safe."

"Thanks, Bear," Battle replied. "I wish this wasn't the only road from the facility. It's the easiest place to set a trap."

Tomorrow was their day off, and on the ride back to the facility, Dent said he needed a break. After keeping track of all the crews and schedules, it felt like he had been running nonstop all day. Drew was busy with the new leadership team, creating regulations and guidelines for Freedom, and he only checked with Boxer and Dent in the morning to make sure all the crews were on schedule.

Dent said, "Something seemed different this week, especially with a couple of the road crews. It felt like everyone was staring at me behind my back."

Boxer turned in his seat. "I noticed that too. It was like everyone was keeping their distance. I wonder if Karl started spreading rumors among the crews. I'm glad Bear is watching the road to the facility. It saves me from worrying about driving into a trap." Boxer turned back to watch the road.

"If we don't have any plans for tomorrow, maybe we could scout around the old farm?" Dent suggested.

"I don't think that's a good idea," Battle said. "Lester is probably on alert for sightings of a gray rat or a bear. Besides, I'm going to meet Ray. He asked if I would teach him some moves to take down an opponent."

Boxer was surprised. "Ray asked you to teach him to fight?"

"He said he would feel a lot safer if he knew how to defend himself," Battle explained. "I may show him my sweepers and how to use them. He could make his own for defense."

"What would be a good defense weapon?" Dent was curious.

"One of the best weapons is a strong staff, long enough to keep someone from getting in close, but not too long to carry. Some of the larger trees have excellent limbs for this purpose." Battle seemed to enjoy sharing his knowledge.

"Would you help me make a staff and show me how to use it?" Dent asked.

"Are you afraid of getting pancaked by Lester?" Battle teased.

"Ha-ha," was Dent's reply as Boxer stopped the transport next to the facility and Bear stepped from the trees.

Dent hurried inside to check on Wren and make sure she understood Aunt May's instructions. He found Wren busy cutting vegetables to put in a pot, and when Dent asked if she needed help, she huffed that she had everything under control. Dent glanced around the room. Wren had four different tasks going at once, and he worried that it was too much for her, but seeing the glare she gave him, he backed out of the kitchen. Next stop was the communication room to check on Manx.

Grand Pierre and Manx were discussing one of the monitors, unsure of what to do. Dent walked over and asked, "Did Francine leave any instructions for how to change the settings on the equipment?"

The tall man sighed. "No, she did not have time."

Dent looked around. "When the room was cleaned, were there any documents? There may be operating manuals for the equipment."

Grand Pierre pondered Dent's question and nodded. "I saw Argies carry a box in the back. Many of the papers looked torn, and some were scorched by the fires. I'll look tomorrow." Then he told Manx, "I think we have done a much as we can today. You have learned everything Francine told me."

CHAPTER 28

*W*ren's first dinner was a comedy of errors. Everyone told her the meal was great, just not a lot of it. The vegetables in the pot burned, and the salad bowl tipped onto the floor when she reached across the table to stir the smoking pot. The soft rolls that Aunt May usually made came out like hard rocks. And something happened to the berries: a red-looking slime bubbled in the bowl when she mixed the ingredients for dessert.

Boxer told Wren to schedule her work, complete one thing at a time, and not try to be like Aunt May until she became more proficient at cooking. His remarks earned him a menacing glare from Wren.

Battle held up one of the rolls and praised Wren, saying that the hard roll could knock someone out if thrown correctly. This earned Battle a roll missile aimed at his head, which challenged his reaction time to save his head from being bonked.

Bear growled, or his stomach did. No one was quite sure which.

Manx told Wren she had done better than Manx ever could, which helped Wren feel a little better.

Dent didn't utter a word, which was strange, but he was extremely smart and knew when to keep quiet.

Wren said she was sorry the dinner was ruined, but the others praised her efforts and said that the next meal would be better—they hoped—causing Wren to finally smile.

Suddenly Boxer stood up and raised his fist, signaling for quiet. He had heard something. He made a circling motion with his hand, and Battle and Bear raced from the room to check the perimeter. He looked at Manx and Wren and motioned for them to get to the lab. He quietly told Dent to get Grand Pierre from the comm room.

In an instant, Boxer was alone, and he silently stepped to two small windows in the outside wall to listen. The windows were placed high at the top of the wall to stop anyone from seeing inside, and he was glad the facility had been built that way. Anyone outside would not know who was inside or what room they were in.

Boxer could tell that intruders were sneaking up the road behind the facility where the transport was parked. They were trying to mask their steps, but Boxer heard them anyway.

Grand Pierre hurried into the room, followed by Dent. "What's happening?" he whispered.

"We have visitors coming up the road behind the facility," Boxer replied.

Battle came into the room, startling the others, as he'd not made a sound until he spoke. "Bear and I counted about twenty men sneaking up the road. They are all wearing masks to hide their faces and carrying pieces of wood wrapped in oil-soaked rags. I'm sure they are going to try to set fire to the facility."

"Lester has finally made his move," Boxer said and walked from the room toward the rear entrance. Battle and Dent followed him, not sure what he was planning to do.

Grand Pierre turned and loped as fast as his long legs would allow back to the comm room.

Boxer told Battle and Dent to wait inside as he opened the door and stepped out. In the dark, Boxer could see the men slinking around, thinking they were hidden.

"Lester, show yourself. We know you are behind this." All movement stopped when Boxer called out.

Finally, out of the tree line stepped a hooded figure, and from the way he slunk forward, Boxer could tell it was Lester. The cloth covering his face had two holes cut out for him to see. Others stepped up and surrounded their leader, all wearing the same crudely made masks. The eye holes were cut differently for each mask—some were slanted, some round, and others oval—but hatred filled the eyes that glared at Boxer.

Boxer taunted Lester. "You can hide behind that mask, but we know it's you. Why don't you leave before someone gets hurt?"

"We're not the ones hiding. You are a freak, and you and the other freaks should leave before you get hurt." Lester raised the piece of wood soaked in oil and shook it. His bravado increasing as his gang of masked thugs gathered around him. "You should have left with those other tall weirdos. You are all mutants, and we are going to burn down this place with you inside."

Dent turned to say something to Battle, but he was gone. Dent stepped up beside Boxer. He wasn't as big or strong as Boxer, Battle, and Bear, but he was fast, and if they were attacked, he could hold his own—he hoped.

Suddenly someone yelled *help*, causing Lester and his gang to look around. Then another man in the back screamed. Dent knew that Bear and Battle, unseen in the dark night, were attacking the men at the rear.

Dent whispered to Boxer, "All we need to do is twist the masks around their heads, and they won't be able to see anything."

Then another loud scream echoed in the dark.

Lester yelled, "Light the torches, and burn the place down."

Boxer leaped from the porch, ran to the nearest hooded figure, and in one move kicked his legs out from under him, causing him to crash to the ground. Boxer picked up the piece of wood and knocked the masked man out cold.

Dent started to run from the porch to help Boxer, but Grand Pierre placed his hand on his shoulder, stopping him. "Wait here with me," he said. "It shouldn't take long."

Dent wasn't sure what they were waiting for. It was three against twenty, minus the ones that Bear and Battle had already taken down. Were they waiting for the three to take out the others or for the others to come and take them out? Grand Pierre didn't seem worried, so Dent decided not to worry either as he watched the madness developing from the doorway.

Another loud scream echoed in the dark as the masked hoodlums tried to light their torches. A few managed to get theirs lit, and they ran forward and threw them at the facility.

Dent decided that the goons needed more practice because the torches didn't even reach the building. They just lay burning on the ground, giving off an eerie light. Dent heard Lester yell, "Get their wheels!" Three men raced to the transport, pushed it over, and set it on fire. The seats quickly flamed and engulfed the transport. It happened so fast that there was no time to save it.

A horn blasted, and two bouncing lights came up the road. The lights were moving so crazily, it was hard to watch them. By now Lester had lost half of his gang. The ones not lying on the ground, moaning, had run away.

The old truck jerked from one side of the narrow road to the other as it hit one tree and bounced to the next. Finally the truck stopped just short of the parking area, wedged tight between two trees.

Drew and Ray jumped from the truck and were handed weapons by men riding in the back. There were six men in the back, plus Drew and Ray. Now Lester was outnumbered.

Lester yelled, "Retreat," and ran back into the trees, followed by the few remaining masked goons that had escaped Bear and Battle's rear attack.

Drew looked at the hooded figures sprawled on the ground and ordered, "Tie them up and take them back to Freedom so they can answer for causing trouble." He bent over a figure and pulled the mask off. "I'm not surprised to see you, Karl."

Drew walked over to Grand Pierre. "After I received your signal, we got here as fast as we could."

"Lester is getting braver, and I'm worried about what may happen," Grand Pierre told Drew as the two stood and looked at the burned transport.

"If you're worried, move back to Freedom where you will be safe," Drew suggested.

"My friend, it's not us that I'm worried about, but Lester and his growing gang. He doesn't understand what may happen if he continues to try to harm us. These children have powers that have not yet been tapped. Even I am not sure what may happen. I have taught them control, but when they are threatened and have to fight for their lives . . ." Grand Pierre shrugged.

The children spent the next day at the facility. It was their day off, and they discussed what to do to prevent future attacks on the facility.

Battle commented, "I don't think Lester will attack again with all of us here. Even with all the guys he had with him, he wouldn't have succeeded. Ray said Drew is going to make an example of the four they took back to Freedom."

"Maybe we should stay here from now on," Dent suggested.

Boxer pondered that. "All that will accomplish is to postpone the showdown that is coming."

"It would look like we are afraid and hiding in the facility," Battle commented.

Manx spoke up. "I didn't like hiding in the lab while everyone else faced Lester. I'm not afraid of him or his followers."

"Manx shouldn't have to babysit me," Wren added. "I can take care of myself."

"I'm not sure we've accomplished anything except to decide that we're not going to hide," Boxer stated. "Tomorrow Battle, Dent, and I will go back to the work center, like normal."

"Lester has spies on the crews," Dent pointed out, "and I feel like we are not welcome by some of the men. Lester may have caused them to be afraid of us and to join his gang of goons."

"Drew, Brion, and Ray know differently and will stand up for us," Battle replied.

It was settled. Tomorrow they would go back to the work center and continue to help with phase two of the rebuilding of Freedom.

CHAPTER 29

$\mathscr{I}$t had been a quiet but busy week. There had been no further sign of Lester. Drew kept his word, and Karl and the three men who had raided the facility stood before the new leadership council. When they admitted what they had done, they were assigned duties at the work center under Sola's direction. Drew made it very clear that if they caused any further trouble, they would be banned from Freedom and never allowed to return. To be banned was the highest form of punishment in Freedom, and having to live at the work center was their form of detention. From the frightened looks on the men's faces, it was clear that they knew they were in serious trouble.

The final road crew returned and reported their progress. Dent updated the charts and was looking forward to having tomorrow off. He went out front to walk around.

Boxer was waiting for his last team to report in. When Battle and Ray returned, they would drive the transport back to the facility. It had been a wise decision to lock up the second transport because now it was their only transportation. Each night Battle would lock it in the storage room.

Dent worried about Manx and Wren. He knew he would be more at ease at the facility with them than he was while working in Freedom. He pondered a big question: when the rebuild was over, what would the future hold for Grand Pierre and the special ones?

Dent did not feel comfortable in Freedom, and he could sense a separation from the people that grew more each day. Fewer men would come and talk to him. The feeling was not the same as it had been before the bear incident, and he felt that it was all his fault for being caught in the caves. They others didn't blame him, and as Boxer said, their secret would have eventually been found out.

Dent was deep in thought when Marta interrupted. "I'm looking for Karry. Have you seen her?"

Dent shook his thoughts aside and replied, "Not today, but we've been extremely busy with end-of-week updates."

Marta looked puzzled. "I can't imagine where she could have gone. Maybe she became bored and went home, but she always tells me. I have bread baking and can't leave. Would you check my house? It's just one street over."

Dent agreed to check on Karry and thought about letting Boxer know, but Marta was worried, and it was a short way to her house and back.

Dent answered, "I'll go and check and come right back."

Marta sighed with relief as Dent ran down the road, and she returned to the kitchen.

Boxer placed the colored markers for the maps into a box and started to push the chairs back under the table. Suddenly he stopped and listened. It was the distress signal from Manx's bracelet, which gave off a slightly higher sound than Wren's.

Boxer glanced around for Dent but didn't see him. He decided he couldn't wait for him. He had to get to Manx. She would not have signaled unless it was an emergency and she was in trouble.

Boxer could tell that the sound was coming from the orphanage, and he wondered why Manx would have gone there. Maybe Lester had raided the facility, captured Manx, and taken her there. Boxer now worried about Wren as well.

He ran outside and stopped beside the transport. It was the one that had been rebuilt and was even slower than the one Lester's hooded goons had burned, if that were possible. Boxer knew he would make better time if he ran, so he ran down the road toward the orphanage. The bracelet continued to send the silent signal.

"Are you sure this thing is working? I can't hear anything, and I'm tired of rubbing it." Lester snarled at Vera, who stood looking out the window of the small pod the special ones had lived in at the orphanage.

Vera answered, "It's what Karry told Jonne when she asked Karry how she got out of the basement. Jonne had said she was sorry. That it was your idea, and stupid Karry believed her." She gave a nasty laugh and glared at the young girl seated at the old table with her hands tied securely together. Karry's small chin quivered with fright, but she didn't say a word.

Trying to get back on Lester's good side, Vera had told him about the bracelet Manx had given Karry, and Lester had come up with a plan to get back at Boxer. Lester's dislike of the other children was nothing compared to his hatred for Boxer for making him look like an idiot in front of the robots. He had almost been killed by the rogue leader when there was no sign of the two girls in the basement of the old building.

"Barten, make sure the guys are watching the road to signal if they see Boxer," Lester ordered as he tightly gripped Karry's arm and continued to rub the silver bracelet.

When Lester had tried to pull the bracelet from Karry's arm, she had cried out that the bracelet only worked when it was on her arm, and he had believed her. Karry was more afraid of losing the bracelet than she was of Lester or Vera. She was confident that Boxer and Manx would come to her rescue, just as they had done before.

"There's the signal. He's coming," Barten whispered from the broken door of the small pod.

Lester's gang had been attacked when they'd raided the facility, and Boxer had known they were outside in the dark. After that, Lester had decided that Boxer and the other mutants must be able to see in the dark. This time he had his followers hidden behind buildings and trees and carrying weapons.

"He's in the yard." Barten kept his voice low.

Boxer stopped and looked around. The signal from the bracelet had stopped, but he couldn't see or hear anyone. He leaned over, breathing hard, his chest heaving from his frantic race to the orphanage.

"It's a trap!" Karry screamed at the top of her lungs.

Boxer tensed as Lester's gang appeared from behind buildings and trees to surround him. They carried weapons they had made or stolen, and they were anxious to use them.

Lester slapped Karry hard across the face, knocking her and the chair to the floor, and ran outside with Barten close behind.

Lester yelled, "Tighten the circle. Don't let the mutant escape."

Boxer quickly counted twenty men slowly stepping toward him with their weapons raised, ready to do him harm.

"Kill him!" Vera screamed from the pod. To harm Boxer would cause Manx pain, and she hated Manx as much as Lester hated Boxer.

Boxer circled around, looking for a weak link in the men as they came closer. He was trapped and couldn't fight off twenty armed men by himself. He could do major injury to some, and kill if he had to, but it was not something Boxer wanted to be forced to do.

One of the guys started to swing a pole with a large rock hanging from the end. He swung the rock at Boxer. Boxer ducked and was hit from behind by a thrown rock that glanced off his shoulder. More rocks were thrown, hitting him and causing pain but not breaking any bones.

A guy lunged forward and jabbed a long sharpened spear into Boxer's leg, drawing blood. Other men lunged at him with sharpened sticks, and a man almost as wide as Battle rushed toward him, carrying one of the chains made to bind the rogue leaders.

Boxer had no choice but to jump toward the charging man, and in an instant he changed into the large black dog. The startled man stopped, his mouth dropping open in fear as the snarling dog jumped directly at him. The large dog leaped over the man and ran away from the armed men.

"Don't let the mutant escape!" Lester screamed and raced after the black dog.

Boxer made it to the hidden tree circle and ran inside. He had been seen going into the trees, so he knew he could not stay here, but his leg was hurting. He glanced down and saw blood gushing from a wound. The sharpened stick had done its job. Boxer had no choice. He howled a loud distress signal from the hidden tree circle.

Startled by the loud howl, which was repeated, Barten stopped and gasped, "Do you think the creature is dying?"

"Only one way to find out," Lester said. "Circle the trees, and don't let the mutant escape." He ordered his gang to surround the trees because none of the men were brave enough to enter the darkness inside the circle of trees where the large dog waited.

Dent went to find Marta. He had searched her small house and found no sign of Karry. Because of the latest event with Lester and his band of masked goons, Dent was worried. He was in the empty kitchen when he heard Boxer's distress howl, and when it was repeated again, he knew something bad was happening.

Marta hurried from the back room and asked, "Did you find Karry?"

"No. She wasn't there, and the house was locked tight," Dent said. "Karry didn't go home." He knew Marta was worried and wasn't sure how much to tell her, but Marta knew of the problems with Lester. "Something bad is happening. Boxer called a distress signal, and I must go. I will look for Karry, and the others will too. Try not to worry. We'll find her." Dent turned and ran to the empty scheduling room to see if Boxer had left any clue as to where he had gone, but he found nothing.

Dent ran outside and looked down the road in the direction Boxer's distress call had come from. He realized that Boxer was in the tree circle and in need of help.

Dent was trying to decide the fastest way to get to Boxer. Changing wasn't an option; as the gray rat, he would never make it there in time to help Boxer. He hurried to the repaired transport and decided he could run faster than it could go. He started to run down the road, when a small bird with a red breast flew around his head and landed behind the transport.

Wren stepped out and gasped, "Do you know what is going on? We heard Boxer's distress call. Bear and Manx are coming through the forest and sent me to see if anyone was at the work center."

"Karry is missing," Dent said, "and Boxer left the work center when I went to check Marta's house. His distress call came from the tree circle."

Dent wasn't sure how much to involve Wren, but she was one of them, so he told her, "Change and fly to the tree circle and let Boxer know that Manx and Bear are coming through the forest, and I'll be there as fast as I can."

Before Wren could change, three loud honks sounded as the old truck came barreling up the road.

"Tell Boxer that Battle and I will be right behind you. Fly," Dent ordered. Wren made two fast hops, and the small bird flew toward the tree circle.

Dust swirled as Battle jumped out of the old truck before it came to a stop. "What's happening?" he gasped.

"We have to get to the tree circle," Dent answered quickly. "Something's happened for Boxer to send a distress call—and Karry is missing again."

"Jump in and hang on," Battle told Dent. Then he ordered Ray to drive to the orphanage and double time it, and the old truck fishtailed down the road.

Lester, Barten, and the armed men stood outside of the tree circle, unsure of what might happen if they stepped inside. None of them paid any attention when a small brown bird flew overhead and landed on a branch not far off the ground.

Wren could see the large black dog standing at the back of the circle, waiting for Lester and his gang to attack. Wren jumped from the tree limb and changed as she landed on the ground.

The large dog was startled and bared his teeth until he recognized Wren. Wren noticed blood soaking the ground from one of the dog's legs.

"You're hurt," Wren exclaimed and bent down to look at the wound. "I have to stop the bleeding." She tore a piece of cloth from her shirt and tied it around the wounded leg. She had to buy Boxer time to allow Bear and Manx and Battle to get there.

"Stay here," Wren ordered and marched to the front of the tree circle where Lester waited.

Wren stepped from the trees directly in front of Lester, startling him and causing him to jump back. With hands on her hips, she walked directly to him and yelled, "What have you done to Karry? Karry never did anything to you, and this is the second time you have taken her. If she is hurt, you will be sorry."

Wren turned to the gang members and spat out, "You are all terrible! Would you hurt one of your own kids? What if Karry was your sister or daughter?" Some of the gang members looked around, confused. They looked to Lester for an explanation.

Lester blustered, "She's over in the pod with Vera. We'll let her go after we kill the mutt."

Wren smiled to herself. Now she knew where Karry was and that she was all right.

CHAPTER 30

*L*ester was double her size, and Wren firmed her stance in front of him. There was no way she would ever let him harm Boxer. Lester would have to get past her. She could sense hesitation in some of the men.

Lester reached out to push Wren aside, but he stopped when the truck's horn broke the silence. Wren grinned. Battle was coming, and it didn't matter how many men Lester had with him. He would not escape Battle's wrath, especially with Boxer hurt.

The truck came to a sliding stop and spun in a half circle, causing dust to billow up in large clouds. Battle, Ray, and Dent jumped from the truck, all carrying weapons of their own.

Battle had shown Ray and Dent how to make long staffs and had taught them how to use them. The three stepped in front of the truck, their faces masked with determination. They were ready to fight, even though greatly outnumbered.

When he recognized some of the men, Ray yelled, "I hope you realize what you are doing and what will happen if you try to harm any of us. You will be hurt, and if you live, you will be banned from Freedom forever. Drew and more men are right behind us."

One of the men yelled back, "But these are the ones who are causing all the trouble. They brought the robots here."

"Who told you that? Lester?" Ray shouted. "When can you believe anything he says? If you have questions or concerns, there is a new council in Freedom that you can come to for truthful answers. Why hurt the very ones who helped us defeat the robots?" Ray no longer feared Lester.

Another man cried out, "But we all saw him change into a dog. He's a mutant." His words caused the men guarding the tree circle to lift their weapons and shout in agreement.

Another voice loudly exclaimed, "We don't want those kind living in Freedom."

Lester shoved Wren aside and screamed, "Kill the dog!"

When Wren struck the ground, she jumped up, changed into the brown bird, flew straight up, and began an assault on Lester's head. With her sharp claws she grabbed hold of Lester's long matted hair, and with her pointed beak she began to peck hard at his head, drawing blood with each strike.

Wren knew how to fight—in her own way. Grand Pierre had taught her well.

Lester screamed and jumped madly about, waving his arms around, trying to knock the crazed bird off his head. But Wren was quick. She repeatedly let go and hopped to a different spot on his head to continue her attack. She was determined to stop him from hurting Boxer.

When Wren finally let go, Lester ducked and started to run away, and she had no choice but to dive and grab hold of his ear to stop him. With her sharp beak she tore off his ear lobe, and Lester's ear instantly began squirting blood, coating the side of his face and streaking down his neck. All of the men stood in shock with their mouths gaping open, watching Lester try to defend himself from the attack of one determined little brown bird.

It was the distraction of Wren's attack on Lester that allowed Battle, Ray, and Dent to run from the truck with their long staffs and challenge the men closest to them, each one knocking a man to the ground. With one swift hit to the head from the sturdy poles, the men were knocked out and lay flat on the ground with gaping mouths.

Battle, Ray, and Dent stood with their backs together as Lester's men ran to their friends' aid. When the first men came within the reach of a staff, they went down in the same manner, losing consciousness when the end of the staff connected with their heads. This caused the other men to stand back, realizing what would happen if they came any closer.

Battle watched the burly man with the chain step forward, swinging the chain in a circle over his head. Battle could tell that the chain and the staff's length were the same. He waited until the high-flying chain flew in a backward motion, took two steps, and slid forward on his knees. He lifted his long pole upward with as much strength as possible, directly between the large man's legs. When the pole struck its target, the large man screamed out in pain and let go of the chain. The heavy chain dropped on top of the incapacitated man, pinning him to the ground.

Battle jumped up, ran directly at the nearest man, and swung his staff. He hit the man in the side and heard the man's ribs break. Ray and Dent ran up beside Battle and challenged the dumbfounded men who watched the groaning burly man secured by the heavy chain.

The men instantly dropped their weapons and turned to run into the forest—just as a huge, angry bear leaped from the trees. In fear, the men whirled around to escape the snarling bear and faced Battle, Ray, and Dent with their pain-inflicting poles. The frightened men dropped down to the ground and covered their heads with their hands.

Bear didn't slow down. He ran toward the tree circle, and with his large paw he sent a man flying high into the air. The man turned a double somersault in midair, landed in a strange position when he hit the ground, and didn't get back up. Bear stopped in the middle of the tree circle, stood up on his hind legs, and roared out a challenge to Lester and his gang: come on in, if you dare.

Boxer had collapsed on the ground. Wren had stopped the bleeding from his injured leg, but he had lost a lot of blood. When Boxer saw Bear enter the circle, he knew he was safe. He gave a low howl to thank Bear for once again saving his life.

Lester had his own troubles. His ear was spurting blood from the missing lobe, and with all the blood that ran down his face and soaked his shirt, he thought he was dying. He kept ducking, trying to avoid Wren's sharp claws and lethal beak. He had patches of hair missing from his bleeding scalp, and he yelped out in pain each time Wren pecked at his head.

Barten was unharmed and backed away from Lester to avoid the crazy little bird. He circled behind the old truck to escape the madhouse that Lester's trap had turned into. After seeing Wren change into the small, aggressive bird, and Boxer turn into the large dog—and seeing that the bear had returned—Barten jumped into the back of the truck and hid.

Wren had seen Bear enter the tree circle to guard Boxer, and she knew this was her chance to rescue Karry. She flew toward the small pod, leaving Lester with his bleeding ear and hole-pecked head, just as Manx leaped from the forest, stopped, and looked around.

Manx saw Vera run into the pod, hissed loudly, and raced toward her. Manx and Wren reached the front of the pod at the same time. Manx jumped against the door, but Vera had managed to block the door from the inside.

Wren dropped down and changed. She told Manx, "Follow me. Vera doesn't know about the door in back, and they are holding Karry inside."

Wren raced around the side of the pod with Manx right behind her.

Wren stopped at the small door and motioned that she would open the door to let Manx enter first. Wren knew that Vera and Karry were inside, but she wasn't sure if there was anyone else. If there were others, Manx would take care of them, and she would get Karry to safety.

Wren took a large breath and pulled. The door swung open, and Manx leaped inside the pod. Wren stepped in after her. They saw Karry lying on the floor, not moving, and Wren hurried to her friend. Manx hissed, and her fur puffed up.

Vera turned from the window where she was watching, and her eyes widened in fear. Her hands flew to the side of her face, and she screamed at the sight of the hissing yellow cat. Vera shoved aside the cot that was blocking the door and pushed it open.

Manx leaped across the room, landed on the cot, and grabbed the back of Vera's dress. As Vera ran from the pod,

Manx's sharp claws shredded the material and left deep scratches down Vera's back.

"Manx, help me lift Karry!" Wren shouted, crouching on the floor. "She's alive, but she's tied to the chair."

Manx wanted to chase after Vera, but she turned back to help Wren. Vera could wait, for now, and Karry needed her. She jumped from the cot and changed. Then she helped Wren lift Karry and the chair from the floor.

Karry opened her eyes as Manx untied her hands. "I knew you would come." She grinned at Wren, the side of her face welted from Lester's hand print. "I just pretended to be asleep so Vera and Lester would leave me alone."

"Good thinking, Karry," Wren said as she helped her friend stand. Between Manx and Wren, Karry walked from the small pod.

Outside, the battle was over. Manx glanced around for Vera but didn't see her. Everyone who had not run off was lying on the ground, moaning or kneeling with their hands over their heads.

"Boxer is hurt," Wren told Manx and Karry. "I need to see if he is okay." She ran toward the tree circle.

Lester was dazed and stumbling around, holding his head in his hands. He was still seeing stars from the crazy bird attack. When he saw Wren coming toward him, he pointed and screamed, "Stay away from me."

True to himself, Lester turned and retreated to the old truck. He jumped inside, scooted behind the steering wheel, and started it up. He jerked the lever down, and the old truck zigzagged down the road.

Ray watched Lester escape and shouted, "Lester is getting away!"

Battle turned to see the old truck disappear around the curve in the road.

"No, he's not!" Battle yelled and handed his staff to Ray.

In two swift steps, Battle changed into a wide, armor-plated mastiff and chased after Lester.

"Amazing," Ray exclaimed.

Battle was not as fast a runner as Boxer, but he had stamina, and he knew he would eventually catch up with the truck. Lester turned onto a small road, heading for the narrow trail that led to the caves.

Battle was gaining on the truck, mainly due to Lester's bad driving. Lester was having trouble keeping the truck on the road. He drove into ruts on one side and then swerved to the other side, slowing down the truck. As the truck made the turn onto the narrow trail, Battle ran up.

Lester looked out the window and gasped at the size of the armor-plated gray mastiff. He recognized the animal's piercing blue eyes. At the orphanage he had sat across the table from Battle during meals.

Battle slammed into the driver's door, causing the truck to slide off the trail and roll over. Battle heard Lester scream as the truck started to tumble down the steep hill. On the second roll, Barten flew from the back, hit the ground, and rolled after the truck.

Satisfied that Lester's threat was over, Battle turned and trotted back to the orphanage. He reached the tree circle and changed. He watched Bear and Wren help Boxer stand up. Boxer looked at Battle. "Thanks for coming to my rescue. Wren told me that Karry still had Manx's bracelet."

Wren said, "Grand Pierre is almost here with the transport, and we can take Boxer home to get well."

"I've just lost some blood. I'll be okay," Boxer replied. But Wren was adamant that Boxer would need rest and she would take care of him.

As they stepped from the tree circle, Drew and Ray came up. Ray asked Battle, "Did Lester get away?"

Battle frowned. "What do you think?" he said, which caused Ray to laugh.

Grand Pierre stopped the transport. He had hurried to the work center as fast as his legs would go. Marta had met him and told him to get to the orphanage, for Lester was causing trouble again.

Grand Pierre looked around and shook his head at all the men lying on the ground. "Oh my," he said.

Drew stepped up. "My men will lock these troublemakers up and make sure they answer for what they've done. Most are good men, and I don't understand why they took part in something like this. Thankfully, Karry is not badly hurt. I'll take her to Marta myself."

"I'm sure Lester told them lies about the special ones," Grand Pierre said. He looked at Battle and asked, "Where is Lester?"

Battle answered, "He's probably at the bottom of the mountain—and Barten too." Then he told them about the truck rolling down the hill and Barten hiding in the back. "I'm sorry about the truck," he added.

Ray spoke up. "The old truck was about to be scrapped anyway. With the new fuel source the scientists showed us how to make, we can get the other vehicles running again."

Wren pulled on Grand Pierre's sleeve. "We need to get Boxer back to the facility."

Grand Pierre ordered Boxer to be placed in the front. The others could ride on the bench seat or in the back, since there was no cage on the spare transport. He agreed to meet Drew the following day at the work center, and then he climbed into the transport and drove away.

As the transport rolled down the road, the special ones could feel everyone staring at them. Nothing would be the same, and they felt even more separated from the people of Freedom.

It was a quiet ride back up the mountain to the facility.

Bunny's SOS

CHAPTER 31

$\mathcal{I}$t was dark by the time the transport made its final turn and rolled up beside the facility and stopped. The special ones climbed out stiffly, their legs cramped from not being able to move during the slow ride from the orphanage. Bear growled as he stretched, saying that next time he would walk.

Battle helped Boxer from the transport and practically carried him to his bed, with Wren hovering over the injured Boxer to make sure he was tucked in tight. Wren turned to Grand Pierre. "Is there anything more we can do for Boxer? He's lost a lot of blood and is very weak."

Grand Pierre placed his hand on Wren's shoulder and replied, "Rest is the best thing for Boxer right now, and plenty of food to replenish his energy. His body will replace the lost blood, and his condition is not as bad as it looks. I checked his vital signs before we left the orphanage, and his heart is pumping enough blood for a good pulse. He just needs to rest for a few days."

Grand Pierre patted Wren's shoulder and looked at the other children. "You did what was required to save Boxer," he told them. "You worked as a team to protect each other, and I am proud of each of you." He paused for a moment and then said, "I will meet with Drew tomorrow at the work center and sort out what happened with Karry—and Lester's part in it. I'm not sure what the future will hold for us in Freedom. Now to bed, and get some sleep." After a final check of Boxer's vital signs, the tall man turned and walked from the boys' dorm.

Dent came up beside Wren and assured her, "Don't worry about Boxer. I'll keep a close watch on him tonight." Then each of the children found their beds, collapsed into them, and fell into exhausted sleep—with the exception of Dent.

Grand Pierre did not go to his room. He knew he would not sleep. He was concerned about the future and the special ones' welfare, now that their secrets were revealed. Instead he went to the comm room to check on the equipment. Neither he nor Manx had looked at the readouts that day. He had left the facility right behind Bear and Manx and had loped down the narrow mountain road to the work center as fast as his long legs would allow.

Grand Pierre quietly shut the door to the boys' dorm as he had done when he'd left the girls' dorm. All the children were asleep. Boxer's breathing was good, and his pulse was strong. The healing powers the children had inherited from their Ulterion regeneration ability, combined with their animal restorative properties, was amazing. He had watched the children as they grew up. Whenever they were injured, it did not take long for them to heal and return to the practice sessions. Maileen had marveled at their quick recovery time, saying she had never seen anything like it on Ulterion.

Grand Pierre greatly missed Maileen and the other scientists and their in-depth discussions regarding their work at the secret facility. The children were highly intelligent, each inheriting distinct cloned characteristics combined with their animal traits. Somehow the large mastiff dog that was combined with Battle's military clone had created a wide armored-plated animal with massive strength. Grand Pierre had puzzled over the reason for this for a long time, but with all of the research material destroyed in the raid, it was a puzzle he would never be able to solve.

Dent was the exception, for he had mastered all the skills. The written language on Ulterion had not used individuals characters for as far back as Grand Pierre could recall. Their written communication had advanced to a single picture or diagram that could hold the same amount of information as a page of text. He wanted to test a theory on Dent. If the boy was challenged, would he be able to communicate with Bunny and the other ulta-minds? Grand Pierre sighed out loud. He wished he could have this discussion with Francine because he missed her most of all.

Dawn was breaking when Grand Pierre drove the transport from the facility down the narrow road to the work center. He wasn't sure how to approach Drew regarding the special ones and their abilities. Grand Pierre had seen that the men involved in the attack on Boxer—those who had lain on the ground, wounded—would recover from their injuries, which caused him to wonder why. Why had the special ones held back? And why had Boxer allowed himself to be harmed? Each of the children had the ability to escape harm, even if it meant killing their attackers. Boxer could easily have escaped his injury, but he had held back. Even Bear had maintained control of his massive strength, and this greatly surprised him. Grand Pierre decided he would asked the special ones about this when he returned from Freedom.

Grand Pierre finally reached the work center, and he was worried about whether the aged transport would have enough fuel for the trip back. As he stepped from the transport, he could smell Marta's cooking, and he realized how hungry he was. He had not eaten since first meal yesterday. He smiled when he thought about how Wren's cooking had improved. The rolls she baked now were soft like the ones Maileen had made, and they went well with the wild berry spread Wren had accidently created.

Grand Pierre walked into the work center and followed the aroma to the kitchen. Drew and Ray were seated at a table, enjoying a steaming cup of the strong, brown brew they drank each morning. Drew glanced up at Grand Pierre as he sat down and noted, "Piers, you look like you didn't get much sleep last night."

Grand Pierre uttered, "More like *no* sleep. I may try a cup of that coffee that gets you going in the morning. You look in need a double dose yourself."

Marta brought Grand Pierre a large mug filled with steaming coffee and told them, "Breakfast will be finished soon, and I'll bring you each a plate." She turned to Grand Pierre and said, "Tell Boxer and the others how grateful I am to them for rescuing Karry again. I'm so sorry Boxer was hurt. Lester and his kind should be put in a cage and never allowed out." Marta turned and stomped back to the kitchen.

At the mention of Lester, Grand Pierre gave Drew a questioning look. Drew explained, "Some men found the truck, along with Lester and Barten, at the bottom edge of the caves. They carried them back to Freedom, but neither will be walking soon, if ever. Both were pretty banged up from the truck going over the hill. The rest of Lester's gang are locked up, and the council will decide what to do with them after a review of their actions. The main problem is that most of the men were not aware that Lester had kidnapped Karry in order to trap Boxer. Ray tells me that Lester and Boxer have a history from their stay at the orphanage."

As he listened to Drew, Grand Pierre nodded. "I'm sure the council will sort out the details and deal fairly with the men," he said. "My concern is about how the people will feel about the children now that their secrets have been revealed."

Ray spoke up. "It shouldn't make any difference. You, the other scientists, and the special ones played a critical part in defeating the robots and helping to rebuild Freedom."

Grand Pierre smiled at Ray and told him, "You have been a good friend to Battle and the others, and you know them better than anyone else in Freedom. Too many people living here do not know the children and will fear them because of their special abilities."

Drew added, "Ray and I will go before the council and tell them what Lester did."

Grand Pierre replied, "That is all good, but I have other news to tell you. The children and I will be leaving Freedom as soon as Boxer is recovered enough to travel."

Ray looked startled and started to protest, but Drew spoke first. "There is no need to make a decision yet. I'm sure the council will be reasonable about allowing you to stay in Freedom."

"I am firm on my decision," said Grand Pierre. "I worry about the trouble Lester or his kind could still cause, and if we leave, that will neutralize any further problems from him." He stood up and started to leave.

Drew jumped up and exclaimed, "We will always have someone like Lester to deal with. Running away with the children is not the answer."

Grand Pierre held his hand out to Drew. "Oh, we are not running away," he said. "We're returning to Ulterion."

When Ray heard this, he grabbed the table, stood up, and shouted, "No!" Marta stood frozen in shock, holding three plates of food, and echoed Ray's cry, not believing her ears. Drew and Grand Pierre shook hands good-bye, and Grand Pierre walked to the transport and drove back to the facility.

When Grand Pierre entered the facility, he could hear the children talking and followed their voices to the kitchen. He frowned when he saw Boxer seated at the table. Wren was busy fixing food, but she turned around when Grand Pierre entered. They all stopped talking and watched him walked over to Boxer. "Do you think it is wise to be up this soon?" he questioned.

"I couldn't stay in bed any longer," Boxer answered. "I promised Wren I would sit here until the food was ready and then go back to bed after we eat."

Grand Pierre's voice held concern. "Just do not tire yourself until you completely recover."

"He won't," Wren answered for Boxer, and from the stern look on her face, Grand Pierre knew Boxer would be under Wren's constant monitoring. Grand Pierre thought Wren's actions mirrored that of a mother hen tending her chicks.

"Since we are all together, I have some news to tell everyone," Grand Pierre said. "Please take a seat, and Wren can join us as soon as she is done preparing the food." He pulled a chair from the table and sat down across from Boxer as the others took places at the table. They waited, not saying a word, anxious to learn the outcome of his trip to Freedom.

"Last night after everyone went to sleep, I went to the comm room." Grand Pierre's words caused Manx to gasp, for she had completely forgotten to check the monitors. Everyone looked at Grand Pierre; the mention of the comm room had their attention. "There was a message from Francine," he went on. "It was garbled, but I was able to make out most of it. Our equipment is not that great at displaying the symbols correctly." Grand Pierre paused, trying to decide what to say next.

"What was the message?" Boxer asked.

"Did they arrive safely?" Bear growled.

Grand Pierre held up his hand to stop the barrage of questions and continued. "Bunny is requesting our help. I could not interpret all of the message, but it seems the ulta-minds are trapped below ground and are running out of breathable air. Bunny must have heard their distress calls. Francine is asking us to return to Ulterion and help them. Apparently the war with the rogues is not over."

Everyone sat in silence until Dent asked, "How can we travel in space?" He stared hard at Grand Pierre, knowing that the tall man already had the answer.

Grand Pierre cleared his throat, not usually at a loss for words. "There is a way—at least Francine thinks there is."

Grand Pierre sighed. He was tired after the ordeal with Lester yesterday, the trip to the work center today, and now this new dilemma. "Let's eat our meal before it's cold, and I'll explain while we eat." Wren dished up the food, and everyone began to eat.

Grand Pierre explained between bites about going with Francine and Berne to inspect the warship the robots had arrived in. Berne had concluded that there was no reason the warship could not return to Ulterion. They only needed to update the data in the control panel, and the warship would return to its original location. Berne had said that the ship's technology was the same as theirs. The rogues had not developed any new spaceships, spending their resources on creating a rogue that could regenerate its cells and live forever. Francine had said that the return coordinates were stored in the communication device, and all they had to do was upload the new information. Grand Pierre had had no further conversations about the warship because of the arrival of Aeron and the rush to return to Ulterion.

Grand Pierre had no answers to the children's questions: How were they to update the warship with the new data? Was he sure the warship would fly? What would happen if the warship got off course? Would they survive on Ulterion if the atmosphere was no longer breathable?

Grand Pierre told the children they should discuss this matter among themselves and then sleep on their decision before choosing to take the risk and return to Ulterion—or to stay in Freedom. Grand Pierre said he would meet them in the morning. Each one would have an equal vote to decide what they would do, but he was certain of their decision. Grand Pierre walked to his room, lay down on his bed, closed his eyes, and instantly fell asleep.

CHAPTER 32

$\mathcal{T}$he special ones did not go to sleep but met in the boys' dorm. They all had questions that could not be answered. Could the warship be programmed to fly to Ulterion, or—as Battle suggested—would it miss its target? What was the actual status on Ulterion? Were the rogues in control? Were there more of the robotic machines than Aeron had said there were? If the ultra-minds, the most brilliant scientists, were in trouble, what about everyone else on planet? Bear worried about Bunny and Francine and whether they were safe. With all the unknowns and what-ifs discussed that night, not one of the children mentioned wanting to stay in Freedom where they were no longer welcome.

The following morning when Grand Pierre walked into the kitchen, Wren said, "Breakfast is almost ready." Manx was helping dish out the food, and the boys were seated around the table. Boxer looked recovered from his injuries; color had returned to his face, and his dark eyes looked alert. The meal was late because the children had discussed their return to Ulterion late into the night, and in the early morning hours they had finally fallen asleep sprawled on the floor in the boys' room. Grand Pierre had overslept too, and he felt rested and ready to tackle the day. At least that was what he had told himself when he'd climbed from his bed.

Everyone finished eating, carried their plates from the table, and waited for Grand Pierre to speak. Finally he asked, "Have you come to a decision, or do we take a vote?"

Boxer answered for the special ones. "No vote is required. We are all in agreement."

"Is your decision for Adoran or Ulterion?"

They answered in unison, "Ulterion."

"Good, good." Grand Pierre was pleased. He knew that all of the children had their doubts but were willing to risk their lives to travel to a strange planet and an unknown situation to help the ulta-minds. "We must put together a plan and list all the tasks that need to be accomplished and who is responsible for each task. Boxer will be the task leader and will document each step: who is responsible, and when the task is completed. Dent and Manx will assist me with the technical items. Wren, you are in charge of stocking the warship with the necessary supplies for the trip. Battle and Bear will guard the facility and escort us to and from the warship. When others in Freedom learn of our leaving, they may try to get even for some of the injured men, so we need to be cautious and not let our guard down at this critical time. Each of you go and document what you think needs to be accomplished in your specific area to ensure our safe return to Ulterion. We will meet back here in four hours to combine the tasks and add any details that may have been missed."

Grand Pierre watched as the children stood and left the room. He let out a sigh of relief. He too had concerns about the return trip, as neither he nor the children had the knowledge to fly the spaceship that had carried the robots to

Adoran. Before she'd left, Francine had said she was certain that when the return coordinates were updated, the ship would fly itself. If Grand Pierre trusted anyone with his life and the lives of the special ones, it was Francine. He knew that she would not have requested them to return if she'd had any doubts. Grand Pierre stood and walked to the comm room. He needed to verify the return coordinates Francine had programmed into the communication device.

When everyone met back in the kitchen, it was Dent's list that made everyone gasp. The paper was as long as he was tall, with multiple sheets taped together. Dent had captured even the smallest detail required to fly the warship to Ulterion. The first item on his list was for Grand Pierre, Manx, and Dent: they would go and inspect the warship, as it had been some time since Grand Pierre had been there with Francine and Berne. Dent had searched through the stored boxes from the rogues' headquarters and had removed any papers that referenced the warship. One drawing detailed how to secure the robots to the ship's walls for transport. They would have to hike to the landing site, as it was beyond the mountain that hid the facility, and the old transport would never make the trip. The last action for Dent's first item was for Battle to accompany them to carry the heavy device.

Boxer finished writing all the steps to complete item number one and looked at Grand Pierre, who nodded his head that item number one looked complete.

In a few hours the kitchen walls were covered with papers, each one listing the different tasks to be completed in specific order. Boxer was in charge of each of the lists and was to track them to completion. Boxer understood how critical each item was to the mission, and he was grateful to have Grand

Pierre's assistance. The most critical tasks were the technical ones assigned to Grand Pierre, Manx, and Dent. If they could not figure out how to update the controls of the warship and ensure it was done correctly, the mission would be scrapped.

Wren had done a good job detailing the supplies they needed, even giving everyone the task of packing their personal possessions. Battle and Bear outlined how they would guard the facility and who would be on patrol both night and day. When Battle accompanied the others to the warship, Bear would cover his patrol. Boxer felt at ease having Battle and Bear on guard duty.

Boxer stood and stretched and then bent down and inspected his leg. The wound had almost healed, but he would carry a scar from the sharpened stick. It had been an interesting discussion with Grand Pierre the night before. None of the special ones had an answer as to why they had not used deadly force on the men with Lester.

Battle explained that it had been different from dealing with the unfeeling robots who killed on command. He'd had no problem with permanently disabling them. Battle said that some of the men were friends of Ray's who had been fooled by Lester. Once Lester was no longer a threat, Battle hadn't felt the need to inflict further injury. Everyone agreed with Battle's assessment, saying that once Boxer was safe, they only needed to control the situation.

It took two days for Dent to figure out the control panel on the warship and for Manx and Grand Pierre to align the symbols to match the pattern that Francine had shown them. Each day Battle accompanied them on the hike to the warship and back, in case anyone from Freedom was hiding, waiting to ambush them. But they had been left alone.

Wren spent a day inventorying the medical supplies, and she stored them in boxes ready to load into the warship. One night she sent Bear to gather nuts, berries, and vegetables for the trip. From Grand Pierre's estimate, they would be in flight for four or five days, and Wren needed food that would not spoil during the trip. The rogues did not require food, so the warship did not have storage units for food. Everyone was responsible for their own clothes and sleeping needs. This led to Bear being teased by the others, who said that he would be happy to sleep on the ship's floor instead of a bed. Bear enjoyed his comfortable bed and would miss it, but he would never admit that to the others.

That night after evening meal, Boxer reported that tomorrow they would begin loading the warship, and the following day they would board the warship and leave for Ulterion. On the day of the vote to return to Ulterion, Grand Pierre and Manx had sent a communication to Francine, saying that they were coming. So far, they had not received an acknowledgment. That had been five days ago. When Grand Pierre mentioned it, it only made the children more determined to get to Ulterion.

All of them had finished eating their evening meal and were sitting around the table discussing the day's accomplishments, when Boxer raised his hand and signaled for quiet. He had heard something coming up the road to the facility. It was a new sound, and he wasn't sure what it was, but it was mechanical. He motioned for Battle and Bear to check the perimeter, and then he looked at Manx and Wren. Both glared across the table at him and shook their heads no; they would not hide in the lab. If there was another attack on the facility, they would stay and defend it. Everyone sat in silence until Bear stepped into the room and signaled all clear.

"It's Ray on a contraption he made from one of the robotic platforms," Bear said as they all walked from the room to go and meet Ray. "It's a strange-looking ride, but it got him here."

Dent circled Ray's ride twice before asking, "What gave you the idea to use just one of the tracks from the robot's platform?"

Ray grinned. "Battle told me about the platform spinning on the ground on its side and the man who developed the haulers helped me design this. The small motor is inside the frame that holds the track in place, and I mounted the seat to the frame. I can steer it with this crossbar. It doesn't make sharp turns, but I can go almost anywhere on it."

Ray took a small package from his shirt and walked to Manx and handed it to her. "This is from Karry. She said to tell you thank you for saving her again."

Manx opened the package, saw her bracelet, and slipped it on her wrist. She opened the folded paper inside. It was a drawing Karry had made of a yellow cat. The cat was out of proportion, but Manx could tell the picture was of her. She smiled at Ray and said, "Please tell Karry I love the picture."

After the others went back inside, Ray and Battle talked for a long time. Finally Ray mentioned that it was dark and he should get back. Ray looked up at the stars in the night sky and asked, "Do you think sometime in the future we might meet again?"

Battle placed his hand on Ray's shoulder and replied, "I don't know, but it's a good thought to keep."

"Watch out for the robots when you get to Ulterion," Ray cautioned as he rode off.

The next morning everyone was finishing breakfast when Bear entered the kitchen and told them, "I found no signs that anyone has been around the facility or the warship. I'll go and keep watch as soon as I eat. If I see anyone, I'll signal, but you can start loading this morning."

Boxer stepped over to the list and made a check mark. Then he turned back and said, "If we make one trip today and one tomorrow, the ship will be loaded and ready to go. Tomorrow we will take the final items with us when we leave." His words echoed a point of no return, and they would leave Adoran forever.

↴↳ ↴↳

"Is everything secured?" Boxer asked, looking around the storage room of the warship. Wren had crates of food, containers of water, and medical supplies stacked on one side of the room. Each of the special ones' personal items were buckled in their assigned areas, making use of the sturdy straps that had held the robots on their flight to Adoran.

After checking one final time, Bear gave Boxer the signal that everything was good.

"We are ready when you are," Boxer told Grand Pierre.

Grand Pierre, Dent, and Manx completed the transfer of data to the warship's control panel. Dent had spent hours reviewing the ship's technical manuals, memorizing the various signals that would blink if something needed attention or—worst case—stopped working. After one final check of the flight coordinates to make sure they aligned with the ones

Francine had left them, Dent turned to Grand Pierre and said, "It's a go."

Dent and Grand Pierre agreed that there was no chance for a test flight because they were unsure of the fuel requirements to reach Ulterion.

Grand Pierre turned from the control panel and announced, "Please take your places and buckle in. I'm not sure how smooth our takeoff will be. Once we have cleared the Adoran atmosphere, you will be able to move about." He turned back to the control panel and told Dent, "Start the engines."

Dent held his breath in anticipation as he turned the power switch. The warship shuddered after years of sitting idle. Then the ship seemed to come to life, and with a shake, it rose from the ground. Dent looked out the window as the ground below became distant. He knew there was no going back.

When the ship began to gain speed as the engines accelerated and Adoran grew smaller and smaller, no one said a word. Each one was wondering what the future would hold for them.

PART III

The Return

CHAPTER 33

"Grand Pierre, do you know how long it is before we reach Ulterion," Wren asked worriedly. "This is the last of the food I was able to bring."

Grand Pierre turned from the warship's control panel and saw the concern on her face. He smiled at the youngest of the special ones. Her care and concern for the others was obvious. "I'm not sure," he said. "It's hard to determine the distance we have traveled. If Francine's calculations are correct, I would say within the next six hours, give or take." He shrugged. It was as good an answer as he could give her.

Dent was seated next to Grand Pierre and leaned out and told Wren, "We all could afford to lose a few pounds, especially Bear." This caused Bear to growl. Dent grinned and turned back to the control panel.

For the past four days since the warship had lifted from the planet of Adoran, Dent had been diligent in monitoring the controls. The only time he was not watching the flashing lights was when he caught a few hours of sleep and Grand Pierre took his place. Dent explained to the others that sleep was not a high priority for him and that he could get by with a few hours a day or night. It was not something he required. Grand Pierre commented that the larger the animal, the more sleep it required, which explained Bear's reluctance to rise early—and why no one ever volunteered to wake him. Bear liked a full night's sleep, and then some.

Manx looked up from the communication device, shook her head, and sighed. "Still no reply from Francine," she said. At regular intervals Manx sent a message to Francine that Grand Pierre and the special ones were on their way. This was so that Francine could track their progress.

Boxer unhooked the belt securing him and floated to one of the small, round windows that ringed the ship. The windows were coated with layers of grime, and he could not see anything but a blur as they moved through space. A row of lights that ran around the ceiling was their only light. Anyone but the special ones would have had trouble seeing in the dark ship. Grand Pierre had grumbled about the lack of light and spent most of his time seated at the control panel where it was brighter. There were windows at the control panel, but all maneuvering was done by the built-in guidance system. Other than watching the blinking lights, there was nothing else to do, unless something went wrong.

Boxer watched the blinking lights and asked Dent, "Do you know where to land the ship when we arrive—or even *how* to land it?"

Dent looked at Boxer. "It's a little late to ask those questions now," he said, causing Grand Pierre to chuckle and the others to stare with anxious expressions.

To ease their concern, Grand Pierre explained, "Francine programmed the landing coordinates, and the warship has automatic procedures that will take over and land the craft. I am not concerned about the landing. I'm more concerned about what we may find when we do."

Battle asked, "What should we expect when we arrive?" Grand Pierre did not have time to answer because the control panel suddenly lit up in various colors.

"We have action on the bridge!" Dent yelled. Then he added, "We must be getting close. The ship is adjusting course and speed." He could feel the ship make a slight turn, and then red lights began flashing in a circle on the panel, creating a red dot trail as one light lit after the other.

"Secure yourselves," Grand Pierre ordered as he turned to the control panel. The warship jerked as if it had run over something, and Grand Pierre said, "We have entered the Ulterion atmosphere."

The spaceship slowed and seemed to dip and turn at the same time. Then it felt like the bottomed had dropped out as the landing legs were lowered. The engines changed to a muted roar, and the spaceship slowly descended to the ground. The ship wobbled when the legs touched the planet's surface and continued to rock back and forth as the legs became secure. The engines whined as they shut down, and the lights on the panel changed to a light blue. No one moved. They sat in silence, not sure what was coming next.

Grand Pierre turned from the controls. "Welcome to Ulterion. Apparently we have arrived."

"And in one piece," Dent added. He grinned, exposing his two black teeth.

Boxer unlatched his harness and asked, "What now?"

"We need to use caution," Battle replied. "Any response from Francine?" He looked toward Manx, who shook her head.

Bear growled, "We need to find Bunny."

The special ones watched Grand Pierre lean over the control panel and look out the window. It was day, but the view outside was dark and hazy. Grand Pierre turned and asked, "Boxer, can you hear anything?"

Boxer intently listened and replied, "No. I don't hear any sounds or movement."

Grand Pierre stood, stepped to the back of the ship, and pushed the release button to open the exit door and lower the ramp. When the ramp touched the ground, Grand Pierre hesitantly stepped out of the warship and looked around in shock. "It is worse than I feared," he said.

Single file, the special ones followed the tall man out of the spaceship and down the ramp, looking around at all the destruction. The air was hazy, masking the daylight. The landing area was buckled and full of holes. There were no other spaceships on the open area that had once been a hard landing surface that could hold a dozen ships. Boxer looked around but did not see the small silver spaceship that had returned for the scientists on Adoran. Among all the piles of debris, one of the piles could have been the Ulterion ship.

"No wonder it took the warship so long to stabilize," Dent commented as he stared at all the damage.

Battle stepped beside Grand Pierre and asked, "Which way do we go? We need to find cover and not stay exposed in the open. Our landing may have alerted the rogues."

Grand Pierre motioned to Manx to bring the communicator, and he checked it again. "No response," he said and sighed.

Battle pointed across the landing area. "That building looks to be in better shape and less ruined than the others." The others stared through the haze and could see several buildings made from some type of metal. All the roofs had caved in, and most of the walls were lying on the ground.

Grand Pierre agreed. "Boxer, take the lead. Bear and Battle, bring up the rear. Everyone stay on high alert. There may be robots hiding in the buildings."

Boxer motioned for quiet and single file and then silently ran toward the building. As he ran, he listened intently for any noise that would give away the presence of robots. The others followed behind as they cautiously made their way across the torn-up surface. When they reached the side of the building, Boxer signaled to Bear and Battle to circle the building, and each ran off in a different direction. The others stood with their backs to the wall of the building, careful not to make any sound that could give them away, and waited for Bear and Battle to return from their reconnaissance. Bear and Battle appeared at the same time, and both gave the *all clear* sign. Manx exhaled a loud sigh, not realizing she had been holding her breath.

Boxer whispered, "Let's get inside." He quietly moved around the side of the building and entered through an opening that had once been a door. After they were inside, he looked toward Grand Pierre and whispered, "What's our next move? Apparently Francine did not receive our communication and is not aware that we are here."

Grand Pierre looked around the ravaged building and sadly shook his head. "This was one of the atmosphere units, but the equipment has been ruined."

Dent walked over to get a closer look. "These look like monitoring systems."

"They were used to control the air quality," Grand Pierre explained.

"They can't have been working for some time," Boxer noted. "The air is barely breathable."

"Things are much worse than I thought," Grand Pierre said with a sigh.

"This planet is nothing like Adoran," Wren remarked. "Adoran was beautiful, with trees and flowers and blue sky."

"Long ago Ulterion was a lush planet like Adoran," Grand Pierre told Wren.

"Didn't anyone care?" Wren grumbled.

"For too many years the people were caught up in their own pursuits and did not protect the planet," Grand Pierre explained. "They were intent on having their own way, and they used any means to get it, even if it meant destroying the environment."

"Quiet," Boxer ordered. He signaled that he had heard something and motioned for them to take cover. Grand Pierre and the others hid behind the ruined equipment, silently watching Boxer creep to a broken wall, make his way outside, and disappear around the corner. It seemed to take forever before he returned, for waiting was not something the special ones excelled at—except Battle.

Francine appeared in the blown-out doorway and exclaimed, "Piers, you made it."

Grand Pierre stepped from behind a piece of equipment and called out "Francine" and hurried to her. The special ones watched Grand Pierre hug Francine tightly, but they made no comment about the embrace. Two men stepped inside the building. By their looks, they could have been younger brothers to Grand Pierre. Both were dressed in gray uniforms and carried strange-looking weapons strapped around their shoulders. Neither man said a word as they guarded the door. They were part of a military unit.

"I could not respond to your communications because most of our equipment was destroyed by the robots," Francine said. "They attacked one of our underground entrances and rolled bombs inside. I was able to receive, but I could not reply. Manx, you did an outstanding job of sending the updates, and I was able to track your progress. I'm so glad everyone made it safely." She smiled at the special ones.

Bear stepped forward and growled, "What about Bunny? Is she okay?"

Francine looked at Bear and answered, "Bunny is fine and is waiting for us, but we must hurry and get underground."

CHAPTER 34

$\mathcal{F}$rancine told everyone to follow the soldiers; it wasn't far to one of the underground entrances. One sentry led the way, and the other brought up the rear, and neither said a word. Battle could see some type of transmitting device attached to their uniforms, and each sentry had a receiver in one ear. Battle knew the sentries were on high alert and would not break silence without cause. Their concentration was on getting everyone safely underground. Welcoming the special ones to Ulterion was not their job.

The sentry led the way, zigzagging between bombed-out buildings. They stopped at a structure that stood alone at the far end of the line of buildings. They carefully checked the surrounding area and, after verifying that there were no robots inside, pushed aside a rusted grate that was hidden behind the building. One sentry leaned down and turned a handle, and a round metal plate slowly lifted up. The sentry warned, "The steps are steep. Hold on to the rail." Francine led the way down the steep entrance.

"This must be an escape hatch," Dent whispered to Manx as he followed her down the dark, narrow stairs. Wren and Boxer came next, followed by Bear, Battle, and Grand Pierre. The sentry moved the grate back to cover the entrance and secured the hatch. The only way the hatch could be opened was from the inside. The steep stairs ended in a long corridor that was dimly lit by small recessed orbs. Francine led the way to an open area that connected with three other passages. The lead sentry stepped up to Francine and told her they would return to their posts. After Francine thanked the guards for their assistance, they walked down one of the corridors.

"Once you learn the underground routes, you will be able to find your way around," Francine said. She pointed and explained, "Each corridor is labeled with a symbol of where it leads, and if the symbols are doubled or tripled, they will eventually branch off. Once you are settled in, I'll have someone teach you how to find your way around. Underground, you can reach all the various facilities and laboratories if you follow the symbols."

Francine led the way down a wide corridor and eventually stopped at a door with a symbol over the top. She turned and explained, "Piers said that you would feel more comfortable staying together in your own living chamber." Francine opened the door and stepped into a room with a sitting area and a table with six chairs. She pointed to a door on one side. "The boys' beds are in that room, and the girls' beds are there. All the items you need have been supplied."

Wren gasped. "We left our clothes and medicine on the ship!"

"Our medicine is far advanced," Francine said, "and your new uniforms are suited for the underground environment, lint- and static-free. You must wear them at all times. Now, Piers and I must go to meet with the controller. Welcome to your new home." She turned and walked from the room, and Grand Pierre followed her.

The special ones looked around. The sitting room was small, and the walls were bare, giving the room a vacant feeling. The furnishings were basic and did not look comfortable. Manx turned to Wren. "Let's find our beds," she said and opened the door to the room where the girls would sleep. It was half the size of the sitting room, with two beds built into each side. Each bed held a mattress, but there were no colorful quilts or pillows.

Drawers were built next to the beds, and Manx opened one, anxious to see the uniforms they were to wear. She lifted out a light, one-piece garment that zipped in the front. It looked much like the blue one Francine wore but was beige in color. The uniform had multiple pockets, and straps at the wrists and ankles. In the next drawer she found shoes—more like slippers—with rubberized strips on the bottom. She held up the uniform and shoes and looked at Wren. "Lint- and static-free. What more could we ask for?"

Wren wrinkled her face. "I'm not sure I like it here. And I don't like those uniforms. They're ugly and will make us look like boys. If I hold out my arms and take one step either way, I can touch the walls of our room." She plopped down on one of the beds and bounced. "At least the bed feels comfortable," she said.

Manx had not known what to expect, but she still felt disappointed with their new home. Even the caves back on Adoran had been fun and comfortable. She could tell that Wren was not happy either. "Let's go see if the boys' room is any better." She held her hand out to Wren.

When the girls stepped into the sitting area, all the boys were standing around. Manx looked at Dent, sure he would have something to say. Dent frowned, shook his head, and said, "Our room may be big enough for Bear. I'm not sure where the rest of us will sleep."

Boxer added, "The room is frugal. I don't think we'll be spending a lot of time here."

Battle said, "It feels military."

Bear growled.

They were all grumbling about their "underground digs," as Dent called it, when they heard a knock on the door. Wren hopped over, opened the door, and exclaimed, "Bunny!" Wren pulled the blonde-haired girl inside and hugged her. Everyone hurried over to greet Bunny. Bear lifted Bunny and cradled her in his large arms. Bunny reached out and placed a hand on the side of Bear's face, and tears sparkled in her eyes.

Bear set Bunny back down, and Manx asked, "Where are you staying?"

Bunny signed that she was staying with Francine.

"Come and sit down," Manx invited. "We have dozens of questions, and maybe you can answer them." She pulled Bunny to the sitting area, and the girls sat on the built-in sofa. The boys pulled the chairs from the table.

Wren reached over and took Bunny's hand and asked, "Do you like it here?" Bunny wrinkled her nose and then signed that it was okay.

Manx noticed that Bunny's suit was yellow. It was Manx's favorite color, and she asked, "Why is your suit yellow and ours is this blah color." She made a face when she mentioned the color being "blah," making Bunny silently laugh.

Bunny signed that yellow was for the ultas and that each team was given a different color.

"When we are assigned to a team, we will get colored suits?" Manx confirmed, and Bunny nodded her head.

Battle said, "I wish Francine would return and let us know our assignments."

"Francine said they were to meet with the controller," Dent said. "Bunny, do you know the controller?"

Bunny nodded, made a large circle with her hands, and signed that the controller was in charge of everything.

"He must be the big cheese in this underground maze," Dent remarked.

Bunny laughed and signed that she had missed Dent's funny words.

Bear growled, "I'm hungry. Where is the kitchen?"

Bunny looked puzzled and then signed, *no kitchen*, causing Bear to gasp, "Where do we find food?" Bunny gave Bear a puzzled looked and signed that in the morning everyone was given their day's supply.

"What? We don't get food until tomorrow morning?" Bear complained loudly, and Bunny nodded that he was correct.

"I think we are going to find many differences living here," Boxer told the group. "It won't be like it was on Adoran. We'd better prepare ourselves for a lot of changes."

Bunny nodded her head, agreeing with Boxer.

"When Francine sent for us, she said that the request came from you and that the ulta-minds were trapped underground and needed help," Battle said. "What can you tell us?"

Bunny's face became solemn, and she looked down.

"If it will upset you, you don't have to tell us," Battle added quickly.

Bunny looked up and shook her head. She signed that she could hear the ultas in her mind. She wasn't sure what they were saying, but she could tell that they were in trouble.

Francine had alerted the controller, and he had sent a military unit to check on them. They found that the robots had sealed the ultas' escape hatch and were guarding it. The ultas' communications were damaged when the robots broke in and bombed the underground facility. The blast sealed off the ultas' research unit, and the escape exit was the only way to get them out.

Battle had one final question. "Can you still hear them?"

Bunny signed faintly, which told Battle that the ultas were in trouble and running out of breathable air.

Battle looked at the others. "Maybe we can get to the ultas from outside and open their escape exit and free them. We just need to be shown where to go."

Bunny quickly signed *no*; the robots were guarding the exit.

Battle looked at Bunny. "That's too bad for the robots. We know how to take them out, and they won't be expecting us. We need to find Grand Pierre quickly."

Bunny stood up and motioned for the others to follow her. She would take them to the chamber where she lived with Francine. Maybe Grand Pierre would be there.

"It beats sitting here, waiting," Battle said, and he followed Bunny out into the corridor just as Grand Pierre came walking toward them. Everyone moved back into the small room, and Battle held the door open.

Once inside, Grand Pierre told them, "The controller will assign each of you to a team. Wren will be the exception because of her age. Manx will assist Francine, and Wren will accompany her. Bunny is also staying with Francine, since the ultas are sealed off. The boys are considered adults and capable of assisting in their assigned areas. There have been no children born in over fifty years, and there are no facilities left to take care of them."

Battle asked, "Does the controller understand the need to act fast because the ultas may not survive much longer?"

Grand Pierre replied, "The controller said there is a team trying to clear the damaged corridor and reach the ultas, but the equipment is old and has not been kept up, so they have not been successful."

Battle said, "We can rescue them."

Grand Pierre sighed. "The controller wasn't interested in you or your special talents, or the failed project on Adoran. That is what he called it: a failed project. He didn't think any of you would be of value to Ulterion, and he gave Francine trouble for sending for us without letting him know because of the added burden of housing and feeding us. With the dwindling population, there has been no need for further expansion. The controller said we are in survival mode and dealing with the results of the extended war with the rogues. I will learn tomorrow about your assignments and will see you then." Grand Pierre turned and left the room.

Battle clenched his fists and told the others, "We can't let the ultas die, no matter what the controller said. If we can get outside and find the hatch the robots are guarding, I'm sure we can rescue the ultas."

"It sounds like we have our first mission on Ulterion," Boxer said. "We can follow our own scent back to the escape hatch."

"I understand the signs to find our way around underground," Dent said. "It's not that difficult, and I can teach you to read and speak Ulterion."

"It's critical that we find our way underground and understand what is being said," Battle said, "but that will come after we rescue the ultas."

Bear said, "I can find my way around once we are outside, and Bunny should be able to hear the ultas more clearly. Then I can find the exit." Bunny nodded her head and signed, *Count me in*.

Dent grinned. "Let's do this. The Secret Six plus one Bunny." He held out his hand with the palm up, and one by one the others stacked their hand onto his until the stack was seven high.

The Choice

CHAPTER 35

$\mathcal{T}$he mission wasn't as detailed as Boxer wanted it to be, but they all understood the tasks they were responsible for. They were aware that they were on their own, especially after the controller had made it clear that their help was not wanted. The plan was as complete as they could make it without any maps of the outside area.

The special ones waited for Bunny to return from her chamber after Francine fell asleep. She had signed that everyone stayed in their chambers at night, so the long corridors would be empty. When she returned, they would find the exit they had entered earlier that day. Once outside, Bunny would listen for the ultas, but she would not be able to communicate with them, as she had not learned their language. By learning the direction their thoughts came from, Bear would have an idea of where to start looking for the escape hatch the robots were guarding.

Boxer looked at Wren and told her, "You will wait in the chamber. You don't have an assignment."

Wren glared at Boxer and firmly answered, "I am a member of this team just like everyone else, and I will take part in the mission!"

From Wren's glare and tone of voice, Boxer knew that Wren would not stay behind, and he relented. "You can stay with Bunny and keep watch when we go to rescue the ultas."

Dent looked at Manx, and his look clearly said that Wren had won that battle.

After the tension lessened, Bear quietly asked Boxer, "Why are you against Wren coming on the mission?"

"If anything happened to Wren, I could never forgive myself," Boxer admitted. "I've watched out for her since we escaped the attack on the laboratory. I feel responsible for her."

Bear nodded his shaggy head. "I understand. I feel the same about Bunny."

There was a tap on the door, and the special ones quietly lined up. With Dent in the lead, they made their way to the exit. After they'd climbed out the hatch, Battle closed it and pulled the grate back in place, as there was no way to secure it from the outside.

Boxer listened and then motioned the others to follow. He led the way around the side of the damaged building. Through the haze, he faintly made out the row of buildings they had passed that morning.

Boxer whispered, "From the position of the buildings, it looks like the underground city is aligned with them. Bear, take Bunny to the closest building, and see if she can hear the ultas. If not, continue on to the next one. Be careful. There may be robots hiding."

Bear nodded that he understood. He lifted Bunny in his arms and silently ran toward the first building.

It was eerily dark outside. The residue from the underground exhausts caused the air to move about like ghosts floating low to the ground. At times, various colors could be seen in the exhaled chemicals. Wren shivered, and Manx placed her arm around Wren's shoulders. Manx didn't like being outside in the gassy, swamp-looking scene either.

Manx looked up, not sure what she was expecting to see through the thick smog. Was she hoping to see one of the moons that circled the planet? On their return in the warship, Grand Pierre had told them that Ulterion had three moons, one very large and two smaller ones. At times when there were breaks in the atmosphere, he had been able to see the larger moon, but the air had become so bad that the smaller ones could only be seen from the large telescope located on the high bluff above the city. He added that the robots had destroyed the telescope before he'd left on the scientific mission to Adoran. Manx sighed. She could see nothing beyond the black mist.

Bear reached the nearest building and set Bunny down. She stood statue-like and listened. Then she looked at Bear and motioned that she thought she had heard a small sound. Bear glanced toward the next building, and not seeing any movement through the thick haze, he lifted Bunny and silently ran to the next crumbling structure. He set Bunny on the ground, and she squeezed his arm and nodded: she could hear them.

Bunny turned her head until she could clearly make out the direction of the sound she heard in her mind. She pointed to the way the communication was coming.

Bear studied the area. There were no buildings in the direction Bunny pointed. He memorized the torn-up ground and, satisfied that he could find his way back, lifted Bunny and silently ran back to the others.

Bear told Boxer, "I can find the ultas' exit, but there could be robots hiding in the last three buildings at the end of the road. We need to scout these buildings before we rescue the ultas."

Battle whispered, "Even if the robots pick up our movement, they may not react if we don't match their programming."

"I don't want to take that chance," Boxer replied. "Let's change and search the buildings in animal form. The robots on Adoran were not concerned about animals, and they ignored the cats and dogs as non-threats."

"Do you think there are any animals left here?" Manx asked. "If the robots detect a strange being, wouldn't they report it?" But no one knew the answer.

"I agree with Boxer," Dent said. "We'll be able to maneuver better as animals, and when we reach the buildings, I can get in without being seen."

They agreed to change and make their way to the buildings at the far end of road. As the gray rat, Dent would sneak in and see if there were robots hiding there. Wren would stand watch and wait with Bunny for them to return.

The first two buildings were empty, and after Dent confirmed that there were no robots hiding there, the others went inside and looked around. Battle changed and pointed at the ground, noticing indentations made by the guards' platforms: hard evidence that robots were guarding the ultas' exit.

The third building was more open and farther away, and the wall facing the ultas' exit was missing. Boxer, Battle, and Bear were large animals, sure to be noticed when they neared the building.

Manx changed and said, "We need to create a diversion. Something to draw the robot out of the building."

Dent swiftly changed and suggested, "What if we throw something against the other wall of the building so the guard will go and investigate? Once it's outside, Battle and Bear can get in unseen."

"It could work," Manx said.

"Give me a few minutes," Dent said quickly. He changed and scurried out a hole in the wall, disappearing before anyone could protest. It would be impossible to see a dark-gray rat in the dark-gray haze.

Battle said, "If I have a clear line of sight, I can use my sweeper to cut the wires beneath the back of the robot's neck, like I did on Adoran. We can get inside while the guard goes to investigate, and surprise it when it comes back. Bear, can you get close enough to grab the guard's head and bend it forward?"

Bear growled his response.

Boxer heard a faint whistle, changed, and said, "Dent is in place, and I will be more useful with my hands."

A loud thunk, like something hitting a wall, broke the silence. Boxer, Battle, and Bear crept outside and watched a platform roll from the building. It stopped and turned from side to side, searching with its built-in spotlight. When the platform rolled away to investigate, Boxer took off running, with the others close behind.

Boxer stopped at the side of the building and leaned out; the guard had not returned. He motioned the others forward and crept inside the building.

Battle took one of the sweepers from his pocket and extended the razor-sharp blades. Boxer and Bear crept to the far wall, and Battle hugged the side where they'd entered. If Bear could bend the guard's head forward, Battle would launch the sweeper under the metal plate.

After investigating the noise and not finding anything, the guard turned around and rolled too close to the corner of the building. One side of its platform sank into a large hole. It took the guard a couple of tries, rolling forward and then backward, to get out of the hole. Finally the guard rolled into the building—and was startled when a huge, hairy animal rose up, snarled loudly, and slammed two massive paws down onto its head to bend it forward.

In a split second, Battle launched the sweeper. The whine from the sweeper was the last sound the guard heard as its exposed wires were cut. Bear changed, and Battle stepped over and removed the sweeper from the guard's neck. Bear grabbed the guard's head in his hands and twisted until the head was pulled loose from the body. Bear glared at the head, wires dangling from the neck, and threw the head into the blackness.

Dent ran over, stared at the headless guard, and exclaimed, "Great!"

Manx walked over and asked, "Why is there only one guard watching the ultas' escape hatch? On Adoran they traveled in pairs."

Dent answered, "Francine mentioned that communication with the ultas is down, so maybe the rogues didn't know it was them trying to escape."

Battle said, "Boxer and Manx, go around back and stand watch. Bear, Dent, and I will find the exit. Signal if you see or hear anything. With the guard off-line, he may have been on a reporting cycle. We must hurry and rescue the ultas in case other guards are sent to investigate."

Manx and Boxer ran to the back of the building, and Manx changed and jumped on top of the crumbling wall to stand watch. Boxer stood below Manx, listening for any sound that would signal more robots coming.

Bear stepped from the building and studied the blown-up ground, looking for the way Bunny had pointed. When he saw the formations he had memorized, he motioned for Dent and Battle to follow.

Bear almost missed the exit hatch because it was concealed under a pile of rubble. He halted and pointed to the debris.

Battle whispered, "The ultas must have been discovered trying to escape; some type of bomb created all this mess." He began pushing clods of dirt and rocks away from a round metal cover, much like the one at the opposite end of the underground city. Bear and Dent helped, and once the debris was away from the cover, Battle reached down, pulled on the release lever, and slowly lifted the cover.

Dent whispered, "Let me go first. If the ultas see Bear coming toward them, they might die of fright."

Battle stood aside to allow Dent to descend the narrow steps. It was complete blackness at the bottom of the steps. The robots' attack had not only sealed off the ultas' laboratory, but it had destroyed their energy source, which meant no lights or air flow.

Dent paused and listened, but he heard only silence. Slowly he stepped into a corridor. The corridor led to a domed room. Dent was surprised at what he could see, but he didn't have time to investigate further. He walked to the opposite end of the large room, where double doors stood ajar. He paused and thought he heard a scraping sound. He pushed open one of the doors and stepped into a room filled with tables, shelves of equipment, desks, and chairs. He took a breath of the stale air, coughed, and spoke the Ulterion word for *attention*.

The Ulterion language did not have a word for *hello*. Aunt May had said they didn't waste time speaking nonessential words. Dent called "attention" again and said his name was Dent and that he was here to bring them to safety. *Rescue* was another word that didn't translate. As Dent waited in the doorway, a man with the same build as Grand Pierre slowly stood at one of the desks, holding onto the desk to steady himself.

Dent looked at the ulta and again repeated that he was Dent and would bring them to safety. He wasn't sure of the translation for *robots*, so he announced that the rogues were gone but that they must hurry. The room stayed silent. This ulta was the only one who had stood up. Frustrated, Dent yelled, "Can anyone understand me? We need to go."

The ulta steadied himself and haltingly walked toward Dent, trying to come to a decision about the strange being standing there. Dent had an idea and said, "Piers, Maileen, Francine, Jacques—I came with them from Adoran."

The ulta nodded his head. Dent never heard a word the ulta communicated, but more ultas began standing up.

Dent said, "We must hurry." He motioned with his arm, and the ultas started stumbling toward him. Dent wasn't sure if the ultas could see in the dark, so he kept a monologue going as he led the way back through the domed room to the exit.

"Others like me are outside. Follow them," he repeated over and over. When Dent reached the steps, he called to Battle and Bear. "There are about twenty ultas coming out. They are not in good shape, and you may have to help them out."

CHAPTER 36

*I*n their weakened condition, the ultas climbed the steep stairs slowly. Dent was diligent in urging the ultas to keep climbing. The ultas willingly accepted Battle's and Bear's assistance and were not hesitant about being lifted from the exit by two strange-looking creatures. The ulta who had stood up first waited until the others made it out before he began climbing.

Dent asked him, "Is everyone out?" The ulta nodded his head as he climbed the steep steps.

When Dent climbed from the exit, Battle told him, "We must hurry. Manx signaled that she saw something."

The ultas huddled together, taking large gulps of air. They were tall and very thin and were dressed in yellow, one-piece suits. Their suits were dirty and stained from days of being trapped underground without power, water, or fresh air. One of the ultas collapsed, and Bear caught him before he hit the ground. He lifted the unconscious scientist and started toward the building with the headless guard.

Bear called, "Follow me."

Battle grabbed hold of another ulta who tripped on the broken ground. Dent counted seventeen ultas stumbling behind Bear.

When they reached the building, Boxer and Manx ran up. Manx quickly said, "I saw something at the end of road, like a light flickering, and then it disappeared. It happened so fast, I'm not sure what it was."

With the ultas safe inside the building, Battle allowed them a short rest, giving them time to recover from their ordeal. The ulta who had waited for the others looked at the headless guard and then at Dent and nodded his head. Dent knew he was thanking them. He pointed to his companions and said, "We are glad to assist."

Battle pointed to Boxer, Manx, and Dent. "Follow the road. It will be easier for the ultas to walk and to help the ones who can't keep up. Bear and I will watch the rear."

Dent told the ultas to follow him, reassuring them that he and his friends would get them to safety. Finally able to breathe air that was not stale, some of the ultas had regained their strength as they staggered forward in the darkness. Between them, Dent and Manx supported a scientist who could barely walk, and Boxer held an ulta under each arm. The going was slow, and it seemed to take forever to reach the escape hatch.

Wren and Bunny ran from the cover of the building to meet the strange procession. Wren exclaimed, "We were becoming worried. It's almost daylight!"

Wren and Bunny each took an ulta by the hand and led them around the building to the escape hatch. The others followed behind.

Battle removed the grate and opened the hatch. "Dent, tell the ultas to hold on to the rail. The steps are steep."

Dent repeated Battle's words, and one by one the ultas slowly descended. The tall ulta waited to go last. He paused and stared at Bunny, and she gave him a hesitant smile. After everyone was inside, Battle pulled the grate back and secured the hatch. The scientists were in bad shape, and each of the special ones helped steady them as they slowly crept down the dark corridor.

When they reached the area where the corridors met, Dent said, "We need to get the ultas to medical. Bunny, can you find it?"

Before Bunny could answer, the area was brightly lit by spotlights pointing directly at them. Behind the blinding light stood sentries, all carrying weapons pointed in their direction. Dent stepped forward and held up his hands. "Do not engage your weapons," he said. "The ulta scientists are in need of medical assistance."

A commotion came from down the hall, and the guards moved aside as a tall man pushed his way to the front and shouted, "There is no threat!" Grand Pierre looked at the scientists being supported by the special ones. He turned to the guards and ordered, "Get the ultas to medical." The guards lowered their weapons and hurried to help the exhausted ultas.

Francine hurried up and exclaimed, "The ultas have been rescued!" She looked at the special ones and stated, "You were able to do what the rescue team could not after days of trying. The ultas have been saved, thanks to each of you."

Battle asked Grand Pierre, "What gave us away?"

"Apparently, the second time the hatch was opened, the sentry on duty decided to sound the alarm. When the alarm went off, I hurried to your room and found it empty. I knew then that you six—no, seven—were the cause of the alarm." Grand Pierre could not stop himself from smiling. "You have saved the most brilliant minds in Ulterion."

Grand Pierre walked with the special ones. The corridors were crowded with other Ulterions coming out of their chambers at the sound of the alarm. Manx noted all the differently colored one-piece uniforms. Grand Pierre stopped and talked with some of them, and the special ones received many astonished looks.

Back inside their chamber, Grand Pierre asked, "What caused you to move so quickly in the rescue?"

Battle explained, "Bunny's contact with the ultas was becoming so faint that she could barely hear them. We knew if they weren't rescued immediately, they would not survive."

Boxer added, "With the controller's attitude toward us, and the ultas' situation, we felt we had to move fast."

There was a rap at the door, and Grand Pierre opened it to see a courier from the controller standing there. He spoke in a curt manner, turned on his heel, and left. Grand Pierre closed the door and said seriously, "The controller called a meeting of the section leaders for tomorrow and has summoned all of you. The section leaders report to the controller, and each manages a team. In the morning after the daily rations are dispersed, we will convene in the administration chamber. Bunny will show you where to report for your day's ration. Each of you has an assigned code based on your individual requirements. Now, you should get some sleep."

Grand Pierre stopped at the door. "My special ones, you never disappoint me. Your mission tonight was a great success."

The following morning the special ones were waiting when Bunny knocked on the door to their chamber. That was what the living quarters were referred to, and each chamber was identified by a specific symbol above the door. The color identified the corridor, and the symbol identified the specific room. It was sort of like a numbering system, but the symbols meant locations, not numbers. As Dent tried to explain how the symbols worked, Bear shook his head and growled that there was no way he would ever understand the strange language.

Bunny stood in the doorway and signed, *Are you hungry?* She didn't have to repeat the question, as they all crowded into the corridor. The distribution center was in the opposite direction from the exit hatch, and as they followed Bunny, the special ones took interest in seeing more of the underground city. Whenever they met another Ulterion in the corridor, the person would stop and give them a slight bow of thanks. The rescue of the ultas had made the special ones the focus of attention.

Bunny reached the end of the corridor, turned right, and came to an area where three corridors ran together. She stopped and signed. The color blue with this symbol meant *technology*; green with another symbol meant *services*; gray with still another symbol was for *military*.

The technology symbol was made up of five circles, each connected together to form a larger circle. The military symbol was three straight lines stacked one above the other, and the services symbol was a pyramid.

Bunny motioned for the others to follow as she walked down the green corridor to reach the distribution chamber. She stopped at a wide doorway and motioned them to go inside. The room was filled with walk-up booths connected to tubes that came from the walls. Ulterions waited in lines at the booths, and when their turn came, they entered a code on a keypad and waited for their nutritional requirements to be delivered in a packet. They picked up their daily allotment, put it in a pocket, and walked out of the chamber.

"Where do they eat their food?" Wren asked.

Bunny signed, *While they work.*

Wren sighed. "I wish Aunt May could cook for us."

Manx said, "I'm not sure there is anything on Ulterion to cook."

Dent heard Manx's comment. He and Bear would have to make a night trip back to the ultas' lab. He wanted to confirm what he had seen in the underground dome.

A station became empty, and Bunny showed them how to enter their code to receive their supplement for that day. Someone must have entered their specific characteristics of height and weight because Battle and Boxer receive two packets, and Bear three. Dent, Manx, and Wren each received one from the station. Bunny retrieved her packet and motioned for the others to return to their chamber. They would wait there until it was time to meet the controller.

Back in their chamber, and after removing the packets from their pockets, they sat down at the table. Bunny demonstrated how to open the packet. She signed that when a packet was empty they were to place it in an opening by the door. The opening was a tube that delivered the packet to the distribution center to be refilled for the next day.

Wren opened her packet, released the straw-type end, and took a small sip. She looked surprised, took another suck on the straw, licked her lips, and said, "It's not bad. Sort of sweet and salty at the same time."

Hearing Wren's comment, the others opened their packets and sucked down the contents. After downing his second packet, Bear gave a large burp, making everyone laugh. "It's better than starving to death," he growled.

A knock on their door startled them. Grand Pierre leaned inside and asked, "How was breakfast? Not exactly what you are used to, but it has all the required nutrients for the day. Are you ready to meet the controller?" Grand Pierre waited at the door as the special ones stepped from the table.

The Controller

CHAPTER 37

$\mathcal{T}$he special ones followed Grand Pierre down a series of corridors until the last one ended in a U-shaped room. The front of the room was raised into a platform, and a long white table filled the length of the platform, with white, padded chairs behind it. Behind the platform, secured high on the wall, was a row of monitors, and all were blank. Grand Pierre walked down one side of the room filled with rows of white, bucket-type chairs attached to the floor. He turned down a row, and when he reached the middle of the room, he sat down and motioned for the special ones to do the same. The chair's height did not allow Wren's feet to touch the floor, and she felt around for a way to lower her chair.

Grand Pierre leaned out. "Sorry, Wren. The seats do not adjust. The center was not designed for small ones."

The only color in the room came from various colored one-piece suits worn by the team leaders as they entered the room and took their places at the table, leaving the center chair open. Each of the leaders, except one, carried a device that resembled the one Manx had found in the rogues' headquarters. The one leader who did not carry a device was dressed in a yellow jumpsuit, and Dent recognized the tall ulta who had waited for his team to reach safety.

At the back of the platform, a door silently slid aside, and an Ulterion in a white suit stepped forward and announced, "Rise for the controller."

The large room was silent as the leaders stood at attention. Grand Pierre and the special ones did the same. An Ulterion in a stark white suit stepped out of the doorway and made his way to the table and sat down. He was bent over, and the white suit hung loose on his thin frame. Once the controller was seated, the leaders took their places at the table. Grand Pierre stayed at attention until the controller looked at him and nodded. Then Grand Pierre sat down, and the special ones followed his lead.

The controller's expression was not welcoming as he stared hard at each of the special ones. Deep wrinkles lined his long face; rows of medals were pinned across his chest; and behind the penetrating blue eyes radiated a keen intelligence. The controller was responsible for everyone's survival. After what seemed a very long minute, the controller spoke in a low voice that echoed around the room through hidden speakers.

Dent understood what was spoken and whispered to the others, "He's calling for order." The controller continued speaking and then paused. Grand Pierre stood, responded in a clear voice, and pointed to the special ones.

Again Dent whispered, "Grand Pierre is explaining why we acted so quickly to rescue the ultas." When Grand Pierre finished speaking, he remained standing as the controller considered his words.

Suddenly various symbols filled one of the monitors on the wall. The controller paused and then nodded to the ulta leader seated at the table. The leader looked recovered from his ordeal of being trapped underground for so long. Across the front of the ulta's yellow suit were various patches.

As Grand Pierre watched the screen, he turned to the special ones. "The ulta leader is thanking you for rescuing his team. He said that many would not have survived the night, and everyone is making progress and should be able to return to work in a few days."

The ulta leader stood at the table and looked at the special ones. He placed his hands together and made a slight bow. The special ones stood up, placed their hands together, and bowed to the ulta leader.

The controller said something to Grand Pierre. Grand Pierre sat down, and silence again filled the room. The controller turned to the leaders at the table and began a quiet discussion with them.

Dent whispered to Manx, "The ulta leader must be able to use his mind to control the device that communicates with the screen."

Manx silently nodded in agreement, amazed at the ulta's ability.

The controller turned in his chair to face Grand Pierre. "I may have misjudged the value of the experiments, and I have decided to assign each of them to a team based on their skills. The team leaders have agreed that their input may be of value—because of their knowledge of how to defeat the robots, their ability to move above ground and not be detected, and their ability to execute missions. The one called Battle will join the military unit. The one called Boxer will be placed with the leadership and planning unit. The one called Bear will be assigned to the services unit. The one called Manx will be assigned to the technology unit. The youngest will stay with Francine until she can be assigned. The one who inherited all skills will work with you. They will report to their teams tomorrow and meet their leaders when this meeting is over."

Grand Pierre had a faint smile on his face as he placed his hands together and made a slight bow. He wished Francine had been able to join the meeting, but he and the special ones were the only ones who had been invited. The remainder of the meeting was filled with updates from the leaders as they reported on the status of projects and any issues that required the controller's attention.

After the last monitor lit up with symbols, the controller stood and made a slight bow to the leaders, signifying that the meeting was over. The controller shocked everyone when he turned to the special ones and bowed. After the controller left the room, Grand Pierre escorted the special ones to meet their team leaders.

Grand Pierre introduced Battle to the military commander, who wore a steel-gray one-piece suit with rows of medals across the chest. The commander looked at Battle and said, "I am grateful for your assistance in the rescue of the ultas, but it was a risk, and the scientists could have been killed."

Battle responded, "We all felt the risk was necessary." After a pause he added, "The small victories win the war."

Grand Pierre hesitantly interpreted Battle's words, concerned about the commander's reaction.

The commander considered Battle's response and seemed to make a decision. "Your knowledge of the robots and your inherited skill of military tactics will aid us in defeating the rogues. I will greet you tomorrow in the command center." The tall leader turned and walked from the room.

Grand Pierre exhaled the breath he had been holding.

Battle turned to Grand Pierre. "Thank you for all the years of training and pushing us to be our best. I look forward to joining the military unit and my new commander."

Bear was relieved to learn that Aunt May was a section leader in the services unit, and that he would be assigned to her team. The services leader explained all of the machinery, both electronic and mechanical, that the unit was responsible for. Then he added that most of the broken equipment was outside, and Bear understood. His inherited mechanical skills, and the fact that he could go outside at night without being discovered, made him the perfect fit.

The services leader left the room, and Manx walked up beside Bear. "You will look stunning in a forest-green jumpsuit," she said, causing Bear to growl in her ear.

Dent walked with Boxer to meet the leadership and planning leader. Grand Pierre had already informed the leader of Boxer's outstanding ability to oversee the total mission, even to the smallest detail. The leadership team had not had a new member in years, and Boxer, who stood as tall as the leader and resembled the Ulterion, even with his dark hair and eyes, was most welcome. The leader looked at Boxer with tired eyes that had seen too many failures during the years of war with the rogues. He clasped his hands together and bowed.

Boxer and Dent returned the gesture. Dent said, "I like the burnt-orange color of the leadership team suits the best."

Boxer asked, "What color will you be wearing? Grand Pierre wears white, like the controller."

Dent shrugged. "I'm not sure. Since I will be assisting Grand Pierre, white would go well with my black teeth." He grinned at Boxer.

The special ones returned to their room without having to be shown the way through the huge underground maze. There they found a pile of suits of various colors sitting on the table, and they hurried over.

"The blue suits are for Manx and Wren," Battle said as he handed Manx the suits the technology team wore.

"Let's put on our new suits and see how we look," Wren said eagerly, and everyone agreed to change clothes and meet back in the sitting area.

When they'd returned to the sitting area, Manx commented, "My suit is too snug. I'll ask Francine for a size larger and save this one for Wren."

Dent walked a circle around Manx and remarked, "I like the fitted look." Manx hissed at him, secretly enjoying his comment.

When Bear walked from the boy's room, he was bent over, pulling at the crotch of his jumpsuit. The sight of his big, burly shape encased in the too-tight forest-green material stretched beyond its limit was comical, but everyone knew better than to laugh out loud.

Wren gaped, wondering how Bear had managed to zip it, and exclaimed, "If Bear sneezes, that suit will shred to pieces."

"It must be the largest size they have," Boxer remarked. "The length might work, but Bear is twice as wide as any Ulterion."

Bear grumbled, "With those skimpy packets of food we get each morning, I will probably be skinny before long."

"I don't think your losing weight will affect the width of your shoulders," Boxer said as Bear continued to tug at his crotch. "Since you're in services, ask Aunt May who makes the suits and request larger ones."

"Why don't we sit at the table and finish our skimpy packets?" suggested Dent, who was dressed in white, and everyone pulled a chair from the table. When Bear sat down, they all heard a long ripping sound, which caused him to growl.

The following morning, Grand Pierre had his hand raised to knock on the door when Boxer opened it. "I have been waiting for you in the distribution area and began to wonder where you were," he said as the special ones walked into the corridor.

"We were up late learning the symbols and how to speak their meaning," Boxer explained.

"That's good," Grand Pierre responded. "I was going to join you today in the leadership chamber. Dent, please show Bear where to find Maileen, and then accompany Battle at the military unit for the rest of the day. Bunny is waiting for Manx and Wren in distribution and will take them to the technology center. For now, Bunny will stay with Francine. She is not comfortable joining the ultas at this time. We will meet back in your chamber at the end of each day to review your assignments."

"Even though we are thought of as *experiments*." Manx hissed.

Grand Pierre smiled down at Manx and patted her shoulder. "Ah, Manx, don't be so touchy. Everyone will soon learn just how special all of you are."

CHAPTER 38

The days seemed to race by for the special ones. They joined their assigned teams, and with Dent's nightly lessons, they were able to understand what was being discussed. Because they'd risked their lives to rescue the ultas, they had been accepted by their teams and felt comfortable in making suggestions or commenting on a topic being discussed. Life fell into a routine. After receiving their packets for the day, they would join their teams until it was time to return to their chambers. The scientists and assistants were dedicated to their roles and did not take time for other activities.

After the workday was over, Grand Pierre would come to their chamber for a debriefing session. He wanted to make sure there were no issues they couldn't handle. The sessions with Grand Pierre made the special ones aware of all the problems the controller faced, from dwindling food supplies to air quality issues and depleted fuel sources.

The military unit was now restricted from going outside during the day. For some reason the platform guards had doubled patrols and were hiding in the destroyed buildings across from the entrances—all programmed to kill. The commander told Battle he was concerned by the increase in patrols and the unknown reason for guarding the entrances.

But with the outside surveillance monitors destroyed, he had no way to find out.

The special ones sat in their chamber discussing the day's events with Grand Pierre. Dent commented, "It's just as the controller stated: we are in survival mode. There has been no new technology development or expansion in years. The expedition to Adoran was the last one, and that was twenty years ago. We are years younger than anyone living here … if you call it living."

Battle suggested, "We need to turn things around, begin an offensive. We have been part of our teams for weeks and haven't accomplished anything."

Bear asked, "What can we do to change things?"

Boxer took a piece of chalk from his pocket, stepped to the back wall, and wrote "Mission Objectives" at the top of the wall in Adoran. He looked at the others and explained, "If someone comes in and sees our list, they won't be able to read it. For now, we need to keep it to ourselves. Agreed?"

The others nodded their agreement, even Grand Pierre.

Battle went first. "First, we need to find out the rogues' military strength: the exact number of platforms and tall soldiers. They are exactly like the ones on Adoran, which tells us that the rogues have not improved their military in years. Second, we need to find the rogues' headquarters. No one in military knows where it is—or the number of rogue scientists still alive and in command of the robots."

Boxer wrote Battle's items on the wall.

Then Bear added more items to the list. "The equipment outside that supplies air isn't working. The air inside is barely within limits. If it becomes worse, it will become toxic to everyone living underground. I've studied the maps for the buildings, and I can investigate at night to determine if anything can be fixed. The fuel to maintain the laboratories is delivered by tubing and is unreliable. The scientists' equipment keeps shutting down, ruining what they are working on. I need to know what the fuel is and how it works before I can repair the outside delivery system."

Grand Pierre told Bear, "I will ask Berne. He is highly skilled in fuel uses."

Manx added, "The communication equipment was damaged by the raid that sealed the ultas in their lab. Francine said the outside monitors have been destroyed, so they can't track the robots or communicate when anyone goes outside."

Boxer finished writing and turned to Grand Pierre. "Would it be possible to build repeaters like you did on Adoran? Bear and I could go out at night and hide them in the buildings."

Dent added, "If we build the repeaters and find the frequency the rogues use to communicate with the robots, we can track them to their control center."

Grand Pierre nodded. "Good point. I've wondered why the attack centered on the communication center. I will talk with Francine and determine if we have the required materials to build similar repeaters."

Dent continued. "There was only one guard when we rescued the ultas. We need a way to tag the robots to count and track them. The rogues could be experiencing fuel shortages, but without the ability to monitor them, there is no way to know how many are actually functioning."

"Interesting," Grand Pierre muttered thoughtfully.

Wren spoke up. "Bunny said the ultas are worried about their labs. She can understand them now. They are worried about the plants they grow for the packets, and they have developed a new food source. The plants need light and air to survive."

"That's great. No packets," Bear growled.

Dent remarked, "With everything we've listed, the days of living underground may not last much longer, and I don't think the Ulterions are equipped to live outside. Sometimes I think no one cares because they can't do anything about their situation."

Battle looked at the list and shook his head in amazement. "We have a lot of items to complete before we can create an offensive plan against the rogues."

Everyone agreed with Battle.

Dent said, "It's time to begin nighttime surveillance and find some answers."

Grand Pierre stood and looked at the long list of items filling the back wall. "You have identified the critical issues," he said.

↓↳ ↓↳

Manx finished the project she was working on in technology and told Francine she was going to her chamber to clean up. She had been clearing out the bombed communication center, and any equipment that looked useable or could be salvaged for parts, she had placed in boxes to take to the new area.

Bunny and Wren had returned to Francine's chamber, since there was nothing else they could do to help Manx.

The special ones' chamber was quiet when Manx entered. She walked to her bedroom, opened the door, and could tell that Bear had recently been in the room. She noticed something sitting on her bed and walked over. She smiled as she picked up the package and looked at all the colors. She knew what to do with the pieces of chalk Bear had gathered from the waste bins placed throughout the city. It was the same chalk Boxer had used to write their growing list of items on the wall behind the table.

Manx dumped the pieces onto her bed and pushed up the sleeves of her blue suit.

Everyone had returned from the work teams and was waiting for Grand Pierre, with the exception of Wren. The door opened, and Wren skipped into the room, holding the tall man's hand, looking happy.

Wren looked at everyone and exclaimed, "Bunny and I had the most fun today. We saw Aunt May and told her we didn't have anything to do, so she took us to this place that looked like our old barn. Aunt May said it was where she used to go, but that was years ago. There were ropes to climb, swings, and mats to jump on. The walls could change into pictures, but when we tried them, nothing happened. The blank walls almost looked like being outside."

Grand Pierre explained. "Maileen took you and Bunny to the old exercise room. I had no idea it was still there. Now, let's review today's activities—although I bet Wren had the most fun."

Manx updated them on communications being moved to the new area. The move was finished, and she was helping find parts to build repeaters. "We need a stable power source to test one to see how far the signal reaches," she said. "Then Francine can determine how many to build. Francine should have the first repeater completed next week, but finding enough parts is a problem." Manx looked at Grand Pierre, but he had no further questions.

Bear reported that all the outside transports had been destroyed, and the inside ones used to move equipment were becoming low on power. He asked Grand Pierre if he had talked to Berne, and Grand Pierre replied that he had not seen him.

Dent reported that last night he and Bear had gone out and scouted the area beyond the landing field and had come to a high mesh fence. From the vibrations in the fence, they could tell that it was electrified. The fence was high, and climbing it wasn't an option, since they could get shocked.

Manx asked how high the fence was. Dent said it was too high for her to jump. Wren suggested she do a flyover.

Boxer interrupted, saying they needed more information about the fence and its purpose before involving Wren, which caused Wren to scowl at him.

Dent added that the fence hadn't been there long. The dirt around the fence was fresh from digging, not packed hard like the rest of the area.

"No one in military has mentioned the fence," Battle said. "Tomorrow is a day off, and if we leave tonight, we can reach the fence by first light. If we can determine what the rogues are planning, it would be valuable information for the commander."

"What if we run into a robot?" Boxer said. There's no place to hide."

"Wren could fly and keep watch from above and warn us in time to escape," Battle answered.

"If the rogues recently built the fence, there must be a reason," Manx said.

Grand Pierre cautioned, "If you go, it is only to gather information and report back."

Their meeting was over, and Wren, tired from her day of climbing, swinging, and jumping, opened the door to the girls' bedroom—and let out a very loud squeal.

Manx grinned and looked at Bear. "I put the pieces of chalk to use."

Everyone hurried to find out what had made Wren shriek.

"This looks like the forest around the farmhouse," Battle exclaimed as he looked at the bright-blue ceiling and the walls covered in trees with big, green leaves and brightly colored flowers. There was a purple flowering tree beside Wren's bed.

"I'm glad you left the vivan out," Boxer told Manx. He recognized the purple flowering tree and remembered Wren's close call with the winged hunter.

Wren hugged Manx. "It feels like home. Thank you."

"Thank Bear too," Manx told her. "He brought me all the colors."

Wren pulled Bear down and gave him a long hug around his neck.

"Outstanding, and done with detail," Grand Pierre exclaimed as he inspected Manx's artwork.

The Fence

CHAPTER 39

It was an hour before daybreak when Boxer woke the others. With the exception of Wren, they had stayed awake late to talk.

When everyone was at the door and ready to go, Boxer verified their situation. "Dent, how far past the landing field before we reach the fence?"

Dent thought for a minute "About a ten-minute run. Bear and I were looking for robots and came upon the fence by accident."

"You didn't see any guards?" Boxer asked again, wanting to make sure before he decided the route they should take.

"No, but if they've discovered their returned warship, they could be in the area," Dent answered.

"We'll avoid the landing strip and circle around it," Boxer said. Once we're past the warship, Bear will take the lead to the fence. We should be there before light." Then Boxer signaled *quiet* and *go* and opened the door.

The night was pitch-black as the special ones climbed from the exit hatch, and Battle pulled the metal grate across to hide it. Boxer signaled for them to stop while he listened. He heard no sounds to indicate that robots were around, but unless they were moving, there would be nothing to hear.

With Boxer in the lead and Bear bringing up the rear, the special ones silently ran from the shelter of the building.

The night air was chilly, and Manx wished she had the coat she'd brought with her, but it was in her sack in the warship. She shivered at the thought that the robots might have found their sacks. The rogues would know the number of travelers that had arrived from Adoran because Grand Pierre had packed one too. From their clothes, containing hair and fibers, the rogues could figure out a way to program the robots to scan for them. Once the mission to the fence was over, she would mention to Boxer the need to clean out the warship, if it wasn't too late.

Boxer stopped to listen for any sounds before changing direction toward the fence. He didn't hear anything to signal that robots were near, and he circled around the end of the landing field. Once they were past it, Bear would take the lead.

Bear let his instincts guide him, and about fifteen minutes later he stopped when a high mesh-link fence extending in both directions came into view.

Boxer inched closer to the fence and heard the vibration. From his keen sense of hearing, Boxer made out each individual pulse radiating through the fence. He stepped back and whispered, "It's a low-voltage sensor used for monitoring. But what would the rogues monitor this far away? The voltage is so low that no one touching it would notice it. It's a good thing Dent picked up on the vibration and didn't touch the fence and give himself away."

As it became lighter, they could see that the fence extended in both directions as far as they could see. The dirt beneath and around the fence was soft. Boxer scooped up a handful and let it drift through his fingers.

Dent pointed. "I can see where the fence ends at those far mountains."

"I haven't noticed any mountains," Bear growled, "but with the hazy atmosphere it's hard to see past arm's length."

"I can't see where the fence ends in the other direction," Manx said, puzzled. "It's too far to tell. And there's nothing on the other side of the fence but fields of dead grass."

"It doesn't make sense why the rogues would build a fence out here," Battle commented. "And it's even strong enough to hold Bear's weight. We need to find where it originates. That might give us a clue as to its purpose." He picked up a rock. "Let's test Boxer's theory and make sure the fence won't harm anyone." Battle tossed the stone at the fence. It hit the fence and bounced back, not causing any sparks.

As they stood looking at the fence, Wren said, "There's enough light now for me to fly and find where the fence ends."

Boxer scowled at Wren, but Battle agreed. "It's the best option to get information," he said. "Wren, don't overextend your flight, and if you see a robot, return fast."

Wren nodded, held out her arms, and ran forward. She changed into the small brown bird, gained height, and flew away.

"Let's wait over there." Dent pointed out a large hole, an area caved in from clearing the ground around the fence. The hole would provide cover while they waited for Wren to return.

It seemed like hours, but it was only a few minutes. All of them were tense as they waited for Wren to return, worried about Wren flying off by herself.

Boxer stiffened. "The signal in the fence has changed. It's pulsing faster, like something is shaking it."

At Boxer's warning, they stood up and looked in the direction Wren had flown. They heard a series of three sharp chirps echo and then repeat.

Boxer shouted, "That's Wren's danger warning, and the fence is vibrating more. We need to get away from here, now."

Manx gasped. "What about Wren?"

Battle ordered, "I'll wait for Wren. Get to the mountains and hide. You can run faster if you change, and you may not be detected by the robots. We don't dare to go back the way we came."

Boxer started to protest, but Battle told him, "There's nothing you can do if you stay here. If you want to help Wren, get to safety."

Everyone but Battle changed and ran toward the distant mountains. Dent, holding tight, rode on Bear's shoulder.

Battle didn't know what to expect or what the increased humming in the fence meant. He reached into his pocket and removed a sweeper. It was the only weapon he had. He could operate the military weapons, but they were bulky to carry. He wished he had one now.

Battle heard Wren's warning chirp once again, and in the distance he saw the small brown bird flying fast. As Wren came close, she folded in her wings, dropped to the ground, and changed.

Wren yelled, "Battle, hide! One of those guards is riding on top of the fence and coming fast. You can't outrun it. Hide!" Wren held out her arms, jumped high, changed into the brown bird, and flew straight up.

Battle knew his only hiding place was the caved-in ground. He ran and jumped into the hole and made himself as small as possible. Battle wasn't as tall as Bear, but he was almost as wide and completely filled the space. He kept his head down and heard a whining sound. He wanted to see the fence-riding robot, but he didn't dare to expose himself to the guard's scanner.

Wren would be safe. The robots were not programmed to scan overhead.

Battle could hear the fence shake from the robot's speed. Then it stopped to search the area where the stone had hit the fence. The fence had clearly been set to warn the robots when anything touched it. Dent's animal-like sense of hearing had stopped him and Bear from trying to climb it. Battle wondered why there was a fence being guarded all the way out here.

Battle heard the rollers start up and could tell that the guard had rolled past him. He decided to risk a glance and lifted his head. It was as Wren had described. A robot guard was on the top of the fence, but the platform was different—smaller, with rollers mounted front and back that moved the guard along the fence. This guard was armed like the platformed guards on Adoran, with built-in weapons and search beams. The guard rolled on toward the mountains, but it was going slow, searching the area beyond the fence. The guard did not turn around and search the empty fields behind it.

When the robot finally started back, Battle collapsed himself into the hole to avoid the guard's scan. He heard the guard stop to report in the same metallic voice he'd heard on Adoran. "All clear. No sign of Ulterion soldiers." Then the guard rolled back the way it had come, gaining speed and causing the fence to shake.

Battle waited to make sure the fence-riding robotic was out of sight. He climbed from the hole just as Wren flew down and changed.

"That was close," she said. "That horrible thing was coming down the fence before I could reach the end. I flew back to warn everyone. It would have killed all of you." Wren was breathing hard and bent over to catch her breath.

"Let's get out of here and find the others," Battle suggested. "How about a ride on my shoulders like we did on the farm?"

Wren grinned as Battle lifted her onto his wide shoulders and jogged toward the mountains. It had only been a couple of hours since they'd left that morning, but it felt much longer.

When Battle and Wren reached the edge of the mountain, Boxer, Manx, and Dent stepped from behind a boulder. Battle looked around. "Where's Bear?"

"He went to scout around while we waited," Boxer said. "We saw the guard riding the fence, and I'm glad you were able to escape its scan."

"I must have set off an alarm when I threw the stone at the fence," Battle admitted. "Thanks to Wren, we were all able to survive."

Battle looked up at the mountain and said, "Let's find Bear and explore the area before we head back. I need to let the military commander know about the fence and the new kind of guard."

When the group reached the top of the mountain they looked back toward the fence. The landing field and buildings were barely visible in the haze.

Battle studied the scene and said, "Now it makes sense." He pointed. "If the robots take control of the underground city, the fastest way for the Ulterions to escape is toward the fence. All outside transportation vehicles have been destroyed, so they would have to run to get away. The back of the city extends under that high ridge, but there's no way for them to get over the steep rim. The rogues must be planning an invasion, so they've built the fence and the armed guard."

"What would cause the Ulterions to evacuate?" Manx wondered aloud.

Bear stepped from the snarl of trees carrying a branch in his mouth. Small purple fruit hung from the branch. Bear changed and looked happier that he had since they'd left Adoran.

"Across the top, the mountain drops into a valley. There aren't a lot of plants, and the trees all look deformed, but I found a number of these bushes. I thought Aunt May would know what they are and if they're safe to eat. There may be water, but I can't be sure unless I cross the valley." Bear picked up the branch and turned one of the fruits in his hand, inspecting it.

"Don't even think of eating it until Aunt May says it's safe," Manx warned.

Bear growled, "I can't wait to chew real food again and not suck it through a straw."

Dent stepped beside Bear and whispered, "I know where to go on our next night trip."

Boxer turned to the others. "We're ready to head back. It's light, so we need to stay hidden."

"And be *careful*," Dent finished for him, causing everyone to laugh and easing the tension they all felt. It had been a while since they had recited their Cs.

The group reached the area beyond the landing strip and saw the warship they'd arrived in. No guards were in sight. Suddenly Boxer signaled a stop and motioned that he had heard something. A loud bump followed by a thump broke the silence. A platform guard had been hiding behind the warship. One side of the platform was stuck and could not gain traction on the torn-up ground.

After watching the guard bump two more times, Dent whispered, "Do you think we should go help him?" Manx punched him in the arm.

Finally the guard stopped rocking back and forth and spoke into a microphone attached to his shoulder.

"He's calling for help," Boxer said.

"Too bad we can't help him," Battle responded.

Before a minute passed, a second guard rolled up.

"I wish we had a way to tag them," Dent said with a sigh. He watched the second guard extend a metal pole with a hook on the end. The hook caught the frame of the stuck platform, and the second guard reversed and pulled the stuck guard from the debris.

"I might have an idea," Battle said as they watched.

As the two platforms rolled away, Boxer heard one guard say, "You will be reprimanded for getting stuck."

When the guards were out of sight, Boxer motioned *go* and circled around the bombed-out buildings to the one at the far end that hid the exit.

After the special ones were safe inside and Battle had secured the hatch, Manx said, "All our sacks are still in the warship. If the robots find them, they will know about us."

"Bear and I moved those weeks ago and stored them where the robots can't find them," Dent told her.

"Nice of you to let us know what you and Bear do on your nightly excursions," Manx grumbled.

"You were sleeping when we got back, and with everything else going on, I forgot to mention it," Dent responded.

After they were inside their chamber, Battle said, "I need to go to military headquarters. The fence is a trap to kill soldiers. If the soldiers had found the fence, they wouldn't have been able to tell that it had sensors. They would have been caught in the open and killed by that fence-riding menace. The rogues don't know we've found the fence, so we can use it to our advantage."

"I don't feel safe underground," Bear huffed. "If the robots learn about the hidden exit, there will be no way for us to escape."

"That's why we need the repeaters," Boxer said as he looked at the long list of issues written on the back wall. He added the fence and rider to the growing list.

CHAPTER 40

The following week everyone was busy, especially the technology team. Manx and Francine worked late into night to complete the first repeater. They ran tests underground, and the signal didn't travel far. The problem with testing underground was that the signals couldn't penetrate the thick corridor walls. Francine said it should have double the range outside, and tonight Bear and Boxer would take the repeater outside to determine if Francine was correct. Once Francine knew the repeater's range, she could determine the number of repeaters required to cover the area the guards patrolled.

Dent helped Battle design a way to tag the robots. Based on his nightly reconnaissance with Bear, he said that the guards didn't scan behind their platforms, only from side to side as they looked for a scientist or sentry to kill. At night the platforms were less in number because the military unit could not communicate with the command center and stayed underground. Two was the number of platform guards Dent had spotted on night patrol.

The issues the controller faced were growing daily in number and urgency. The military commander was worried because the robots were becoming more aggressive and had increased their day patrols, halting all repair efforts on the damaged systems. If the sentries went beyond the ultas' exit hatch, they were chased away.

The commander was concerned about the fence, and Battle discussed with him why the rogues had made the effort to build the sturdy fence and rider, other than to trap and kill the soldiers. Battle had become a respected member of the military unit, and the commander valued his input.

In the services unit, the major concern was the air quality of the underground city. Bear complained that if the air became any thicker they could wear it.

Grand Pierre reported that the ulta scientists were anxious to get back to their laboratory and check on the food sources. The ingredients for the packets were almost depleted.

It was late when Manx entered the chamber. She was tired and looking forward to her bed. She was shocked to see the others sitting around the table, and from the look on Wren's face, she knew something was up. She stopped in the middle of the room. "What is going on?"

Wren jumped up, took her hand, and pulled her to the table. The purplish fruits that Bear had found sat in the middle. Wren explained, "Aunt May said the clumes are safe to eat and taste a lot like the berries we picked on the farm. Everyone is waiting for you before we eat them. We each get one, and Aunt May took one for herself and for Grand Pierre and Francine."

"What are we waiting for?" Manx picked up one of the clumes and took a bite, and purple juice ran down her chin.

"Tonight Bear and I are going to test the repeater," Boxer said. "We'll wait until just before light. The robots won't be expecting anyone to be outside." He wiped juice from his chin as well.

"Be careful," Manx said as she finished her clume. "When the signal drops to half strength, stop and determine the distance between you and Bear. Francine said we have enough parts to build ten repeaters, and depending on their range outside, we may be able to monitor the extended area the robots have started to patrol."

"I wonder why the rogues started guarding the area beyond the ultas' exit," Dent commented. He looked at Battle. "How are the trackers coming?"

"We've completed ten," Battle reported. "If we can get them anywhere under a guard's platform, they'll attach to the metal like a magnet. Each tracker will emit a different signal so we can tell them apart and determine where they are. And then we can take the war to them." He grimaced.

"How large are the trackers?" Dent asked.

"They're about the size of a small, flat stone and very light," Battle replied.

"The platforms are high enough off the ground for me to sneak underneath and secure the trackers. If a rat comes from behind, they won't notice." Dent grinned.

Manx spoke up with concern in her voice. "No. You could get squashed by a platform."

"I'll be careful and not become a flat rat. I'll only place the trackers while the platforms are watching the entrances. Besides, I'm the only one who can get close without being seen." Dent tried to easy Manx's concern, but she wasn't smiling.

Battle considered the idea. "It could work," he said. "Tomorrow night I'll bring a tracker, and we can test your plan." Manx scowled at Battle but didn't say any more.

"Let's get some sleep," Boxer said. "Bear and I will leave before dawn." He stood, ending the conversation.

The following morning Francine became excited when Boxer told her how far the signal reached. She quickly calculated the distance and said there were parts for enough repeaters to cover all outside entrances and the landing area near the warship. She asked Boxer to obtain a map of the outside buildings and meet her in the communication center—and to bring Bear. The three of them would decide where to hide the repeaters.

"I can't wait to tell Piers," she exclaimed. "When we start monitoring their communications and find their frequency, Piers can program the interruption signal. The technology team should have the repeaters finished by the end of the week." Francine hurried away to find Grand Pierre.

At the end of the day, Battle walked into the chamber and over to Dent. He handed him a round silver object and asked, "Can you carry it?"

Dent balanced the small disk in his hand. "It shouldn't be a problem, and I don't plan on carrying it far."

"Do you want to try to attach one tonight? Battle asked.

"I'll take it with me when Bear and I go out. Bear wants to look at the buildings, and I want to inspect the fence again." Dent placed the small round disk in his pocket and looked at Manx. "If you're not ready to go to bed, I want to show you something." He held out his hand, and together they walked out of the chamber.

"Where are we going?" Manx asked.

"Haven't you heard about curiosity and the cat?" Dent grinned.

"Ha-ha," Manx answered.

Dent led Manx down a corridor, and the farther away from the housing chambers they went, the more the corridor widened. Finally Dent stopped at a wide door and told her, "Close your eyes."

Manx gave Dent a scowl before she shut her eyes. She heard him open the door, and then he took her hand. "Don't open your eyes until I say so."

Dent led her a few steps ahead and then closed the door behind them. Manx heard typing on a keyboard and could sense the room becoming brighter. Then she heard sounds she had not heard in a while.

"You can open your eyes," Dent said.

Manx gasped as she looked around. She was in the exercise room, and the walls were covered with trees. Birds sang in the background.

"I thought you would like this mode best," Dent said. "There are a couple of other modes, but they're just colors or abstract lines that move around. The Ulterions used to spend a lot of time here. Aunt May said she can remember climbing the ropes when she was younger."

Dent led Manx to a wide platform held by two ropes attached to the ceiling. He sat on the platform and patted the seat next to him. Manx sat down and tucked her legs up. Dent pointed a controller at the panel where he'd typed in the codes for the forest scene, and the platform started to circle the room.

"It's like riding with Grand Pierre in the transport on learning trips." Manx leaned back, closed her eyes, and listened to the birds singing as the platform circled. She sighed. "This is great. Thanks for bringing me."

"I thought you could use a break," Dent said. "You've been working hard helping Francine build the repeaters."

"Are you suggesting I've been under a lot of pressure—and acting like it?" Manx teased.

"Well, you haven't been yourself lately—kind of grumpy from working long hours." Dent held his breath, waiting for Manx to punch his arm.

"I'm sorry," Manx said. "But everyone is working so hard. I hear them talk about the air getting worse and now running out of food. I can't understand why anyone would choose to live this way." She sighed.

Dent reached for her hand. "I agree. Come look at this."

Dent aimed the control device to stop the platform and then pulled Manx to one side of the room. He punched a button, and a panel slid to one side, revealing shelves that held balls of various sizes. He handed Manx a ball and then took another. "Watch this."

Dent threw the ball toward the panel, but before the ball hit the panel, it bounced back, and he caught it. Manx threw her ball and caught it when it bounced back. Manx laughed and asked, "How does it work? There's nothing between us and the wall."

"It's some kind of energy field," Dent said as he threw his ball again. Manx and Dent devised a game where they would throw the balls and catch the other one's. It wasn't long before they bent over laughing, totally exhausted.

"When did you have time to come here and figure out all of this?" Manx asked as she looked around. "Wren said nothing worked when she was here."

"At night when everyone was asleep," Dent answered. Then he added, "Years ago the Ulterions' lifestyle was totally different. They developed amazing things, like this amusement chamber. Because of the war with the rogues and trying to survive, all this amazing technology became unimportant.

Later Manx and Dent returned to their chamber, happier than they had felt for a long time. Before Dent went to sleep that night, an idea popped into his head. He would ask Grand Pierre about it tomorrow.

Trackers

CHAPTER 41

The night was blacker than usual when Dent and Bear climbed from the exit. They would use hand signals to communicate. Dent motioned for them to circle around the landing strip to reach the far buildings near the ultas' exit. This route would keep them away from the main road, which the guards patrolled at night.

Francine had said that at one time the buildings had been used by the ultas to grow plants for food and to conduct experiments on new food sources. The ultas had developed highly nutritional plants that met all their diet requirements. When the war with the rogues escalated, the rogues had purposely destroyed their food source, causing the ultas to move underground. Now their underground laboratories had been sealed off by the explosion, and there was no way for the ultas to check on their experiments or to harvest the plants required for the daily packets.

Each night one of the two guards on patrol hid in one of the three crumbling buildings, and Dent decided it would be easy to sneak up on the guard there and attach the tracker. Dent continued to wonder why the ultas' hatch was important enough to guard every night. Perhaps the rogues were not aware that the ultas' entrance underground had collapsed from the bombing. The second guard on patrol would roll in front of the three underground entrances and scan the area. The guard repeated these steps throughout the night.

There were three entrances to the underground city: a large main entrance and two smaller ones. At each end of the city, an escape exit or hatch had been installed. The rogues guarded the escape hatch located by the ultas' labs but not the one at the other end, which the special ones used.

The main entrance was used by the services unit. The wide doors allowed the larger transports to move equipment in and out of the city, but as Bear reported, all the large transports had been destroyed, along with most of the outside buildings and equipment required to maintain the huge underground environment.

There were two smaller entrances located on either side of the main one. The entrance close to the ultas' corridor was where the communication center was located. It was this entrance where the robots had attacked and damaged most of the equipment.

The other entrance was used by the military unit. During the day, the platform guards were easy targets for the sentries, but the guards did not stay out in the open. They hid in and behind the buildings, waiting for an opportunity to kill anyone who dared to come outside.

It was still a few hours before daylight when Dent crept to the back of the nearest building and changed into the gray rat. He picked up the small round disk with his teeth and scurried inside through a hole in the wall. He glanced around, saw no guard hiding there, and went out through the same hole.

Dent hurried to the second building, holding the tracking device in his teeth. Through the damaged wall, Dent could see that the building was empty. The third building was farther away, and to reach it he would be exposed as he ran. He listened and then scurried across the ground. He stopped at the back of the building and looked for a way to get inside.

The building was more intact that the others, and Dent could not find a way inside. He ran around to the front just as a beam of light lit up the ground, and a patrol rolled up and stopped in front of him. Dent froze. He didn't dare move and give himself away. The guard aimed its light toward the ultas' exit, scanned the area, and shut off the beam. In a metallic voice, the guard reported no sign of movement. For some reason the exit was not being guarded.

As the guard sat there, Dent crept up beside one of the wide tracks that circled the platform. As he was trying to decide the best way to get underneath the platform, the guard turned, and the platform rolled backward toward Dent. He acted fast—for he had promised Manx that he would not end up a flat rat—and jumped into a wide indentation in the dirt, made when the guard rolled up.

This would be his only chance to attach the tracking device. Dent scurried forward to reach the metal bar that held the tracks in place. He raised up on his back legs and touched the metal bar with the small round device. Instantly, as Battle had said, the tracker clamped tight. Dent turned to scurry away, but then the platform started moving above him. It was a game of cat and mouse, with Dent running one way and then the other, trying to keep from being squashed by the heavy rollers. Luckily for Dent, the guard did not move fast, and he was able to avoid becoming a flat rat. When the platform straightened, the guard rolled away down the road. Dent watched from the deep rut until the guard disappeared and then scurried inside the building to make sure there was no guard inside. The building was empty. Dent changed and signaled Bear, who instantly appeared in the doorway.

"That was close," Bear said. "I wasn't sure what to do, and you never gave a distress call."

"It was too close, and don't tell Manx." Dent breathed heavily. "I wonder why there was only one guard tonight? Since we have the opportunity, I want to check out the ultas' lab. I don't think the guard will return soon if he has to complete the patrol route himself."

An hour later, with his arms full of containers of strange looking plants, Dent told Bear, "This is the last load we'd better take. We need to hide everything before the guard returns." The plants were the experiments the ultas were worried about, and he wanted to save them before they died from lack of light. "We can check tomorrow night, and if the exit isn't guarded, we can rescue more plants."

"Where should we take them?" Bear asked, and Dent said he had an idea.

It was daylight when Bear and Dent crept back to the hatch, anxious to get inside and avoid being seen by the robots. When they reached their chamber, both collapsed in their beds. Bear and Dent were still sleeping when Battle came into the room and nudged Dent. Dent opened his eyes and saw Battle, who looked like he was going to burst with excitement.

"The tracker is working!" Battle said. "We tracked the guard to an area beyond the landing field. It may be where the fence ends. Did you check the fence last night?" Battle asked.

Dent sat up and mumbled, "We ran out of time. It was getting light, and we needed to get underground. I'll check it tonight. Let Bear sleep. We had a busy night." He yawned and scratched his head. "There was no guard at the ultas' exit, and I'm not sure when they stopped guarding it. The platform I tagged was the only one on patrol. Bring me another tracker, and I'll take it with me tonight."

Dent climbed out of bed and followed Battle from the room. "I need to find Grand Pierre and tell him about an idea I have," he said.

Battle started down a different corridor and turned to Dent. "Your mission last night was a success, and we know the trackers work."

Dent smiled. Praise from Battle was always earned, especially this time, and he hoped Manx would never find out how close he had come to becoming a flat rat.

Dent and Bear climbed from the exit just after dark, avoiding the area where the platform patrolled, they ran for the buildings by the ultas' escape hatch. After a quick check of the three buildings, just to make sure there was no guard lurking, Bear and Dent hurried to open the hatch.

They had completed three trips in and out of the ultas' laboratory, with one of them always on watch, when they heard a noise coming from beyond the buildings. They hid and waited until they were sure the guard wasn't returning, and then they began carrying the plants to hide them with the others they had rescued.

Their plan for tomorrow night was for Bear to carry the rescued plants to the valley on the far side of the mountain. Bear had gone back to the valley and had found plants growing wild, like the sparse-looking clume bushes. Bear said that the farther he went, the healthier the vegetation became. Dent decided that some of the toxic exhaust fumes had drifted across the steep mountain.

Dent set the pots he was carrying on the ground. He had noticed that the wilted plants they'd rescued on their first trip had looked dead but were starting to look better. If only half of the rescued plants survived, the ulta scientists would not have to start over with their experiments. Dent would take Bunny with him and talk to the ulta leader to find out what the plants needed to survive.

All efforts to clear the corridor to the ultas' laboratory had stopped. The services crew reported that the damage was too great, and removing any more of the debris would cause the corridor walls to collapse. Now the ultas were desperately trying to find other sources of nutrients for the daily food packets.

Bear and Dent completed their last trip with the plants. It was almost daylight when Dent said, "I told Battle I would check the fence tonight. The military commander thinks the rogues are planning something and that the fence is involved. Besides, I have an idea and need your help."

Bear's response was a low growl, sure that once again Dent was going to get them in trouble.

Dent ignored Bear and continued. "When we get to the fence, lift me up. I'm going to place a tracker on the top, and when ol' fence-menace rolls over it, the tracker should attach itself. If it works, Battle will be able to tell where the fence ends. Besides, the guard tonight didn't stay in one place long enough for me to tag it."

Bear growled again.

When they reached the fence, the area looked deserted. Dent and Bear rested in the caved-in area where Battle had hidden last time. Dent took the tracker out of his pocket and whispered, "Ready." They crept to the fence, and Bear knelt down while Dent climbed on his wide shoulders.

Bear warned, "Don't step on my hair." Underground, Bear tied his brown hair at the back of his neck, but when he was outside he untied his long hair and shook his head, causing his hair to fly around.

Bear raised up, holding Dent by his legs to steady him, and stepped close to the fence. Dent leaned forward, reached up, and carefully placed the tracker on top of the fence.

Bear stepped back, and Dent jumped from his shoulders and said, "I hope this works."

"Let's get out of here," Bear said, not bothering to lower his voice. "We're too exposed."

It was the increased humming of the fence that startled them, and both dove into the caved-in hole as two platform guards rolled up to the fence. Another robot stood on the back of one of the platforms. It looked exactly like the tall leaders on Adoran. The robot stepped from the platform and spoke into a communication device attached to his uniform.

The humming decreased as the fence-riding robotic stopped, and the tall leader issued orders. Dent dared to peek as the fence-rider handed a bundle of long silver cylinders to the tall leader. The tall leader placed the bundle on the back of a platform and stepped back to retrieve another bundle from the fence-rider. This continued until there were four bundles, each containing four cylinders, stacked on the back of each platform. The tall leader said something that sounded like "return to base," and the fence-rider rolled back in the direction he'd come from. The tall leader stepped onto the back of a platform and issued orders, and the two guards rolled away.

Dent understood the reason the fence had hummed so loud. It was because of the extra weight of the cylinders. He was glad for the sound, for he and Bear would have been discovered without it. Dent and Bear waited as long as they dared. It was daylight, and their only escape was to follow the fence to the mountain. They ran in that direction.

"We'll have to wait for dark before we can go back," Dent huffed when they reached the mountain. After he caught his breath he said, "I wonder what those long tubes are for." He pondered for a minute and then added, "They didn't stop at the landing area. They just kept going, but where to?"

Bear pointed. "We're close to where we hid all the plants. Keep watch and signal if you see any guards. I'm going to get the plants while we have the chance."

The day was half over when Bear carried the last of the plants to the mountaintop where Dent stood watch. Then they spent the rest of the day carrying the plants over the mountain and down to the valley.

Bear picked a bunch of clumes for them to eat while they rested. Dent wiped purple juice from his chin and thought. He knew what they must do once it became dark, but he wasn't sure how to tell Bear.

$$\lor\!\!\!\!\lor \quad \lor\!\!\!\!\lor$$

Dent and Bear had not returned last night, and now the day was almost over. Manx paced around their chamber like a caged cat, causing Wren to worry. Wren told Francine, and

Francine told Grand Pierre, and now both were standing in the special ones' chamber.

Manx clasped the tall man around his waist and said, "Grand Pierre, I'm so worried. You know how Dent and Bear can be. I'm afraid they've done something really stupid."

Battle walked into the chamber and heard Manx and tried to reassure her. "Last night they tagged the robot riding the fence," he said, "and we tracked the signal until it stopped moving. Besides that, Boxer went outside a few times and did not hear a distress signal from either of them."

"What if they're hurt and can't signal—or worse," Manx wailed.

Battle said, "They probably couldn't make it back and found cover. If they were at the fence, that's a long way to return."

Grand Pierre agreed with Battle and told Manx not to worry. He was sure they would return later that night. Manx suggested that she and Boxer go and search for them, but Grand Pierre replied that it was too dangerous with the increased patrols. Finally Manx agreed to wait, but she knew she would not rest until Dent and Bear returned.

CHAPTER 42

$\mathcal{I}$t was dark when Dent and Bear made their way down the mountain, taking extra caution, aware of the robots' activities at the fence. Before they left, Dent was able to get Bear to agree to his plan. Dent wanted to check the warship. He had not been there since he and Bear had removed the sacks of clothes, medicine, and anything that might give the rogues information about who had arrived from Adoran. They had left the warship as empty as they'd found it on Adoran.

When they reached the place where Bear would keep watch, they listened for the guards. They heard no sound of movement, so Dent changed and scurried toward the warship. He reached the ramp that extended from the ship and decided to be cautious. Using his long nails to keep from falling, he climbed up the underside of the ramp. When he reached the top of the ramp, he looked over the side and saw a pulsing beam running across the top of the ramp. The rogues had set a trap, and if the signal was broken by someone entering the warship, the robots would attack.

This was a valuable piece of information he could relay to Battle. The rogues were not as sneaky as they thought—at least not as sneaky as one gray rat. Dent grinned as he backed down the ramp and scurried back to where Bear waited.

It was almost light when Dent and Bear secured the hatch to the underground city and climbed down the steps. They were both exhausted from missing two nights of sleep, especially Bear. When they entered the corridor, Manx exclaimed, "It's about time," causing Dent to jump with fright.

"Manx, you scared me!" Dent's voice shook. "Why aren't you asleep?"

"That's where *I'm* headed," Bear growled and pushed his way past Manx.

"Do you think I could sleep not knowing if you were all right?" Manx snarled.

Dent sighed. "I'm sorry, but we couldn't get back before light and didn't want to risk being seen." Dent reached out and took Manx's hand, and they hurried down the corridor after Bear.

Bear had not been quiet when he'd entered the boys' room, and Boxer and Battle were waiting for Dent when he entered the chamber.

"Bear said you have important information," Battle said, "but he was going to sleep, and no one was to disturb him."

"Let's sit at the table before I fall down. We've had two very eventful nights." Dent collapsed into a chair.

When everyone was seated at the table, Dent told them about finding the ultas' exit unguarded, and rescuing and hiding the plants. Then he described the trip to the fence and placing the tracker on the top, almost being discovered by the platforms, seeing a tall leader riding on the back of a platform, and having flashbacks of Adoran. He described the fence-rider delivering eight packets of cylinders, and the tall leader stacking them on the platforms and rolling away.

By then it had been light, and he and Bear had run to the mountain to hide.

Battle was confused. "What is inside the cylinders, and what are the rogues planning to do with them?" He discussed possibilities with Boxer and Dent, and when they were finished, Dent told them of last night's discovery. "Once it was dark, we circled around the landing field. Let the commander know that the warship has a signal beam at the top of the ramp to alert the rogues when someone goes inside."

Dent continued, "We went to the ultas' exit. Past the buildings, there is no cover to hide behind. When we were removing the plants, we heard noises coming from that way. Bear waited while I changed and went to investigate. Here's where it gets interesting. The road ends at the steep bluff, and I got as close as I could without being seen. I counted four platform guards and five tall leaders. Four of the leaders steadied rods on the ground, and the platforms pounded on the rods to make holes in the ground. It looked like they had been doing that for days, which must be the reason there's only one patrol at night. The fifth tall leader patrolled the area, searching up and down the road." Dent paused to catch his breath.

Boxer and Battle looked at each other, trying to make sense of Dent's story. Boxer asked, "Could you tell what they were doing with the holes?"

Dent shook his head. "They were still pounding when I left. The leader almost caught me in his search beam, so I decided it was time to get out of there."

Boxer asked another question. "Did you see the cylinders the fence guard delivered?"

Dent thought about that. "No, but the area past the road is rocky, and they could be stacked there. Where else would they take them? The cylinders are clearly what the holes are for."

"Too bad we can't steal one of those cylinders," Battle muttered.

Dent yawned. "That's why we didn't come back yesterday. I felt it was important to find where the robots were taking the cylinders. Now I think I'll join Bear and catch a couple hours of sleep."

Boxer told Dent, "Don't wake Bear or go out tonight. Francine said the repeaters will be finished tomorrow, and Bear and I will hide them tomorrow night. Bear will have another full night's work."

Dent was happy to take the night off, and he went to bed.

Battle stood up. "I need to report to military command," he told Boxer.

"And I need to find Grand Pierre," Boxer responded. "I'm not certain, but I have an idea of what the holes and cylinders are for."

Manx hadn't said a word, but the look on her face said that she was worried about the survival of the underground city.

It was the following day before Bear turned over in bed, stretched, groaned, swung his legs to the floor, and stood up. He stumbled to the door, opened it, and spied Dent sitting at the table.

"I've been wondering if you decided to hibernate for a month," Dent said. "Wren saved our packets, and you have two days of nourishment to suck down." He pushed the packets to the end of the table as Bear sat down, still groggy from sleeping so long.

"Grand Pierre is trying to figure out what the rogues are doing, and Francine is scrambling to finish the repeaters so you and Boxer can hide them tonight," Dent explained.

Bear sucked down a second packet and burped loudly, causing Dent to fan the air in front of him just to annoy Bear. Bear gave a large yawn and picked up another packet.

Dent rambled while Bear finished off his two-day supply of food. "Grand Pierre is working with the tactical team to see if an idea I had could protect the entrances in case the robots throw bombs again. Boxer is reviewing the plans of the city with the design team. Hey, you know what? If you are less than sixty years old, you are considered to be young, and Grand Pierre, Francine, and Aunt May are some of the younger Ulterions. The controller is over one hundred years, and Aunt May thinks he may be closer to two hundred."

Wren entered the chamber, followed by Bunny, and exclaimed, "Bear's awake! No one wanted to wake you, so we let you sleep."

During the past weeks, Wren had experienced a growth spurt, and she was almost as tall as Bunny, who was now as tall as Manx. Francine said Bunny had reached her full growth, even though she was shorter than the other ultas. Wren was now eleven years old, and Francine had discussed with Grand Pierre the idea of placing her with a team when she turned twelve. Because of Wren's caring nature—and her not displaying any specific skills—Francine worried about where to place her.

Dent was the only one without a specific team assignment. "I'm GP's sidekick," was his response when asked about it.

Wren sat down at the table and looked at Bear. "Boxer is bringing the repeaters to our chamber." Bear stared back at Wren, not saying a word.

Bunny stood beside Bear and signed that she was glad he was okay and that she had been worried about him. Bear smiled at her.

Dent said to Bear, "I can go with you and Boxer tonight and watch for the patrol."

Bear finally spoke. "There is just the one patrol. The other guards are busy pounding holes. Besides, Boxer can hear the patrol coming, so we can avoid it."

Boxer entered the room carrying two heavy-looking packs and set them on the table. He told Bear, "There are four repeaters in each pack. The technology team is still working on the last two, but I didn't want to wait until they finished. We should leave soon to get them hidden before light. They will cover the area the robots patrol at night. Tomorrow night we can hide the last two repeaters."

Bear stood up and slung one of the packs over his shoulder. "I'm ready." He looked at Bunny and told her, "See you later."

Boxer picked up his pack, smiled at Wren, and followed Bear from the room.

"I hate waiting," Wren grumbled as she watched Boxer and Bear leave the chamber.

"Boxer will be fine," Dent said. "He has Bear to take care of him."

Wren and Bunny attacked Dent, and as he fended off their playful punches, he fell out of the chair and landed on the floor, laughing. Manx and Battle walked into the chamber.

Dent sat up and looked at Battle. "If you have a tracker with you, I know how to tag the night patrol. I want to put a tracker on the road, and when the patrol rolls over it, it will attach to the frame. Is the patrol tonight the one I tagged before?"

"No," Battle answered. "It's located where the holes are being made. Find where the ruts from their rollers are deepest and place the tracker on the highest ridge between the ruts. It will give the tracker a better chance to attach to the crossbar." Battle reached into his pocket, took out one of the small, round disks, and handed it to Dent.

"Feel like a walk in the park?" Dent ask Manx, and she answered, "Of course."

It didn't take long for Dent to find a good place for the tracker, and when he and Manx returned to their chamber, Battle was waiting. "Military command is watching the monitor and will contact me if the second tracker starts signaling."

"It shouldn't be long," Dent told him. "The guard was turning around by the ulta buildings when we left."

From a speaker built into the wall, a sentry reported, "We now have three of the guards tagged and being monitored."

CHAPTER 43

$\mathcal{T}$he haze in the night sky was breaking with streaks of light. Day would soon follow.

Boxer and Bear entered the special ones' chamber and saw Battle and Dent sitting at the table. Neither had gone to bed, their minds filled with worry for Boxer and Bear. Boxer and Bear were coated with dirt and grime from crawling around, on top of, and over the destroyed buildings to hide the repeaters.

Boxer gave a thumbs-up to Battle. "The repeaters are installed. There was only one guard on patrol, so it was easy to avoid. As soon as I change into a clean suit, I'm going to the communication center to see if Francine was able to make contact with the repeaters."

Manx walked from her bedroom and told Boxer, "I'll go with you. I'm anxious to find out if the repeaters work."

When Boxer and Manx entered the communication center, Francine was seated in front of a row of monitors with dials across the front. Each monitor was programmed to connect to a specific repeater. Francine was busy turning each of the monitors' controls to different positions, watching for a light to blink green for "receiving" or to stay red for "no contact."

Francine looked around. "Good work, Boxer. I've made contact with six of the repeaters." She pointed to a large screen, "As soon as I identify the frequency the rogues are using, we can interpret the signals that order the robots. The robots communicate with the rogues verbally, but all communication from the rogues are by programmed signals." Francine turned back to the monitors.

Boxer and Manx stood and watched Francine. Manx asked, "Is there anything I can do?"

"Watch those last two monitors, and let me know when you see a green light," Francine answered without turning around.

"I'll be in strategy and planning," said Boxer as he left the room. "Call me when you find their frequency."

That evening Grand Pierre and the special ones were seated in their chamber, waiting for Battle. Because of all the activities, they had not reported on each team's accomplishments for days, and there was a lot to catch up on. Grand Pierre's face looked strained, and his shoulders slumped. Clearly the situation of the underground city was critical.

While they were waiting, Dent told Grand Pierre that he was concerned because the controller had no escape plans for the city. The controller had told Dent there was no place to escape to because the rogues had destroyed everything above ground years ago.

Grand Pierre sighed and said he was unsure if the Ulterions, who had lived underground in a controlled environment, could survive above ground. With the ultas unable to access their plants, there was a food shortage, and the extra nutrients stored in distribution had been depleted.

Grand Pierre admitted that the current situation for Ulterion was dire.

Battle entered the chamber, looking exhausted, and sat down at the table. Grand Pierre asked, "What is your update?"

Battle reported, "We tracked the tagged platforms to an area where the fence-rider stops. The commander thinks it is the rogue headquarters and is trying to determine a way to investigate, but the area will be heavily guarded if the rogue scientists are there."

Grand Pierre replied, "Once Francine identifies their frequency, she can tell where the signals are coming from. This would confirm if it is their headquarters."

"Francine has tested over half of the possibilities," Manx reported, "and I'm sure that tomorrow she will have identified their frequency."

"What if we go back to the mountain and climb to the other side?" Bear suggested. "The rogues are not scanning that side of the fence, since there is no way the Ulterion military can get over it. We could follow the fence until it ends."

Battle explained, "On the other side of the fence, the ground is flat and covered with dead grass. There is nothing to hide us. Besides, the mountains are far away, and it would take too long. I don't think we have much time."

"I can fly from the mountain," Wren suggested, "and if I stay high enough, the robots won't notice me."

Grand Pierre nodded at Wren. "It is a workable solution."

"Tonight I can carry Wren to the mountain," Bear said, "and she can fly at first light."

"I'm coming too," Boxer said firmly, causing Wren to scowl at him.

Battle asked, "Grand Pierre, is the communicator we brought from Adoran working? Boxer could give the commander an immediate update."

Grand Pierre said that the communicator was operable and agreed that Boxer, Bear, and Wren could leave tonight. At first light Wren would fly to where the fence ended to determine if it was the rogues' headquarters.

Boxer, Bear, and Wren climbed from the hidden exit and carefully made their way to the mountain edge where the fence ended. Bear found a place to sleep. He had carried Wren on his shoulders to save her energy, and Boxer had carried the heavy communicator. Boxer and Wren waited behind a boulder for daylight. Only Bear's snoring broke the silence.

When as it was light enough for Wren to fly, Boxer cautioned, "Stay high until you reach the end of the fence. Don't fly too low and expose yourself, even if you need a closer look. I'm not sure if the robots will recognize a small bird as a threat."

"Don't worry, Boxer. I will be careful and cautious," Wren teased.

"Don't take any chances," Boxer warned.

Wren hopped, changed into the small brown bird, flapped her wings to gain height, and flew away.

꙳Ꙭ ꙳Ꙭ

The following morning Francine pushed open the door to the special ones' chamber where Grand Pierre was waiting. She exclaimed, "I have the rogues' frequency. We are receiving streams of data, and from the tagged guards, we can determine what they do on a specific command." Francine's face glowed with excitement.

Grand Pierre leaped from the table and gave Francine a very big hug.

Battle stated, "This is great news. I need to let the commander know." He quickly left the chamber.

↓↳ ↓↳

Battle, Dent, Manx, and Grand Pierre sat in their chamber. They had completed their day's assignments, and all were anxious to hear from Boxer. Dent reached out and took hold of Manx's hand, knowing she worried about Wren, trying to reassure her.

Grand Pierre held a receiver that would type out Boxer's message.

Suddenly an alarm echoed through the corridors, and Battle jumped up. "I need to get to military command."

Grand Pierre stood and handed the receiver to Manx. "Monitor for Boxer's update, and when you receive it, get it to the command center immediately." He followed Battle from the chamber.

Battle and Grand Pierre raced down the long corridors until they reached the main entrance where the military commander stood surrounded by armed sentries. The commander turned to Battle. "Six platforms are coming down the road, rolling in pairs. The spotter said that each guard is carrying one of those cylinders."

Grand Pierre asked the commander, "Have you engaged the energy fields?"

The commander nodded. "They'd better work."

Grand Pierre silently hoped that Dent's idea worked as planned.

The platforms stopped, placing two guards at each of the entrances. Battle looked at a monitor and noticed that tagged guards were among the six. One sat in front of the main entrance, and another was at the communication entrance. The six guards sat in plain sight, taunting the Ulterions to come out in the open.

Manx rushed up carrying the receiver and told Grand Pierre, "Boxer sent the update."

Manx handed the receiver to Grand Pierre, who read the report and then ordered one of the sentries, "Take this to the command center and upload it. It has information regarding the rogues' headquarters."

There was movement outside when one platform from each of the pairs rolled forward and stopped directly in front of the entrances. In sync, each guard twisted the cylinder to activate it, pulled its arm back, and threw the cylinder at the entrance. The three guards waited and were caught off guard when the hissing cylinders hit the invisible nets—the same kind used in the exercise room to play ball—and bounced back toward them.

One of the guards reached out and caught the sizzling cylinder. It exploded, blowing the guard to pieces and leaving only the platform. The other two guards started to roll backward but weren't fast enough. The cylinders landed in front of them and exploded. One platform was blown over, crushing the guard beneath the heavy frame. The tracks on the third platform were blown to shreds. The guard tried to get away, frantically swinging its arms, unable to move.

Cheers rose from the sentries as they watched the robots destroyed by their own bombs. The remaining three guards had not moved. Battle heard one guard reply, "Order received," and then the three guards twisted their cylinders and threw them. The cylinders flew high, up and over the entrances, and landed on the hard ground that hid the city below. Then the guards turned and sped down the road toward the ultas' exit, two of them with trackers that reported where they were going.

The commander ordered, "Disengage the nets, and immobilize the platforms."

The sentries grabbed their weapons and ran outside, just as the bombs on the top of the underground city exploded, shaking the corridor walls.

Watching the sentries disable the guard spinning on the road, Dent commented, "We took out three platforms with their own bombs—and no causalities for us."

Battle stood next to Dent and wondered, "What purpose did that serve? The rogues should have known our military would be expecting another attack on the entrances."

Dent had figured out the rogues' plan. "Without the nets, our only defense would have been to go outside and fight. The second guard was there to deliver the kill shot." He looked at Battle. "If the rogues had succeeded, they would have trapped everyone underground. They must not know about the exit we use."

"The situation is under control," Battle said. "Let's find out what information Boxer sent."

Boxer's message was streaming across one of the monitors in the command center: "Large metal building, no windows, single door. Stacks of items outside, could be parts for robots or weapons. Outside, four tall leaders, two platforms, one fence-rider. No cover close to the building."

As he watched the monitor, Dent said, "Wren did a good reconnaissance. Too bad there weren't any windows so she could see inside. A fortified metal building will be hard to destroy. Fire won't work on it like it did on Adoran."

The Final Battle

CHAPTER 44

It was dark when Boxer, Bear, and Wren reached the building that hid the exit to the underground city. They had stayed close to the mountainside to avoid being seen, although they had not seen any guards on their return. Boxer signaled for quiet and listened. Then the three climbed silently down the steep stairs, and Bear secured the exit. When they entered their chamber, Battle, Grand Pierre, Dent, and Manx were sitting at the table.

"The military commander was impressed with your report," Battle said. "He said that the information was valuable. He is certain the metal building is the rogues' headquarters."

"Wren did all the work," Boxer said.

Wren stood beside Grand Pierre and shrugged. "They didn't even notice me. I wish I could have seen inside the building, but there were no windows."

Grand Pierre told Wren, "Sit down, and tell me everything you saw. No detail is too small."

Wren sat down, closed her eyes, and began recalling. "The fence ends at the metal building. On the ground were piles of what looked like pieces from those platform things. There were no trees for cover to let me get closer. There were more piles of parts to make the tall guys—legs and arms and even heads stacked on the ground. Yuck! That fence-rider was there, and two platforms were moving parts between the piles. The tall guys looked like they were trying to fix the broken guards. The tall guys walked funny, sort of jerky. I was getting tired from circling, and I'd seen as much as I could, so I flew back."

"The rogues have not developed new robots in years," Battle explained. "The guards and leaders on Adoran were identical to the ones here, and they were at least twenty years old. The rogues are making repairs from other damaged robots."

Grand Pierre agreed. "The increased patrols to keep everyone underground is because the rogues do not want us to know how many robots are operational. Mention this to the commander."

"I'll let him know first thing in the morning," Battle replied.

Grand Pierre patted Wren's shoulder. "You have done very well. Isn't it interesting how one small bird can contribute so much? No one else could have gathered that much information without being seen."

Grand Pierre looked around the table and told the others, "We have had an eventful day and need to sleep. Who knows what may happen tomorrow?"

Manx was fast asleep when she thought she felt her bed shake. She decided she must be dreaming and turned over.

Dent threw open the bedroom door. "Something's happening."

Manx jumped from her bed and shook Wren as a muffled sound shook the walls. Alarms began blaring from speakers in the corridors.

Grand Pierre entered the special ones' chamber and exclaimed, "The rogues have begun setting off the cylinder bombs in the holes they have been digging. The repeaters have identified a platform hiding outside each of the entrances, waiting for the sentries to come outside and investigate."

Dent was confused. "But the holes are too far away from the city to cause damage," he said.

"The corridors have been weakened from previous attacks," Grand Pierre explained, "and if the steep ridge on the side of the city collapses and causes a rock slide, the walls will not be able to withstand the added pressure. Aunt May looked at the terrain maps, and where the robots have planted the bombs, there is an underground fault that runs under the ridge. To collapse the ridge—that is the purpose of the holes. The second attack was to seal the entrances."

Suddenly there was a second muffled blast that rattled the walls.

"They're trapping us like rats in this underground maze," Dent said.

"It's a devious plan," Boxer declared, "and if it succeeds, the rogues will have won."

Battle gravely stated, "The final battle for Ulterion has begun."

Francine threw open the door. "Manx, we need you in communications. Time is running out to disrupt the rogues' orders." Manx followed Francine from the room.

Battle raced to military command as alarms continued to blare, and Grand Pierre and Dent ran behind him.

Bear growled as he left the chamber. "I need to find Bunny and get her to safety outside."

"Take Wren with you," Boxer said. "The girls will not be able to fight the robots." He took Wren's hand and pulled her out of the chamber behind Bear.

"We'll meet you at the exit," Boxer called out as another blast echoed and the walls shook. Bear took off to find Bunny.

Boxer opened the exit hatch and looked out. Satisfied that it was safe, he pushed aside the grate and climbed out. Wren, Bunny, and Bear followed him. Boxer listened, separating the sounds: the robots rolling back and forth in front of the entrances, the cylinder bombs going off, and the blaring alarms. He detected no sounds near the old building where they hid.

Boxer looked at Bear. "You and Wren change," he said. "Bunny can ride on your back, and Wren can fly. If Bunny stays low, she won't be noticed—nor will Wren if she stays close beside you. Take them to the mountain's edge. They can climb to the top and hide."

Wren started to protest, and Boxer sternly told her, "There is no other choice. You and Bunny need to get to safety. Besides, Bunny needs you."

Boxer looked around the side of the building and told Bear, "Go that way to the mountain. It will take longer but will be safer."

Bear nodded and changed into the huge brown bear. He knelt down, and Boxer lifted Bunny onto his back. He told her, "Hold on tight. It will be a fast and bumpy ride." Bunny buried her arms securely around Bear's neck.

Boxer looked at Wren and told her, "Stay safe, and keep Bunny safe."

Wren reached up and hugged Boxer. "I'll wait for you on the mountain. You stay safe. I love you, Boxer."

Wren changed, and Bear leaped from behind the building and loped toward the distant mountain. Boxer watched Bear increase his stride as he ran with the slim girl holding tight to his neck, her long blonde hair blowing behind. Wren flew close to Bear, and Boxer watched until Bear made a turn that hid them from sight.

Boxer looked toward the main entrance, making sure the robots had not seen Bear. Then he climbed down the hatch, not bothering to pull the grate over it. He knew that before the day was over they would need the exit.

Boxer ran to the command center to join the others amid the chaos of the blaring alarms, shaking walls, and gunfire from the sentries as they desperately fought to keep the platforms from getting inside.

At the main entrance Battle could see that the sentries were at a disadvantage. They needed a direct line of sight on the robots for their weapons to be effective. The robots were stationed at the entrances, waiting to kill anyone who came out. Three soldiers had tried to make it out, but all had been wounded—one seriously, who would not survive.

Battle turned to the commander. "We need to get all nonmilitary personnel to safety."

The commander looked at Battle and asked, "How?"

"The rogues don't know about the exit by the living chambers," Battle explained. The commander looked at him with a confused expression, and Battle added, "They can escape through the exit and run to the mountains."

The commander sighed. "We have no way to protect them, even if you can convince them to go outside."

"It's the only hope they have," Battle said.

Grand Pierre stood by, listening, and knew that Battle was correct. He told the commander, "Maileen and Jacques can lead the people to safety. They have the knowledge to survive outside."

"If we create a diversion, the robots won't notice," Battle said.

Another blast shook the walls, and the commander asked Battle, "What do you have planned for a diversion?"

"A smoke screen to hide the escape," Battle answered. "If we set the far building on fire with oil that creates rolling black smoke, the robots will think the bombs caused something to explode. Since they don't know about the exit, they won't bother to investigate another burning building."

Battle had the commander's attention. "It could work," he admitted. He turned and ordered two sentries to take oil containers to the exit and wait for further orders.

Then the commander told Grand Pierre, "Find Maileen and Jacques, and let them know the plan. I'll announce that all nonmilitary personnel must evacuate immediately—and where to go."

Grand Pierre turned to go and find Aunt May and Jacques.

After hearing the commander agree to have all nonmilitary personnel meet at the escape hatch, Dent hurried from the main entrance to check on Francine and Manx. He stopped at the entrance to the communication center and watched Francine quickly turning dials to different settings while Manx monitored the screens. Dent didn't want to interrupt, so he backed away and hurried to the exit.

Frightened scientists were filling the corridor, each clutching a few special items that would be lost forever when the walls collapsed. Battle was standing at the exit steps when Dent hurried up. "Is there anything I can do?" he asked Battle.

Battle said they were checking the chambers to make sure no one was still inside—when suddenly the hatch rattled. Battle and Dent jumped back, expecting a robot to drop a bomb. Both exhaled a sigh of relief when Bear climbed down, looked around at everyone, and growled, "What's going on?"

Battle asked, "Are any robots nearby?"

Bear shook his head, and his hair flew wildly. "No. I checked before I climbed down."

Battle turned to the two sentries and ordered them to set the selected building on fire. Time was running out for the plan to work. The two soldiers picked up the oil and climbed the steps.

Battle looked at Aunt May standing at the front of the line and asked, "Ready?" Aunt May nodded and gave Battle the signal for *mission go* that Grand Pierre had taught them back on the farm.

Battle had briefed Aunt May on the mission details. Hidden by black smoke from the oil-soaked building, she would lead the Ulterions from the city to the mountains. Jacques would bring up the rear, making sure everyone kept up. When everyone reached the mountain, they would climb to the top and wait with Wren and Bunny.

The ultas were the last of the scientists to climb from the hatch, followed by their tall leader. Dent noticed that some of the ultas did not look fully recovered and might have trouble keeping up.

Battle watched the old building. It was almost burned to the ground, and he hoped the smoke would last long enough to hide the scientists until they were out of sight where the path turned.

"There are so few of us left," Grand Pierre uttered when Battle and Dent climbed back down the hatch.

"Now they have the chance to survive," Battle replied.

"How much of a chance, I wonder?" Grand Pierre said. "Plans should have been made and supplies hidden for an emergency like this. It was arrogance for the controller to think that the underground city would always protect them."

Then Grand Pierre told Battle that the controller was in the large conference room. He would not leave the city, and a few of the older Ulterions had joined him. The controller would rather give in to defeat than try to survive outside.

CHAPTER 45

*B*oxer had an idea and told Bear, who agreed it might work, and they went to find the commander and Battle and told them. The commander took a communicator from a sentry and handed it to Boxer. "Take this. We will contact you when the platforms start your way."

The commander gave Bear two square-looking bombs. "Bury these where the platforms will run over them," he said. "Once they are triggered, they will explode. Bury them, set off the alarms, and get away." Boxer and Bear nodded and headed for the exit.

Boxer climbed the steps and looked out. Smoke wafted from the burned building, but it was not enough to cover their escape. He waited until he heard gunfire from the military, which was intended pull the robots to the entrances. Then he and Bear raced toward the landing field, with Bear being extra careful that he didn't stumble.

They reached the warship, which was rigged to signal when anyone entered. Boxer stopped. Bear handed him one of the explosives to bury and then continued to the fence. Bear was smoothing the ground over the explosive when Boxer ran up.

"I tripped the sensor in the warship and jumped over it to get out," Boxer said. "The rogues will think soldiers are inside." He glanced around, checking the area for guards.

Bear stood up, looked at the fence, and gave a low growl. He jumped against the fence and then gave it a good shake. He looked at Boxer. "That should get their attention. Let's get out of here."

Boxer and Bear ran to the far end of the landing strip and hid behind pieces of the destroyed runway. The communicator in Boxer's hand vibrated. It read, *Two platforms and four leaders coming your way.*

Boxer and Bear waited, and then Boxer heard the fence begin to vibrate. The fence-rider went rolling by, and Bear whispered, "The rogues think the scientists are trying to escape over the fence."

Boxer motioned for quiet and pointed ahead. Two platforms, each carrying two tall leaders, came into view. One of the platforms turned and headed toward the warship, anxious to attack the unsuspecting sentries they believed were inside.

Boxer's keen sense of hearing heard fence-rider report, "No sign of sentries by the fence." Then fence-rider ordered, "Search the area in both directions."

One of the platforms had made it to the fence, and Boxer and Bear peeked around, anxious to see if their plan would work.

One of the leaders answered in the familiar metallic voice: "Why do we need to search if there is no one around?"

"Orders," fence-rider responded.

"The ground looks disturbed over here," the tall leader started to say, but he said no more.

The explosion was massive, the sound so loud that Boxer and Bear covered their ears. Bear's long hair flew straight back from the wind created by the explosion.

"Wow!" Bear exclaimed as he gaped at the enormous hole in the fence. Parts of fence-rider started to rain down from above.

Another huge explosion shook the ground, and the warship lifted up into the air. When the pieces fell to the ground, they glowed orange, smoldering from the heat of the blast.

"Those scientists sure know how to build bombs," Boxer exclaimed. "There's nothing left of the warship but small pieces of metal."

Bear counted aloud. "That eliminates the fence-rider, two platforms, and four of those tall things." He smiled and looked at Boxer. "Now what?"

Boxer looked back at the way they had come. After the explosions, the robots would be watching the area. There was only one way for them to go. "Let's go find that metal building Wren spotted."

Battle and the commander were watching the monitor, waiting for Boxer and Bear to report, when Dent left military command. He wanted to check on Manx.

He walked into the room just as Francine shouted, "I found out how the rogues are commanding the robots! They are using a sub-signal. That's why it took so long to find it."

Francine and Manx were seated in front of a row of monitors, and Grand Pierre was standing behind them. "Outstanding!" he exclaimed.

Francine turned around. "We're ready to scramble the signal. Manx, lock each panel to the correct setting."

Grand Pierre watched the monitors fill with streams of data as the rogues issued orders. He studied the monitors and then typed codes into the communicator he held. "That should scramble the commands," he said. He handed the communicator to Francine, who immediately connected it to the control panel.

After the explosions at the fence and warship, the fighting became even more intense as the remaining platforms began to force their way inside the entrances. When the platforms rolled ahead, the sentries had direct line of sight.

Battle guarded the main entrance, armed with a large weapon, and the commander fought beside him. The tall leaders stepped into the entrances, holding metal shields. The military weapons could not penetrate the thick shields, and because of the robots' strength, the force of the hits did not stop them.

As the tall leaders came close, a bullet ricocheted off a shield and hit the commander. The commander collapsed, and Battle pulled him away from the entrance. Blood was gushing from the commander's neck. The commander reached for Battle and tried to speak.

"Save your strength," Battle told the brave commander.

The commander pulled Battle closer and whispered, "We will not survive. Get everyone out." And his hand fell to his side.

Battle had no time to grieve for the solider he admired. He stood and saluted, signifying that the commander's last order would be carried out.

Everyone in the communication center could hear the intense fighting. Francine's hand shook as she handed Grand Pierre the communicator. "Uploads are complete," she said and rested her head on her arms.

Grand Pierre placed his hands on her shoulders. "You have done much."

A tall leader with a gun suddenly appeared at the door and said in a metallic voice, "Now you die."

Manx gasped and reached for Dent's hand.

The tall creature turned and scanned Manx and Dent. Then it scanned them again. "What are you?" it said. Suddenly the leader's arms began to jerk.

Manx and Dent watched in horror, waiting to be killed.

At that moment Battle raced up and instantly assessed the critical situation in communication. He grabbed his last sweeper out of his pocket, released the razor-sharp blades, and threw the lethal missile. The blades hit the tall leader in the neck, causing sparks to fly from the deep gash as the wires were severed.

The leader stumbled to the floor and looked up at Manx. "I don't want to die," it said.

The walls shook violently, and Battle yelled, "We must get out now." He pulled Grand Pierre and Francine from the room as the ceiling began to collapse. Dent and Manx ran from the room as the ceiling crashed to the floor. Battle led the way through the crumbling corridors, and billowing dust filled the air.

They reached the main entrance and could see the sentries outside attacking the platforms that had been disabled by the corrupted commands. The beams supporting the entrance began to shake violently and twist sideways. Battle ran ahead and ordered the soldiers to push the platforms inside and get to safety.

Everyone raced across the road, swerving to avoid large holes in ground, and stopped beside the crumbling buildings. A few soldiers who had been able escape the destruction ran toward them. The soldiers were bloody and hurt, but none had given up the fight.

A violent rumbling shook the ground, and the underground city imploded, leaving a massive depression. Everyone watched in stunned silence as densely colored fumes began to float above the flattened city.

Dent held Manx's trembling hand. She looked at him and said in a shaky voice, "He didn't want to die. He was forced to do what he did. How can anyone do that to their own kind?"

Dent didn't have an answer for the evil that had caused so much pain and destruction.

Grand Pierre was watching the fumes that rose from the sunken city and exclaimed, "Get away from here! Those colored fumes from the labs are toxic and will kill us all."

"We must get to the mountains!" Dent yelled above the roar that came from the exploding laboratories.

"Have you heard from Boxer and Bear?" Manx worriedly asked Grand Pierre.

Grand Pierre pushed a symbol on the communicator. "Boxer, are you there?"

Grand Pierre sighed in relief when he heard, "Bear and I are at the metal building. We can't get inside because the door is sealed."

Battle told Grand Pierre, "Get everyone to the mountain, and tell Boxer I'm on my way." Then he turned and ran behind the building.

Dent kissed Manx and held her close. He stepped back, smiled at her shocked expression, and said, "Help Grand Pierre get everyone to safety." Then he raced after Battle before Manx could argue.

Battle and Bear were puzzled. They stepped back from the secure metal door and looked around. Something was wrong. Why were there no guards outside the metal building?

Boxer said, "Maybe the rogues ordered all the guards to attack the city, and they're not worried about anyone finding their headquarters."

Bear looked around and growled, "I feel like I'm being watched."

Movement from one of the piles of broken robot parts caused them to spin around. A tall robot had been watching them from behind the pieces of arms, legs, and heads. He was having trouble standing up and was frantically trying to aim a weapon in his shaking hands.

Bear gave a loud roar and charged. At full speed he tackled the robot, knocking it to the ground, and the gun flew into the air. Boxer ran over and picked up the gun and aimed it at the robot. The robot lay on the ground, not moving. Bear had broken its neck. Boxer pulled the trigger, and the blast from the weapon blew the robot to pieces.

Boxer and Bear were looking at the smoldering pieces when Battle rushed up with Dent right behind. Boxer pointed. "It was hiding in the scrap pile and tried to ambush us."

Battle looked around to make sure there were no other robots hiding. Then he looked at the building and asked, "You couldn't get the rogues to open the door?"

"I pounded on the door and told them the war was over and to surrender," Boxer explained, "but there has been no response from inside."

Battle shrugged. "They've had time to surrender. Stand back."

Battle changed into the wide, armor-plated mastiff, lowered his massive head, and charged the door. When Battle crashed into the door, the sound was almost as loud as the blast by the fence, and the door exploded inward.

The huge mastiff was too wide to enter the narrow opening. Battle changed and stood at the door and ordered, "You have lost the war and must now surrender."

No response came from inside, so Battle stepped through the door and into a pitch-black room. Boxer, Bear, and Dent entered behind him.

The special ones stopped in the middle of the dark room and looked around. Along one wall were rows of monitors and communication equipment, similar to the ones Francine and Manx used. The opposite wall held what looked like medical equipment. There were three long tables hoisted upright. Beside each table hung wires and tubing from the various pieces of equipment.

Three unrecognizable creatures were standing in front of the communicators, frantically pushing and turning controls, trying to contact their metal creations. The creatures wore long coats with exposed connections to the wires and tubes that delivered their life-sustaining drugs. Once they had been tall, but now they were shriveled and bent over. Hoods covered their heads, and gloves encased their twisted hands.

Battle glared menacingly at the three remaining rogue scientists, the last of their kind, and started toward them.

Dent held out his hand and stepped forward to stop him. "The war is over," he said. "The robots have all been disabled."

The three robed figures stopped their frantic punching at the controls and slowly turned to look at Dent. The reason Boxer had heard no response was that all three of the pale, wrinkled faces were covered by masks that continually pumped air to their lungs. Three sets of eyes glared at Dent. The middle rogue pointed a bent finger, and Dent could read the question in his eyes.

"We came from Adoran," Dent explained.

The rogue began to move toward Dent, not walking but rolling. As he neared, Bear gave a low, menacing growl. The rogue instantly stopped, and his long coat swung to the side to reveal a platform with a stand that held the rogue upright. Dent wondered how old these rogues must be. They must be hundreds of years old, maybe survivors from the first conflict that had separated the rogues from the Ulterions.

The middle rogue nodded to the rogues on either side of him. His crooked hands shook as he lifted a lever from inside the platform. He looked up, and Dent could see defeat in his eyes, and he realized what the rogue was going to do.

"Stop!" Dent yelled. He heard a click. The rogue had armed an explosive. "It's a bomb!" Dent turned and raced for the door behind the others.

Dent barely made it outside when the building exploded. He could feel flames scorching his back. All four boys ran until they were safely away from pieces of hot metal falling to the ground. They stopped and looked back at the sizzling remains of the building.

"They chose to die rather than surrender," Boxer said.

"It was their choice." Battle was satisfied with the outcome.

Bear emitted a triumphant growl of victory.

The Future

CHAPTER 46

The four boys walked beside the fence toward the mountain. They were jubilant, feeling a sense of relief, and it was a feeling they had not felt in ages. They were discussing the three remaining rogues, wondering how old they were. The rogues had not found a way to renew their bodies and live forever. Instead they had created metal monsters. The Ulterions had never been a threat to the rogues. It was the rogues' own greed that had changed them into unfeeling creatures.

Suddenly a small brown bird swooped down, buzzed around their heads, and landed. Wren changed and ran to Boxer. He caught her in his arms.

"I've been so worried!" Wren exclaimed as she tightly hugged Boxer around the neck.

A yellow cat leaped from the rocky mountainside to the ground and changed. Manx looked hard at each boy and hissed. "You survived the blast, and nothing looks broken. Grand Pierre has been trying to contact you."

"I dropped the communicator when we ran from the building," Boxer said. "It was destroyed in the blast."

"You could have changed and howled a *situation okay,*" Wren scolded. "We would have heard you." Boxer agreed.

Manx walked over to Dent and held out her hand. "We heard the blast from the mountain and became worried when Grand Pierre couldn't contact you."

Dent explained. "The rogue leader set off an explosive, and we were barely able to get out. The only damage is to the hair on the back of my head—or the lack thereof." Dent turned and Manx saw his scorched hair.

Manx sniffed and told him, "You smell like a burned rat."

Dent grinned at Manx, exposing his two black teeth.

"Did everyone get to safety?" Battle asked Manx.

Before Manx could reply, Bear growled, "Where is Bunny?"

"Bunny is fine and is anxious to see you," Wren chirped, and Bear sighed with relief.

"Grand Pierre said the scientists who made it out of the city should survive," Manx said, "but there aren't many of them left. The old ones refused to leave and stayed with the controller. Grand Pierre said they were afraid of the future." She started climbing the steep mountain, not letting go of Dent's hand.

"What about the ultas?" Dent asked worriedly.

"Not all of them made it to the mountain," Manx told him sadly. "The long run was too much for them. Bunny said the ulta leader is very sad."

When the special ones reached the mountaintop, Bunny ran to Bear and hugged him around the waist. Bear felt her slim shoulders shudder and knelt down. "No one was hurt," he said. "We are all fine."

Grand Pierre hurried forward and anxiously asked, "What happened at the rogues' headquarters. We all heard the blast and worried about your safety."

"The rogues decided to go out with a bang instead of surrendering," Boxer replied.

Grand Pierre nodded. "I thought as much. Surrender was never a part of their plan."

Battle saw the few soldiers who had made it out huddled together. No one had escaped injury. He walked over, bowed to each one, and thanked them for never giving up.

Grand Pierre stepped up, placed his arm across Battle's shoulders, and looked at the soldiers. "The military commander told me that if he did not make it out alive, Battle was to take over command of the military."

Every soldier stood, some having to help their comrades up, and saluted Battle. Battle firmed his shoulders and saluted Grand Pierre, signifying his acceptance.

Grand Pierre told them, "We do not know what the days ahead hold for us, but with Battle's leadership and you brave soldiers to protect us, I do not fear the future."

The people who had escaped the city were sitting around in groups, recovering from the long race to the mountain and the steep climb to reach the top. Bunny was sitting by the ulta leader, trying to comfort him. They all looked sad and unsure of what to expect.

Dent noticed the small group, walked over, and bowed to them. He said, "You are in for a big surprise once we get across the mountain."

The ulta leader looked at Dent and nodded, signifying that the ultas would place their trust in the special ones in the days ahead.

Bear walked over to Dent. "We need to get off the mountain before dark. I'll let Grand Pierre know to get everyone moving."

Dent told the ulta leader, "We will go slowly and help anyone who cannot keep up."

The sun was fading as the last of the exhausted procession climbed from the rocky mountainside. Boxer stood on a ledge and counted the survivors. Including the special ones, the number barely passed one hundred.

Boxer gazed across the valley below him. It was wide and stretched far, and he was thankful for Bear and Dent's nightly prowls to discover the valley.

Dent found Grand Pierre and led him aside to explain. "Bear and I carried coverings for shelters and mats for bedding, as much as we had time for. Bear found some utensils and pots for cooking in an old storage area. Beyond that rise is a small stream, and the water is good to drink. You need to assemble a team to erect shelters. There is plenty of wood for fire if it gets too cold."

Grand Pierre was shocked and stammered, "You and Bear have done all this?"

Dent grinned. "We made a few night trips, but Bear worried that if the controller found out, we would be prevented from going outside."

Grand Pierre replied, "I'll put Maileen and Jacques in charge of food and shelter."

Dent laughed. "I'm sure Bear was thinking of Aunt May's cooking when he found the pots and pans. I know he will be happy to chew food again. I need to find the ulta leader."

Dent left Grand Pierre to get everyone organized, and he noticed Bear and Battle building a fire. He found the ulta leader and motioned for him to follow. He led the leader to a clearing not far from where they were to camp for the night. Dent pointed, and the ulta leader gasped and looked confused.

"Bear and I rescued most of the plants from your laboratory," Dent explained. "They are doing well with the sunlight and water. There should be enough food for us to survive until you can grow more crops, and there are lots of clumes and other fruits that grow wild in the valley."

The ulta leader placed his hands together and bowed, and Dent returned the gesture.

The fire was roaring, giving off enough heat to warm everyone seated around it. Grand Pierre was busy making sure there were enough shelters and beds for the night. Manx was watching the fire and eating a clume when Dent walked up.

She handed him one and said, "Bear picked enough for everyone to eat tonight."

Dent and Manx sat by the fire, and Manx softly said, "It's so peaceful here, it reminds me of the farm."

Bear returned from another clume run and gave the fruit to Aunt May to pass around. Bear took Bunny by the hand and led her to an open area where he picked her up and swung her around, causing her to laugh and her face to glow in the firelight.

As they watched Bear and Bunny spin in a circle, Dent told Manx, "That's the first time I've ever seen a bear dance."

Wren saw Grand Pierre standing by himself and walked over. "You look worried."

"Oh, no, I'm not worried," Grand Pierre replied. "I was thinking."

Wren took hold of his hand and admitted, "I don't think I will miss living underground, even if we don't have a lot of things. Francine said that all of their technology has been destroyed."

Grand Pierre smiled down at Wren. "I agree. After spending so many years living on Adoran, it wasn't easy for me to be confined underground. I'm sure we will survive without the use of technology."

"Will you be the new leader?" Wren asked the tall man.

Grand Pierre answered, "Maybe for a short time. Once everyone is settled and has a place to live, we will need a leader capable of understanding everything that is required to survive."

Wren asked, "Who?"

Grand Pierre answered, "There is one who has the knowledge."

"Oh, you mean Bear," Wren chirped, causing Grand Pierre to gulp.

Wren laughed at Grand Pierre's reaction. "I know you're talking about Dent," she said. "We know he inherited all the skills, and he can talk to the ultas, but he said not to let Manx know, or she will punch him in the arm."

Grand Pierre laughed. "You are indeed my special ones."

The End

ACKNOWLEDGMENT

The author would like to thank the staff at AuthorHouse for all their assistance to make *The Special Ones* special! This is a team of professionals in the publishing business.

*S*ynopsis for Book 1: The Twins of Fairland

Twins separated at birth are reunited. As they get to know each other, they discover an ancient magic hidden for years. They team up to protect the hidden kingdom of Fairland alongside their unique animal guardians. When they are challenged by a forgotten enemy with dark powers, they must trust and depend on each other. Tre and Skylin are guided on their journey into unknown territory by Mallrok, a mystic shaman. The twins may look alike, but are very different in other ways. Together they complete each other as the Twins of Fairland.

Join the Twins of Fairland on their journey of discovery filled with rescues, hidden kingdoms, magical powers, and forgotten enemies.

The Twins of Fairland is a well crafted, easy to read story for the preteen/teen reader.

*S*ynopsis for Book 2: The Twins of Fairland II

In the sequel to The Twins of Fairland, the magic continues when Tre discovers an ancient curse placed on the Lineage of Currin. Queen Laurel, Tre's mother, is the last of the line of queens of Currin and is threatened with revenge by the dark spirit riders of Lothan. Tre and his twin sister, Skylin, must lead the people to a new land and escape the destruction of Fairland.